D0341124

PROMISED
LAND

9/18

PROMISED LAND

A Novel of Israel

Martin Fletcher

Thomas Dunne Books
St. Martin's Press 🔀 New York

THOMAS DUNNE BOOKS
An imprint of St. Martin's Press

PROMISED LAND. Copyright © 2018 by Martin Fletcher. All rights reserved. Printed in the United States of America. For information, address St. Martin's Press, 175 Fifth Avenue, New York, N.Y. 10010.

www.thomasdunnebooks.com
www.stmartins.com

Library of Congress Cataloging-in-Publication Data

Names: Fletcher, Martin, 1947– author.
Title: Promised land : a novel / Martin Fletcher.
Description: First edition. | New York : St. Martin's Press, 2018. | "Thomas
    "Thomas Dunne Books."
Identifiers: LCCN 2018018488| ISBN 9781250118820 (hardcover) | ISBN
    9781250118844 (ebook)
Subjects: LCSH: Jewish fiction. | Brothers—Fiction. | Israel—
    History—1948–1967—Fiction. | GSAFD: Historical fiction.
Classification: LCC PS3606.L486 P76 2018 | DDC 813/.6—dc23
LC record available at https://lccn.loc.gov/201801848

Our books may be purchased in bulk for promotional, educational, or business use. Please contact your local bookseller or the Macmillan Corporate and Premium Sales Department at 1-800-221-7945, extension 5442, or by email at MacmillanSpecialMarkets@macmillan.com.

First Edition: September 2018

10 9 8 7 6 5 4 3 2 1

For Amnon and Tamar
Who gave me Hagar
And lived through this

לאמנון ותמר
שנתנו לי את הגר
שחוו את הדרך

PART ONE

PETER and AREN

All Peter wanted was a change of clothes. But Mama stuffed more and more trousers, sweaters, and shirts into his suitcase. A raincoat, ties, and belts. Her hands trembled. It was as if the more she gave him, the more of her went with him.

But Peter didn't want clothes. He wanted photographs, diaries, his favorite books. He didn't want more pants, he wanted memories, his father's wooden pipe carved like a lion's head: something to hold on to.

Whatever she put in, he pulled out. Mama started to weep, Pappi coaxed her away. Finally, Peter, almost as tall as his mother, embraced her. "Forgive me, Mama," he whispered, glancing over her shoulder at his little sisters on the steps. Renata and Ruth wiped tears from their eyes.

When the Quaker lady opened the car door for Peter, his brother Aren jumped inside and wouldn't get out. Aren's little hands gripped the seat as he cried, "Don't take the bag, take me instead. Take me with you."

The Quaker lady didn't know what to do. She was large, wore a black-and-white bonnet that covered her brow, and was not used to tantrums. But when her eyes met the father's, she tried to smile in sympathy.

How awful, to give up a child. But the way things were going, keeping him could be even worse. They were running out of time. The poor people.

They had decided to say good-bye at the house rather than risk a scene at the train station, but Aren wouldn't get out of the car.

"Me too," he cried. "I want to go with Peter. Why can't I go too?"

"You will, you will," his brother said, hugging him. "I promise, when I get to America I'll get all the papers and send money and you'll come too. Everyone will."

Tears streamed down Mama's face, and Pappi rubbed his eyes. The girls held each other.

In the end Mama and the girls said good-bye at the house and Pappi and Aren drove with Peter to the station in the big black car. In the backseat Pappi slipped off his silver watch and strapped it onto Peter's wrist. Even on the last hole the leather strap hung loose. "Wear it," Pappi said. "Be punctual wherever you go. Polish your shoes. Be polite and say please and thank you."

"Please and thank you," Peter said, but they couldn't smile. He added softly, "It's yours, I'll give it back one day." His father squeezed his hand.

Aren held the other so hard it hurt; still Peter didn't pull away.

"Why can't I come too?" Aren murmured, defeated.

The Quaker lady tried to explain, looking at their miserable faces in the mirror as she drove. "America won't let in many Jews, my dear, but we have special permission for a few children. We'll try to get you onto the next list. Don't worry. Everything will be all right."

"Of course," their father said. "Aren, you're next, and then when you're both in America it will be easier for the rest of us to get papers. Isn't that right, Frau . . . I'm sorry, I didn't get your name?"

"Frau Bildner. Yes, that's right. You're thirteen, Peter?"

"Almost fourteen."

"You'll like the family we found for you. And, Aren, they will find someone to sponsor you too. Near Peter. How old are you?"

"Twelve and a half. Almost."

"Don't worry. Everything will be fine."

At the train station Aren tried to cling to his brother, while Peter cuffed Aren around the head and gave him two of the butter biscuits Mama had baked for his journey. Pappi and Frau Bildner watched the brothers hug. Her lips quivered and Pappi had to look away.

There were whistles and clouds of steam and people rushing with trolleys piled high with cases, and men in black leather coats with swastikas and guns scanning faces, examining papers while their dogs strained on leashes.

All along the train, guards pulled up the iron steps and slammed heavy doors as passengers waved from windows. Peter leaned out too as the engine lurched forward and picked up speed. In one hand he gripped the paper with the name of the person who would meet him in Hamburg and take him to the ship for America, with the other he waved to his father and Aren. He wanted to shout, "I love you," but was too embarrassed. "Good-bye," he called, the wind whipping his hair. "See you in America!"

Pappi tried to shout, "Go west, young man," but his voice caught. "We'll see you there, I promise."

With a long thin whistle and a screech of wheels the great metal machine rattled around the bend and Peter was gone, a trail of smoke rising behind him.

Everything about Wisconsin was large and strange, though the Wilsons tried hard, and so did Peter. They allowed the Jewish boy to keep a night-light. He didn't cry much, but Peter often dreamt of his family. Everything he did was to make them proud. He worked to learn English, do well in school, excel at sports.

Walking to the yellow school bus on snowy winter mornings, glancing often at his father's watch to be sure he wasn't late, he imagined hugging Mama at the Madison station, and seeing his father's delight when he gave Pappi back his lion's-head pipe. How he would enjoy their surprise when they saw his big new home with the lawn that went all the way down to the street. Mr. and Mrs. Wilson would give them lemonade, they would meet his new brothers, Chuck and Bud. They called him Pete. He would give Aren his comics, and he and Aren would share a room again. His father had promised: "We'll join you in America."

But they didn't.

For when Aren and his parents and sisters were finally put on a train, it did not go west, but east.

TAMARA

Tamara threw back her head and shrieked into the wind, her bare feet over the side of the sailboat, racing water smacking her toes. Spray stung her cheeks, her long dark hair flew like a cape. Pascal, in shorts and shirt, pushed the rudder hard into the wind. She gripped the gunwale as the little boat spun and shot back toward the western bank of the Nile, toward the Pyramids and the Sphinx, into the setting sun.

Tamara studied Pascal with his back arched, straining to hold the rudder. His chest swelled, his biceps bulged, his feet were planted wide, every sinew fighting the wind. She tried not to look between his legs.

This is the last time, she thought, enjoy it while you can. She kicked at the water, as if to annoy her mother, who had warned her for eighteen years against the bilharzia virus that lived in the murky brown waters. She felt like kicking her mother, and her father.

Tomorrow they would leave Cairo for good. She would never see Pascal again. She glanced down at him, at his shorts, and quickly looked away. She felt herself flush. If only she could kiss him, just once. Should she do it, just slide over and kiss him? Here, right now on the boat. Free the sail, release the rudder, bob with the waves, do as he wanted, as she did too. Should they? Now? Here? In the clutch of the mighty river. What a memory! The sun would sink in minutes, night would quickly fall, they would be alone in the dark, drifting with the current, in each other's arms.

She squirmed at the thought and found herself leaning toward him. But did he want to kiss her too? There was only one way to find out. But no, she didn't dare. The wind dropped and they settled into a gentle glide toward the bank. Pascal's chauffeur, Suleiman, waited at the jetty, holding open the back door of the black Mercedes.

Instead of driving home, they strolled one last time beneath the sycamore trees that lined the Nile. Children played at the edge of the water, couples sat on benches, impatient for the dark. Lights twinkled across the dark water. Only when dusk enveloped them did Pascal take her hand. "This is it, then," he said with a heavy sigh.

"Don't say that."

"Will you write?"

"Yes, yes."

But could she? Could she send letters from Israel to Egypt? There would be no way to communicate. She would lose him. She would lose everything. She loved Cairo, her home, her friends, the fragrances of tamarind and jasmine, the roasting of shawarma and river fish, the music and drumming of the night. And especially Pascal. She knew it wasn't true love. They'd hardly touched. It was the tension of discovery, the fear of it too. The unknown, the forbidden. He was a year older, nineteen, a boy, really, but what a boy. Tamara squeezed his hand and looked around. Could she for once be brave? Be foolish? In the darkness of a tree she stopped and at last pulled Pascal to her. Why hadn't she before? His lips were warm and firm, he tasted of the pomegranate they had shared, she liked it. They kissed, searching, and then, with the craving of a first embrace, a kiss of desperation, their last, their only kiss. She felt him tremble.

How jealous her friends were when she had met Pascal in the open-air cinema. He was dazzling in his tight black shirt. Later they had all gone to Groppi's for pistachio cassata, where he had said, "This ice cream is sweet and creamy, just like you." Her friends had howled with laughter. Creamy! Stop! It hurts!

"We'll meet again. In Paris. Or I'll come to Jerusalem," he said, his heart beating against hers. "Nothing will change."

Oh yes it will, she thought, everything will change. Who would she be in six months, in a year? Who knew what would happen in her new home? But the uncertainty emboldened her too. Instead of words, she felt herself pressing against him, she felt his body responding in turn, felt him growing against her belly. Her skin quivered, she felt a thrill. Move away from him! But no, why? She'd probably never see him again. She pushed against him, feeling the shape of him, while he held her tighter. Only after moments passed and her senses were on fire did she pull back.

If only she could stay, even just one day more.

It was her father's fault, though she shouldn't blame him. He was a Zionist, rounded up with a thousand others. After ten months' detention, beaten and starved, he had emerged a sickly man.

He had only been freed from the camp on condition he left the country, and that was fine by him. Being a Jew in Egypt was hard enough before the war with Israel, but since then it had become unbearable. The Jews were all but annihilated in Europe, her father said, we can't wait like fools for the same to happen here.

No, she couldn't blame her father; there was no life here for a Jew, not since the Jews won the war and had a country next door.

Through the window's lace curtain Moïse watched as the Mercedes drew up. The one good thing about losing everything, he thought, was that his daughter wouldn't see that boy again. He should never have sent her to that Catholic school. They had turned her head with all that money, the car, the boat, the villas. His parents were Catholic bankers, loud and ostentatious, as far from his world of academia as a camel from the ocean. True, the Collège du Sacré-Coeur had given her a good education, and thank God she had just graduated, so she could go to Israel with her diploma. It would help her go to college there. But that boy . . .

He suspected they had kissed, and God knows what else.

His wife took his hand. "Are they still in the car?" Rashil asked.

"Yes."

She felt his fingers ball into a fist, and she squeezed. "Stop it. Tomorrow we go to Israel. Thank God."

TAMARA

SIDNA ALI, ISRAEL

February 1950

The cold stung, the canvas was slick with sleet, it pricked Tamara's skin as she peered out of the tent. She had never seen her breath's vapor before, or the fluffy white stuff. "Ima," she hissed to her mother, "look, come quickly."

Shivering, drawing her coat tightly to her throat, Rachel, who had renounced her Arab name of Rashil, crawled over the sleeping forms to the opening of the crowded tent. "Aiee," said one, turning over. "Careful!" cried another. Rachel stared with surprise at the white earth, and stretched out her hand to receive the snowflakes, which melted in her hand. She brought the moisture to her lips, and grunted. *"Elohim shmor aleynu,"* she muttered. "God protect us," her favorite new Hebrew phrase. Rachel turned and crawled back into the tent they shared with three other families. With a loud sigh she drew her blanket over her head.

"Sssshh," someone said.

Excited, Tamara pulled on both pairs of socks, slipped into her sandals and coat, gathered her long black hair beneath a headscarf, which she wrapped around her face, and emerged from the tent like an Eskimo from her igloo. Her feet crunched on the crisp earth and at first she didn't notice the cold. She stood still in the row of tents and let the drifting snow tickle her eyelashes and dust her head and shoulders, and felt a lightness in her heart. She smiled at her footprints, like animal tracks, thinking, My first snow. Who would have thought it, snow on the cactus. Everything is new and different.

At that moment, from between two tents at the end of the row, a group of men in hats and coats appeared, walking toward her, talking loudly. They paused briefly at a mess of canvas and ropes where two tents had collapsed in the wind, and continued. As they passed she said, *"Boker tov."*

"Good morning," the one in front responded. He pulled his hat over his eyes to keep out the snow.

"What are you doing here?" she asked. "So early."

The same man answered. "We're looking to see how bad the conditions are here. It's freezing, the last time we had snow like this was in 1870. We may have to move you all somewhere else."

Keeping step with them, Tamara said, "I never saw snow before, not in Egypt."

"Well, it's crazy weather," the first man said, pulling his coat tighter at the throat. Tamara noticed his leather gloves and woolen scarf. She looked down: and his warm boots.

"The poor babies," Tamara said.

"Yes," he said, "people are dying, not in this camp yet, but in other places."

"There's nowhere to go," she said. "We've tried."

"That's the whole point. We have to build houses, and fast. It's even worse in the Arab refugee camps; there are more deaths there. Exposure. The cold. A roof collapsed from the weight of the snow."

The group passed another row of tents, pointing at heaps of frozen garbage, kicking at empty food crates, stamping their feet, cursing the cold.

"Is that where you're from, Egypt?" the man said. His gloved hands were deep in his pockets while Tamara blew on hers, enjoying the sight of her breath.

She looked up, emerald eyes and long black eyelashes, her face half-hidden by a scarf of black and gold.

"How old are you?" he asked.

"Nineteen. And you?"

"Twenty-five."

"Where are you from?" she asked, taking him in now. He looked bulky beneath the heavy coat.

"What makes you think I'm from somewhere? I'm from here."

"Not with that accent. Anyway, your Hebrew is hardly better than mine."

He laughed. "Germany. But my Hebrew is much better than yours."

"Not for long. And your accent is terrible."

Another man grinned. "Arie," he said, "be careful of that one."

Snowflakes turned to raindrops as low leaden clouds blew in from the sea over the cliff at Sidna Ali, ten miles up the coast from Tel Aviv. Mist curled between clumps of eucalyptus trees and hugged the minaret of the ancient mosque, once the heart of a Bedouin encampment, now a transit camp for Jewish refugees from Arab lands. The men were swarthy and some wore knives in their waistbands, while the women were exotic and fair—certainly Tamara was in the eyes of Arie.

Rain pelted down now, drumming on the tents, a torrent rushed over the ridges of icy mud. As they fled to shelter in the metal hut that served as an administration office, Arie guided Tamara with his hand in the small of her back. A man blocked the doorway and barked in German, "Halt! She can't come in."

"Of course she can." Arie pushed his arm away. "It's pouring outside."

"So she must go back to her tent," the man said in Hebrew. "If she comes in they'll all want to and what a mess that would be."

Tamara froze at the open door, her cheeks red from the cold, and now also from humiliation: These *yekke* German Jews think they're so superior. Cold air blasted into the heated space that was sour with sweat. "Hurry up, shut the door," the man said.

She turned on her heel; they can keep their stinky room.

But Arie pulled her back by the hand and closed the door after her. "Who are you, anyway?" he said, pushing his chest toward the man. "You'd make this young girl go outside into the cold and rain? You're here to help them, you . . ." He caught himself. "Move over," he said, and pressed himself into the cramped hut, still holding Tamara by the hand. "Here," he said to her, "it's nice by the stove."

Warmth rose from the kerosene heater, which had two kettles of water boiling on its grill. The man who had objected to Tamara's presence grimaced but kept his silence, while the others stamped their feet and held their hands out to the heat.

Arie squeezed Tamara's hand before releasing it, and as he glanced at her, he couldn't help a grin. All he could see under her scarf were her deep green eyes, and one of them slowly winked.

Two hours later, as a gleaming Tamara emerged from the narrow shower stall in Arie's building and padded barefoot to his room, she could hardly believe her luck. A hot shower in a warm bathroom, with soap and dry towels. The stuff of dreams. If only she could bring her whole family here. With her wet hair piled in one towel, her body wrapped in another beneath her overcoat, she found herself walking behind a slim young man in a cap and jacket. He stopped at Arie's door and took out a key. Surprised when he suddenly halted, Tamara bumped into him. He was surprisingly solid. "Oh, *slicha*!" she said, sorry. The man looked over his shoulder and quickly smiled, with teasing eyes. All he had felt was her softness. "That's the best thing that's happened to me all week," he said.

"Are you going into that room?" she asked, and added, "of course you are, you're opening the door."

She stood before him, and began to blush. "Me too," she said.

"You too? You too, what?"

"Me too going in."

At that moment the door opened and Arie said, "Tamara, so you met my brother, Peter, already, come in. Quick, out of the corridor, you'll die of cold."

Tamara entered the room, followed by Peter, who raised his eyebrows at his brother. Arie grinned and shook his head. Brother talk for: No. Not yet. Unfortunately. Peter followed her with his eyes, a smile slowly forming. No words needed: Now that is one beautiful girl.

Tamara made a spinning gesture with her hand and the brothers turned around while she dried herself with a small towel, leaning over the little electric heater. She grinned, surprised at herself: she had better not tell her parents about this, half-naked in a room with two strange men. Her father would kill her. But times are changing, Israel is not Egypt and thank God for that. And living with other families in the tent for so long meant she had given up on privacy.

Looking at the door, his back to her, Peter asked in German, "Who is she, what's she doing here?"

"I found her at the immigrant camp at Sidna Ali," Arie said, staring at the window, straining to see Tamara's body in the reflection. He couldn't make out much but he liked what he saw: a pale shape blurred by raindrops sliding down the glass.

"And of course you invited her for a hot shower," Peter said.

"Well, it worked last time," Arie said. "That Moroccan."

"You're a snake. Do her parents know she's here?"

"Are you crazy? They'd skin me like a rabbit."

"How old is she?"

"Nineteen."

"She looks younger. Well, at least give her a good meal."

"And a good time?" Arie said with a laugh.

Peter said, "I have to go, I just came to get my stuff."

"Where to this time?"

"Don't ask."

"How long for?"

"Who knows."

"What's the job?"

"You know I can't say. Stop asking."

Tamara said, "Are you talking about me?"

"Yes," Arie said. "Peter thinks you are beautiful. So do I. Can we turn around?"

"Not yet, and don't peek or you'll turn into a pillar of salt." She congratulated herself on learning that new Hebrew phrase.

Still looking at the door, they heard a knock, saw the knob turning, and the door opened.

"Arie, you're late," Natanel Ben-Tsion said, entering the room. "And now I can see why," he continued with a smirk.

"Turn around!" Tamara shrieked.

"I'm so sorry," he said, "I didn't see anything. Well, not enough. Arie, come on, they're waiting . . ."

"Oh no, I totally forgot. Peter, you know Natanel; he works at the city council. I have to leave for a bit, we have a meeting. Tamara, wait for me, all right, I'll be back as quickly as I can." He slapped Peter on the back. "Don't do anything I wouldn't do."

"So I can do what you would do? I'll be gone when you get back. See you soon."

"Stay safe. How long will you be gone this time? Is it a dangerous one?"

"No, of course not, it never is." Peter chuckled and pulled his brother into his arms. They embraced, each stealing a glance at Tamara, who was checking the dampness of her clothes. Then Arie was gone.

"This is the best I can do," Tamara said at last. "My clothes are all wet. Do you mind if I stay like this?"

Peter turned. "No," he said, his voice catching. "It's fine."

Tamara's hair dangled in damp braids across her honey shoulders, bare but for the towel that covered her to her waist. As she moved, her skirt revealed the swell of her stomach. The moment hung. She knew that Peter was examining her, and she felt naked. And oddly excited. In Cairo her father could beat her for less. But here in Israel . . . she marveled at her daring. Each movement of her arm pulled at the towel, which she held firmly in case it fell away. Each tighter grip swelled the outline of her breasts and revealed more of her belly, where Peter now gazed. She saw him swallow. She trembled, yet felt safe with this handsome, embarrassed young man.

She didn't know what to say as they stood before each other, closer than an arm's length. Peter, made bold by the sweetness of the moment, took her hair into his hand. "It's wet," he said.

"Yes."

"Would you like me to brush it?"

Tamara swallowed, her breathing quickened. She hesitated.

Peter walked to the bathroom and returned with a hairbrush. He pulled up a chair. "Here, please sit down."

Tamara looked from Peter to the chair. She knew she should leave, but her blouse was wet and her coat was still dripping. And, really, what harm could it do? As long as nobody knew.

She sat stiffly in the chair with her back to Peter, who gathered her hair in one hand and slowly brushed with the other, tenderly, rhythmically. She relaxed, rocking gently to the movements of his hand, as in a slow dance. As he pulled through each strand and ended each stroke with a flourish and a sigh, he placed a hand on Tamara's forehead, to steady her, and he felt her lean into his hand, as if giving him permission. Tamara, lonely for so long, felt herself in secure, strong hands, and allowed herself to drift into this intimacy. The gentle pulling at her hair, the resting of her head against his warm hand, such familiarity with a stranger was thrilling, yet somehow reassuring. She felt safe. They were silent, the only sound Peter's quickening breath.

He placed each gleaming bunch across Tamara's naked shoulder. He gazed at his shiny handiwork, and at the soft swell of Tamara's breasts, where she had relaxed the grip on her towel. Twice, in her dreamy state, the darkness of her nipples had been revealed.

Peter smiled and pulled up the towel. Gently, Tamara removed Peter's hand from her head. "Thank you," she whispered. "I think I feel more relaxed than I ever have since I left Cairo." She squeezed his hand and stood, searching for her blouse.

"When was that?" Peter asked.

"Nine months ago." Her voice was wistful, soft and sweet.

As he watched her he felt himself stir. How he wanted to rip away that towel, take her innocent face in his hands. But how could he? A beautiful refugee girl who trusted him. Could he even touch her? He knew Arie would. His heart raced.

He was twenty-seven and didn't have a girlfriend; he was leaving on another mission, who knew when he'd have another chance? And so beautiful . . . he leaned toward her.

And as for Tamara, when Peter leaned into her, cupped her head in his hand, brought his lips slowly to hers, his eyes closed, her own eyes closed too, and her lips met his. She felt as if she were in a dream, melting into him, turning her back on Egypt. She had never felt like such a woman. Her towel slipped away, and her naked breasts were against him. His shirt was rough.

As her fingers dug into his flesh, she returned his kiss and the room swayed. They sank onto the bed. A voice in Tamara's head whispered Stop, leave, now! But just then Peter unbuttoned his shirt and pulled her to his strong body. At first she shrank from his searching touch, until in wonder, she discovered him too. He pulled at his pants, and at her skirt. Her thoughts vanished, and she felt only gratitude and heat and elation. She gripped his buttocks and soon felt pain, but for a mere instant, she wanted this, needed this, more than anything ever before. She was escaping the tent, the camp, her horrid life, and finding freedom. Everything forbidden, all that was withheld from her, she embraced now with all her soul and all her might, until his tremors went through her. She heard his call as from far away, then they shuddered together and it was over.

She was panting, gripping him so hard that he had to prize her fingers apart. Her heart raced against his until slowly their breathing eased and her mind began to clear again.

And when it did, lying at Peter's side, she thought only, over and over, *Ya Allah*, Tamara, oh Tamara! What have you done, why did you do this, you're a crazy girl. For a moment, there she was with Pascal on the boat, wind in her hair, water whipping her toes. She saw Peter, and felt herself recoil. Who is this man? She felt damp between her legs and wished she could ask for another shower.

She examined her hands: they were trembling. Was this a telltale sign? When she got home, would anybody know what she had done? Could they see? She had shamed herself and her family and, in Egypt, she could be punished and beaten, or worse. But wait, no, this was Israel, and after nine months living in a tent, who had the right to judge her? She didn't belong to anyone. Still, nobody must ever know.

They dressed quickly and in silence, afraid Arie would return, each astonished at what had occurred.

Tamara could not meet Peter's eyes, while he could not take his eyes off her. Each time he tried to say something a half-formed word emerged, like a grunt: he had no idea what he could say, for he knew she had broken all the taboos of her world. All he wanted was to hold her and look after her.

He looked at the door, knowing he wouldn't be back for months. He couldn't call Tamara, he couldn't tell her why, and there was nothing he could do about it. He felt the thudding of his heart; he had never felt this way before, anxious and pained: the sense of a beginning, cut short before it began.

Peter held his arms out to Tamara but she backed away, confused, until she saw the pleading in his eyes and came to him.

He held her to his chest, stroked her hair, kissed her eyes, brought her fingers to his lips, made his promises, and left.

PETER

Tel Aviv, Israel

February 1950

The next day, in a small room at 85 Ben Yehuda Street in Tel Aviv, Peter checked his suitcase one last time, making sure his clothes had no Hebrew labels, that his toiletries were clean of all Hebrew lettering, that nothing he wore or carried could identify him as a citizen of Israel. All he kept was his watch, his father's Swiss Longines, that he never took off: his security blanket. He checked that he had the right passport and that it matched his driving license, library card, identity card, and ration book, all in the name of Willimod Stinglwagner, Munich importer of medical products. It was such an unlikely German name that he felt it had to sound genuine. *"Nennen Sie mir Willi,"* he would say. "Call me Willi."

That was for Germany. Here at the Office he was better known by his code name: Wolf.

Satisfied, Peter closed the case and lay on the bed, pulling on a cigarette, still tingling from Tamara. What a body, what a beauty, what a girl. He just knew Arie would be all over her, and there wasn't a thing he could do. He must not go to see her, he didn't even have an address to write to. Any slipup could be deadly.

He waited to be briefed by his handler. He only knew that he'd be working on his own, or almost on his own. Nothing new there. He had been a secret agent for years, with America's OSS in Europe, then for Shai, the Jewish Underground in Palestine, and now for Israel.

At a tap on the door Peter sprung to his feet, ready to be taken to room seven for the briefing. Instead, in walked Reuven Shiloah himself, holding a large brown envelope. Peter stepped back, put out his hand, withdrew it. "Reuven," he said. "Sir. I'm sorry, I wasn't expecting . . ."

"Relax, Peter, sit down," Shiloah said. "I came myself because this won't be the usual."

"'The usual.' There's such a thing?"

Shiloah didn't smile. He rarely did, and certainly not now. The prime minister's special adviser was a legendary master of the dark arts. He had founded the pre-state secret service, formulated many of Israel's defense doctrines, and was the most trusted of David Ben-Gurion's secret warriors. He gave nothing away. It was said that when a taxi driver asked where he was going Shiloah told him to mind his own business.

Shiloah sat to Peter's left, and as he began to speak, Peter couldn't take his eyes off the scar below his right cheekbone. He hadn't seen Shiloah since the man had been hit in the face by shrapnel from an Arab car bomb in Jerusalem. The thin reddish welt that twitched as his jaw moved and his unwavering stare through round-rimmed spectacles made Shiloah appear almost fiendish.

Peter shifted uncomfortably, leaning back as the big man edged closer; the spymaster's presence was overwhelming. Fortunately Shiloah rose and began to pace, but his first words made Peter's heart miss a beat. "This could be a long operation, Peter. . . ."

Long? Tamara flashed before Peter, bare shoulders and swelling breasts, honey skin, sparkling eyes, and wet hair, their bodies a perfect fit.

"And a difficult one . . ."

Peter tried to focus.

"I'm not going to say more than I need, but you know about our problem with Yanai center? With our own people there?"

Peter nodded. Yanai was the code name for the Paris station. It was the talk of the bureau. Black market, cheating on expenses, agents living high on the hog, clumsy meetings in luxury hotel lobbies, in short, everything the austere socialists running the country despised, and to make it worse, serial incompetence and meager results.

"Yes, I get the picture; we all do," Peter said. Out of loyalty to a friend in the Paris team, he added, "Isn't it true, though, that they need to make money on the side to finance their activities because their budget is much too low? That's what people are saying."

If looks could kill, he was dead.

Shiloah sneered. "The short answer is No. The long answer is that I will deal with them all, be sure of that." His tone changed, short and blunt. "But that is not the point. This is a very sensitive and dangerous time for Israel, and we must focus on what is most important." He sat down and fixed Peter with his notorious stare.

"I want you to go to West Germany, and report back only to me. No contact with anyone else. Our European organization is compromised by those clowns in Paris and this is too sensitive a mission to take a risk. You must know that Ben-Gurion is convinced we're on the brink of another war. Me, I'm not so sure. But we must be ready for anything. I have a special mission for you. Long-term." He took a bundle of photographs from his envelope, set them out on the bed, and looked up at Peter. "I trust only you with this, nobody else."

For whenever Reuven Shiloah had an especially sensitive mission, off the books, when he needed someone with loyalty, discretion, as well as cunning and special fighting skills, he called on Peter Nesher.

The young man had first caught Shiloah's eye toward the end of World War Two, when Peter Berg was a twenty-two-year-old officer in the American OSS, the Office of Strategic Services, and Shiloah was trying to win American support for the Zionist enterprise. He also had discreet feelers out for potential allies inside the American operation.

Peter fit the perfect profile: a Jew who had escaped Germany at the age of fourteen, lucky to be sent to safety in America. He spoke perfect English with a flat Midwest accent, as well as German. At the age of twenty he had fought his way through Europe with the 45th Division of the US Seventh Army, winning the Silver Star for gallantry: he had led an assault on a machine-gun nest but ran out of ammunition; he jumped the last two gun-ners and stabbed their throats with his bayonet. He was among the first units to liberate the Nazi concentration camp in Dachau, where he had searched desperately among the survivors for his family, who came from nearby Munich. He searched in vain. Finally, because of his cunning, bravery, and fluent German, he had been tapped by the OSS to work on secret mis-sions among the German population, and then farther afield.

Shiloah thought he had the perfect background, experience, and skills to spy for the Jews of Palestine. But at that time, in 1945, Peter had turned him down. He said he already had a job, and owed America, and wouldn't cheat on them. Nothing would budge him, no threats, no entreaties, no bribes.

But in 1947, two years after war's end, Peter, by now one of the founding agents at the CIA, had been shocked to learn that his younger brother had survived the concentration camps after all. He went to search for him in Palestine. And it was Shiloah who found, within hours of Peter's appeal for help, that his brother, Aren Berg, was living in Tel Aviv under the Hebrew name of Arie ben Nesher. It made sense. The root of the German name "Aren" was the same as the Hebrew "Nesher": Eagle. To celebrate, Peter took the same family name and became Peter Nesher.

Peter told Shiloah he would be forever in his debt, and a conversation had ensued that Peter would never forget, even if he sometimes came to regret it.

"Why forever? Pay me back right now." Shiloah had said.

Surprised, Peter had answered, "If I can, of course."

"Oh, you can. The question is, will you?" Shiloah launched into his re-cruiting speech, which rarely failed. "Do you want to serve your people? Because we need you now. Our battle in Palestine has barely begun, Jews are fighting for our very existence, as we have not fought in two thousand years. Could the Nazi massacres happen again? Of course they could, if the Arabs had half a chance. But this time we will not be led like lambs to the slaughter. We will fight back and defeat our enemies. We will build our Jewish state, and defend it for eternity. The question is, do you want to be part of the greatest Jewish enterprise since the Jews were forced into exile?"

He followed up at the jugular. "Do you want to avenge your murdered parents? Your slaughtered sisters?"

They were walking in shirtsleeves along the busy Tel Aviv promenade on a glorious sunny day, which only emphasized their good fortune, the freedom they enjoyed in contrast to the horror of the camps, which had taken the lives of six million Jews.

"For every Jew you see around you here in Palestine," Shiloah had said, "nine were murdered. Can you imagine such a thing?" He stopped and took Peter's hands. "Spread out your fingers. Now close all but one." Peter did, leaving the index finger of his right hand. "That last one standing is you, safe," Shiloah went on. "But for how long? And don't you owe a debt to the dead? Why, of all people, did *you* survive? For what?"

Men and women were laughing and splashing in the calm sea and sunning themselves on the sandy beach. Boys played paddleball, the rat-a-tat of solid rubber on wood like gunshots mingled with honking cars and calls of *"Artik, artik,"* from the dark-skinned men selling fruit ices. "Nine dead bodies for every one here," Shiloah said, shaking his head. "Can you imagine? Never again."

They paused, watching a boy chase a girl, kicking up sand, and the silence lengthened. "Well, do you?" Shiloah insisted. "Want to avenge your parents? By protecting our country?"

Instinctively, Peter rubbed his leather watch strap. "How can I say no?"

"Wrong answer."

Peter turned to the older man, who had become something of a friend, and had to grin. "How's this? Of course. Of course I do. Very much. This time the answer is yes."

"That's better," Shiloah said, taking Peter's hand. "Come with me."

They had crossed the beach road and walked past the low homes and shops to Ben Yehuda Street, a tall, powerful middle-aged man with graying hair and spectacles, accompanied by a slim, tough man half his age. Two men with a purpose. Shiloah had guided Peter to the secret headquarters of the spy agency, Shai, the same nondescript apartment building at number 85 where Shiloah was now, three years later, showing Peter the photographs.

Shiloah grunted involuntarily. They made even his stomach curl.

"Horrific, but we don't choose our enemies. And sometimes not our friends," the spymaster said, gathering up the evidence. He repeated: "You leave in the morning. No contact from now on with anyone in Israel but me. Everything you need is in this envelope. People, profiles, addresses. You won't travel with it, you will receive it again on location, sealed. In each case our goal is the same. And be very, very careful. These are killers."

That night, torn between duty and desire, Peter decided Shiloah would never know he had had one last contact, and if he did, he'd approve. Peter took the stairs down to the office on the ground floor, where he found two sheets of paper, two envelopes, and a stamp. He sat at a desk and in the pool of light from the swivel lamp wrote a short note to go inside the first envelope: "Arie, my brother, please give this letter to Tamara." He didn't add anything else, Arie would understand that he could give no information about where he was.

Inside that envelope he folded the second envelope, addressed to Tamara, with a second brief note. In case her family read it, he wrote as discreetly as he could:

My Dear Tamara,

Stay away from my brother! But seriously, I want you to know how special our brief time together was. I hope that you will wait for me to return. I don't know when that will be and this may be a lot to ask, but I feel and pray that I can ask this of you.

Peter

It was past midnight when he slipped the envelope addressed to Arie into the Frishman Street postbox and returned to his room at the Office. His suitcase ready for the early call, his papers in order, Peter fell into a deep, satisfied sleep, dreamt of Tamara, and woke with the sun as Wolf, alias Willi Stinglwagner.

TAMARA and ARIE

Arie and Tamara were trying to cross Allenby, one of Tel Aviv's busiest streets. Their drive into town along the narrow coastal road had been harrowing enough, with all the hooting and gesturing drivers, but here, buses and cars billowing blue fumes competed with groaning engines, honking horns, and the curses of pedestrians. Women pushing prams dodged the vehicles, Arabs in keffiyehs peddled coffee from steaming urns, offering warmth in the morning frost. Tel Aviv, less than forty years old, was chaotic, improvised, inventing itself day by day.

Tamara was almost overcome by the din and the tumult, but not quite. Laughing, she took Arie's hand and pulled him through a break in the traffic to Nachalat Binyamin Street, where Arie had said there would be a surprise.

By the tree in the little square where Nachalat Binyamin met Allenby, they looked up at the rounded prow of the notorious Polishuk House, which looked like a beached boat in the center of town. Its surprising shape and small round windows like portholes distinguished it from the bleak, angular buildings everywhere else. It was known as "The Monstrosity" but was also the home of Naalei Pil, Elephant Shoes, and here Arie held the door open for Tamara.

It was icy outside and warm inside and just for that Tamara was grateful.

But when Arie sat her down and asked the salesman for a pair of Bata shoes in her size, she was surprised. "For me? Really? No, I can't."

"Come on," Arie said. "You need them, you deserve them, it's muddy in that camp, and cold. You've just got sandals. Anyway, try them on, see how they feel."

But even as he spoke, Tamara had pulled off her sandals and was waving her feet. Thank God she had darned her socks last week.

When the man returned with three pairs to try, Tamara hesitated. "You know, Arie, in the camp everyone wears sandals. The rich people wear better sandals. What will people think? Can I really go back in these?"

Arie put his hand on hers. "Yes. Yes, you can."

She selected soft leather boots in two-tone black and dark gray with low heels and a straight toe. She trailed her fingers over the leather, thinking of her escape from Cairo with just the sandals on her feet, but dismissed the image. "You're right, I really do need these, thank you so much, I don't know what to say." She squeezed his hand. She shouldn't really accept them, but what a relief they would be.

In another shop in the same building Arie wanted to buy her a knee-length burgundy wool coat with a fur collar. When she tried to object, Arie overrode her, saying they must buy it because soon Israel would introduce rationing for shoes and clothes, and then they wouldn't be able to buy anything. It was now or never. And, anyway, he added, what's the point of saving money, who knows if there'll be a tomorrow? And also, why freeze when you can be warm? It was hard to disagree with anything Arie said.

Relishing the comforting soft fur against her throat and her snug new boots, Tamara clung to Arie's arm as they walked along Sheinkin Street. Feeling hard muscle through his coat, she only now realized how strong he must be. Amid the strangeness and bustle of town, she felt safe.

They entered Café Stern, akin to a kibbutz dining room, with its crowded tables, familiar faces, and miserable coffee. Sarah Stern, the gruff and beloved owner, shrugged off complaints, saying she'd serve better coffee if her clients asked for it, but they didn't.

"It's bitter, this coffee," Tamara said with a grimace. "I make better. But mmmhh, wonderful poppyseed cake, though. And that reminds me," she added, leaning forward, forking the last moist black crumbs into her mouth. "I shouldn't ask, or maybe I should. The boots. The coat. Isn't this very expensive for you? I really shouldn't have accepted them."

A thought had disturbed her and now she knew what it was. Walking to the café, they had passed shouting children throwing snowballs, and when Arie had playfully thrown one at her, without thinking she had turned her back and didn't join the fun. Now she suddenly understood why, and it made her sad. It was the children back in the transit camp: children of the desert, from Yemen, Morocco, Egypt, Libya, Iraq. They weren't bundled up in warm clothes, playing in the novel snow in the streets, or skiing down the slopes of Mount Carmel in Haifa or sledding the streets of Jerusalem. They were curled up in bed with frozen toes, shivering in thin clothes under a single blanket. It wasn't fair. Why couldn't they be out playing too, with gloves and woolen hats?

Setting down her fork with a louder clang than she had intended, Tamara demanded, "Your car. What do you do? I mean, all the money. How do you make so much? And if you're so rich, why do you live in one room with Peter? And, anyway, when is he coming back?"

Arie gazed over Tamara's shoulder and around the room, through the bluish haze of cigarette smoke that rose from every table. Behind the wooden counter Sarah held out two cups of fresh coffee to a waiter. The door and windows were closed against the cold while outside, a flurry of snow whitened the stacked tables and chairs.

Why did he still share a room with his brother? He knew that splitting the rent helped Peter; he earned peanuts with the government. But it was more than that. What was it? Duty? No. Guilt? No. Or, maybe a bit of both, and more. They were family, it was just the two of them now, all the others had been murdered in the camps, as far as they knew. Every day began with a twinge of hope: Maybe today someone would turn up. It happened all the time. Everyone knew someone whose relative, mother, father, sister, cousin, believed dead, suddenly knocked on the door, or a letter appeared in the post: Are you so-and-so from so-and-so?

And then there was this, clear to Arie, even if Peter did not fully understand: at home, in their little shared room, Arie could be himself. Outside, he was the new Israeli—ambitious, powerful, clever, funny. But he could never mention what drove him: the camps. If he did, people's eyes dropped, they looked away, as if it was a crime that he was still alive. What did you do to survive? So he buried his pain and his shame. But at home with Peter he was safe, he could be himself, be the younger brother, short of temper and manners, and while Peter could never fully understand, at least he didn't judge him.

Peter could only say: There, but for the grace of God, or rather the Quakers, go I.

Their childhood ended when Peter was randomly chosen to go to America, while he had to stay behind. Peter had promised, on that last day, at the train station, to bring them all to America. But how could he? He was only fourteen. Arie knew Peter had felt guilty then, and still did now. He had left his family to their fate in Germany, while he went to live in safety and luxury. But wouldn't I have done the same, Arie thought, if I could have?

Yes, they didn't share just the room. They shared everything, and nothing. They had each other and nobody else. They weren't yet ready to let go.

And, as a matter of fact, he also didn't really have much money to spend, he put it all back in the business, even if he'd told Tamara there was no point saving.

He heard her say "Well, is it a secret? Where do you get so much money from?"

"Have you finished your coffee?" he asked, draining his cup.

"Yes."

"So come with me, I'll show you something."

As they drove, Arie prepared Tamara. "When I was in your camp the other day, when we met, you know what we were doing there, right? Me and the other men?"

"Looking at the way we live."

"Yes, but more than that. The government wants you out of there, and not just you. There are more than half a million immigrants like you, and almost all go through the transit camps. You're supposed to be there a week or two, three at the most, yet you've been there for months and some are approaching a year; there's nowhere to go. We have to build, and fast. There are more Jews landing at the ports every day, tens of thousands a month, so many our Jewish population doubled in less than three years. All these people need homes, jobs, schools, clinics, transport, clothes, food. Some-one has to provide all that, so there are fortunes to be made. By doing good work. It isn't just about making money. We're building a country, we're in a hurry, and it isn't always pretty."

As if to prove him right, a car on the outside made a sharp right turn, pulling across Arie, causing Arie to swerve to the left, toward an oncoming truck, which hooted and skidded as its driver hit the brakes. As he straight-ened Arie hooted too, and all three drivers shook their fists. "Welcome to Israel," Arie said with a tight grin.

"Ben Zonah!" They heard a fading shout, "Son of a bitch!" Dozens of men and women lined the road, hitchhiking and shouting good-natured insults at cars that ignored them.

They turned east off the new tar road at the one gas station in the dunes between Tel Aviv and the rising town of Herzliya. They bumped by orange groves until the rutted track ended at a building site, a blunt, elongated structure rising from shrub and sand.

Trucks unloaded, others exited with debris, and workers swarmed over the three-story building that was nearing completion. It was long and squat, with a stucco exterior: roughly mixed cement, Arie explained, cheap, easy to apply, low maintenance, weather-resistant. The last of the concrete blocks and steel girders were still visible as workers laid rows of bricks.

"We're close to the end," Arie said, winding up the window against a blast of cold air. They watched from the warmth of the car, the engine throb-bing. "Five buildings with their own entrances, all connected at the first floor, three levels, eight apartments on each level, a hundred and twenty apartments. Built in eight months. Not bad. Another acre and a half to build on. Roads, maybe a playground, shops. Who knows, maybe your family will move in."

With her sleeve, Tamara wiped moisture from the window and looked from the buildings to Arie. "And?" she asked. "You work here?"

A smug grin. "Sort of. I own it."

Tamara's mouth widened. "Really? no . . ."

"Really, yes. With my partners. And another site like it. They should all be ready in eight weeks. And we're breaking ground on two schools."

"But . . . but, you're so young."

"So what? That's just it. Everyone's young. It's a young country. Two years old, and half of that we've been at war, and nobody thinks the fighting's over. We have a lot to do in a very short time. Think of it. Two years ago the country's main export was oranges. Total Israel exports were six million dollars. But now the sky's the limit. And I aim to be part of it."

"But . . . if you own all this, why do you live in one room?"

"Well, first of all, I don't have much cash, I . . ."

"But you bought me shoes. And a coat. Why, then? I knew I shouldn't have accepted . . ." She flushed with embarrassment.

"No, no, don't worry." Arie laughed. "I have plenty when I want, but mostly I don't want. Every penny I make goes back into the business. We build fast and cheap. Walls and a roof, that's all that counts . . ." In his excitement, he spoke so fast Tamara could barely follow. "I'm in construction, but there's a lot more too. I import materials for construction, some foods, some . . . there's such a shortage of everything: plumbing. Copper. It's so expensive, America's using it all for the war in Korea. You can't find anything here. Everything's rationed."

Tamara listened with a growing smile of bemusement. She had never met anyone like him. If he had been a refugee in the camp, they would all have been in houses long ago. He didn't stop talking. "There was a fire in a mill in Haifa and now there's not enough bread. I have a friend, we're going to start a bakery. And everywhere you look they're planting trees. I know someone at the Jewish National Fund, they're going to plant six million trees, one for each Nazi victim; someone has to provide them, the seeds, or saplings, or whatever you call baby trees, they have to come from somewhere, that's a great business too, and . . . well, anyway, there's a great future here for anyone who wants to work. And I want to work. And of course, you have to know the right people. And I'm getting to know them."

"But how did you start? You said you came here with nothing."

"I worked, I saved, I bought a small piece of land, against that asset the bank lent me money to build, I sold, did it again, and it all just grew. As long as I can pay the bank interest, I can keep borrowing. And because the country is growing so quickly, the projects become bigger, and, well . . ."

"Well, I'm surprised," Tamara finally interrupted him. "If I'd known all this, I'd have asked for a woolen hat and leather gloves as well!" She shouted out a laugh. "I'm joking."

After lunch back in town Arie left Tamara alone in the Romanian restaurant for twenty minutes, saying he had some quick business to attend to. She drank mint tea, observing the crowd of European women in warm coats and woolen scarves. How snug they were, all bundled up against the cold, chatting over their coffees and cream cakes. A special treat back in the camp was black bread soaked in the juice of stolen oranges. How long had they been in Israel? When would she have a home of her own, and money for meals in a place like this? It hardly seemed possible.

It made her sad, thinking how little she had, and how much she had lost. She often thought of Pascal and the River Nile. Egypt, so far away, was closed to her; Israel, not yet open. She felt neither here nor there. Unwanted, almost unseen. It was horribly hard, living in the tent. Worst of all was the cold and the rain, they had had no idea it would be like this. She longed to be warm, to live in an apartment like Arie's. As for Peter, it was only three days but it already seemed like a long time ago. He had just walked away, saying he couldn't call, and he hadn't written. Why not, why so secretive? Was he married? Didn't he love her? She didn't want to ask Arie about him again. It had been a big mistake. A big, beautiful, crazy mistake.

Her mood lightened as she saw Arie passing in the window, smiling to himself, and entering the restaurant. She felt a rush of warmth; he was so positive, so enthusiastic, how lucky she was to have met him. He removed his coat, hung it over the back of his chair, bowed like a gentleman, and, with a serious face, handed her two small packages. She accepted with an inquisitive glance and, her smile growing, unwrapped the layers of soft tissue paper, to reveal a woolen hat and leather gloves.

Tears came to Tamara's eyes, her lips quivered, and she gripped his hand.

And later, in Arie's room, when Tamara described her family's life and escape from Egypt, one family among twenty thousand Jews, a second Exodus, there were more tears. When she was fourteen, louts from the Muslim Brotherhood, rampaging through Cairo's Haret el Yahoud, the Jewish quarter, punched her in the face. "It didn't hurt, I was too surprised. But they went crazy, they set the synagogue on fire, they even destroyed a hospital and they beat all the Jews they could find." During Israel's war with the Arabs in 1948, her father was fired from the university, men spat at her mother and called them dirty Jews. She lost her Arab friends.

Growing up, Tamara was like a sister to Nanu, their cleaner's daughter, a Muslim, and Tamara smiled as she recalled how they would walk hand in hand, exploring the streets near home. Nanu called her Tameri, because it was close to Tamara, and meant "My Beloved Land," meaning Egypt. But Tamara's voice caught as she remembered how disturbed she was when even Nanu had called her *Sahyuni*, Zionist, which in King Farouk's Egypt was a curse. That was when Tamara knew it wasn't her beloved land anymore. She felt like a rock had been thrown into the still waters of her existence.

When they left Egypt she had hardly felt the stifling heat of the buses as they rattled north across the sandy roads, ferried across the Suez Canal, and slowly made their way through the Sinai Peninsula into Israel. Little Ido and Estie, her brother and sister, slept most of the way, but she couldn't, she was too excited, imagining her new home among her own people: open arms, smiling faces, new friends.

But from their big warm house they had moved into a leaky, cold tent.

Worse, these Jews from Europe who ran the camps for the Jewish Agency didn't speak a word of Arabic and acted superior in every way. Her father, a professor of Arabic literature and philosophy, couldn't talk with them, and now laid irrigation pipes. It was like being a Jew in Cairo, only a different form of insult. And as for the other Jews in the camp, mostly from Morocco and Iraq, they kept to themselves, leaving the few Jews from other countries, like her family, feeling like segregated minorities. In short, little had changed except they had swapped their middling status in life for one at the bottom.

It all came close to breaking her father, who struck out at her in frustration, while all her mother did was line up at the soup kitchen, cook, wash clothes, and wail. Ido, he of the boundless appetite, grew thinner and thinner. And even her sister, Estie, six years old, who in Cairo had always been laughing and playing, seemed lost and alone in the strange tent city.

After almost an hour of describing her life to Arie, Tamara wiped her eyes. "I'm sorry, I shouldn't carry on like this," she said. "My family wasn't killed, like yours." Arie held her in his arms, sighing, for he couldn't very well try to take her clothes off now. He stroked her hair, kissed her forehead. "It's all right," he said. "I'll find you a new home very soon. Your father will work in a school or maybe even a university, your mother can work too, if she wants, and you can study if you like. Do you want to?"

"First things first. My Hebrew must be much better. What we need now is food on the table. Then I'll think about tomorrow."

"But what do you want to do today; right now?" Arie answered, hoping she'd stay the night anyway. He felt Tamara hesitate as she turned to him, a smile playing upon her lips. His heart leapt, was this it? He was glad he had opened Peter's note to Tamara and torn it up. Stay away from my brother, indeed. All's fair in love and war, dear brother.

On the drive back to the camp, Tamara chuckled at how Arie had leapt to his feet when she said that if she was late home her father would kill them both.

Instead, her parents had stared at her new clothes. Everyone had. After Arie dropped her off at the entrance to the transit camp, all heads had followed her as she'd walked along the muddy tracks in her new leather boots and long burgundy coat. She lowered her eyes in embarrassment. Part of her wished she had hidden her gifts. What must everybody be thinking? It made her look like a bought woman. And as her mother shyly touched her woolen hat with one finger and then tried on a leather glove, and smiled at her father as she playfully extended her hand, palm down, to be kissed, Tamara thought, how far have we fallen? After we had everything we could possibly want in Cairo, now look how excited we get at a hat and gloves. In Cairo her mother would have been angry and made her return the gifts. Here, they just wanted to be warm.

That night Tamara struggled with sleep, troubled by the rain's patter on the tent, aware of each sigh as her parents gathered their blankets tighter. Ido coughed, again and again, as if he'd choke; she hoped he wouldn't get pneumonia. Estie, of course, slept like a rock. The moonlight, diffused through the canvas, glinted on her mother's thinning gray hair that bunched from beneath the new woolen hat. What had Arie meant, she wondered, when she had asked again if he had heard from Peter and when he would return. At first Arie had ignored her questions. When she insisted, adding mischievously how handsome Peter was, Arie had answered abruptly: "He'll call whenever he wants to. But I don't know when he'll be back; you never know with him. It could be days or weeks or months."

And then he puzzled her with the words: "I'm building the country, Peter is defending it."

ALIAS VERONIQUE

BRUSSELS, BELGIUM

April 1950

———

A s soon as he had arrived in Europe, Peter Nesher called Veronique, a woman with an instinct for the weak spot of a man. On their last mission together she had understood, at the last moment, that the young German parliament member she had been sent to seduce was a closet homosexual. With no time to find a male replacement, she disguised herself as a handsome boy, and still lured him to the trap.

Her improvisational genius made her perfect for Shiloah's first target: Dr. Lothar Genscher, a man with a secret. And a bad back.

Veronique secured a position as a masseuse in the parlor that the burly thirty-six-year-old engineer frequented in the Brussels suburb of Ixelles, and the appealing brunette immediately became his favorite.

The music was soft, the oil warm, the fragrance delicate, as Veronique gently kneaded Genscher's back, stimulating the tissue around each vertebrae. Her hands glided down his sides, until they fluttered over his gluteus maximus muscles, and she giggled again: "I'm hopeless, I'll never understand."

His voice faded as Genscher struggled to explain the cutting-edge field of electronics, until the firm circular motions of her hands banished any remaining thoughts of electrons and semiconductors, reducing him first to contented silence and soon to sighs and groans of pleasure as he struggled to control a different energy flow.

She rejected his invitations to dinner, but after several more massages, of growing intimacy, he managed to overcome her reticence, and she consented to meet him at the bar and grill of her choice, in Le Berger hotel, on the Porte Namur side of the opulent, seventeenth-century market square. It was an outwardly respectable establishment, but the hotel's art deco suites doubled as discreet hideaways for illicit couples, whose comings and goings could be concealed by an elevator that exited directly onto the street.

Two nights later, in the smoky grill, Veronique, devouring her steak au poivre, was full of humor and vague promise, elegant yet earthy. Dr. Lothar Genscher, who over wine, cognac, and calvados became Lothar, which became Lotto, was quite swept away. In their wood-paneled alcove the masseuse, with her revealing lace décolleté and solicitous serving of the French cabernet, was the picture of desirable youth, struggling yet again to understand the work of the company he had founded, Elektro SPRL. Her peals of laughter at the intricacies she was failing to grasp melted his heart. After all, even his wife didn't understand a word of it.

Leering at her across the candles, which sparkled in her eyes and brought a flickering glow to her cheeks, he thought, she's beautiful. Beautiful but limited, with a pedestrian background, as he had learned over dinner: Born in Brussels, she had spent the war safely at home with her mother while her father fought the Germans in France and Germany, only to be killed in the last month of hostilities. She hadn't finished high school, but earned a hairdresser's diploma. Then, because of the "opportunities," she learned to be a masseuse and now hoped to graduate from this dreary suburb to a "better-class salon" closer to the Grand-Place, the market square, where the real money was. She looked at him with a coquettish air, expectant, it seemed to him.

Exquisite but transparent, he thought, like so many of her age, their youth lost in the war. She should stop playing hard to get. Basically, she's just looking for a rich husband.

Fortified by the thought and the alcohol, Genscher said, "It's getting late." He drained his third calvados, and settled his glass back on the table. "And I hope you don't mind, my dear Veronique, but I took the liberty of booking a room here. It's small but interesting with exceptional art deco touches. I wonder, would you care to join me there? For another drink?" He took from his jacket pocket a key attached to a wooden disk, showing the number six. "It will be quieter there."

Veronique surveyed the silent room, her lips curling into the hint of a smile. "Art deco touches?" she said at last, drawing out the last word.

"Yes," he said, with a lascivious grin. "Lots of them."

"Well, I could certainly do with another drink," she said with a sudden laugh, gesturing toward the empty wine bottle and the half-empty bottle of apple brandy. She leaned forward, and his eyes dropped to her cleavage as she whispered, "I don't want to go up together. You go first and I'll follow in five minutes. Don't close the door."

Genscher leaned across the table to kiss her on those luscious full lips, but she pulled back with a wink. "Slowly, Lotto, slowly," she said. "All good things come to he who waits. In five minutes, then, upstairs. Room number six."

As he undressed, Dr. Lothar Genscher surveyed himself in the full-length mirror that faced the bed. He turned to his profile and patted his belly, sucking it in. His light-brown hair was thinning and receding, his brow was creased, but still his chest was powerful and his arms were strong. He watched himself shrug off his shirt and trousers, and smiled with satisfaction. Lothar, well done. He had fantasized over the bimbo downstairs for weeks, and now he would have her, every juicy part of her, those breasts, those legs, those hands.

Genscher closed his eyes with a deep sigh and removed his underpants, regretting how little time he had. He had told his wife he was at a business meeting and he should really return home before she became suspicious. Not that he cared. He turned to examine the bedside lamp and its base of sculpted stone. It supported a naked marble nymph whose outstretched arm held the stained-glass lampshade. He turned off the main light, leaving the room dimly lit in hues of blue, green, and red. He lay naked on his stomach, covered himself with a sheet, and waited for the masseuse. His masseuse. Beautiful young Veronique, with those magnificent young breasts. He didn't have time for more drinks.

Two minutes later the door opened slowly and he felt the slightest breeze of cooler air whisk his neck. The door closed gently and he heard the click of the key. A smile of anticipation spread across Genscher's face, resting on the soft pillow, as light footsteps approached the bed.

Another click and the room was in darkness. He shifted, and waited. A shiver of suspense ran down his back. She knows how to do this!

He felt a prick on the base of his neck. A sharp fingernail? She'll caress him, all the way down. But the prick felt sharper, and then pressed down. He realized it may cut him, and his breath caught. He began to struggle, to twist around, but a weight pressed him into the bed.

He gasped in fear at the man's voice.

"If you move I will cut your spinal cord." This was said in a voice so calm it could have been ordering a steak. "You will be paralyzed for life."

Genscher froze. He heaved, trying to suck in air. With an effort, Genscher raised his head and turned it so he could breathe. His guts were on fire.

"I'm going to turn on the light," the man continued in German. "Don't shout; nobody will come. Don't try anything, I won't kill you, but I will maim you and it isn't worth it. I just want to talk to you. You can turn around."

He slid off Genscher's back and drew up a chair while Genscher pulled the sheet to his neck to cover his nakedness, which made him feel even more helpless. "Who are you?" he said. "What do you want? Where is Veronique?"

"You are married," the man said, showing the eight-inch blade in his lap.

"What? Is that what this is about? Are you crazy? You scared the life out of me. Put that knife away. And what do you care? Who are you, anyway?"

"My name is Willimod Stinglwagner. Call me Willi," said Peter Nesher.

Genscher almost laughed. "What sort of name is that?"

"Bavarian. You think this is funny?"

"Actually, yes. Get out of the room. You think you scare me because you'll tell my wife about Veronique? Go ahead. You think I care? Anyway, there's nothing to tell. So I had dinner with my masseuse, so what? Now get out of here." But as he spoke Genscher pressed back into the soft headboard of the bed.

Peter leaned forward, placed the knifepoint high up Genscher's inner thigh, on his femoral artery, and pressed until beads of sweat appeared on Genscher's brow. "If I cut here you'll die in minutes," he said. With his other hand Peter pulled his jacket aside to reveal the butt of a pistol strapped to his side. *"Noch immer so komisch?"* Still find it funny?

Genscher shook his head and managed to say, "What do you want?"

"The thing is, Monsieur Genscher," Peter said, "you're not who you say you are, are you?"

Genscher looked at him with loathing.

"Does your wife know?"

"Know what?"

"Do you miss them?"

"Who?"

Peter pulled a large manila envelope from his pocket and drew out a photo. A woman stood against an ivy-covered wall watching two children playing at her feet. It was taken from a distance but was pin sharp.

"Why, Elisa, Uwe, and Friedrich of course."

Genscher's jaw dropped and he went white. He looked from the photo to Peter and back again, and grabbed the picture.

"Keep it," Peter said. "We have plenty more. Take it home. Maybe your wife here would like to know about your wife there. And about your two little boys. They do look sweet." He could see Genscher's mind racing as he looked at the photos.

"Again I ask you, what do you want?" Genscher said. "You want to blackmail me? For what? Is this about my research? Because if it is, all you have to do is knock on my door. It's for sale, we are a commercial company."

"Ah, that's it. Precisely. But the opposite. We don't want you to sell your research."

"So what do you want? Do you really think I can be blackmailed? Do you know how much I miss my family in Germany? I would give anything to go home, to live with them again."

"So why don't you?" Peter said, tapping Genscher's leg with his blade. "And by the way, please cover yourself." Genscher had let the sheet slide down, revealing a white chest covered in matted black hair. "Well? Why don't you?"

Genscher remained silent, looking at the photograph of his family. Peter knew what he must be thinking. They're five and seven now, it's a recent photo, what else do they know about me? And, who are They?

Peter switched to English, his Midwestern drawl. "You speak English?" he asked.

"Yes."

Peter knew Genscher had studied at MIT before the war. He had been an outstanding electrical engineering student, but had answered the Nazi call, summoning him home to the Fatherland.

"So," Peter said. "Bigamy."

"A minor crime. I'll divorce and go home. I'd be glad to."

"I don't think so."

Genscher waited. What did this man have to do with Veronique? Where was she? She must be working with him or she would have entered the room by now.

"Let's get down to business," Peter said. "Shall we, Herr Braun? Hans-Dieter Braun. SS-Sturmbannführer Hans-Dieter Braun?"

Genscher tensed. So he knows that too. So what? What can he do? There were thousands of Nazis like him, tens of thousands. Only a handful had been arrested, and even fewer served time. It's ancient history now—fascism is over. Today a new Europe is being built, and old enemies are united against the new threat of communism. Germany needs experienced people who can get things done. He felt his chest subsiding with relief. It's time at last. He could finally go home, face the music, live with his family, live his real life.

Peter sized him up. His hair was thinner, the silly little mustache was gone, he seemed stockier, but there was no mistaking him from the other photos in the brown envelope. This was the same little bastard all right. Peter quashed a sneer and the instinct to punish. Israel needed this man.

"That is indeed my name," Genscher/Braun said finally, and waited.

Peter had been through this before. Their arrogance knew no bounds. Sniveling bullies, all of them. But when they broke, they shattered. They cried, and begged.

Peter waited. Genscher broke the silence. "So you will give my name to the authorities. And when they arrest me, if they do, I will say I obeyed orders. I was an honest soldier for my country, which is the truth. And I will go home to my family. That is the worst that can happen to me."

"If that's true, then I'm curious why you haven't done that already," Peter said. "Could this be why?"

And fixing him with his eyes, Peter withdrew the next photo from the envelope, waiting for the Nazi's reaction. He pulled out half a dozen more pictures and laid them on the bed, one next to the other, lined up like a firing squad.

Genscher's eyes widened, then he gasped. He seized one photo, then the next, and the next, looking at Peter with shock, and then back at the photos. They shook in his hands. He hurled them to the floor. He was trembling, and beneath the sheet his legs twitched.

"You will be put to death," Peter said. "Either by the courts or by the people." He couldn't blow his cover by saying aloud what he thought: Those who feed on Jews, choke on them.

He gathered the evidence from the floor, and offered it to Genscher/ Braun, who turned violently toward the wall, his whole body shaking. "It was so long ago," he managed.

"Oh, not so long. What, seven, eight years? Anyway, I doubt that matters in your case," Peter said, sliding the photos one by one back into the envelope. "That is you here with the knife, isn't it? And here, cutting the baby from the mother's belly? She's screaming, it appears. Who wouldn't? It's quite a series of photographs, don't you think? Technically, very proficient. Well lit. And there are more, as you can see. The one with you laughing over the female corpse is particularly sharp and clear. With your boot on her naked breasts." He tapped Genscher's knee again with the knife. "These photos are your death warrant. But perhaps not yet. And maybe never, SS-Sturmbannführer Hans-Dieter Braun. But if you want to survive you must do what we want you to do."

PETER and ALIAS KARLA

STUTTGART, GERMANY

June 1950

Günther Steinhoff was next on Peter's list. A rising star in the Wies-baden mayor's office, with his eyes set all the way to the federal capital in Bonn; his wartime sadism on the Eastern Front, fully documented by Shiloah's sources, exposed him to blackmail.

It had taken five weeks of identification and pursuit, two weeks of meticulous planning, three days of pressure and coercion, and half an hour in a hotel room, but instead of the recruitment of an agent, it had led to the flash of a hunting knife, now rusting in the River Rhine.

Afterward, Peter walked briskly to Wiesbaden's Hauptbahnhof, the main train station, where he called Karla, alias Veronique, who was waiting by the phone in the hotel. He told her to leave town immediately and to meet him at 5:00 P.M. at the Ritterhof Hotel in Frankfurt, which she knew meant 6:00 P.M. at the Weinstube Adlerberg in Stuttgart.

He sat at a window seat, staring out onto the rain and the glistening lawns of Schlossplatz, toying with his linsen and spätzle, his favorite local dish. He had little appetite; he was replaying the disaster in his mind, wondering where he had gone wrong.

He should have realized that an SS intelligence officer could not be broken as easily as the others, and that he was a lot smarter. Where had he failed? It wasn't his American English; that was flawless. His preparation and documentation were immaculate. He had even showed Steinhoff his CIA card, which was a perfect forgery, down to the embossed government seal and the tortuous signature of the director, Roscoe H. Hillenkoetter.

Maybe it really was true that the SS could smell a Jew. Either way, Steinhoff sentenced himself to death when he sneered that the CIA would never hire a Jew like Stinglwagner.

"You are an Israeli, aren't you?" Steinhoff had said. "You think I'd work for your stinking country?"

It wasn't the insult that made Peter wait for the right moment to glide behind Steinhoff's back, seize his head, and slit his throat. It was his instructions from the Mossad chief. Nobody, under any circumstances, Shiloah had told him that first February evening in Tel Aviv, must know that Israel was building a spy network in Germany. Any hint could dilute German support for the Jewish state just as Konrad Adenauer, the German chancellor, was beginning to say that maybe the new Germany should take responsibility for Nazi crimes and compensate the Jews, some kind of financial reparations for lost lives and property. It could mean German blood money, hundreds of millions of dollars that Israel badly needed. For Israel, German guilt was an economic asset.

That's why Shiloah had warned him always to make the pitch in the privacy of a hotel room, where quick action, if necessary, could be taken, unobserved. Preferably in the afternoon, after the maid had cleaned the room, so he would have a full day before the body was discovered. The DO NOT DISTURB sign could buy a few more hours.

Shiloah had ordered: If a target realizes this is a false flag operation, if he works out you are an Israeli, kill him. He deserves it anyway.

Those words were in Peter's mind as he sprang with the knife: He deserves it anyway.

He had felt a flash of doubt, instantly banished, and a surge of adrenaline that had all but lifted him from the ground. He was a soldier at that moment, bayonetting the gunners, not from a meter at the end of a rifle but gripping Steinhoff's hair in his hand. An instant of godly power, a hint of regret overcome, and it was done. He had pushed away the gurgling head and stuffed a towel into the hole.

So far, Peter reflected, watching the rain from inside the restaurant, I've caught one and killed one. Not a good average. Must do better. Four more on the list. At this rate he'd never see Tamara again, and the thought prompted a deep sigh.

"What's wrong?" The woman now called Karla, alias Veronique, hung her coat on the hook by the table and placed her hat on it. She swung onto the bench opposite him.

"So what went wrong?" she asked, after ordering a beer. The nearest diners were two tables away but she still lowered her voice.

When he told her, she said only, "Good. It's better that way."

He knew what she meant. They'd been arguing for months, even though it didn't affect their jobs. It was a moral question and it wasn't clear who had the high ground. Karla thought there was no such thing as an ex-Nazi; once a Nazi always a Nazi, and that if they discovered a truly evil person, they should kill him, not offer to work with him.

Her belief was shared by many in the Israeli government. But Shiloah, and presumably his boss, the prime minister, David Ben-Gurion, believed blackmailing high-level ex-Nazis, making a pact with the devil, made sense if it helped the country, which needed all the help it could get.

It was a moral quandary that had not yet been resolved in Jerusalem, but Shiloah believed the country's situation was too dire to delay. So, while the politicians dithered, the agents acted off the books.

Which made it lonely. With all his being Peter became his cover, the German Willi Stinglwagner, medical products importer. He had to think in German, dream in German, be a German, nothing could break his cover. How true the warning had been during his brief training: When you're an agent in the field, don't worry about it affecting your home life because you won't have one. He couldn't contact the embassies, or local Israelis who could ask awkward questions, or go anywhere they frequented, or phone home, write, or communicate in any way with his brother or, more important, with Tamara. It had been months since he had met her, and he had fallen off the map. He couldn't chance a call. Orders were strict. Right before the War of Independence the Arabs had caught an entire Jewish spy cell in Jaffa just because two of them had been overheard speaking Hebrew on tapped phones. Three were executed.

All he could do was lie in his hotel bed, smoke, and dream of Tamara. Would she wait for him? Why should she? Just because he had asked her to in the note he'd given to his brother? What did Arie tell her about him? He tried not to imagine his brother courting her. Arie had money, he loved to party, while he, Peter, couldn't even keep a dinner date. Or give a reasonable excuse for not turning up. His whole life was a lie. Everything was a conspiracy, everyone had an ulterior motive, he was always one false step from catastrophe.

Or killing. True, for his country. But where was the line between exacting justice, and murder, and who set it? Shiloah once asked him if he wanted to avenge his parents, and he had said yes. What else could he have said? But when does that revenge end? How many can you kill? Isn't the true revenge just existing when the Nazis wanted to wipe them out? Building their own country instead of again scattering across the globe? But if it is, someone must defend it.

"Hello? Hello? Anybody home?" Karla was peering into his face. "What did I just say?"

He gave a smile of embarrassment. "I have no idea, sorry. I was thinking . . ." He raised his glass and clinked against hers. "Prost."

"Cheers. Well, I just told you a very funny story and you missed it. Your loss."

He enjoyed Karla. She was funny, clever, sharp. Her real name was Diana, and her namesake in ancient Rome, she loved to point out, was the goddess of the hunt, the moon, and childbirth. A British journalist with a German father and a French mother, she was trilingual. During the war the British had interned her father for a year on the Isle of Man, afraid that "enemy aliens," even Jews, could be German spies, but he was freed in 1943 in time to join the British Army Intelligence Corps.

She had survived the London Blitz with her mother, who worked as a translator for the BBC, while supporting General de Gaulle's Free French movement. It was her mother who got her started in journalism, and it was her father's contacts and experiences that gave her something to write about. But it was Peter who'd recruited her.

Her work as a freelance journalist was a perfect cover for her long periods on the European mainland. And her classic beauty: high cheekbones, full lips with a ready smile, green eyes that gleamed, and long, soft auburn hair that bounced as she walked, made heads turn. But it was her focus that had won Peter's attention, when he first sat opposite her at a lunch in Paris. Her brow had puckered in absorption as she hung on to his every word, her look of admiration and appreciation was flattering, pleasing, charming. It had made him feel the most important man in the world. And there was no way that she meant it: Peter had thought, I'm just not that interesting. It's an act, a brilliant act. We need someone like her. Beautiful, calculating, and above all, able to suppress a yawn.

From that meeting, and several more, had been born a fruitful cooperation in the service of the State of Israel, for with very little training, Diana Greenberg had become a genius at entrapment. She could lead a man to the gallows and make him think the noose around his neck was the latest fashion in neckties.

One tipsy evening in Amsterdam, Peter had told Diana about Tamara and he came to regret it. Over a bottle of wine she had told him about her special friend, a schoolteacher, with a sweet little house in the Home Counties with a white wooden gate and a blue front door. He thought she was a journalist, a sensitive writer of human-interest stories. That's the person he fell in love with, who he wanted to marry. He was sweet, but he didn't dare tell his parents she was Jewish. "Can you imagine if they knew what I do for you?" she said to Peter with a high-pitched laugh. "Anyway, I'm thinking of moving to Israel."

And, as for Peter, he felt stupid when Diana had asked him how long he had known this wonderful girl he missed so much. First he had hesitated, recognizing the absurdity, then answered, the last word rising as if in a question: Two hours? Diana's eyes, always large, had widened further as she'd absorbed the import of what he'd said. She brought her hand to her mouth to suppress a giggle, but couldn't help herself and it came out as a hoot, and then she had burst out laughing. "I'm sorry," she tried to say, but it emerged as a yelp, and she repeated, "you've known her for two hours?" and he began laughing too. He couldn't stop, nor could she. They had fairly rocked with laughter, gasping and helpless in the quiet family restaurant, gripping their sides, while couples with children tut-tutted their disapproval.

How stupid can you be? Two hours! He didn't even know her family name. Or how old she was—did she say nineteen? Did she still know he even existed?

He knew only one thing for sure: For him, two hours were enough.

TAMARA and ARIE

HERZLIYA, ISRAEL
March 1950

After Peter had left, Tamara hadn't known what to think. She certainly felt different: Could she be pregnant? She shivered at the thought and, with no word from Peter, she felt abandoned. He said he couldn't contact her. Why not? Of course he could, if he wanted to. Arie had said so.

Nobody must ever know what she had done, especially her parents, who would never understand her moment of weakness, that beautiful moment of passion. In Israel, everything had changed, values were upside down. The strong became weak, respect was an empty word, European Jews ruled. This land had promised so much and given so little: They still lived in a tent with no real work.

And now here was Arie, bearing presents and promises. Could she tell him about Peter? No, never. Arie was kind and generous and sweet. Could she love Arie, after making love with his brother? Or was Arie's wealth turning her head, a ticket out of the misery of the camp?

Whatever was happening, it was happening fast, though not as fast as with Peter, thank God. She had resisted Arie once, and since then he hadn't tried again. They snuggled together on the bed, to keep warm as much as anything else, and that was all. Sometimes they dozed, but mostly they talked. And she already knew that for all his humor and strength, Arie was in pain. If she needed somebody to speak to, Arie needed it more.

It was a joke that had made Arie talk about the bluish, vein-like numbers, 126497, tattooed on his forearm, and then Tamara wished he hadn't.

She had laughed when he told her his name had been Aren Berg before he changed it to Arie ben Nesher, which meant Lion, son of the Eagle.

"How noble," she had said, "how powerful. King of the jungle, master of the skies. The New Israeli."

"If you think that's funny," he had replied, "what about my friend Dov, remember him, the taxi driver?"

"What about him?"

"Paul Kokotek was his name in Poland. Here he's Dov ben Arie, Bear, son of Lion. And then there's Sammy Schnitzler, you don't know him. Here he's Natanel—Gift of God. Everyone reinvents himself here; it's wishful thinking. It's like a snake shedding damaged skin. No more diaspora Jew, here, they're reborn as fighters, at least in name."

It was cold that evening as they had huddled beneath the blanket by the little electric heater, its one bar glowing red in the dark, like a warning.

"You're strong," Tamara had said, thinking of nothing but the hardness of his body. But she had felt his body tense and he went silent. What is it? she thought.

"You don't know how right you are," he had finally replied. She had said, "What do you mean?"

In the same way he had to eat, had to sleep, had to breathe, sooner or later he had to tell someone something; it was too much to bear alone. Outside, he was a *hevreman*, one of the guys, while inside, he was drying up.

Indeed, he had been strong: a fighter. In Auschwitz, where Jews fought Jews and if you won you lived to fight again, like a gladiator. In Rome, if you lost, you were fed to the beasts. In Auschwitz, you were fed to the ovens, and you rose to heaven in a column of smoke.

It had been nearly six years since the SS had abandoned Auschwitz a gasp ahead of the Soviet troops. But for Arie, liberation did not mean he was safe. There would be a different danger, it would be payback time. Already, he had seen packs of inmates kick and beat SS guards to death while their Russian liberators cheered.

Tamara had sensed the tension in Arie's body as he forced himself to break his vow of silence. His voice was low, she strained to hear. "I mean . . . you're right. I was . . . strong, a fighter. They made some of us fight." He spoke haltingly, as if hearing each word for the first time, describing a nightmare, something he barely believed, a horror divorced from the safety of this moment by the heater with the girl he was beginning to love. "The Kommandant, the guards, they arranged boxing matches, you got extra food, you didn't have to work so hard, they kept us alive so we could fight to the death, or near death." Now it was Tamara, hanging on every word, whose body went tense. "I kept winning, so I kept fighting, and I stayed alive. For months, that went on. I don't know how I was such a fighter, I was always bigger and stronger than everyone else at school, but it wasn't about winning. It was about surviving; I suppose I wanted to stay alive more than anyone else did. It was like a dogfight, all the guards yelling, drunk, betting. We were an entertainment for the Nazis."

Tamara could hardly breathe as she listened. Her breath came in sharp intakes, she felt the hair rise on her neck, barely comprehending that the body next to hers, the hand that gripped hers too tightly, the feet that lay over hers, this kind man could have done such things.

"They didn't let us stop until there was blood. A lot of it. I don't know how many I beat. I as good as killed them, they were bleeding on the ground and were taken to the ovens, or they were shot. But it was them or me. That's the truth." He stopped suddenly. He breathed in as deeply as he could and heaved the deepest sigh she had ever heard.

"Yes, I was strong. So I got more food. And the other Jews didn't like it. They hated me. But I lived. And now here I am." He paused. "Here we are." He sighed again, and felt relief, but not for long. Now he felt shame. And fear, as Tamara lay silently beside him. He had exposed himself. For what? It could only harm him; he shouldn't have said a word. Just because she said he was strong?

He pushed her hand away.

She felt tears in her eyes, and noticed herself edging away from his tense body. He was breathing fast, almost panting. Was he feeling it now, was it still so real? She couldn't imagine such a memory, such a reality, such a life.

And he said he had only been a fighter for a few months. What else had he done to survive for years? He had said that her worst nightmares were better than what he woke up to each morning. Now, beneath the cozy blanket, he had uncovered his soul: how he must suffer.

Yet after a few minutes, when she glanced at him, she saw that his eyes were closed, his face was relaxed, his breaths were shallow and easy. He had unburdened himself and she wished she could do the same. There was nobody to tell: Her period was late and she was frightened. She had been irregular for months because of all the changes in her life, the new diet, but . . . but now it was different. She had made love with a man.

She heard Arie mutter something. "What?" she whispered, "I couldn't hear."

He said it again. She moved closer, put her ear to his mouth. "I can't hear."

His breath tickled. "I said, thank you."

ARIE and TAMARA

———————

O ne afternoon the car wouldn't start.

"You don't know much about cars, do you?" Tamara said, as Arie kicked the tire for the third time.

"I know enough to know I should never have bought this *shtuck dreck,* this piece of garbage. . . . It's something to do with the battery. Or the ignition. Or the carburetor. Or whatever. How should I know?"

"What's *shtuck dreck?*"

"Yiddish. You don't want to know. Let's get a taxi."

"Never mind, we don't have to go."

"No, you'll like it. I really want to take you there."

"But you haven't said where. And what about the car?"

Arie liked his car. He had bought the 1945 Ford Prefect from a friend who had bought it from a British businessman who left when the British army pulled out in '48. "It's a 100E, four-stroke ignition, very fast acceleration," the friend had told Arie. "Zero to eighty kilometers an hour in less than twenty-six seconds." Arie loved to put his foot down and feel the thrust, and race other cars. Tamara would grip the sides of her seat and beg him to slow down.

"I'll fix it later. Or sell it. Right now, I've got something much more important to do. Come on. It's a surprise." They walked to the phone box two streets away and called for a cab.

In the taxi Arie mused, as usual, about what he should do next. "Cars. That's the future," he said. "You know there's only about thirteen hundred miles of road in all of Israel. We need to build more road and then there'll be more of everything. More road construction, more cars, more spare parts, more gasoline, more gas stations, more garages, we're growing so fast it doesn't matter what you do, everything is growing, you just have to be on board, grow with it. You know what they say, a rising sea lifts all ships."

"Unless it sinks them."

He laughed, and almost shouted: "But it won't. I could make a fortune just importing parts to fix my own car."

Tamara had never met anybody with so much ambition, with so many ideas. He told her that a week earlier he had visited a poultry farm as workers slaughtered chickens. He watched as they plucked the feathers and threw them into bags. There were piles of them, and when he asked what happened to the feathers the farmer told him they were thrown into a garbage pit somewhere. That made him think of the feather beds he loved in Germany and another business idea was born. He would collect chicken feathers and manufacture luxury pillows and quilts.

And Arie told her that the reason he'd been at the chicken farm in the first place was to find out what the birds ate. He wanted to collect discarded food in towns and sell it as animal feed.

The taxi dropped them at the cliff just north of the Sidna Ali transit camp, or *ma'abara*, as it was also known. Rows of white tents crowded along hilly dirt paths.

"What are we doing here?" she said. "This is where I live."

"You'll see."

It was a fine sunny day, a relief from the winter chill. She followed him as he picked his way down a ravine lined with bushes and thorns that led to the deserted beach. "I love it here," he kept saying.

The water was almost as blue as the sky and gentle waves caressed the sand. They took off their shoes and walked along the narrow beach until the way was blocked by jagged sections of ancient brick walls that had crumbled into the sea.

"You know why I love it here so much?" he said.

"Why?"

He dragged his foot through the sand and watched the little gully fill with water. "Because not far from here is where I first set foot on the Holy Land. Four years ago. The boat anchored fifty yards offshore and we waded through the water at night so that the British wouldn't see us. No lights. There was a British police post up there." Arie gazed toward the hilltop and then pointed out to sea. "There were about three hundred of us, so-called illegal immigrants, on the tiniest, ricketiest boat you've ever seen, she made it all the way from Italy, and we were half-dead when they threw the anchor overboard. They told us not to waste a second and run for it or, rather, swim. The water was almost over my head. Half of us carried the other half. I was carrying an old man, and his suitcase. I didn't have anything. Luckily, there were Jewish boys waiting to help us; I don't know if I would have made it otherwise. When I made it to land I almost dropped the old man, I was in such a hurry to kiss the sand. And now this is where I come when I need to be alone."

Tamara smiled. "But you're not alone."

Arie's eyes shone. "Nor do I want to be. Not anymore."

He took Tamara's hand and helped her clamber over the rocks. On the other side he walked slowly, with care, eyes fixed to the ground, but after a minute it was Tamara who called out, "Look what I found." On one knee she inspected an oblong object in a color she had never seen. It was a transparent sky blue, opaque in part yet smoky too, with delicate ivory streaks, the size of half her thumb and smooth as a ball. It sparkled as she held it up and turned it in the sunlight.

Arie laughed. "That's what I wanted to find. There are lots of them here sometimes, after storms, and that's a nice one. Do you know what it is?"

"A stone. It's beautiful. I've never seen anything like it."

"Ah! Because it isn't a stone. It's a piece of glass. More than a thousand years old." He told her its history: The rock and sections of smashed brick walls piled on the sand were remains of a Byzantine glass foundry that had fallen into the sea when the cliff collapsed a thousand years ago. It had produced glass for most of the Eastern Mediterranean. The foundry's waste products were dumped into the sea and today, those ancient chunks of discarded glass, smoothed by centuries of currents and sand, polished by the constant battering of the water, lay hidden among the sand and pebbles of the ocean floor. A storm or high seas caused turbulence that freed the shards from the grip of the seabed and washed them to shore.

Arie took the glass gem from Tamara's hand, wiped it on his shorts, put it to his mouth, and kissed it. "It's the most beautiful piece of glass I've ever seen," he said, "and it was found by the most beautiful person I've ever known. You're so lucky to find it, but I'm even luckier." He took Tamara's hands in his. "Because I found you."

Tamara lowered her gaze, unsure what to say. She felt the heat of her cheeks. Her bare feet and spread toes sank into the sand as waves sucked back into the sea.

"You know what I would like to do?" he said.

"Yes. Find lots of these, of all sizes and shapes, and make beautiful rings and necklaces and earrings, in settings of silver and gold, and sell them, and get rich quick."

Arie roared with laughter. The sun glinted in his eyes. "That's a great idea, maybe I will. Why didn't I think of that! But, actually, I was thinking of something else."

With the sheer cliff of Apollonia looming above them, birds hooting and swooping over the waves, Arie sank to one knee and said: "I'll make it into an engagement ring. I know we haven't known each other long and this is crazy, but, Tamara, I'm alone and you're alone, I love you, will you marry me?"

PETER

TEL AVIV, ISRAEL

August 1950

———————

The tense young man called Willi Stinglwagner boarded the plane in his dark suit and Peter Nesher got off. Blistering heat shimmered off the tarmac, beads of sweat rolled from Peter's hairline, but he swung his heavy bag like a bunch of feathers. He couldn't wait to change into shorts and a short-sleeved shirt. He looked proudly at the letters "El Al" painted in blue on the converted DC-4 that had flown him from London to Lod Airport: Israel, my country, my home!

Peter smiled to himself as he presented his passport to the bearded Jew in the booth, back among his own people, but minutes later, outside the arrival shed, he recoiled at the yelling, sweating mob of porters grabbing at his case, the cabdrivers and lollipop vendors pushing and shoving for business.

A familiar voice yelled and the Office driver elbowed his way through, leading Peter to the car, where Peter sat back with a deep sigh. It was sweltering, but, thank God, he thought, no more Germans. For now, anyway. Three days earlier he had received the message to return home quickly, and had rushed to London to catch a direct flight on Israel's new national airline.

But even as he relaxed among his own, a painful thought inserted itself: Own? Who? He was happy to see his brother again, his best friend in the

world, but who else? He had had no time to make friends. He could barely
summon up a vision of Tamara. Would he even recognize her in a crowd?
The note he had left for her seemed pitiful now. It had been half a year. If
once he had dared hope she would wait for him, he had dismissed that
hope months ago. He had lost her, he knew that. But . . . maybe . . . part of
him held on to a vestige of hope like a drowning man grabs at a twig.

Waiting all afternoon in the familiar anteroom at the Office in Ben-Yehuda
Street, Peter wondered why Shiloah wanted to see him so urgently this
time. He hadn't even been home yet. In Germany he had sent regular reports directly to Shiloah: the Info File, on who he had recruited, what they
had said, how they could one day be activated; and the Ops Report, the
nitty-gritty details about where the meetings were held, who knew about
them, what else had happened in the meetings, especially the two that had
gone badly. He had even submitted his expenses report; although they were
all taught to lie, steal, and cheat for Israel, God help them if they did the
same for themselves. They operated on a shoestring, forever fighting for
bigger budgets, which is why the high living of the Paris office was so dis-
tressful. The reports were all routine though.

It was not routine for a lowly operative to have a private meeting with
the big boss just when rumor had it a massive reorganization of the secret
services was under way. Unless Shiloah had another below-the-radar job in
mind. Peter groaned. All he wanted was to go home.

That thought made him squirm: He had transformed one chance en-
counter with a complete stranger who probably didn't remember he existed
into an imagined love affair. But that was six months ago, and he had gotten over her. Or had he? Peter lay on the daybed, one hand beneath his
head, the other hanging over the side with a cigarette, staring at the ceiling. It was embarrassing. He must be very hard up to concoct a phantom
affair out of such thin gruel.

But: He could still feel the softness of her body when he'd stopped and
she had bumped into him in the corridor. He remembered, how could he
not, her delicate hands pulling her coat to cover her bare throat; her naked
feet; her coy and shy smile and how she blushed when she said she was en-

tering the same apartment. And then, inside, everything about her. Dressing while he and Arie looked away. Her saying, "Now you can turn around." She had looked so beautiful, with her shiny big eyes, her wet hair around her shoulders, and then, holding her hair, enjoying every damp strand, its soapy fragrance, his hand cupping her head, her naked shoulders, her breasts barely covered by the little towel, a moment of such intimacy, the memory of which in his lonely bed had helped him fall asleep many a time. So tender, young, and exciting. And then, they had made love, gloriously. She didn't say, and there had been no blood, but he was sure it had been her first time.

Still, it's over. In his note he had asked her to wait, but so what? He wondered where she was. What she was doing.

And Arie. What crookedness was he up to now to get rich? Was the apartment a mess?

Yes, that was the one certainty in his life, when he got home he'd have to clean up. The thought made him chuckle. It would be good to see his brother again.

At the tap on the door he stood and accompanied the girl to Shiloah's office, a bare impersonal room: a simple wooden desk, four chairs, two landscapes of Jerusalem, and the obligatory portrait of the country's leader, his white mane framed by a halo of light. On a side table sat a cheap *hanukiah*, with a pile of colored candles next to it, which reminded Peter that it was Hanukah; he would be home for the holidays. He had better buy some presents. But who for? Arie? He's already got everything.

Shiloah came in, pointed to a chair, and didn't waste words. "That Steinhoff bastard, what happened?"

Peter replied in kind. "It was clean. Quick. Quiet. As I wrote in the report, the hotel was close to the train station, that's why we chose it, so I took the first train that left, it was going north to Hamburg. I got off at the next stop and made my way by bus and another train to the fallback rendezvous with Veronique. Why? Is that a problem?"

"No, not at all. Pity it came to that, that's all, we could have used him, but no, no problem. You did well, what you had to do. I want to talk to you about some things. Veronique. Karla. In other words, Diana Greenberg."

Peter leaned back in relief. It wasn't another job. He could stay home, for now, anyway. He caught himself and sat straighter. Shiloah wouldn't miss a thing but could get the wrong impression. With him you always had to be raring to go.

"Tired, Peter? It was a long job."

"Not too much. But well, it's nice to be home for the holidays."

"Good. Enjoy it. While you can."

Peter tensed. Maybe he wouldn't tidy up the apartment, after all. It may not be worth it.

"First, I'm going to tell you something that I don't want you to repeat," Shiloah said. "It will all come out in due course, but I want to make sure you continue to be available to me for special operations. The prime minister has instructed me to reorganize the intelligence community. I'm sure you've heard that already. I'm bringing all foreign intelligence gathering under one roof: The Institute for Intelligence and Special Tasks. It's a bit of a misnomer, though, because for now, at least, I have to be sensitive politically. So the institute will gather the information while actual foreign jobs will still be carried out by military intelligence, which will have the new name of Aman.

"I will head the new institute. It will be known as Mossad. Now, some jobs must remain secret, even from Aman. And that's where you come in. You will be my first operational hire. For special ops, answerable directly to me. No title yet. Do you accept?"

Peter felt his nerve ends tingle. He's looking right through me, he thought. He knows I'd never say no. His brother flashed into his mind. His response would be: What's the pay raise?

Peter stood up. He didn't know why, but he looked Shiloah directly in the eyes and saluted. A rigid American salute, palm out, fingers together, thumb snug along the hand, he snapped his right hand till the tip of his forefinger touched his right eyebrow, just as he did in the 45th. It wasn't a gesture of servility, but of respect and trust, and it was about as un-Israeli as you could get. Here, to show respect to an officer, you didn't punch him.

Shiloah said, in a laconic voice, "I take it that's a yes."

Peter dropped his arm to his side, and thought better of shaking Shiloah's hand. "I couldn't be more honored, sir," he said.

"Good. Consider it done. The paperwork will be drawn up in due course and until then, this stays between us. Only one other person knows about this: none other than David Ben-Gurion himself. He knows you did important work in Europe, especially in Germany. He appreciates your discretion and, shall we say, decisiveness in the heat of the moment. Let's leave it at that. For now."

Shiloah went on to the other item. "Diana Greenberg. She's asked to move to Israel. But she's valuable in Europe."

Peter suppressed a smile. "She certainly is."

"Tell me about her . . ."

"You've read in the reports what she did. Invaluable. But beyond that, what can I say? She's beautiful, sexy, intelligent, I'd say a keeper."

Shiloah raised an eyebrow, and said with a sniff, "Tell me more that relates to her fieldwork, where she could serve us best."

Peter had left his apartment with a backpack, and now he returned with the same backpack, unopened. The clothes he really traveled with, European suits and ties and shirts, he had returned to the office rack, ready for the next slim agent of average size who needed to melt into a European crowd. He searched his pockets for the key to the apartment and found it caught in the paper packaging of the little present he had bought Arie at the bus station. By chance, the day was Sunday, December third, in the Hebrew calendar, the twenty-fifth night of Kislev, the first day of Hanukah. He was looking forward to surprising Arie and lighting the first candle together.

But it was Peter who was surprised. The flat was neat and tidy, the surfaces clear, the sink empty, the beds made, as if nobody lived there, and indeed that was almost the case, for Arie had moved out. Peter found a note beneath a saucer on the kitchen table dated two months earlier:

Peter, Welcome Home. A lot has happened. Come to see us right
away at 224, Dizengoff, top floor, apartment 8.

Us?

It was six o'clock in the afternoon and still muggy, so after a brief cold
shower Peter dressed in his light clothes: white shirt, khaki slacks, and sandals, remembering at the last moment to take the little gift. He walked along
Rothschild Boulevard, in the shade of the ficus trees, stopping for a quick
iced soda at a corner kiosk, and continued the length of Dizengoff to the
corner of Arlozorov Street.

The cafés along Tel Aviv's main shopping street were beginning to close,
as families prepared at home for the Hanukah meal. Only Café Kassit was
crowded with its usual bohemian crowd. The roads were all but empty of
cars and buses. The few people he shared the streets with hurried along
bearing plates of covered food, their contributions to family meals.

Peter walked slowly, savoring the calm, shedding one skin and growing
another, from secret agent to upright civilian.

He looked left as he passed Keren Hakayemet Street, the boulevard
where the prime minister lived when he wasn't in Jerusalem, and thought:
The Old Man knows I exist. Strange how much has happened, and how
fast. A boy in Germany, and in America, a soldier in Europe, and now an
agent of the secret service of the Jewish State of Israel, which didn't even
exist two years ago. How did that happen? Where did the time go? He was
twenty-seven, and all he really wanted was to be in love.

He thought of his mother, the last time he saw her, thirteen years earlier, tearful, yet beautiful. He couldn't bear to think of her behind barbed
wire, abandoned and filthy and terrified, starving and beaten. He had
searched for her, and everyone else, among the diseased survivors of Dachau
when his 45th Thunderbird Division had liberated the concentration camp,
but he had found none of his family. Later he heard she had been murdered
in Latvia, and his father in Riga. Three of his four grandparents were ex-
terminated in Auschwitz, taken on the same transport from Lodz. His
grandfather on his mother's side had jumped from the train and was shot

while fleeing. Renata and Ruth, his two younger sisters, were on no lists, they had simply disappeared, like millions more. His cousins, aunts, and uncles? Surely someone must have survived, besides his brother?

The only thing he knew for certain was: Never again. Then there was nowhere to run to. Now, there is: Israel. And he would do all he could to defend the Jewish haven. He straightened as he walked.

He reached the squat building at number 224. There were balconies with flowers. It must be an upscale building, he thought, otherwise the tenants would have turned the balconies into bedrooms. But of course Arie would only live in the best; his greatest fear was to be mediocre.

And again he thought of the note: Us. Who is "Us"?

He climbed the stairs and from each apartment heard voices, laughter, music, all the family sounds he craved. A baby cried and a dog barked. It made him feel even more alone. Through a thin door he heard a child's shrill voice: "It's mine, give it to me!"

Peter reached apartment eight on the top floor and his heart beat faster. What would he find? He felt breathless, and it wasn't from exertion, but anticipation. After all he had been through, now he was nervous? He cleared his head and rapped on the door, which seemed to be shaking.

Immediately a little boy opened it and looked up at him, a ball at his feet.

"Shalom," Peter said.

"Are you Peter?"

Surprised, Peter nodded. "Yes. Yes, I am. How did you know?"

"I am Ido," the boy said and hugged Peter's leg. Peter looked down and stroked his head.

"We've been waiting for you. Every day. Did you bring me a present?"

"Yes, I did," and Peter gave him the present he had brought Arie. "Try not to open it yet, though. Can I come in?"

Ido took him by the hand, through the living room, and to the balcony, where a dozen adults were gathered and children played on the floor. There was a tantalizing aroma of sizzling meat. Arie, with his back to Peter, was flipping steaks on the barbeque. But Peter wasn't looking at him.

He was numbed by the girl sitting between an older couple. She was as he remembered, beautiful, and sweet, he could feel the beating of his heart;

the two hours that were still ticking in his breast. Tamara stood slowly, staring at Peter. Her breasts heaved as she said, quietly, "Arie." She had put on weight, or more likely, Peter knew immediately, she was pregnant. He felt a shiver of dismay.

There was a hiss of meat as Arie basted four chicken wings and Tamara said again, "Arie." This time he heard and saw her staring and turned and saw his brother. His look went quickly back to Tamara, then settled on Peter. He stabbed the meat and left the fork in the heat, as a slow smile came to his lips that grew and took over his entire face.

"*Sof sof!*" he said. At last!

"Arie," Peter said. "Barbeque? Can this be? For Hanukah?"

"I got hold of two plump chickens. Too good not to eat. Fresh. And don't worry. We'll have latkes too. With apple sauce. Just like Mama made. Sour cream too. Well, no cream, but still . . ." Arie spread his arms and shouted to all, "Peter, it's my brother Peter, at last he's come home." All heads turned, and the couple at Tamara's side, who he now realized must be her parents, jumped up, beaming. The father grabbed his hand and pumped it in welcome. Everybody was talking at once, Ido began to unwrap his present while his bigger sister, Estie, shouted, "What about me, what about me, where's my present!"

Arie pulled Peter into his arms while Peter felt a stab of pain.

So. " Us" is Tamara. Of course it is.

"You're married, then?" Peter said, holding Arie away, looking at him as if he must have changed.

"Oh yes, to the most beautiful girl in the world. And soon to be a father. Three months to go, inshallah." If Allah wills it. He beamed at Tamara and she smiled back shyly, her hands resting on her belly. "You'll be an uncle," he said.

"But I'm the older brother, I'm supposed to do everything first."

"Well, too bad, if you stayed in one place long enough, maybe you would. We married very soon after you left. Can you imagine? Crazy." He smiled at Tamara. "Crazy, but the best thing I have ever done."

Peter felt like vomiting. "How many months?" Peter asked, patting his stomach.

"Six. It's going to be a big one, that's for sure."

Peter nodded, looking at Tamara, who looked away.

Arie lowered his voice, as if speaking to a conspirator. "How did it go this time?"

"Good. All good."

"But half a year? That's crazy. And no problems? Can you say anything?"

"No, to both. How about you?"

"You can see," Arie said with a grin. "You do remember Tamara, of course."

"How could I forget?" He felt his blood rising. Was he blushing? He hoped not. Should he go to her? Kiss her on the cheek? Congratulate her? After a nodded greeting, he tried not to glance over again and failed. He just caught Tamara's eye as she tried to avoid his. He felt faint. They had made love and never would again.

"What is it?" Ido shouted, pulling at Peter's trouser leg. He was waving the present, a little silver hand on a chain.

"It's a *hamsa*," Peter said, gathering himself. "It's for good luck. See, it's an open hand, five fingers, *hamsa* means five in Arabic. It's against the evil eye, it means that God protects you."

Arie pulled him by the arm. "Let me introduce you to everyone."

There was Tamara's father, Moshe, a professor of Arabic literature and philosophy, who pointed out sadly that such subjects didn't yet figure highly in the Jewish state's needs.

"If Moshe is my father-in-law and we're brothers, that must make him yours too, is that right?" Arie said. "Or uncle-in-law. Is there such a thing?"

"Probably not, but I'll take it," Peter said. "Any family is better than none."

He accepted a glass of orange juice from someone, and asked, "So, are you teaching now?"

Moshe laughed. "No, I work for a new company that makes feather pillows and bedcovers. We hope to export heavy feather bedcovers to the Arab world, where ten months of the year they die from the heat. Next we'll sell them sand." He hooted with laughter. "Arie is nothing if not a dreamer."

Peter liked the old man, who he guessed to be around fifty. He complimented him on his Hebrew, while Arie broke in, "You'll see, we'll export to

Europe and America. We have to create jobs. And with the export subsidies the government is offering, we can't lose. They're paying me to work, they're desperate for foreign exchange."

He took Peter by the elbow and they leaned over Rachel, Tamara's mother, who was sitting on the sofa next to Tamara. Rachel spoke passable Hebrew, but she hadn't found a job and didn't particularly want one, although they could use the money. She said she was busy at home with her two smaller children, Ido and Estie, who loved school. She took Peter's hand and covered it with her other and said she knew a nice young girl for him.

"What about me?" Arie said with a guffaw.

Rachel ignored him. "But first, eat," she said to Peter. "We hardly get by on rations, while here, Arie always has a full fridge. We don't even have a fridge. Eat while you can."

With the egg sandwich Rachel pressed on him in one hand, Peter now found himself before Tamara, who was looking up at him, and in embarrassment he offered her the sandwich. She declined, so he took a bite and chewed. When he could speak, he congratulated her: on the marriage, on the baby to come, on her new home, this lovely apartment; in fact, he was thinking, all the things I'd love to have. With you. Oh, why didn't you wait? He put his lips to her cheek, and inhaled the sweet fragrance of lavender. Did he smell of egg?

Sitting to the side, bemused by the tumult, was an American couple with one child who had moved to Israel but were finding it too tough and said they may give up and go back to Cleveland. He was in car spare parts but there weren't enough cars, there wasn't enough volume to make a decent living. Arie called out, "Anyone who leaves America to make a decent living in Israel should have their head examined."

Next to them was Arie's friend, Natanel Ben-Tsion, the former Sammy Schnitzler from Frankfurt, who, usefully for Arie, worked in the Herzliya city hall. His position of trust there was helpful for Arie's local business ventures. Ben-Tsion didn't have any family and wanted to celebrate Hanukah with nice people. He added, after a dramatic pause, "So I don't know why I came here." They laughed and moved on.

Arie said, "I saved the best for last. Apart from Tamara, that is."

Peter had noticed the young man staring at him but had been distracted by meeting his new family-in-law. Arie beckoned to the man, who approached with a bottle of beer and a broad smile. He had an expectant look, and he raised his eyebrows as if waiting to be recognized.

"So," Arie said. "Peter, do you know who this is?"

Peter smiled back, looking from the young man to Arie and back again. "Should I?"

"From München. We used to play together in the garden," the man said, and waited. He was a couple of years younger than Peter, twenty-four or -five.

Peter crinkled his eyes, made a show of struggling with his memory, and finally shook his head. "I'm sorry, *klum*, nothing." And then, "Wait. Wait."

Something was falling into place . . . children. Playing in their large garden when the Nazis banned Jews from parks and pools. A tree, a branch, falling. Shouting. His mother running to see if he was hurt. A child crying. The boy. Peter put his arm on the man's shoulder, his mouth opened, his eyes widened, and he stretched out the name: "Wolfie?"

The man nodded, swigging the beer.

Peter said, "The branch broke and I fell on you? Everyone was shouting at the same time. Oh no! It's you, Wolfie. I mean, oh yes!"

Wolfie and Arie hooted with laughter. Everyone was looking. Peter fell into Wolfie's arms.

His old neighbor. "But what happened to you? How did you survive? When did you come here? How did you find Aren? Sorry, Arie? What about your family? Your parents? And what is your brother's name again . . . ?"

"Was. Was my brother's name," Wolfie said.

Arie said, "Slow down, another time, lots to hear, Peter. The main thing is he's here with us. Let's light the candles. Celebrate the miracle. Miracles. Tamara, to you goes the honor of the first blessing."

Moshe said, "The first candle of the first Hanukah of the first year of marriage. And the first baby soon. Inshallah. Many more, inshallah."

"You mean, *Bezrat Hashem*," Tamara said, "this is Israel," and everyone laughed.

As they gathered around the silver *hanukiah* on the windowsill facing the street, as was the custom, Tamara lit the first candle of Hanukah. As she did this she recited the same prayer her ancestors did on the same day for thousands of years, and her voice was soft and firm:

Baruch Atah Adonai Ehloheinu Mehlech Haolam Shehasa Neesim Laavo-teinoo Bayamim Hahem Beez'man Hazeh.
Blessed are You, Lord our God, King of the universe, who has granted us life, sustained us, and enabled us to reach this occasion.

Didn't enable enough of us though, Peter thought, looking from Arie to Wolfie, who were chanting the prayer with closed eyes. He could barely summon the faces of his mother and father, or Renata and Ruth. Not a day passed that he didn't think of them, if for only an instant, but as shadows, they glided past like silent birds, and they were gone. Still, who would have thought it? The family was all but wiped out. When he left he had just a brother. Now he came back to a brother, a sister-in-law and her parents, her brother and sister, plus a niece or nephew on the way. And even an old neighbor. Lonely no more. Or, more alone? His stomach clenched.

"Amen," they said, and as he gazed at Tamara, over the dancing flames, it occurred to Peter: Light and life returns, that's the miracle of nature. And so a nation is rebuilt, family by family. But for all the gains he saw around him, he felt only a sickening sense of his own loss.

Tamara and Arie kissed in the flickering of the *hanukiah*, and Peter had to look away.

ARIE

A rie's appointment with the legendary Pinhas Sapir was for 3:00 P.M. in his office just off Jerusalem's busy Jaffa Road, half a mile from the ancient wall that divided Jewish Jerusalem from the Jordanian Old City. He arrived half an hour early and killed time by eating a cheese *boureka* in the corner café, but then missed the unmarked finance ministry among the buildings along the lane; by the time he found it he was breathless and anxious. He was surprised by the modesty of the building, and even more surprised that the director-general of the ministry, a solid man with a bald head and thick glasses, received him in his underpants.

"Sit down," Sapir said, pulling on his trousers, "Lovewy day." Arie had been warned not to laugh at the lisp, although Sapir himself did, but he should laugh as much as he liked at Sapir's Yiddish zingers, which he sprinkled throughout his conversation to create a bond of Jewishness with rich Israel donors from America.

But Arie didn't want to give money, he wanted to get it. So he had boned up on Yiddish phrases for exactly the same reason Sapir used them.

"I'm no *tokhis leker*," Arie began, when Sapir bluntly asked what he wanted. "I'm no ass licker, but I've come with a proposal that I think would benefit Israel's economy and which I think would qualify for government support." He paused, unsure whether he should continue while Sapir buttoned up his pants.

"Nu," Sapir said roughly, "*mach schnell*," which was so close to the German that Arie understood the Yiddish immediately: Hurry up. Arie was beginning to regret using his brother's sway to meet the finance ministry's number two. He should have gone through the regular channels, the officials he already knew. But everyone knew the quickest way to a government loan guarantee, and often the only way, was through Sapir himself. Two of his new Yiddish phrases came to mind: the "*alte kacker*" doesn't like the "*pisher*"—the old fart doesn't like the little bed wetter. But this was Arie's chance so he plowed on. He already understood he had better not waste a word with this crude yet critical figure who all but ran Israel's economy. It was some comfort to know the tough Zionist Sapir, meaning sapphire, was born Koslowski.

Arie launched into his spiel, his words speeding up as he strove to deliver his message. "My company wants to bring work to the people, not people to distant empty places where there is no work. The government policy of moving immigrants to border areas to secure the borders while providing homes is important, but without work and schools they cannot stay there." Slow down, he told himself, he was almost breathless, rattled by Sapir's intense gaze. "What I want to do is something complementary. I want to turn wasteland near towns into productive land." He thanked his partner Natanel for that word; it sounded specific and constructive but was vague enough. "It will guarantee pleasant green areas as towns grow, and families could even have their own allotments of land where they can grow their own produce, teach their children to farm. Our claim to the land will be all the stronger as we cultivate it rather than allow it to lie fallow."

Arie had been practicing all these Zionist talking points: education, land, people, jobs, and he smiled. He'd hit them all. Except one, he suddenly realized, the most important. Security. "And it will make the cities safer. And that isn't bupkes." He loved the sound of that Yiddish word, which meant "nothing" or "trivial."

"So what do you want from me?"

"Um . . ." Arie recovered from the blunt question. "I need a government guarantee for a bank loan to help buy the land; it wouldn't even be expensive, it's wasteland. And I need help with the Israel Land Authority." He breathed deeply before continuing, for now came the true pitch. "I have found the perfect location, a large tract of neglected state land on the western edge of Herzliya, near the sea, a forty-five-minute drive from Tel Aviv. Preferably I'd like a loan to buy. Or to lease it. The government is doing nothing with the land."

He squirmed as his armpits dampened. There was no way to know how Sapir was reacting. "I also am a Mapainik," he said, trying to smile, trying to ingratiate himself as a supporter of the leading political party, Mapai. "We need government investment, not government management."

"You mean you want government money to help you get rich."

"Doesn't everyone? Why not? They say, a rising sea lifts all boats."

Sapir finished tying his shoelaces and sat up. "So, have you finished?" he said.

"No, but isn't that enough for now?"

"How old are you? And from where?"

"Twenty-eight. From Germany. Munich."

"Married?"

"Yes, two children, twins. Two years old."

"Sabras? Born in Israel?"

"Of course. A boy and a girl."

"How perfect. Listen, boychik. It's true there are problems, of course there are. We shocked ourselves by fulfilling our dream, we have our country, it's a miracle. But what is the reality? An Israel of rationing. Waiting in lines. We lack water, food, electricity. First not enough people and now too many. So things take time, but this is a unique opportunity in the history of the Jewish people. What is the name of your company?"

"Feather Products Limited."

Sapir laughed in recognition. "You make pillows, cushions, feather beds from cast-off chicken feathers. Original. A good blue and white innovation. But you've expanded, right?"

"Blue and white?"

"Colors of the flag."

"Of course. Yes, that's just a small business, but growing, I should add. I kept the name, it amuses me. It's really a holding company now, of course without stocks, it isn't a public company, but it's like an umbrella company for various companies I set up. Construction, import-export, mostly building materials. But I'm really interested in local projects, manufacturing." And he added, "Creating jobs." He almost said, to build the Jewish state, but that would have been too much.

Sapir asked more specific questions about turnover, profits, growth potential in the various fields, and then took out his little black book. Arie felt weak with tension, his heart beat faster. He suppressed a grin. Everyone knew Pinhas Sapir was forever noting numbers in his famous little black notebook, from which it was said he managed the entire Israeli economy. It was also said that, for him, true poetry was a line of numbers, and Arie badly wanted to be among them. Was Sapir making a note to remind himself: Loan guarantee to gifted young entrepreneur?

But Sapir had a proposal of his own. "Why don't you take your energy and knowledge and set up in a developing town where the immigrants are? Small-scale farming in the central region has its value, and it's true that people there need jobs, but people along the borders need them more, and we need the people to stay there. You'll get a government subsidy much easier there than near Tel Aviv."

"What business did you have in mind?"

"Textiles. You'll get rich, the people there need jobs and it's a labor-intensive industry. We have excellent contacts worldwide with the *schmatte* trade, so you'll have a ready-made market. The government will always keep ownership of military-security industries, and natural resources, but we'll help other manufacturing industries. What do you say? Interested?"

"Of course I'm interested. In principle. But what I say makes sense too. How about a deal? I go wherever we agree to set up a textile business, and you provide the approval for the agricultural land. That way we're both happy, and that is the basis of any good deal."

"You've got chutzpah, and you're a little too smart for your own good, boychik. But it sounds good. Leave me your details and your proposal. We'll work on it. Be in touch in a week."

They shook hands, and Arie had the opportunity to pronounce the Yiddish phrase he had practiced dozens of times, and prayed he would find useful: *"A groysen dank dir."* Huge thanks to you.

"Gey gezunterheyt," Sapir said, waving at the door. "Go in health. And stop trying so hard to use Yiddish phrases, it doesn't suit a German *yekke.*"

IDO and ARIE

It was a surprise to everyone that Tamara's little brother Ido, who Rachel always said would lose his head if it wasn't fixed to his shoulders, still had the gift that Peter had given him when he had returned from Europe two years earlier: the silver hamsa, the little hand with a deep blue glass eye glowing in its open palm. The good luck charm hung around his neck on the same silver chain, and each time Rachel unhooked it to wash her son or put it back she would say: *Elohim shomer alaycha,* God protect you.

Ido was six years old now, and loved to play to the crowd. He would kiss the hamsa and raise his eyes to the heavens, which made everyone laugh. "I feel lucky," he would say, and that made them all hoot with laughter. "From your lips to God's ears," Rachel would say.

And it was only after the stabbing that everyone realized: It was the one day Ido wasn't wearing his hamsa to ward off the evil eye.

Moshe had taken Ido and his sister Estie to the beach at the Jaffa end of Tel Aviv for a *Yom Kef,* a fun day out. The children played in the low waves until the sun was high, when they walked to the shade of the Carmel Market for hummus and falafel. Moshe loved it because you could refill your salad as often as you liked, and he liked to do so often.

They arrived late when the food market was thinning out before the

Sabbath. Dogs scavenged through offal and the poor rummaged for discarded vegetables, while the last of the shoppers crowded around Yossi's pita stall for a quick lunch. Moshe bumped into a colleague from the school where he now taught twice a week, and together they jostled forward, inch by inch, as Yossi yelled "*Yalla, Yalla,* fresh falafel, forget about grandma, this is the real thing, don't panic, plenty for everyone."

It was a zoo. Few understood the new currency, which had just changed from Palestine pounds to Israeli lirot, from the British occupation currency to the Israeli freedom one; the banknotes had new colors and pictures, while the coins were too similar. People loved having the first Jewish currency in two thousand years, but they fumbled with the change, afraid of being cheated. To make it worse, half the crowd were new immigrants who barely spoke Hebrew and called out in languages from Parsi to Bulgarian to Spanish. One young woman who was crammed against the counter dropped her change and cursed loudly in French because in the crush she couldn't bend to pick up her coins.

Ido and Estie were holding hands in the narrow alley, watching vendors pull down their striped awnings. Trucks backed up through thick exhaust fumes to reload the unsold produce. As the heat cooled the unsanitary odors became less pungent.

Just as it was finally Moshe's turn to ask for pitas with hummus and falafel and extra salad, there was sudden shouting in Arabic and Hebrew and yelling and a woman's scream. A man in a jalabiyah and one sandal ran between two carts. He was shouting in Arabic, *Allah Akhbar,* God is great, and raced down the alley straight toward Ido and Estie. Sunlight flashed off the blade in his hand, it was long and red with blood. The screaming penetrated the din at the falafel stand and everyone looked around and saw the Arab coming fast. Moshe yelled. "Ido! Estie!" He tried to force his way through the press of people. He screamed and his friend and everyone else pushed to the side to get out of the way. Now everyone was yelling "Stop him!" in every language. A man darted forward and looked as if he would tackle the Arab but stopped dead. The Arab was tall and young and desperate, his legs pumping as he waved the dagger above his head. His face was contorted in fear and fury, drops of sweat flew from him. He was closing on Ido and Estie, looming above them. Estie put her hand to her mouth and screamed. Ido, still holding her other hand, pulled her sharply out of the man's way and as the Arab passed them Ido stuck out his leg. The Arab was too fast and strong to trip and his motion pushed aside the boy's leg, toppling Ido, who spun to the ground. But the Arab lost balance, his forward momentum twisted him to the side, his legs crossed, and he crashed sideways into a metal pole supporting an awning, which shook and twanged like a Jew's harp. He caught himself but the impact made him drop his knife. For an instant he was unsure whether to bend down to grab the knife or run without it. Seeing this, the man who had wanted to intervene regained his courage and sprang onto the Arab, pinning him to the ground, pounding him with his fist, and others joined him.

They heard shouts of "Stop him, the murderer!" from the direction he had come. More running feet and a woman fell on the Arab, beating him mercilessly about the head with a stick, hitting other Jews in the process.

Moshe pulled her away, shouting "Enough," and he tried to protect the Arab from the enraged crowd as the woman shouted, "He stabbed my husband, kill him, kill him!" Now the crowd was cursing Moshe, calling him an Arab-lover. They pulled him away so they could get at the Arab again but two policemen ran up, handcuffed the bleeding man, and pulled him to his feet, leading him away, leaving the crowd shouting, some laughing in nervous excitement.

Panting heavily, Moshe pulled Ido and Estie into his arms while one man said, "What kind of Jew are you, protecting that bastard? The boy has more guts than you do."

And indeed, Ido was the hero of the moment. Everyone had seen him try to trip the big Arab and that had led to his capture. Estie was shaking and crying and Ido had his arm about her shoulder, silently comforting his older sister.

"He's my son, he's only six," Moshe said between gasps, kneeling by his children. His colleague said, "You should be proud of him," and Moshe said, "I am, I am."

"He's got more guts than you have," someone said again.

"And what did you do, then?" Moshe responded, but stopped himself.

This was no time to fight. "It's true though," he said, ruffling Ido's hair, "he's a gutsy kid."

At home Rachel put ice on Ido's leg, which was red and sore, and tried to bounce him on her knee, even though he struggled to get off. He was too old for that and was silent and glum. Rachel wanted to say, Never do anything like that again, but she couldn't because in the country they lived, who knew what the future held? There were terrorist attacks all over the country every week. Israel's secret weapon was the resilience of its people. They didn't panic or run away, they fought back. But a boy? A six-year-old boy? Well, hopefully soon there would be peace.

It was then that Tamara noticed the *hamsa* was not around Ido's neck. He wouldn't let anyone bathe him anymore and had forgotten to put the *hamsa* back on. Tamara said, "But where is the *hamsa*? You see, God protects those he loves even without it," and that is when Ido spoke for the first time. His wide brown eyes looked up at Tamara and he said, in a small voice, as if talking to himself, "I didn't want the bad man to hurt Estie," and at last he burst into tears.

It took ten weeks for Pinhas Sapir's Finance Ministry bureaucrats to rubber-stamp what it took Sapir one minute to decide: Feather Products Ltd.'s proposal to turn wasteland into small-scale semi-urban farming was sound and desirable fiscally, socially, and politically. Arie got his deal.

He called his friend Natanel Ben-Tsion, now a leading member of the local Mapai party branch and, more relevantly, head of Herzliya's Land Use and Planning Committee, asking to meet immediately.

Two hours later Arie ordered coffee and blueberry cheesecake at Kapulsky Café near Herzliya city hall. A moment after the surly waitress slammed the cake to the table, Ben-Tsion slapped him on the shoulder from behind, pulled out a chair and with a two-handed thump on the table, which rattled Arie's coffee cup in the saucer and spilt the coffee, sat down heavily. "What a day," he said, dabbing at the spreading dark stain with a paper napkin. He used Arie's teaspoon to sample the cake, but before he could launch into his trials Arie said, "It's just beginning. Sapir came through."

"With the land?"

"Yes."

"Terrific. Wow. Okay, so what's next?"

"Exactly as planned. We now have permission to develop all the land, ninety-two dunams, into agricultural space. Papers are being drafted, I'll take care of that. We'll clear it, flatten it, put in water piping, fencing, enough to make it look like Feather Products is serious. What you must do is immediately begin the process to rezone the agricultural land into residential. We can build a whole subsection of town, and if we really can build higher than usual, like you said, four stories, . . . can we?"

"Yes, I'll take care of that." Ben-Tsion laughed and drained his orange juice. "So basically, you got the land for bupkes."

"Yes. Free."

"Two more juices," Ben-Tsion called to the waitress. "To celebrate."

"What about the Canadian? Any news?"

"Yes. I got his answer yesterday. He's worried, and it should work. I'll write back this afternoon. I'll confirm the accuracy of your assessment and let him stew."

The adjacent plot of land, another eight dunams on the eastern side, jutted out of the square ninety-two-dunam plot like the pointed roof of a house. From the land registry Arie had found out that a Canadian had bought the land in 1932, presumably as an investment for the future, but had never paid his land taxes. So Arie, assuming, correctly as it now turned out, that he would get the land license, had written to the Canadian in Winnipeg a month earlier, pointing out that the man's investment had gone south and was barely worth more than the taxes he owed. The land in question now abutted a larger parcel that was becoming farmland, an urban green belt, and would never be worth more than it was now, which was little. However, his company, Feather Products Ltd., which needed space for greenhouses and sheds, was offering to buy it from him at current market price. Arie pointed out that when it would be surrounded by farmland, it would be worthless. At most he could grow lettuce. Arie proposed that the Canadian not take his word for it but write and ask the Herzliya municipality what the long-term master plan was for the area. Arie helpfully provided the correct name and department to address the request for information: the chair of the Herzliya Municipality Land Use and Planning Committee, Mr. Natanel Ben-Tsion.

Their secret plan was to build a shopping center on the Canadian's land, to serve the new housing community.

The two friends sat back, sipping juice and coffee. Arie took out a cigar and began to unwrap it, but Ben-Tsion laid a hand on his forearm, looking around. "Don't smoke that here. Where did you get it, anyway? It's too conspicuous. People don't have enough to eat and here we are *fress*ing blueberry cake and smoking cigars. People will notice, ask questions. Don't show off."

"Nonsense," Arie said, pulling the wrapping off with a flourish. "What's the point of living if you can't enjoy life? Anyway, I have to go, I have to see a man about a textile business. Come to the house for Shabbat dinner on Friday. And bring that girl you were with last night, she's sweet."

"You can talk, Tamara is . . . Well, all I can say is, you don't deserve her. You shouldn't mess around."

"You say a lot of things. Just write that letter today, I want those eight dunams before he finds out the land is being rezoned. And I want the rezoning to be quick too. How long will it take?"

"Hurry, hurry, that's Arie Nesher. It'll take a few months. So slow down, we'll get there. And, seriously, my advice—Tamara is too lovely to lose."

"Don't worry, my friend. Just bring that girl. Peter's bringing his new English squeeze too."

TAMARA

Tamara was possibly the only housewife in Israel still obeying the austerity rules of the old Ministry of Rationing and Supply, which put the entire state of Israel on a diet. Nobody expected much more than 0.2 ounces of noodles per person for dinner. But if her guests couldn't be guaranteed a good meal, they were never short on drama.

A year earlier Arie had come home with two kilos of prime rib for Shabbat dinner, promising the feast of a lifetime, and in front of all the salivating family members Tamara had thrown the meat to the floor. "No black market food in my kitchen," she had shouted at Arie, "I've told you a thousand times."

Arie had stormed out but at least he had a sense of humor because he returned three minutes later with two eggs and a lettuce and yelled, "Here, make dinner for eight with this."

She had shouted back, "It's ten, can't you count?"

For the weekly Sabbath gathering, Natanel brought his new girlfriend, Yasmine, a young Moroccan with almond eyes, olive skin, lips like ripe peaches, and a body even more delicious. The poor culinary metaphors were Arie's. Everything about her, he told his friend, made him want to eat her up.

"Too bad," Natanel said, "you've got your ration at home."

"That's one thing the government can't decide for us."

"Maybe in your case they should."

Tamara's voice came from the kitchen. "Arie, where are the matches for the candles?"

"I don't know," Arie called back as he sat down, offering a cigarette to Yasmine.

There was a knock on the door and Diana Greenberg entered, followed by Peter. "I heard you, I've got some matches," Diana shouted in English to Tamara, and more quietly, to nobody in particular, "do you mind if I smoke?"

"Everybody else is," Peter said. "Hello, Natanel, how are you, and who is this? I'm Peter."

"I'm Yasmine."

Diana's smile to Yasmine was quick and mirthless. "I'm Diana."

Another knock and in came Moshe and Rachel with Ido and Estie, who ran upstairs to find the twins.

"So what's for dinner?" Moshe said.

"Don't ask," Arie said.

"We brought some chicken and roast potatoes."

"Thank God," said Peter.

"Don't be unkind," Diana laughed, on the way to the kitchen to help Tamara. There was a clattering noise from upstairs, a thud, and yelling. Silence followed by a scream, and then laughter. A briefer silence. Another thud, and the ceiling trembled. More laughter.

"The twins," Tamara said mournfully. "As long as there's laughter within two seconds of a scream I know it's all right."

"The same with Peter and me," Diana said.

Tamara chuckled. "How is everything? You've been seeing a lot of each other. People are beginning to talk."

"Don't tell me what they're saying. Put it this way, things move quickly with that man. Very quickly."

Tamara inclined her head in a question but Diana had picked up a knife. "How can I help?"

They chopped vegetables, put them in the grill of the American oven, which took up a whole corner of the kitchen, opposite the fridge, and went into the garden for a smoke.

It was the large living room that opened onto the private garden that gave their new home its rare sense of luxury, that and the cane garden furniture with white cushions, which Arie had imported just before furniture joined the rationing list. The dining room seated twelve people, so Arie and Tamara hosted all the family events. If there were more guests they could spill out into the garden, where there was an American barbeque grill. Upstairs were two bedrooms linked by an outside terrace overlooking the strawberry fields and citrus groves of Kfar Ramat Hasharon, a farming village. In the evening the fields glowed gold in the setting sun. It was half an hour's drive to Tel Aviv but Arie, no farmer, liked the space to play. He could spend hours spraying the little twins in a game he called Germany. He shot the hose pipe into the air and water fell on them like rain, while Daniel and Carmel shrieked and ran in circles. Tamara would call out to them not to waste water, but couldn't help laughing at their gleaming naked bodies darting around the garden.

When Tamara asked what she had meant by "Things move quickly," Diana winked. "I'm good at keeping secrets. It's my job. You'll find out soon."

Tamara poked her in the ribs. "Come on, don't do this to me, you can't tease me like this," but Diana just answered, "Yes, I can."

They finished their cigarettes and with Tamara humming, "she's so beautiful and in love," returned to the kitchen. But they had taken too long. As Tamara placed two bowls of blackened vegetables by Rachel's lemon chicken and roasted potatoes, Arie said, "The vegetables are burned, they're black."

"They're supposed to be, it's an old Italian recipe," Diana said. "Florentine."

They lit the candles and said the Sabbath prayer. Then Arie and Peter argued loudly about Egypt. Moshe and Rachel each took care of a twin as they ate, Moshe next to Daniel and Rachel next to Carmel. The three-year-olds squirmed, jumped down from their chairs, and crawled among the legs beneath the table as Ido and Estie kicked them. Diana was greatly amused at the chaos; family dinner in England was nothing like this. Natanel and Yasmine just held hands.

All of a sudden Arie shouted "Quiet!" and banged a glass on the table. The twins stopped where they were on their knees and the table fell silent. "Thank you," Arie said. "I can't hear myself talk in this noise."

"Lucky you," said Peter. "Anyway, you're wrong. There's no way Naguib or Nasser will make peace with Israel; if they really wanted to they'd have stopped the fedayeen attacks across the border long ago. They know we'll have to react to their terrorist raids. They're trying to provoke us."

"But they're socialists, like our socialist leaders. They have a lot in common," Arie said for the third time. "And they have to make peace, all that talk of leading the Arab world is nonsense, Egypt is dirt poor, all they have is the Suez Canal, and when the British pull out, which they will one day, they'll have to make peace, or they'll have no economy."

"But they hate us," Tamara said. "It doesn't matter if the British are there or not, or if the canal is working or not, they hate us. All the Arabs do. They will always try to destroy us."

"I agree with Tamara," Moshe put in, one hand pointing a finger at Arie, the other trying to hold Daniel's head beneath the table. "Arie, you see everything through the eye of business, where you can make money, and that may be a fair standard for America, Europe, the West, but it doesn't hold here. The Arabs value honor far higher than money and Israel humiliated them in '48. They want revenge, not peace. Peace may come later, inshallah, but first Egypt will need to regain its honor."

"How can they do that?" Natanel said.

"War. No other way," answered Moshe. "Today Egypt is focused on building the country's economy, and for that they need stable relations with Israel but that is just a prelude to the inevitable. You can see how much money they're spending on developing the military, airfields, and the like."

"You mean they have to defeat us in war before they make peace with us? That doesn't make sense," Arie said. "If they defeat us, why would they make peace with us? They'd rather kill us all and we can find peace in our graves."

"Well, I didn't say it was easy. The next thing is . . . Aiiieee! Daniel, don't bite! He bit me! Ow, are you crazy?"

"Let go of my head, then. You're hurting me!" Daniel shouted.

"He speaks very well for a three-year-old," Natanel said.

"Yes, they both do, they're very clever," Tamara said.

"Trust me," Arie said, "there is a way to avoid another war. Business. The closer our economies become, the harder it will be to go to war. We need joint economic ventures, common business interests, like they sell us water from the Nile, we sell them . . . whatever."

"Pots and pans," Tamara said.

"Sandals," Peter said.

"Featherbeds," Arie said with a laugh, "a toast to featherbeds," and they clinked their water glasses.

"The only problem is they'll never do business with the Jews," Peter said.

"They would," Moshe said. "As long as it's secret and as long as there's profit. But I say again, they'll never make peace until they've lost their shame at losing to the Jews."

"All I can say," Tamara said, "is there better be peace by the time the twins reach army age, because I'm not sending them to fight. In fact, right now I'm sending them to bed; it's past their bedtime."

"Inshallah, there will be peace," said Moshe.

While Arie ushered everyone into the garden to smoke and enjoy the cool air, Peter volunteered to help Tamara put the children to bed. He carried them up the stairs, their heads resting on his shoulders, and helped them undress while Tamara prepared the bath. "Parenting suits you, Peter," she said with a smile, and regretted it. She had spent too many hours studying the faces of her twins: Who did they resemble more, Arie or Peter?

As he steadied Daniel and Tamara soaped Carmel, the girl slipped in the bath. Tamara and Peter both grabbed her, and their hands met on the child's thin wet leg. Peter held Tamara's eyes. Briefly she rested her hand on his, a friendly tap, as if drawing a line. As she withdrew, Peter stopped her, he took hold of her hand. "Tamara, there's something I want to tell you," he said. He felt her muscles tense even as her eyes softened. The sweet sadness of "if only" always hung between them: If only he hadn't gone away for so long when they had first met. If only he had been able to contact her. If only she had not been so desperate to leave the transit camp. If only . . . a sigh escaped her lips. "Please," she said. She picked up a towel, wrapped Carmel in it, and handed over the damp bundle with a sad smile. "Here, she's all yours."

But Peter didn't move. "Tamara, please, there's something I have to say to you. I must."

"Don't say it. Please, Peter, don't say it. When it's said you can't take it back." She turned her back on him. "Go. Put Carmel to bed. I'll be right there with Daniel."

Outside, there was laughter from the garden and Arie's raised voice. "Tamara, what are you doing up there? Hurry up."

She gave Peter a light push out of the bathroom.

"Tamara . . ."

"Go."

When Peter joined the others outside, Arie was just explaining his latest coup. He had begun building another two schools but had discovered during stage two of construction, when the concrete was all poured, that there was a problem with the license for stage three, installing all the infrastructure, so work could be held up for months. That would cost a fortune in unscheduled bank interest. To make things worse, there was a shortage of foreign exchange to import key supplies, especially copper. But at the last moment a French construction company had bought his share of the project. Arie had made a big profit, in French francs, and unloaded the headache and imminent interest losses. He had got out just in time.

"Do the French know about the license issue?" Peter asked.

"It's their job to know, isn't it?" Arie said. "They do due diligence."

"Did you tell them?"

"Of course not, why should I? I only sold my part of the project. My partners know, and they stayed in, so they must know something I don't know." That made him throw his head back and laugh, and Natanel clapped him on the back. "Anyway," Arie said, "there isn't much profit in schools." Peter saw darkness pass across Tamara's eyes.

"That isn't right," Peter said. "Aren't you supposed to disclose things like that?"

"You're kidding. I'm happy to be out of it, and wealthier."

"That's plain wrong. You'll get caught out one day," Peter said. "You're lying to them."

"How can I lie if I don't say anything?"

"Lying by omission is still a lie. Remind me never to do business with you."

"Now, now, boys," Natanel put in. "Don't fall out over a few lirot."

"One point five million," Arie said with a broad smile.

"Well, moving on, I too have something to say," Peter said, drawing Diana closer, "and unlike Arie, I'll make it brief. For a change."

Everyone laughed, for Peter was a man of few words. All eyes were on him.

"Diana and I," he began, and he couldn't help glancing at Tamara, whose smile was fading, "are married."

"What?" Arie shouted. He quickly collected himself. "That's fantastic, brother!" He rushed to Peter and hugged him and hugged Diana too. Now everyone was exclaiming and shouting "when?" and "where?" and "how" and "why didn't you say?" and "when's the party?" and hugging each other. Tamara seemed a step behind everyone else, but she kissed Diana and then Peter. "I love you both," she whispered to him, brushing his ear with her lips. "I wish you every happiness, you deserve it." He touched her cheek and had to look away.

"I'm so happy for you both," Moshe said, embracing them. "You're perfect for each other."

"Good choice," Natanel said, beaming.

"Well," Diana said, "it was an easy choice for Peter because he doesn't actually know anybody else."

"Too true," Peter said with a laugh. "Still, we're a perfect match, we'll probably never see each other. I'd like a toast but unfortunately we don't have any champagne."

"Yes, we do," said Arie, heading for the kitchen. "The best. Wait here."

Peter shook his head at his brother's back. "Champagne. Why am I not surprised?"

PETER

TEL AVIV, ISRAEL

October 1953

———

What did surprise everyone was that six months later, Diana gave birth to twins.

"What? More twins?" said Moshe. And Tamara. And Arie. With no history of twins in anybody's family, how was this possible?

Diana had one crib ready as well as a variety of pink and blue clothes, but now she had to double everything. Tamara gave Diana some of her twins' old clothing and Arie presented her with a second crib, while Moshe and Rachel brought cooked food every day for two weeks. With sunken eyes, drawn cheeks, and disheveled hair Diana received visitors in her nightgown, slumped on the sofa, an infant at each breast.

Her most dedicated helper was Tamara, who came twice a day until Diana's mother arrived from England, tut-tutting at the mess, the food, the manners, the heat, and the noise of Tel Aviv. Everything she did was accompanied by a French-accented "tsk, tsk."

"Please come back. She's making me crazy," Diana moaned to Tamara on the phone. "She doesn't know that babies cry. It's all my fault. She says that I don't know how to breastfeed, I don't know how to wash them, I use the wrong diapers, they shouldn't dry in the sun, they'll get germs, I don't eat properly, she can't buy her cornflakes, oh my God, please, help me."

"I'm sorry, I shouldn't laugh," Tamara said, laughing. "How long is she staying?"

"She wants to stay forever. She wants to move here. I need her like a hole in the head. Oh, God, what can I do? She keeps complaining I don't have a meat grinder. For God's sake, I don't have any meat."

"Have you heard from Peter?"

"Twice. He'll come home as soon as he can. But you know what that means. It isn't his fault. It's that crazy job, whatever it is." But few knew better than Diana, on maternity leave from Mossad's European desk.

Isser Harel, the former Shin Bet chief, who had replaced Reuven Shiloah a year earlier as the head of Mossad, was known as a family man, but that stretched only as far as sympathy for Peter, who had to miss his wife giving birth: "Sorry, but this is national security."

Peter didn't object; there was no point. Nothing stood in the way of Little Isser, a driven if unlikely spymaster. His nickname came from his height of four foot ten inches, in contrast with Big Isser, Isser Be'eri, who was head of military intelligence. Little Isser had comically large ears, but there was nothing funny about his glare, which was more piercing than an interrogation light. He was a living contradiction. Aged forty, he looked sixty, yet had the hyper energy of a child. Born Isser Halperin in Russia, his ambition could be measured by the Hebrew name he chose—Harel, Mountain of God.

When he handed over the reins of Mossad, a transition that included a dozen ongoing operations for which there was no paper trail, Reuven Shiloah took Harel aside to outline his most sensitive undertaking: his super-secret sleeper network of ex-Nazis, who were kept in line by one of his most valued and trusted agents, Peter Nesher.

And for Harel, a man who saw conspiracy at every turn, who on his first day at Mossad fired a top agent for skimming expenses, a straight arrow with Peter Nesher's skills and experience was a match made in heaven. Like Shiloah before him, he needed a man close to him who he could trust.

"We are heading for a big mess," Harel had told Peter in September, four weeks before Diana's due date. "And I need you back in Germany to start cleaning up before it happens. Briefly, it's Egypt again, and it's complicated."

Harel had summoned Peter to his office on Ben Yehuda Street, always the prelude to action. It made Peter's stomach turn over. Diana would kill him if he missed the birth. He didn't hear the first few sentences but when Harel had his full attention, he knew right away there was nothing he could do or say. He tuned back in just as Harel was saying:

". . . military intelligence. The loose cannons at Aman want to bomb the British in Egypt and say the Egyptian Muslim Brotherhood did it. Can you imagine anything more stupid? And the Old Man won't listen to me, he's terrified the British will leave Egypt after seventy years and hand over all their military bases to Nasser. Two airfields, weapons dumps, and ammunition, docks, radar stations. Thirty-eight years of British installations. That must not happen. But state terrorism against Britain? Aman is filled with lunatics."

"Can they do that?" Peter asked. "I mean, do they have the people, the expertise?"

"Of course not. But they do have Ben-Gurion's ear."

"I don't get it, or maybe I fear I do," Peter said. "If Britain thinks the Egyptians bombed them, then the British won't pull out. So Egypt wouldn't get the military installations to use against us. Yes?"

"Exactly."

"But what can I do in Germany?"

"I'll tell you. The Old Man is quite right that another war with Egypt is inevitable. But this time there is a very dangerous buildup of Germans in Egypt, senior officers from the Nazi air force, navy, army, intelligence. They are helping Egypt rebuild its armed forces. A strong Egypt can unite the Arab world against us. And Ben-Gurion believes we may not survive against such an alliance today."

Peter waited with a sinking heart. He knew where this was going, Israel had to attack first. And he knew what that meant. It meant he would miss the birth.

"What?" Harel said. "You're shaking your head. You don't agree?"

"It isn't that. To be honest, sir, I was thinking of Diana."

Harel came around his desk and patted Peter on the shoulder. "I know. When is the baby due?"

"Four weeks."

"You'll be in Frankfurt, then. In fact, you'll be there next week."

Next week. A curse word formed. Diana would roast him, and slowly.

There was a knock on the door, followed by a voice: "It's four o'clock, everyone is here."

"Good, coffee for everyone, bring them in."

Peter looked at Harel, raising his eyebrows. Harel said, "This is a sanctioned operation. You'll hear why now. The European desk will work with you."

Diana's group. Peter knew all four analysts who entered the room. They nodded to him and immediately began pouring coffee, waiting for Harel to take command. "Yossi v'Hezie," who got his nickname of "Yossi and a half" because he was so tall, sat opposite Peter. "How's Diana?" he said.

"So far so good," Peter said. "Resting, it isn't an easy pregnancy . . ."

"We miss her," Gingie, nicknamed for her red hair, put in, but before she could continue Harel silenced them with a wave of his hand as two men and a woman entered the room. They glanced at everybody and sat at the table as if they owned it. Peter had never seen them before. Maybe they were the reason Harel was running the meeting himself. Normally a section chief would be in charge.

"You all know why we're here so, Professor, sum up briefly," Harel said.

Yehuda Shur was the chief analyst of the European desk, although his Ph.D. from Oxford was in Arabic history. He had fought in the Palmach, the Jewish pre-state underground army, was among the earliest Shai agents, and could bench-press more than everybody in the room combined. Peter thought of him as probably the strongest man he had ever met. His hands were massive, he had a wrestler's thick neck, all he lacked was a broken nose. But his chief contribution to Mossad was his intellectual breadth.

Yehuda laid out half a dozen folders. "I prefer to stand," he said. He spread his hands on the table and leaned on them, taking a moment to arrange his thoughts.

"First, the individuals. We have a list of seventy-one Germans," he began, drawing a list of names from one of the folders. "We have good photographs of most of them. For example, Army General Wilhelm Fahrmbacher, who served in both world wars. Captain Theodor von Bechtolsheim, a naval genius. Major General Oskar Munzel, a tank commander who developed new armored units for the Wehrmacht. Dozens more like them, veteran fighters and commanders.

"And then there are true Nazis, SS-men. Leopold Gleim, a Gestapo boss in Warsaw. Willi Brenner, who ran the Mauthausen concentration camp. Many more like them, who choose Cairo today because they won't be extradited, and they are paid well to keep fighting the Jews."

Harel interrupted. "Get to the point. That is all obvious; we can read it in the files. Tell us why it is all so complicated."

"America? Russia?"

"Of course," Harel said impatiently. "Why else are we here?"

Yehuda picked up another folder and took out a note. "Israel's scope of operations is limited by global restraints. In other words, our hands are tied. Briefly, our government and Britain agree that we must stop the Germans from helping Egypt. But America does want the Germans to help Egypt, because a strong Egypt will resist Russian expansion in Egypt and wider afield in the Middle East. A weak Egypt will not. So the more the Germans can help Egypt, the more a strong Egypt can help America against Russia. But a strong Egypt is a greater threat to Israel. So whatever we do to weaken Egypt harms our relationship with America. In other words, it's a mess."

"Is this clear?" Harel said, looking around the table, and especially at the three strangers. "We must proceed with extreme sensitivity and caution, yet quickly and effectively." Peter nodded, his lips pursed. So what's new? What do they want from me?

As Yehuda expanded further on the big picture, Harel interrupted again. "All right, thank you, Professor, we'll come back to you about cooperation with the British. And the French. But now, Gingie, you take it from here. Rockets."

Gingie nodded and began in her rapid-fire high voice, which sounded as if she were hyperventilating. Peter had met her many times. She shared an office with Diana and sometimes came to visit in their apartment. A kind woman, but her off-the-chart nervous energy gave him palpitations.

"Apart from aiming to improve every aspect of its military," Gingie said, "Egypt's absolute priority today is rocket science, especially developing medium- and long-range battlefield rockets. They have recruited brilliant German scientists to help them, in particular one Rolf Engel, who developed rockets and antiaircraft missiles for the Nazis. And of course, Egypt has no clear enemy to arm itself against, other than us."

After another thirty minutes of Egypt's military prowess, rocket development, and the grim contribution of German experts, everybody left the room but Peter, whose head was reeling. He poured himself a cold coffee and wondered where Harel would take this. Now he would hear the point of it all: his mission.

Harel didn't waste a moment. "So there you have it," he said. "Nazis are back to killing the Jews. Aman's lunatic answer to the British problem is to bomb them. Now guess what their answer is to the Germans in Egypt?"

"I'd rather not."

"Exactly. They want to murder them, or enough to scare the rest away."

"Would that work?"

"What do you think?"

"What do I think? What do *you* think?"

"I don't think they know how." Harel paused, staring at Peter. The silence lengthened. Peter stared back, becoming uncomfortable. "What do you want from me, then?" Peter said at length. *Surely he doesn't want me to do the killing.*

"I want you to go to Germany, contact your Nazi sleepers, make them contact their sleazebag colleagues in Egypt, find out what progress they have really made, and make them leave."

"How could they do that, if they're working in Egypt legally?"

"Blackmail, of course. And money. What else works?"

"Does Aman know about this?" Peter asked.

"Do they need to?"

"Do they?"

"More to the point is, do you need to know if they know?"

"I suppose not."

"Good. Leave the rest to me."

This is like cat and mouse, Peter thought. Those dramatic pauses. What does he really want? "Frankly, I'm relieved," Peter said. "I thought you were going to say we should kill them, because we can do a better job than Aman."

"Should we?"

"No."

"Peter. Never say never."

That night was hard for Peter and Diana. She wished he didn't have to go. She wished he would be with her when she gave birth, when she brought the baby home, when she fed the baby for the first time, and bathed it, and fell asleep beside it. She knew it would be hard and lonely but, most of all, she was afraid for Peter.

She knew who he would be dealing with, for after all, she had been the first to meet them, to wake their lust, it was she who had brought the Nazi killers to him. She knew what Peter could do, but she also knew what they had done and that they were still capable of anything, especially if scared and trapped. At least one would come out fighting; it was the law of averages.

After they made love she trembled in his arms while Peter caressed her belly, kissing it, whispering to their baby as she stroked his head.

It was a long, beautiful night, and so was the next, but time did not stand still. The next dawn Peter would leave.

That day's first light found him on the closed-off balcony, his hand resting on the wooden slat of the crib that was waiting for their new baby, inshallah. The next generation, inshallah. At last he was beginning to build his very own family that he would love and protect. For each time he discovered some awful new fact about the fate of his mother, his father, almost his entire family murdered by the Nazis, he swore to himself: His revenge would be a large new family, in a safe Jewish country.

With his backpack over a shoulder, he contemplated Diana, curves beneath the sheet, hair spread around her, secure and snug in their bed. Have a safe birth, an easy one, my sweet wife. Peter Nesher kissed her lightly on the lips, and again on the tip of her nose, and the man code-named Wolf, alias Willi Stinglwagner, tiptoed away to blackmail five Nazi murderers.

MOSHE and ARIE

TEL AVIV, ISRAEL

January 1954

————————

As Moshe contemplated his visiting grandchildren at play, he knew only one thing for certain: He could not continue stuffing chicken feathers into pillows. Though he had to admit Arie's offbeat idea was turning into quite a success story. He had expanded into feather-padded winter coats and hats, for export to Germany and Scandinavia, which was like selling sand to the Arabs. And now Arie was thinking of cornering the European market in chicken feathers, which were discarded as poultry waste, and opening up a factory somewhere central, like Belgium or Holland for European sales, but also near a major port like Rotterdam to be closer to the larger markets in America and Canada. The boy had quite a head for business. He was even experimenting with chicken feathers as home insulation for his apartment projects. Moshe wondered: Are there enough chickens in the entire world to support Arie's dreams?

Arie's construction business alone was making him rich. But when he, Moshe, tried to find work in his field, Arabic literature and philosophy, people laughed at him. We're trying to make everyone learn Hebrew, they told him, and you want to teach Arabic? We're trying to forget Arabic. We want to teach Jews from Arab countries how to be Israelis, not the other way around. Forget Ḥassān ibn Thābit and Abū Firās, study Bialik and Alterman.

Moshe didn't have the heart to tell Rachel that he had failed yet again to find work as a teacher, that he had again been politely shown the door of a school building. He found little comfort in Al-Mutanabbī, who ten centuries earlier wrote:

Never did I expect to witness a time
When a dog could do me ill and be praised for it all the while.

Moshe studied his grandchildren, Ido and Estie, playing mummy and daddy with Tamara's twins, while Tamara gave Diana baby advice. He thought, this country is for them, not for me. They already speak good Hebrew, they're learning and growing, they're not in decline. They joined a children's group where Ido was a natural leader and Estie had the best singing voice. Tamara is bringing them up in Arabic as well as Hebrew, and Arie speaks to them in German. Smart parents. Smart kids.

"What is it, Abba?" Tamara said. "You look sad."

"Nothing."

"There's no such thing as nothing," Diana said. "By definition, it doesn't exist. There's always something. What is it, Abba?"

The young mothers, lying on the floor, rolled toward Moshe in the chair. Tamara put her hand on her father's knee. "Come on, what is it, Abba? Trouble with Ima?"

He laughed. "No, not at all. It isn't that."

"What is it, then?" Diana said. "Come on, two beautiful women want to know." She put her hand on his other knee. "I've had enough talking with Tamara about my sore nipples."

"Is that how you talk to your father in England?" Moshe said.

"Yes."

"Well, I have a lot to learn. To tell you the truth, I don't feel so good. It's wonderful to see you all so happy here. But for me and Rachel? I don't know. I can't get work in my field, I'm fifty-two, and if someone asks me what I do with my Ph.D. and professorship, I say I'm in chicken feathers."

Tamara and Diana fell back laughing, and Moshe couldn't help a throaty chuckle as he lit another cigarette. "I just don't feel we belong. I can divide the people of Israel into four, and I'm afraid my place is not a good one."

"What do you mean?" Tamara said with a patient smile. She turned to Diana: "For my academic father, everything has three causes, and four parts."

"I've been thinking," Moshe began, "watching you and the children. This country is for you, not for me. It is for the young. And even you can be divided into four groups. First, there are the Israelis, who were born and grew up here. They fought for their country. Hebrew is their mother tongue, this is their home. The future is theirs. Then there are the Western professionals, academics, from America, Europe. They bring with them their culture and values, and maintain them. You can tell them from their jackets and ties. Then come the European immigrants, concentration camp survivors, who are accepted as weak remnants yet have a place of respect, even if life is hard. Half of them still look sick. But they belong. Then last, and apparently least, there are the people like me: basically, Jewish Arabs. The first three will become one; it may take twenty, thirty years for them to merge, but it will happen. Together, they are the new Israel. But people like me? Dark skin, Arab speakers, desert values? We will never truly be accepted here. I never read a newspaper report on the Arab immigrants that doesn't imply somewhere that we have to be taught to use a toilet. Or that we sleep on the floor under the bed. The only thing people envy are the amazing libidos of the Yemenites."

Diana hooted at this. She had heard the same.

Moshe shook his head sadly. "It could be funny if it wasn't so sad. It starts at the top," he said. "The genius Ben-Gurion. He calls concentration camp survivors 'human dust.' He calls Arab immigrants 'rabble.' All have to be house-trained, like pets, trained to become like 'Us.' The New Jew. Those *yekkes*, in their European suits and ties, spit on three thousand years of Arab civilization because a Jew from Sana'a hasn't seen a ceramic toilet before." He lit another cigarette and exhaled with a sigh. "Chicken feathers!"

Tamara patted his thigh in sympathy, while a thought occurred to Diana: He is a superb analyst. He exactly summed up the people and our tensions. He is Egyptian, an expert in Arab thought and motivations with thirty years of professional experience. He has an acute mind focused on the contemporary world. My God, she thought, the Office could use him on the Arab desk. We need more people like him. In fact, she thought, from what she'd been picking up around the Office about Egypt right before the twins were born, the timing was perfect. And that made her think of Peter, in Germany, and she felt she could vomit from nerves.

Tamara was nervous too, but for a reason closer to home. Later, after Diana had left with her children, Moshe asked her why. She at first said she wasn't nervous, and then said it was nothing.

"Nothing? According to Diana, there's no such thing as nothing," Moshe said. "If you're upset about something, tell me. Or if you like, tell Ima."

"No need. It's four o'clock. I have to take the children to friends. And then I'll go home." They kissed at the door and Moshe called after her, "Come visit again soon."

Moshe could guess what it was about, but didn't say anything. Arie. That boy was trouble. He'd always known it. Smart as a whip, but too ambitious, in every way. He'd never be content, at work or at home.

Tamara had promised herself that she would confront Arie that night. She had kept it all in for too long and her anger gave her headaches. He came home late, he was secretive, he was short-tempered with the children, he ignored her, took her for granted. And he was obsessed with money. How much did they need? But again, he usually didn't get home till after she was asleep.

In the morning, after the children left for school, when Arie said he had an important meeting and didn't have time for the breakfast she had prepared, Tamara couldn't take it anymore. At the door she pulled him back by the arm. His muscles tensed, his arm felt like a club. "Look at me, for once," she said. "We have to talk."

"What is it?" he said, pulling away as if he had been expecting her anger. "I don't have time now."

"You never have time. You're never here. All you care about is money, and more money." Her voice was rising. "And what do you do every night, why are you always so late? You hardly talk to me or the children."

He struggled to keep his voice calm. "Tamara, I don't have time now, really, I have to see someone and I'm late already."

"Who? A woman?"

"Don't be ridiculous."

"Who is she?"

"What are you talking about? I have to go." He turned abruptly, thrusting out his arm as if waving her away. The light brush from his forearm sent her stumbling into the doorframe. He knew he had gone too far, but didn't care. "Enough drama!" he shouted, "I have to go now, and stop chasing me."

Tamara couldn't stop the tears. "What's wrong?" she cried. "What's wrong with us? What's wrong with me?" Arie turned, made a move toward her. "Tamara . . ." he said, but she pushed him away. "Go, then, and don't come back." She slammed the door in his face. Relieved, he continued down the path, started the car, and drove away.

That morning was Arie's third meeting with Yonathan Schwartz, and he was resolved to stop the whole thing right now. If Peter was here they could have maybe handled it differently, but he wasn't, and it could be months before he returned. Arie had been thinking for weeks about what to do, and he always came to the same conclusion. His only choice was to meet force with force.

Schwartz knew about Auschwitz.

They had met by chance in Arie's favorite café on Dizengoff Street, which was so crowded they had had to share a table. It was a hot day, and they were two young strangers, both with long sleeves. Schwartz had stared at Arie's sleeve, glanced at his own, and muttered, "Where?"

"Too long ago," Arie said. "Forgotten." But even as they spoke, each felt a memory stirring. Had they met before?

The man continued in German. *"Wo?"* Where?

"Wie gesagt, zu lange her. Lass mich in Ruhe." As I said, too long ago. Leave me alone.

The man's eyes widened, and he paled, forcing himself not to tremble. He stared into Arie's face until Arie looked away. The man said in German, his voice shaking, "I thought I recognized you. And your voice, the Bavarian accent." He half rose in his chair, and sank down again. He said in a faint voice, "I wondered if I'd ever see you again. I heard you survived."

Arie went stiff. These were the words of his nightmares. The man had a scrawny neck, thinning hair, hooded eyes, and a deep scar by his right temple. He was clearly afraid. And now Arie remembered. But what was his name, dammit?

Arie tried to control his breathing. He stood and, without counting, laid a handful of change on the plate and pushed through the chairs on the sidewalk. At the street corner, concealed by a tree, he turned and saw the man standing at the door, talking to a waiter, pointing to their table and then looking up the street after him. Arie turned to go back to the café, to confront him, convince him he was mistaken, but thought better of it and hurried away.

He carefully avoided the café, but after a week the man had phoned his office, giving his name. The next day he called again, and on the third call, Arie told his assistant to put him through. Schwartz's threats began.

Arie, who was twenty-one when he was liberated, had never been a kapo, but he knew he had gotten away with murder, almost literally. He had never been a block captain in Auschwitz, never bullied fellow Jews, or done the dirty work of the SS guards, but as a boxer, the result had been almost the same. And maybe he had gone too far, living a fighter's privileged regimen of enough food and light work. Maybe he had unnecessarily beaten a few inmates outside the ring, but they shouldn't have insulted him. He knew that one older man whom he had sent to the infirmary never came back, but he was at death's door to start with. But then they all were.

Certainly, if it came out now, Schwartz's story would destroy him, just as kapo trials were haunting the country. Tales of the evil Jews who collaborated with the Nazis filled the newspapers. It was a kind of national cleansing process—the country vomiting its poison in order to feel better.

They would label him a Jew-murderer, and he would be a pariah.

But that wasn't going to happen. He had seen too many people die in the camps, then in the War of Independence. At first he had asked himself, What was the point of all that death? But then he realized the real question was, What was the point of this life? What would he do with his life to make it all worthwhile? He didn't have an answer to that, but what he knew for certain was that the jerk, Schwartz, was not going to ruin it for him.

Twice Arie had given Schwartz money to shut him up but Arie knew it would never be enough. He had to stop the blackmail.

As if that wasn't bad enough, by the worst imaginable luck, after the threats began, Schwartz had seen him hand in hand with Yasmine at the Kaete Dan hotel on the Tel Aviv beach. They'd taken a room there, only to find that Schwartz worked behind the desk. Arie broke it off with Yasmine the next day. He couldn't see her anymore there and she didn't want to meet anywhere else. Only the five-star hotel, with a terrace overlooking the beach, was good enough for her now.

The ending became loud and messy, and he had paid her off also, but so what? It was just money and, after all, he still had Batia.

Two days later at noon, Arie pulled up at the café where he had promised to give Schwartz another wad of cash. But this time he had other plans. He would end this, Arie swore to himself. One way or another, the blackmail stops here.

Schwartz was not happy when Arie told him he didn't have the money yet. But Arie said, "Don't worry, I'll have the cash later on, and then you'll be happy."

Arie had not wanted to arrange anything by phone or letter; only face-to-face. No trail. They arranged to meet again that same evening.

At first Schwartz had hesitated to meet Arie on the rocks near the Yarkon River, he'd have to take a bus there, it was out of the way, notorious as a seedy place of prostitution, and he didn't see the point. But Arie's promise of a bit of fun, at his expense, persuaded Schwartz to turn up as planned. It was dark when he arrived at the clearing, just north of the river where the road ended, and where the ladies of the night gathered between clients.

"I often go there for a bit of fun," Arie told Schwartz. "Come at nine after work, I'll introduce you to Osnat, she's French, genuine blonde, a bonus from me. To celebrate the last payment. This is the last one, right?" Arie said, knowing that Schwartz would never stop blackmailing him.

"Yes, of course, I said so, never again."

You lying piece of trash, Arie thought. You don't even know you're telling the truth.

Schwartz walked alone in the dark from the bus stop. The moonlight was dim, sudden shrieks or groans made him jump. Why had he agreed to come here? What madness made him leave the security of a crowded café on a busy street? Of all the people in the world, he should trust Arie Nesher, who could kill him with his bare hands? He expected to hear Arie's car approaching and peered all about him, seeking a pair of growing lights in the darkness.

"Hello, Schwartz," Arie said, clamping a hand on his shoulder. Schwartz jumped a foot and felt his heart would never beat again. When it did it was so rapid he couldn't talk. Finally, he managed to gasp, "You lunatic, I almost died of fright."

"A good way to go," Arie said. "Clean, quick, painless." He took out an envelope. "Here, let's get this over with, count it, and then we can go find Osnat, and her friend Michal. Not that those are their real names. It's all there?"

"How should I know? I can't see a thing."

"Well, it is, trust me. And it's the last payment. Yes? Shake on that."

They shook hands. Schwartz said only, "I'll count it later," and with a comforting tap put the envelope into his trouser pocket.

"Don't lose sight of your pants," Arie said with a laugh. "Come on, the fun begins."

"I don't think so," Schwartz said. "This is not my kind of place. I'm going back to the bus stop. I'll be in touch."

"Oh no, you won't," Arie said. "You won't be in touch, and you won't be going. Come on, don't be a baby, come with me, Osnat is waiting for you." He took Schwartz's arm and pulled him along. "She's beautiful," Arie said. "All curves and lips. Know what I mean? She's the best at everything you can dream of. Oh my, her ass!" He felt Schwartz's resistance weaken and relaxed his grip. Schwartz kept close to his side, stumbling as he walked into a rut.

"Follow me," Arie said, "she's over here." Arie, who had approached on foot, had already scouted out the area and found a quiet spot over the hill where the sloping earth and rocks would mute any noise. They were soon alone. "That's funny, where is she?" Arie said.

"Let's go back," Schwartz whispered, as if someone was spying on them, edging closer to Arie. "Where are we?"

"Near the sea," Arie said, pushing Schwartz away and, with all his might, he punched him in the solar plexus. There was a sucking sound, Schwartz doubled up and retched, gasping for breath, while Arie twisted his side to Schwartz and smashed him in the temple with the point of his elbow. There was a crashing, tearing sound, like a tree falling through foliage. His world spinning, Schwartz crumpled to his knees and felt his mouth fill with warm ooze. His skull felt like it had caved in. He tried to yell but all that came from his mouth was a rattle and blood. He supported himself with one arm but Arie's knee to his jaw jerked his head back so far and so hard it may have snapped his neck.

Arie took back the envelope of money. With two fingers he felt Schwartz's artery. When he was sure it was still pumping, he whispered into his ear, "That's just a warning. If ever I hear from you again, I'll kill you."

DIANA and PETER

There was quite a stink at the Office when Peter didn't show up for the briefing. His affronted section head, Amnon Sela, filed an immediate complaint. Sela had ordered Peter to come straight from the airport to the planning meeting, because he brought new information from Germany that needed to be considered for their recommendations. But Peter had gone straight home to his wife.

"He's a loose cannon," Sela told everyone. "Who does he think he is? It's unacceptable." Everybody wants to go home to his wife. But first comes a responsibility to the team and the Office.

Sela made sure his accusation went all the way up the ladder, which was his mistake, because the only response from the family man at the top, Isser Harel, was, "Of course he went straight home. It's been nearly five months. He's got children he's never seen. After all, it was just a planning meeting. Who gave the dumb order he should not?"

"Leave it to me," Sela said to his boss. "I'll find out."

Peter's grin grew the closer he got to home. He had boarded the plane at Berlin Tempelhof Airport as Willi Stinglwagner, all dark business suit and decorum, and he hadn't yet had time to change into the khaki shorts and short-sleeved white shirt of Peter Nesher. The taxi driver had asked if he was visiting Israel for the first time.

Peter didn't miss much. When he said he had flown in from Berlin, he saw the driver's grip on the wheel tighten, saw his neck muscles twitch. The driver, stocky, gray-haired, balding, glared into the rearview mirror. Peter smiled back. "Quite a country you've built here," he said in German. The driver held his look a moment and turned his attention back to the road. He didn't speak again until he asked for the fare, which was half again of the real price. Peter paid anyway. Who knew what the Nazis had done to him?

And anyway, he had something to celebrate.

He carried his case up the stairs to his two-bedroom apartment in the same building where he had shared a room with Arie.

On the first landing he paused, waiting for his heartbeat to slow down, trying to control his racing thoughts. It wasn't the stairs, it wasn't getting cheated with the cab fare, it wasn't even seeing Diana again and the anticipation of her warm body wrapped into his, after so long.

No, none of those. He murmured their names, savoring the sounds. Ezra. Noah. Noah, who built the ark. Ezra, the prophet. My boys, he thought, four months and three days old. He floated up the last flight of stairs, a grin occupying his entire face.

He stopped outside his door, and heard the piercing sound of a baby crying. Another one joined in. Lusty lungs, Peter thought. He heard Diana calling out in frustration. A bang and clatter as something fell to the floor. Silence.

After a moment to collect himself, he turned the key and opened the door.

And there was Diana, eyes widening in alarm. She was barefoot, her hair partly pinned up with strands falling over her face, her brow gleaming with sweat. His shirt hung over her baggy shorts like a tent. In one hand she held a brush and in the other a pan full of dust and bits of food.

Her face was a kaleidoscope of emotions. Surprise, which turned to horror, which turned to embarrassment and then joy, and finally she jumped into his arms, dropping the brush and tin pan with a clatter.

"You're early . . . they said you wouldn't be home till late, you had to go to the Office for a meeting . . . I haven't tidied up . . . haven't showered. I haven't . . ." until Peter gently pushed Diana to arm's length.

"I couldn't wait, I love you too much," he managed to say. He looked from her to the bedroom door and pointed with his chin. "In there?"

The smile of an angel came to her. She pulled her hair from her eyes, which shone with joy. She nodded and took Peter by the hand. But first he took off his shoes, he didn't know why, it seemed the right thing, to pad gently and silently into the presence of his dearest twins and meet them for the first time in this life. Before he even crossed the threshold, tears were streaming down his face. Diana touched them in wonder. "I've never seen you cry," she said.

Noah and Ezra, he didn't know yet who was who, lay across each other like puppies, the foot of one in the eye of the other. They had sparse black hair and chubby thighs and looked up at Peter with wide brown eyes. "I was trying to dress them for you," Diana whispered. "But they hate clothes."

"They take after me," Peter said, with a gentle squeeze of Diana's hand. "Here," she said, picking up the top one and as she held him out to Peter, she kissed the baby and said, "Peter, this is Noah. Noah, meet your daddy." Peter took the tiny wriggling thing and held him at a distance, before shifting his hold, until Noah's body pressed against his breast. A thin wail became earsplitting. With all his might Noah strained away from Peter, one tiny pudgy hand using Peter's nose for leverage, and his face turned puce and then scarlet from the effort of crying and pushing.

"What did I do?" Peter wailed as Noah sucked in air between screams.

Diana took Noah from him. "Nothing, he just doesn't know you."

"Ouch. That hurt."

"Try Ezra, pick him up." Diana held Noah with one arm and with the other hand she pulled her shirt open, allowing a full breast to plop out with a large brown nipple, which disappeared between the lips of Noah, who settled and sucked.

Peter looked on in envy and picked up Ezra, who squirmed, grimaced, puckered up his mouth, and began to scream. "Oh no," Peter said. "It was easier dealing with Genscher."

"Lothar Genscher? Never mention his name in this home again. This is a scum-free zone."

"You're right," Peter said, "bad joke. What should I do?"

"Just hold him and walk around till he stops."

Twenty minutes later Peter could barely stay on his feet but Ezra, his son Ezra, was asleep in his arms, his head warm in the crick of Peter's neck and, on the sofa, Noah slept at Diana's breast.

She formed with her lips, "Welcome home, my love."

The next morning all Peter wanted was to sleep, but he couldn't give Sela the pleasure of his missing the nine o'clock meeting. It was a beautiful Tel Aviv morning so he walked, pausing for a black coffee and half a sandwich at the corner *budke*. Dahlia, a worn-looking woman with a working man's cap and a loud word for everyone, had managed the tiny kiosk so long that she still had the list of Indian Assam and Darjeeling teas she had served the British troops in the Mandate days. Many of them had served in India and enjoyed Dahlia's tea and company, without knowing that beneath the wooden floor she had a stash of Haganah pomegranates, slang for hand grenades. She always greeted him with a knowing look; she had fought in the Haganah with half his spy bosses and he wouldn't be surprised if she still had a stash of explosives beneath the oranges she squeezed for his juice.

"Been away keeping us safe?" she yelled as she poured Peter's coffee.

"How's business?" he answered.

"So how was it to see your boys for the first time? Diana was so excited you were coming home. They're so sweet."

Before Peter could answer, the stranger sipping coffee next to him said, "First time to see your children? How old are they? Where have you been?"

Peter answered Dahlia, "They are, they are. Amazing. But I don't think I slept all night."

The woman behind him said, "What do you mean, 'they.' How many are there?"

The first stranger said, "How come you've never seen your own children before?" He shifted on his stool to look at Peter. "Have you been in jail?"

"Jail?" the woman said, taking a step back.

A man walking by stopped in his tracks. "Who?"

"Thanks for the coffee, Dahlia," Peter said. "See you tomorrow."

"Bye, Peter, have a good day."

Thanks, Dahlia, he thought, I'm supposed to be low profile. But he smiled as he walked in the shade, thinking, it is a good day. It's good to be home. He must stay as long as possible. Warmth pulsed through him at the thought of his children, and he silently answered Dahlia's question: Yes, I have been away keeping them safe.

At the Office, apart from a few nods of acknowledgment, it was as if he'd never been away, except for his direct boss, Amnon Sela, who came over to shake his hand. He was all smiles and compliments for the Germany job.

Sela's fake cordiality belied the tension in the room: pursed lips, grim faces, silence. A dozen agents were waiting for Harel, but it was Yossi Duvshani, his number two, who entered the room, carrying just one folder.

He began right away, with a bitter tone. "The defense minister reconfirmed that all foreign operations remain under the army's command." His eyes flashed toward Peter and away again. "We in Mossad will continue to gather information, while the military intelligence arm, Aman, will act on it. In Egypt, Unit 131 is their secret weapon, God help us. So this is a disaster waiting to happen, and it will be up to us to pick up the pieces. Remember, our supreme goal is not to change British foreign policy in the Middle East, but to limit our enemies' ability to wage war on Israel."

After ten more minutes of general business, Duvshani rapped on the table and called on Sela for country reports.

Amnon Sela looked up from his papers. Reporting on Peter's work while Peter was in the room would be uncomfortable, he should have spoken to him directly first, but Nesher had gone home yesterday, instead of reporting to him as he should have, so tough luck.

"I'll start with Germany and Obersturmbannführer Otto Skorzeny," Sela began. "The head of the snake. In World War Two Skorzeny was an SS colonel, head of their special forces. He's the man Hitler sent to rescue his buddy, the Italian dictator Mussolini. Well, he's turned up again. Last year Egypt hired Skorzeny to develop their security services. We have tracked at least a hundred and fifty Nazis, mostly intelligence operatives, who have joined him in Cairo. Many were hiding in South America, especially Argentina, Brazil, and Paraguay. One of them, for instance, is Franz Buensch, who wrote *The Sexual Habits of the Jews*. Peter Nesher is leading the operation against these bastards."

Peter nodded at the unexpected endorsement.

"The trouble is, we are not doing very well."

Peter's stomach churned. He'd been set up.

"We track Skorzeny, we know where he is, we know what he is doing, but we haven't been able to stop even one of those Nazis from joining him. So far." He deliberately avoided Peter's glare. Peter shook his head. Not this again. Money. Sela is obsessed with money.

Sela went on. "When Nasser proposed the job to Skorzeny, he said no. They didn't offer him enough money. Then the CIA stepped in. They want a strong Egypt, to stand up to Russia, so the CIA offered Skorzeny money on top, so then he took the job." He paused before delivering his coup de grâce. "So if we offer him more money, we can buy him out. He'll leave and go home to Spain, where he has his own business. But he mustn't know the money comes from Israel."

Peter couldn't help himself. If Sela wanted to bring this into the open, so be it. "Of course," Peter said, "with our budget, we'll outbid the CIA. Look, we can hardly pay our own salaries. And as for keeping the source a secret, who else but Israel would want to bribe him to leave Egypt? And then it gets out—Israel wants to pay Otto Skorzeny. What a fiasco that would be. Plus there's also the small matter of Israel going head-to-head with America over their Mideast policy. Do we really want to do that?"

"This is not the time or place for that," Sela said.

"You brought it up," Peter answered.

"The fact is, you were supposed to stop Skorzeny and so far, the score is a hundred and fifty to him, zero to us."

They'd been fighting over this at long range for weeks. "Look," Peter said slowly. "Let's put the cards on the table." He looked at Duvshani, who nodded.

"Unit 131 wants to attack British targets in Egypt," Peter said. "We know that one way or another that will end in disaster for Israel. That appears to be out of our hands, thanks to Ben-Gurion's support for Aman. They also want to bomb the Nazis. No bad thing, in principle. But in practice? Kill a hundred and fifty Germans? Working legally in Egypt? This is a fantasy. And Sela's only answer would lead to a fiasco too. There is only one way, and even that is a long shot, and that is what my team and I are working on, with, and I say this sarcastically, the help of Mr. Sela, here."

I shouldn't have said that. I went too far, he thought immediately. "I take that back, there is some frustration in the field," Peter said. "Our hope is that the Nazis we are pressuring in Germany will force Skorzeny and his gang back from Egypt. They'll do the work for us, cleanly, with no fingerprints."

"And it's working so well," Sela said. "If you'll excuse my sarcasm."

"All right, that's enough," Duvshani cut in. "I've read the reports, so has Isser, and we want to proceed quickly in a slightly new direction. Nesher, your Nazis are not doing what they've been told. Not one of them. So we have to up the ante."

"Which means?" Peter said.

"This meeting is over," Duvshani said. "Nesher, Sela, to my room."

When it was just the three of them, Duvshani turned to Peter.

"You have to scare them. Show we mean business. Choose one. Expose his past and eliminate him."

"Eliminate? In Germany?" Peter said.

"Yes. And that doesn't leave this room."

"You mean, it is not all right to kill a German in Egypt, but it is in Germany?"

"Yes, I do. Because your target will not be a nameless rogue in Egypt but a Nazi working high up in the German government, respectable, prominent, it will be a humiliation for Germany to have such an established person exposed and murdered. They will be forced to act against their own people, more Nazis, in Egypt, openly planning to kill the Jews. Again."

"Especially after a list of a hundred and fifty Nazis permitted by the German government to work in Egypt against the Jewish state appears in *The New York Times*, *The Times* of London, and *Le Monde*," said Sela.

"Precisely," Duvshani said.

"Does Harel know about this?" Peter said, knowing he was ruffling feathers.

"Of course he does. Now get to it."

If there was trouble at the Office, there was trouble at home too.

Diana's leave of absence from the Office had stretched from a month to three to five. With Peter rarely home and the twins to care for, and her mother banned from Israel until she changed her ways, Diana could not go back to work. The small apartment was hot in the day and noisy in the evening. None of the neighbors seemed to communicate below a shout. She sometimes found herself longing for her British terrace house, where neighbors were rarely seen and never heard. Here it was like a bus station, and everybody had a different unkind theory about where Peter was, most of them involving women in other towns, especially, for some reason, the desert town of Be'er Sheva. She could have written a book with all the advice she received, none of it welcome.

For Diana to go somewhere with the twins was like provisioning a day's training march for an army brigade. Only Tamara helped keep her sane. On hot days in Tel Aviv, where they sometimes strolled in their clinging, low-cut dresses, not a man walked by who didn't stare or comment. It was on one such morning in a nearly empty café that Tamara laid her hand on Diana's and confided, in a low voice, that she had a little problem with Arie.

Diana laughed. "Oh, you don't say!"

"That's not nice," Tamara said.

"Sorry, I didn't want to be mean. But, really. You don't say!"

"Well, this is different. Listen, I don't know what to do, or think." She told Diana of one evening when Arie had come home late and when she'd asked him where he had been, he had almost shouted, "I've been home all night and don't you forget it."

"It's like he wanted an alibi or something, a real police alibi. Why would he say that?"

"Because he wanted an alibi, you're right. But why? Did you ask him?"

"No. You don't understand. If he doesn't want to talk, he never will.

He's like a rock. He can be so loving and the next minute nasty and hard. So, no, I didn't ask him. There's no point."

"So why are you telling me?"

"Do you think he could have done something wrong? Something bad?"

"Oh, Tamara, please. You know who you married. Of course he could. And it isn't anything to do with a woman or he wouldn't have mentioned it. When was it? Do you remember the exact date? Did Arie leave town that day or was he in Tel Aviv?"

The next day Diana phoned Gingie at the Office and asked her to get the Tel Aviv police to check their logs of that day and the next. Were there any unexplained criminal events? Someone leaving the scene of a car crash? A fight? Anything?

Gingie called back the same day. Of the open files, only one was serious. The body of a male, identified as Yonathan Schwartz, twenty-eight years old, of Tel Aviv, had been found by the rocks north of the city. His head wounds were consistent with a fall. But spots of blood had been discovered nearby. So he must have been bleeding before he fell. Or it could be somebody else's blood. Women who frequented the area at night had been questioned and nobody heard or saw anything untoward. The file was open but no investigation underway.

"Is anything known about this man?" Diana asked.

"Not much," Gingie said. "I asked for the file. He was a single father, one son, nine years old, no sign of where the mother is. He worked at the Kaete Dan hotel as a waiter. A concentration camp survivor."

Diana, who was thinking of any possible link to Arie, asked, "Which camp? Or camps?"

"Auschwitz. There were others but that was the only one he talked about to colleagues at the hotel. They said he was a very nervous, excitable person. That's all the police have at this point. They didn't pursue it. His son is in care with social services."

Everyone knew Arie had been in Auschwitz. He never said a word about it, but then neither did anyone else who had survived there. Voices dropped, eyes shifted, shoulders drooped. The very name began with an expression of pain.

"Did Arie ever go to the Kaete Dan hotel?" Diana asked Tamara.

"In Tel Aviv? Probably. It's a place where businessmen meet. Why?"

"Just wondering."

When Diana asked Gingie if she could get hold of the hotel records to see if a certain person ever stayed there, Gingie said she could do better than that. The secret services used the hotel too. All the best rooms were bugged.

"Really?" Diana said. "Can you get hold of recordings? How?"

"I'd need a good reason. I haven't asked you, but I will now. Why are you asking for all this?"

"I'll get back to you if I need more, all right?"

Later, on the telephone, Diana asked Tamara if she really wanted to know what Arie had meant. "Sometimes it's better to let sleeping dogs lie. I think you should drop it."

Tamara went silent, tapping her fingers. She said, after a while, in a questioning voice, "Sometimes I think I don't know who I live with."

"How is he with the children?"

"Oh, he loves them, he's a wonderful father. But I know he has other women." Tamara sighed, a silent appeal for help.

"You're so beautiful," Diana said. "Men are beyond me."

So Diana didn't tell Tamara what Gingie told her. There was no reason, it could all be just coincidence.

But she told Peter.

After almost two months running the operation from the Office with only short trips to Germany, two months at home with the babies, Peter had never felt so close to Diana, every moment with her and the boys was a pleasure beyond anything he had ever imagined. When they cried he comforted them, when they slept he watched over them, when they rolled over he exclaimed in delight, and all this while holding Diana's hand. At night they all slept in the same bed, and so as not to wake the boys, he and Diana made love on the balcony in the cool air.

But when Diana told him about Arie's apparent demand for an alibi, and what Gingie had found out, his blood ran cold. Diana should have stayed out of it, left it up to Tamara, but it was too late now. He wouldn't put anything past his brother. Of course he did it, whatever it was. Why else would he need an alibi? A car accident? An affair? A robbery? No. His instinct screamed it, every supremely trained sense knew it. The victim, Schwartz, knew something about Arie in Auschwitz and couldn't be allowed to live to tell the tale. Quite an assumption, but what else could Arie be hiding?

Yet, so what? What should he do, if it's true? Turn his brother in? He'd never do that. Warn him? Arie was damaged, whatever the concentration camp equivalent of shell-shocked was, nothing would ever stand in his way, his moral compass was stuck on south, he had nothing to lose because he had already lost it all. Arie had never told him much about how he'd survived in the camps. But he didn't need to, Peter had read all the reports, he knew what it took to survive so long. The nice guys died first. So why challenge him? To stop him doing anything so crazy again, of course.

Tamara. Would Arie ever harm Tamara? No, she's the mother of his children, on whom he dotes. Anyway, why would he? Was he ever violent at home? Tamara had never said so.

And it occurred to Peter, who was he to talk? He was going to Germany to kill a Nazi he was already blackmailing. Didn't that make him worse than Arie? Does the end justify the means?

Best to let it ride.

A week later the whole family came together for a barbeque at Arie's, complete with ribs of beef, sausages from Germany, and piles of salads and sauces. As they milled around with plates of food and beers and orange juice, Moshe revealed his news with pride. "I've got a new job at the foreign ministry," he said, "as a Near East analyst. They're moving their offices to Jerusalem, to help get Jerusalem recognized as our capital."

"I wouldn't hold your breath on that one," Peter said. "But congratulations, that's wonderful."

"How will you get there, though?" Tamara asked.

"By bus, of course."

"And I'm teaching Hebrew to new immigrants," Rachel said, and looked mock-upset when everybody laughed. She could hardly put two sentences together herself.

"Well, while we're all mentioning our new jobs, I'm going back to the Office," Diana put in. "Part-time. Gingie found me a good girl to look after the twins in the mornings. No more tittie-feeds."

Wolfie introduced his new girlfriend, a striking girl called Mayan, born on the same kibbutz as Moshe Dayan, the one-eyed warrior tipped as the next army chief of staff. Natanel was there too. Apparently he'd gotten over Arie stealing Yasmine, who, anyway, had disappeared over the horizon.

The adults sat and smoked on the cane sofas beneath the pergola or milled around the garden, while the children played on the grass. "He's a natural leader," Tamara said proudly as Ido arranged the other children into rows. And look at Estie." The little girl was balancing on the railing like a tightrope walker. "Be careful!" Rachel shouted in alarm, grabbing her by the arm and hoisting her to safety. Then a ball came sailing over the chairs. Ido lashed out with his foot, sending the ball crashing into a jug of orange juice, which smashed to the floor, scattering shards of glass in all directions. "Nobody move," Tamara yelled. "Put your shoes on. And Ido, go to bed! Now!"

At Peter's request, the buffet included hummus, tehina, falafel, and shawarma, the food he most missed when eating the sauerbraten and *kartoffelsalat* of Herr Willi Stinglwagner, Munich importer of medical products.

PETER

The former SS-Sturmbannführer Hans-Dieter Braun, alias Dr. Lothar Genscher, torturer and murderer, now living in Germany with his first family, didn't know how lucky he was: He had been struck off the list, for now. Amnon Sela and the men at the Office decided he should be left to rise in the ranks of Germany's industrialists until he could become more useful. The same applied to two more Nazis hiding in plain sight, one of whom was a Christian Democratic Union member of parliament, and the other a young aide to Cologne's police chief. They were on fast tracks, let them be promoted until their exposure would humiliate the country, if that was ever required, or their position of power gave them access to information Israel needed, or both. One thing was sure: Sooner or later they would pay for their evil past.

The name that Sela eventually gave Peter Nesher's hit team in Germany was infinitely more powerful and controversial. Eight Israeli agents were tracking him around the clock, looking for the sweet spot, a time and place that he regularly could be found. By definition, it took weeks. But everyone had something they did like clockwork. Maybe he left home at exactly the same time each morning, or left work at the same time. Maybe he went for a sauna or met friends for a drink each Tuesday evening at six o'clock on the way home. Or he took a child to her piano lesson, or brought food to an aging parent. The later at night the better. Somewhere quiet and inconspicuous. Visiting a lover? A walk before bed? Some routine that left him vulnerable, when he could be snatched, leading to his filmed confession and silent death.

The team rented a safe house in the countryside of Rhineland-Westphalia, and in different names and places rented five cars, one for the snatch, one for escort, one for backup, and two for the switch.

They procured untraceable weapons from trusted sources, one in Hamburg and one in Munich, opposite ends of the country, and they met in the middle: Bonn, the birthplace of Beethoven, a sleepy backwater now the capital of the Federal Republic of Germany.

Mossad had discovered that Kurt Bohlendorf, the head of protocol of the chancellor's office, a man privy to Konrad Adenauer's complete schedule, who organized state visits and who had access to all relevant private information of visiting world leaders, had spent part of the Second World War as Deputy Reichskommissar, Ukraine. Together with his Nazi boss, Kommissar Erich Koch, who had described himself in his glory days as "a brutal dog," the pair had imposed a German wartime occupation policy in the Ukraine that led to the deaths of 1.3 million prisoners of war in 160 concentration camps. Another three million Ukrainians died of starvation and disease. If Koch was a brutal dog, Bohlendorf was his pitiless bitch.

"And this animal," Nesher said to Yehuda, the muscleman analyst who was now a field agent, "today approves who enters the chancellor's room first and for how long they shake hands. He probably decides on the menu."

"The Germans must know who he is," Yehuda said. "And they don't care."

"All the better. Stay focused on what you have to do."

Yehuda's role before the snatch, which he would help perform, was to put together the cover story on who killed Bohlendorf: revenge-driven Ukrainian nationalists. No Israeli fingerprints. And, to make it all perfect, to add even more to the West German government's humiliation, while following Bohlendorf Mossad had discovered another of his secrets: He was a spy for East Germany, in the heart of the West German government.

This last nugget, though, provoked a furious debate among the team, which Peter knew could only be resolved at headquarters. Was Bohlendorf too important to kill? Could he be more valuable to Israel alive than dead?

While his team continued with the planning and preparations, Peter flew home. This needed a full discussion about whether they should change their plan, and only Harel could decide. Peter wanted to be there.

But while he was in the air, the debacle began.

He heard about it from the Tel Aviv taxi driver leaving Lod Airport.

"Did you hear the news?" the driver said, elbow resting on the open window, a cigarette in his hand, turning down the radio with his other hand, and staring in the mirror. "It was just on the radio."

"Do you mind keeping at least one hand on the wheel," Peter said. "And looking at the road, I have two little children." He smiled as he thought of them. He'd be home in half an hour.

"Those clowns at Mossad," the cabbie said.

"What?"

"Think they're so smart. Let me tell you, the country's going to the dogs. And the puppies are in charge. They don't know a thing. And now this. It's embarrassing."

"What is? And please. Slow down."

"You didn't hear, then?"

"No, I just landed. What happened?"

"Believe me, there's worse to come, there always is." He shook his head. "What's the country coming to?"

"I don't know," Peter said. "You tell me. So what did the clowns at Mossad do?"

"What didn't they do!"

"For God's sake, tell me what happened. Or rather, tell me what the radio said happened. It isn't always the same. And I mean it, slow down."

A car coming toward them took the bend too fast and crossed into their lane, forcing the cabdriver to hit the brakes. "Damn drivers," he yelled, thumping his horn, but the car was long gone.

"It was just on the radio," he said. "The Egyptians are arresting Israelis. Apparently one of our boys was about to put a bomb in a British theater in Alexandria but guess what, the thing blew up in his pocket. Can you imagine that? What happened to his balls? Not to mention his schlong. Oh, it hurts just to think about that." He squirmed in his seat as he spoke, taking a drag from his cigarette. "I hope for his sake it was his back pocket. I mean, who carries a bomb in their pocket? Was it a big pocket? Or a small bomb? And if it was a small bomb, then what was the point? Or maybe it was a jacket pocket. Jackets have bigger pockets. But who wears a jacket in Cairo; it's much too hot. Anyway, when a bomb goes off in your pocket . . . well . . . I hope he has a family already. What an idiot."

Peter was speechless. He was about to say it wasn't Mossad but Aman, but caught himself. "Change of address," he said instead. "Take me to the corner of Ben Yehuda and Smolenskin." He didn't want to stop right in front of the Office, this driver had a big mouth.

"That isn't all. There have been a whole load of arrests. That's a way to run a country? It isn't enough we let the Egyptians arrest one of our ships in the Suez Canal and don't do anything about it? Apparently, there have been a whole string of bombs in Egypt, and the BBC said they may all be related. And now they've got our boy by the balls, literally. I'm telling you, this country is finished."

"Where are you from?"

"Poland."

"Will you go back, then, if it's so bad here?"

"Are you *meshugge*? Crazy? We don't have anywhere else to go. Does that make this paradise, though? The best thing about this place is the breakfasts. Omelet with salad."

Peter paid the taxi and carried his case the last hundred yards to 85 Ben Yehuda. He passed through the identity checks and left his suitcase with the B floor guard. It was a four-story building with five floors. One could not be accessed or even seen from the main staircase, and had no windows. B floor was a box within a box. That was where he went.

The first thing his section chief Amnon Sela said to Peter was, "What's wrong with you? Last time I told you to come here and you go home. This time I tell you to go home and you come here? What is it with you?"

"I'd laugh, but tell me, is it true, what my cabdriver told me?"

"Must be. If a cabbie said so."

"About Egypt?"

"Can you believe it? Come to my office."

Sela closed the door. "Harel hit the roof. He went straight to Defense HQ and now I think they're all driving to Jerusalem. The prime minister wants blood. Says he didn't know anything about it. Everyone's blaming everyone else, of course."

"I came to talk about Bohlendorf."

"Yes, well, we will, but that'll have to wait to get anyone's attention. I think this is the worst thing to ever happen to us."

"Us?"

"Not us, but it may as well be."

"So fill me in. What happened?"

"Aman messed up. Totally. All this month. Letter bombs that did almost no damage in Alexandria. Then two more bombs, against the USIA libraries in Cairo and Alexandria. In hollowed-out books. The acid leaked and blew up the bombs too early. Nobody was hurt. The same in a train station. Freight trains, thank God, nobody hurt. And then this shlemiel today whose bomb went off in his pocket. Anyway, the Arabs are going through the Aman network like a knife through butter. They've arrested a dozen people, all Jews, and it's still going on. God knows where it will end."

"It'll probably end with the rest of Egypt's Jews running here," Peter said, thinking of Tamara and her family.

"This mess is exactly what Harel warned against. Aman just doesn't have the people to do this kind of work. We do, and only we do. Now they've cleaned up all the Aman network, they'll go on trial and we'll all be exposed as liars and crooks; and incompetent, which is worse."

"Just when we need everyone's help against Egypt."

"Exactly. So what was that you were saying about assassinating a top German official in Bonn?"

"*I'm* saying? You too."

It was all anyone was talking about at the Office but it was all at the gossip stage. "Have you heard . . . ?" "Is it true?" "Whose bomb blew up . . . ?" So after learning as much as he could, Peter decided to go home.

Sela told him to wait there till he was called. "This Egypt disaster will take over for a few days, nobody's got time to think about your man."

All of a sudden he's my man, Peter thought. Sela's a piece of work, he's already covering his ass. "Make that our man," Peter said.

The word went to Peter's team in Bonn to put everything on ice, while he picked up his case to go home to Diana, Noah, and Ezra.

But a last word from Gingie at the door rang the alarm. "Peter," she said quietly, laying her hand on his arm, looking around to make sure nobody could hear. "I told Diana, I had a call from the police. They wanted to know why I asked for the file of a man who died months ago. I had to tell them I was doing Diana a favor."

Peter felt his throat go dry, and nodded. "When did they call?"

"Two days ago."

"That's fine, no problem."

But that was the last thing he thought as he took the cab home. The police? This could snowball. Why did Diana get involved? It was Tamara's problem. Gingie shouldn't have asked for the file. It was all right to ask over the phone for information. There's no log. But now there's a paper trail. It was five minutes home by car but in that time he saw his future mapped out: lying to save his brother. He'd have to come up with a cover story for Diana. Why would she have asked for the dead man's file? Ironic, he thought. He, so straight and honest, had become a professional liar. At work, he lived a lie, he lied for his country. How long does it take to absorb those warped values at home? Here he was, desperately seeking a lie that would save his brother, and, for that matter, his wife, who would appear an accomplice after the fact. Poor, dear, Tamara, the innocent. He had to find a story to explain it all. To lie for them seemed the most natural thing in the world.

Or was he wrong? Did his brother not do it? Was there some innocent explanation? There was no way now but to ask him.

To lighten his mood before seeing Diana, he bought her flowers at the corner shop. He took the stairs two at a time, daisies in one hand, suitcase in the other, smiling all the way.

This time she was ready for him. Her auburn hair was long now, with curls to her shoulders, which were bare beneath a clinging silk chemise her mother had sent from London. Its fine lace trim and flimsy straps begged to be slipped over her shoulders. She wore a short cotton skirt that swirled as she turned, and her bare feet moved silently to the sofa where she led him by the hand.

He asked, "Are the boys all right?"

"Yes, they're sleeping. So much has happened."

"Yes, lots to talk about. But it can wait."

"I missed you so much," Diana whispered, taking him into her arms, stroking his neck, kissing him.

"I missed you too, my love." His hand felt beneath her chemise, he slipped his fingers beneath the silk straps and carefully raised them over her head while she wiggled out of her skirt. He always wondered how she did that. And then her specialty, which amused him even more. She stood on one leg, pulled the other foot up her inside thigh, hooked her big toe inside her panties and slowly pulled them down, all the while smiling, her eyes fixed on his. It always made him laugh, as on one leg she slowly revealed herself.

They had half an hour before the boys would wake.

It sufficed, just. He covered her mouth with his hand. "Sssshh," he whispered. And soon she did the same to him.

They held each other tightly, Diana lying on top of Peter, her chest on his, her belly on his, playing with his hair, while he trailed his fingers along the warmth of her damp skin, from the small of her back to the hollows of her knees. She trembled at his touch, even afterward, while he kissed her ear and the curve of her neck, which lay so enticingly by his lips. She felt his peaceful, warm breath, thinking, I have to tell him about the police, and he was thinking, This is so idyllic, I can't let Arie ruin it all.

That evening he sat the boys, ten months old now, in the bathroom sink and soaped them with warm water while Diana tried to hold them still. Ezra was as slippery as the soap, first sliding down into the basin and then climbing onto the counter. Noah picked up everything within reach, the soap, toothbrushes, paste, tweezers, Band-Aids, and threw it all to the floor. He put only one thing in his mouth: the scissors, which he also tried to push into his ear. In between, the twins pushed and pulled each other, their racket merging with Peter's exasperated exhortations for them to behave, and Diana's helpless laughter.

"This is what it's like every day, so you have no sympathy from me," she said when she could talk. "Don't forget between the legs and behind the ears. Would you like another one?"

"Yes. At least three more."

"Triplets."

"How on earth do people cope?"

"Divorce, I imagine."

When the boys were finally asleep, and Peter and Diana could at last rest on the sofa with glasses of juice, it was Diana who brought it up. "The police have asked about, you know, what we talked about. The man who was killed."

"Yes, I know."

"Really? How?"

"Gingie told me. Today, at the office. I was going to mention it now."

"What do we do? I haven't stopped thinking about it. I can't say Tamara asked me to find out. But what on earth can I say?"

For once he was at a loss, just when it was closest to home.

It didn't take long. The next morning there was a sharp knock on the door and two policemen asked if they could come in.

The younger one was built like a boxer, with small penetrating eyes that bored into Diana as his partner introduced the two of them. He was older, more worn, rumpled and wary. He could be right out of a British detective film, Peter thought. He asked the questions while his partner's eyes roamed over every item in the room, and studied him and his wife. This could go badly, Peter thought. What on earth could they say?

"I'll be quick, ma'am," Sergeant Ludlow said. Peter half-congratulated himself. He was right, he's English, probably one of those rare Christian admirers of the Zionists left over from the Mandate period. He'll be sharp.

"I understand you asked your friend in one of the security services to order a police file of a man, Yonathan Schwartz, suspected to have been murdered. I'd like to ask you, why?"

Diana was flustered. If only they'd worked out what to say. Peter was worried. "Does she have to answer?"

"Not right away. But it's better if you do, ma'am," the sergeant said, addressing himself directly to Diana. "This is an official inquiry and you are obliged to answer. If not here, then at the station. This is purely a formality, you understand, I'm sure you had a good reason."

Peter tried to control his heartbeat. He looked at Diana with a hint of encouragement, hoping to look unbothered.

"Of course," Diana said with a polite smile. "I can't really say fully, but it's related to an inquiry of my own as part of my work for a government department. If you know where the inquiry came from, then you know which department."

"Yes, ma'am, I do. But I still need to know what it is about, and I thought you may prefer that I ask you here rather than at your office."

"Well, thank you sergeant, that's considerate, but there is really nothing to hide. We are trying to contact survivors of Auschwitz in relation to an SS guard there. You would need to approach the Office officially to ask why we need the information, I'm not allowed to say, but I can say we were hoping to find out through the deceased man's personal file whether he knew the whereabouts of other survivors who could help us. It concerns a particular guard and we are having trouble finding people who remember him."

Peter looked from Diana to Ludlow, his eyebrow rising imperceptibly. Brilliant, he was thinking. Everyone's looking for someone, and her general description could fit any number of ongoing activities including, for that matter, his own. The Office would confirm it without blinking an eye. Especially if the police inquiry went through Gingie. And he would make sure it did.

"It's purely routine," Diana added. Perfect, Peter thought, she's a genius improviser. Veronique. Karla. She always knew what to say. What other phrase so deftly establishes an equivalence between the policeman's inquiry and her own? They've got the same job, she was saying in code.

"Of course," Sergeant Ludlow said. "Thank you. I suspected something of the kind. Well, that's all I need to know now. Thank you for your time."

Diana tried not to smile at Peter.

But at the door, his hand on the knob, the policeman turned and said, "I'm curious though, ma'am. You have a part-time job. Yet you asked a much more senior person to make a simple call for you. Wouldn't it normally be the other way around?"

Diana forced herself not to swallow. "Uh, yes, and no."

There was an uncomfortable pause as the two policemen stared at her.

"It's a very informal place," Peter put in, "but coordination between security services, even of a minor nature, must go through the proper channels."

Sergeant Ludlow nodded with pursed lips, as if his question had been conclusively answered.

"Yes, of course. Thank you both for your time."

Peter knew what was going through the English copper's head. Mossad? Proper channels? That'll be the day.

Later, on his way to see Arie, Peter's mind was aflame. He just wanted the cabbie to shut up. The taxi driver was angry about German government reparations to Israel. What's one and a half billion dollars for all they did? We shouldn't take a penny, it's blood money. Nothing can pay for six million lives. Or if they insist, then it should be three times that. Maybe I'll get a new cab out if it, he said. This piece of junk has had it. Falling apart. No gearbox."

"Do you mind?" Peter said. "I have a headache."

"Bloody Nazis. Bloody Ben-Gurion. Calls himself a Jew!"

Peter was trying to think straight before he met Arie at Kapulsky. And why always Kapulsky? Probably another crooked deal, did he own it? What a corner they were in, thanks to Arie. Diana had lied to the police. He had backed her up. These were small lies and could be supported, but protecting Arie would lead them to bigger, more serious lies. They were digging themselves into a hole, and maybe it was unnecessary. He had to know. Did Arie kill the man or not? If not, why had he demanded an alibi from Tamara, and so crudely?

At the café Peter walked right to Arie, who was sitting at a front table dominating the entrance. See and be seen. Arie stood and hugged Peter, beaming. "Your timing is perfect," he said. "Welcome home. Peter, this is Nadav Bru . . . well, never mind, Nadav from Bank Diskont. We have just shaken hands on something. I'll tell you about it later. How are you?" He held Peter at arm's length, admiring him. "Sit down, join us, what will you have?"

"Arie, I don't have much time, I thought we were meeting just the two of us."

Nadav rose immediately. "That's fine, Peter, good to meet you. I was just going. Arie, I'll get back to you, don't worry, this is going to happen." He shook hands with them both and left. When he was gone, Peter sat down, leaned forward, and put his hand on Arie's forearm.

"You look serious," Arie said. "Listen, I'm going to get a loan for a huge deal, maybe you'll get a new car out of it, Nadav is the chief . . ."

"I don't care, at this point," Peter interrupted. "Arie, I'm going to ask you once. And remember, this is my job. So don't lie to me."

"All right, all right," Arie said, pulling back his arm. "What is it, why are you so riled up? Relax."

"I'll relax if I get the right answer to my question."

"Fine. What is it?"

Peter looked around, leaned forward again, pulled Arie closer, and whispered in his ear, "Did you kill Yonathan Schwartz?"

"What?" Arie jerked back, his brow creasing, shaking his head. "Who? Are you crazy? What are you talking about?"

"That's not an answer. Did you murder Yonathan Schwartz?"

"Why would you ask me that? I haven't seen you in months, and that's your first question?"

"Arie, I just need a yes or a no. Did you have a fight with Yonathan Schwartz and beat him to death?"

FAMILY TIME

Tel Aviv, Israel
September 1954

Money bought power, even within the family. With the most money and the biggest house, at thirty years of age Arie was beginning to act like the patriarch. His call for a family meal was like a summons.

While Tamara and Rachel prepared dinner in the kitchen, he and Peter drank orange juice as they contemplated the kids yelling and rolling across the floor.

Ido had wrestled Estie to the ground and was sitting on her. Combining their four-year-old strength, Daniel and Carmel pulled him off. They all ended up rolling on the floor, tickling each other and laughing. How bizarre, Peter thought, Tamara's brother and sister fighting her son and daughter, aunt and uncle wrestling with niece and nephew. The minute age difference between Tamara's children and her siblings confused the generations.

Sitting down for dinner, Peter told Ido to calm down. Ido was still breathless and had kicked his sister under the table. Now Peter was telling his brother-in-law to behave.

Tamara came in beaming, carrying a large dish, which Moshe helped place on the table. "Food is ready, and it's just right," she said happily. Arie told her to wait. "I have an announcement."

"Wait till after dinner," Tamara said.

"What for? This is a celebration, they should know what we're celebrating."

"No business during dinner."

"This isn't business, it's pleasure. It is for me, anyway." A glass tinkled as Arie tapped with his fork.

"Ladies and gentleman, your attention, please." Peter and Diana, Moshe and Rachel, Wolfie and Mayan, looked toward the head of the table, where Arie stood with a raised glass. Ido and Daniel were staring at each other, seeing who would blink first.

"I won't take a moment, because we all want to eat this wonderful meal that my beautiful wife has prepared, but I'd like to share with you my latest news. There has been a big development. Feather Products Limited is the new Israel distributor of . . ." He beamed around the table, enjoying his dramatic pause. "Of . . . Peugeot, the French car manufacturer. That means I'll sell their cars, we'll set up garages to service them and sell spare parts, and I hope to expand into gas stations to fuel them and everyone else. As you know, there are very few private cars in Israel but as the country grows, and more roads are built, every family will have one. It's going to be a huge business and we'll be in on the ground floor. And mostly, I'm happy to add, the investment comes from the bank and third-party backers. Very little of Feather Products' money will be needed in direct investment. And the loan interest is favorable. We'll pay it off with profits from car sales. So tell your friends, come buy your Peugeot 203 from me." He drained his glass with a flourish and sat, smiling at Peter.

"That's wonderful," Moshe said. "But I don't know anyone who can afford to buy a car."

"Nor do I," said Peter.

"Well, I do," Arie said. "And Peugeot will be the car of the future here. Now, Tamara, serve the food."

"I hope it isn't cold." Tamara served beef stew in an Italian porcelain tureen, with mashed potatoes that soaked up the gravy, and on matching porcelain side plates a coleslaw salad. The red wine was a nice little one, Arie said, from Cyprus.

"I saw that," Tamara said to her father who had swapped a glance with

Rachel. Moshe laughed out loud. "And I know just what you're thinking," she said.

"What am I thinking?" Moshe said with a wink to his wife.

"You're thinking, where's the rice *kushari*? Oh, what would you give to eat a good rabbit *mulukhiya*?"

Moshe hooted with laughter and slapped Rachel on the knee so hard she yelped in protest. "Indeed, my wife, when will you make *mulukhiya* again for your husband? Real Egyptian food." He turned the salad over with his fork. "What is this anyway, this *yekke* stuff, coleslaw and beef stew. *Ya Allah*, is this Munich or the Middle East?"

"Well, I have to keep my husband happy, right? That's my duty," Tamara said. She caught Peter's eye, who raised an eyebrow as if to say, Is it? "It's excellent, Tamara," Peter said. "Right, Wolfie?"

"I'm staying out of this. I'm lucky to have anything to eat." Wolfie was on leave from his base in the Southern Command, near the Egyptian border. After his compulsory thirty-month service he had signed up as an infantry officer with the regular army.

"On the kibbutz all we eat is cucumbers, tomatoes and mystery meatballs. This is all amazing. Thank you, Tamara, and you, Rachel," Mayan said.

"Well, there must be something right about your kibbutz diet; look at you," Arie said.

Tamara glanced at Peter and rolled her eyes.

As Tamara cleared the plates away and served coffee, Diana, holding her twins, apologized for not helping: "I wish I could but I have a boy on each tittie."

"Don't worry, please," Tamara said. She didn't want Mayan's help either, saying, "You're guests here, relax and enjoy." Tamara didn't want anybody else in the kitchen. She had prepared a surprise for her father. And when she presented it, her face lit up at his reaction.

"Alḥamdulillāh," Praise the Lord! he cried, clapping his hands in delight. "You are your father's daughter after all."

She gave Rachel the first helping, telling her father, "Ladies first, not like in Egypt."

"I agree," Moshe said. "But still, real men don't wait, it is the law of the desert. And of course Ibn Tulun wrote . . ." and he sank his fork into Rachel's slice of *konafa*, even as Tamara served him next.

The dessert was perfect: baked golden brown, a pie from thin strands of pastry filled with double cream and cheese, topped with halved almonds, all drenched in heated honey water.

"Delicious," Moshe said, helping himself to another piece. "Now I feel at home."

Konafa was the favorite Ramadan dessert, for one month Egypt's national dish. It took two and a half hours to prepare and bake.

It was all gone in ninety seconds.

As she contemplated her father licking his plate, Tamara's smile was one of pure satisfaction. But after the children fell asleep on the floor, sprawled across cushions, their limbs all jumbled up, it hurt her to hear him complain.

Wolfie had asked him about his new job.

"It isn't working out for me at the foreign ministry," Moshe said as the adults sat smoking in the garden. The harsh tobacco smell mingled with the sweet scent of citrus carried across the orchards and strawberry fields. "They just don't want to hear me. To them I'm an aging Egyptian professor while they're all young graduates from Europe and America or sabra ex-army officers and they think they know it all. There is a groupthink you can't argue against."

"What do you mean?" Peter asked. "What does the group think?"

"What worries me most is that they're looking for any reason for war with Egypt. Egypt is the bogeyman, the ultimate military threat, and when I disagree they all say it's because I'm from Egypt, that I can't see the wood for the trees. Apparently being an Egyptian is a disadvantage when trying to understand the Egyptians."

"But there is a real threat," Arie said. "Every day there are attacks across the borders, from Sinai, from Gaza, they're killing our people."

"Of course, but it doesn't justify going to war. Anyway, we're retaliating and killing more of them."

Peter listened with interest. Moshe always had a counterargument, and whether he was right or not, it was good to hear the other side. "Doesn't Nasser mean it when he says Israel is the natural enemy of the Arab people? A plague?" he asked.

"Yes and no," Moshe said. "Look, take all his war talk, his speeches, that's all for the Arab street, and then look at what he's really doing. The first thing Nasser did when he took over six months ago was to reduce his defense budget. He moved his troops away from our border. There are not-so-secret peace talks between Egypt and Israel, everyone knows that. Does that sound like someone planning a war? Nasser personally has nothing against the Jews, he grew up next to a synagogue, Jews owned the house he lived in, and they were friends. If anyone is rejecting the idea of peace it's Israel, because we don't want our hands tied by agreements—we want to manufacture excuses to take more land."

"And we need it," Arie put in, getting heated. "We need more land, we're too small to survive more wars."

"True," Moshe said. "But why fight more wars? Isn't it a better solution to give up on more land and just make peace with what we have? Anyway, the Egyptian military is a joke."

They all looked at Wolfie. He should know, he was a paratroop lieutenant near the Egyptian border. He smiled. "You talk. I'll smoke. My lips are sealed."

"Then how can you smoke?" Mayan said, and they laughed.

Arie said, "Still, there are twenty-three million of them and one point five million of us . . ."

Moshe interrupted him. "Take their air force. Out of thirty aircraft, only six can fly at any one time. They don't have spare parts, no maps, no functioning airfields, no ammunition. You know how many tank shells they have? Enough for one hour's combat. One hour. Peter, what do you think?"

"If Wolfie's lips are sealed, mine are sewn shut with steel wire. But look, there's some truth in everything you're all saying. From my point of view, the only thing that counts is that Israel must be ready for anything. War, if we can't avoid it. Peace would be better, but to make peace we have to be strong, and that means preparing for war. But in the meantime, who wants to make peace with us?"

"Egypt!" Moshe almost shouted. "Did you hear anything I said?"

"I did," Peter said softly. "I hope you are right but I fear you are wrong."

"Excuse me for saying this," Diana said, "but Moshe, is the real reason you're upset with the Ministry because you're not part of the Ashkenazi white boys' club?"

"That's just another way to muddy what I'm saying. We're heading for an unnecessary war."

Tamara touched her father on the knee. "Abba, why don't you leave the foreign ministry? Be a journalist. Write for a newspaper. Israel needs to hear different voices and nobody understands Egypt better than you."

Moshe squeezed his daughter's hand. "Well, as a matter of fact, I've thought about that. Maybe I will. If they'll have me."

PETER and ARIE

TEL AVIV, ISRAEL

September 1954

Sunday morning was the one day of the week when Peter and Diana walked to work together, making time to stop at Dahlia's *budke* for coffee and *bourekas*. Regulars crowded around the serving hatch, or fought over the two seats in the shade, and argued over the latest news, a welcome routine in Peter's schizophrenic life.

Today it was *Bat Galim*, a small Israeli cargo ship the Egyptians detained in the Suez Canal. "They put the crew in prison, we have to bust them out," said "the lawyer," nicknamed for his black suit. He was a restaurant waiter. Everyone spoke at the same time, their voices overlaid like a music score: "It's an international waterway, they have no right, the UN must condemn Egypt." "The UN? Huh!" "And what about yesterday, another shooting by Gaza." "Where's the army?" "Where's Ben-Gurion when you need him?"

Two weeks earlier the Old Man had moved to the Negev kibbutz of Sde Boker to leave politics, a claim nobody believed. "He'll be back, you wait and see," the lawyer said.

The new prime minister, Moshe Sharett, was considered a moderate, and as Peter and Diana continued their walk to work, Diana asked, "So, will Sharett change things at the Office?"

"We'll see. Maybe he'll put a halt to the German operation. Part of me hopes so."

Diana nodded. "It's getting too complicated. I just hope you stay at home." But "home" was about to get a lot more complicated too.

Gingie was waiting for them. "That policeman called again. His office is asking for an official response to his specific question: What was Diana working on that required that dead man's file? They said they need to know today."

Diana frowned. "Why today? Did you say anything?"

"Not yet. I'm sitting on it."

"Say it's to do with my operation," Peter said. "And it's top secret, only Isser Harel can approve. I'll talk to Harel."

"Is that true?" Gingie asked.

"Wait a minute," Diana said, pulling Peter by the arm away from Gingie. "You said Arie denied it. Strongly. You said he got angry and didn't know the man."

"Yes, that's what he said. And I don't believe a word of it." Peter said with a groan, "He was shifting around like he had ants in his pants, a sure sign of lying. This is getting us into hot water. Before I speak to Harel I need to know for certain what's going on. I'm going to see Arie now."

"What about the morning meeting?"

"Tell them something came up."

"Sela won't like it."

"What does he like? I'm going now, Arie is in the same café every Sunday morning. If I don't find him now I won't see him till tonight."

Peter did his best to shut out the cabbie; it was something about the price of chicken breasts, then about whether to raise pork in Israel. The rabbis said pigs could live in Israel only if their cloven hooves did not touch the Holy Land, so pigs would have to spend their entire lives on concrete or wooden floors. "Can you believe that?" the driver shouted. "All I have is a dirt floor."

"I have a headache," Peter said. "Do you mind?"

He got out early and walked the last few blocks of HaYarkon Street. Diana always found it curious that Peter could slit a man's throat but couldn't tell a cabdriver to shut up.

Arie was deep in conversation with two men in suits so Peter found an empty corner table and waited to catch his eye. He waved him over. Arie shook his head. Peter tapped his watch repeatedly. Now.

Arie was not happy to be called away from his table. "What is it? To you this is just my café but to me, this is where I do business."

"This is business. You lied to me, didn't you?" He switched to German. "I know you murdered Yonathan Schwartz."

Arie looked around sharply. "Are you crazy? Keep your voice down. And, no, you don't know that. How could you? I didn't."

"Don't lie to me, Arie. I told you, the police are onto Diana, she's getting mixed up in something we know nothing about."

"You just said you know I did it, now you say you know nothing about it."

"Don't play smart with me, Arie, I'm trying to help you here. The police asked Diana why she wanted his file."

"Why did she?"

No point holding back any longer. "Because Tamara told her you asked her to say you were at home the night he was murdered."

"So what? I could have asked for a dozen reasons."

"So give me one. Why did you?"

"Look Peter, I'm sorry, but it's none of your business what I get up to at night. I can tell you this: It wasn't because I killed someone. Who do you think I am?"

"I know exactly who you are, Arie. I know what you've done and I know what you can do."

"Well, I didn't kill that man."

"In that case I can tell Diana to just tell the police the truth. Your wife said you came home late, you told her, if anyone asked, to say you had never left home. She wanted to know more, so Diana did her a favor and asked for the police file for that night, to see if there was any connection to you. That's the truth. And then you'll be the detective's next call. Are you okay with that? Is there any connection to you?"

Arie pursed his lips, linked his fingers, played with his thumbs. Three seconds became ten.

Peter knew this was the moment to be gentle, responsive, encouraging. That's how he would behave if this was work. But this was his brother, whose lies were threatening Diana, and Peter was getting angry. "You're evasive, pensive, nervous as hell. You're lying." Instead of talking calmly, he was losing his temper. His voice rose. "I'm asking again. Is there a connection to you? You want to tell me, or the detective?"

Arie stared into the distance, his face puckered up; Peter knew this was the moment of truth, he had seen it dozens of times.

"Arie. Hello. It's me, Peter. Your brother." He forced himself to lower his voice, or he'd lose the moment. "I know you thought you had a good reason. I don't even need to know what it is. I just need the truth if I'm going to help you."

"Are you?" Arie swallowed hard. Drumming his fingers, he stared into Peter's eyes.

All signs of fear, Peter knew. "Going to help you? Of course I am."

Arie's shoulders slumped, he leaned forward and whispered. "Look, all right. It was an accident, I swear it was. Yes, I knew him, we argued, he ran away in the dark over the rocks. I didn't even see him, I just heard a shout, and I ran home. That's all I know. That's the God-honest truth."

"There was blood nearby."

"Was there? Was it his? Someone else's? Maybe someone else attacked him. Maybe he fell and hit his head."

"His head? Why his head? Was his head beaten?"

"How should I know? I'm just telling you. I panicked and ran away."

"Okay look, I'm not going to ask any more questions. I don't want to know. You never told me this. I'll try to make this go away."

Their eyes held, until Arie looked away.

"I know you're still lying, Arie. You haven't told me the real truth."

Arie bit his lip, his eyes moistened. "Enough of it."

Peter laid a hand on Arie's. "It's all I need for now. But, Arie, another thing." He had been looking for an opening.

"What?"

"Tamara. Stop cheating on her. She's too good for that."

"What, me? What are you talking about?"

"For God's sake, stop lying. Everyone knows. You're hurting her, everyone can see it."

"Peter, mind your own business."

"Is it my business to protect you from that detective? Then this is my business too. It's a package deal." His voice was raised, people were looking. "You have the most beautiful, lovely wife and you treat her like dirt."

"How do you know what goes on in my home? And anyway, you think I don't know about you two? Always flirting with her, those knowing looks, your hands touching, you've never forgiven me."

"You're out of your mind, none of that is true. Anyway, I haven't forgiven you for what?"

"You know for what."

"No, I don't, say it."

"For marrying her, that's what."

"Listen, I love Diana, I'm very happy. Don't slide out of this like the snake you are. I'm telling you, stop cheating on Tamara."

Peter pushed the table and stalked away.

Even though he'd be even later for work, Peter walked back to Ben Yehuda Street, fuming all the way. Bringing up Tamara was a mistake. Arie was a cornered rat, he came out with bared teeth and nails and he was cunning too, he knew just how to go for the jugular. Flirting with Tamara, indeed. He couldn't help feeling sorry for her whenever Arie was rude to her in public, that's all. And when Diana reported back about Tamara's latest fight with Arie, he felt responsible for his brother, as if it was his fault Arie was a disgrace. And now this. Murder. And he's covering up for him. That brother of his will sink them all.

No wonder he was so successful in business, he's ruthless. Peter had said what needed saying but Arie didn't want to hear it. That meant he'd never change. And it would get worse between him and Tamara. What could he do? Speak to Tamara? What good would that do? Arie was right about one thing. It wasn't his business.

Peter hesitated outside the whitewashed Office building, trying to push Arie from his mind. He had to stop using Auschwitz as an excuse for whatever evil things Arie did. And he had to stop feeling guilty that he had escaped it all, and he had to stop babying his younger brother because of it. For how long can the past excuse the present?

Inside the office Peter passed by Diana's desk. "Where's Gingie?" he asked.

"What happened?" Diana said. "Quick, she'll be back in a moment. And, by the way, the police called again, about the file."

He looked up and down the corridor, half-closed the door, and whispered, "Arie says it was an accident. I bet it wasn't, though, he's a terrible liar. Did you tell Tamara what we know?"

"No, of course not, that her husband's a murderer? That's all she needs. Anyway, we didn't know for sure."

"Well we're sure enough now. We have to bury this here. But what did you say? The police called again? Already? What's the hurry?"

"I don't know. Gingie spoke to them. And also, Harel is in the building. To do with the trial in Cairo, and what we do next. And Sela was looking for you."

"All right, thanks." He went out into the corridor and bumped into Gingie.

"At last, there you are," she said. "Harel wants to see you. And there's something else."

"What?"

"The police. The murdered man, Yonathan Schwartz? They've established a connection between him and a man. They have a waiter who saw them arguing in a café, the day Schwartz disappeared. Guess who the man was. Your brother."

Peter felt his flesh crawl. "Oh, crap."

"So they want to interview Diana again, I suppose to gather material before they call for him. It's gone right to the top."

"Harel? Oh, no." It'll take the police precisely five minutes to fill in the dots. And Harel, ten seconds. "He wants to see me?"

"Yes. But that was before the thing with the police."

"Alone? Or there's a meeting?

"Both."

Germany, then.

PETER

BONN, GERMANY

November 1954

Eight o'clock at night. Between the almost full moon, the new fluo-rescent street lamps, and the brightly lit shop windows, it may as well have been midday outside Bonn's municipal swimming pool.

"This is where you want to snatch him?" Peter said incredulously to Yehuda, who sat in the driver's seat of the rented Volkswagen Beetle. "This is what we pay you for?"

Yehuda couldn't repress a snigger. "Well, it was dark when we chose it. But that was eight weeks ago. It isn't our fault you took so long to get the green light."

"Don't get me started."

"The plan was to wait till there's no moon. But they put in special new lightbulbs last week, and we didn't know they light up the Christmas win-dows so early."

"They lose the war and look at those shop displays. The luxury. Amaz-ing. It could be Paris."

"You're kidding. Paris? I've been there. You think they won the war? They've got nothing."

"Nothing? I'd like that nothing. Tel Aviv has nothing."

"Anyway," Yehuda said, "this isn't the place. This is where we start fol-lowing Bohlendorf. He comes out at 8:00 P.M. three times a week like clockwork. Unless there's a government event. He's a very good swimmer, breaststroke and crawl, so he's probably fit and strong. He walks to the corner over there, turns left, and walks in a straight line home. A ten-minute walk. After six minutes he passes a small vegetable patch, somebody's private allotment. It's dark and isolated. I'll take him there. The only problem is we need a quick getaway. If he's five minutes late his wife will come looking, and I mean five minutes, you know what the Germans are like. She'll have her poodle with her, on a leash. Last thing at night they walk the dog."

"The good news is it's a poodle," Peter said. "So let's say she really does come looking after five minutes. Ten minutes to the pool. A few minutes there looking for him. Less than twenty minutes to get him far away before the alarm goes out."

"Yes."

They cruised past the allotment. Two trees shedding leaves, ragged bushes, rows of vegetables, piles of wooden crates, a locked toolshed, a low fence. All bathed in the cold light of the moon, diffused by the tree's thin foliage.

"When does the owner work here?"

"Weekends. Some mornings. No routine, but never in the dark. An elderly couple."

Yehuda turned the corner and Peter got out of the car to stroll back past the snatch site, while Yehuda drove slowly around the leafy neighborhood of low brick homes to pick Peter up outside the pool.

"Okay, it's perfect. You earned your money," Peter said. "Where's Bohlendorf now?"

"In his office in the chancellery. We have eyes and ears there monitoring him."

"Ours?"

"Theirs, who is one of ours."

"Good."

The next day they checked out the safe house, a rented farm alone at the end of a village lane outside Gönnersdorf, an hour south of Bonn, and went over the plan. The snatch cars would be abandoned at the edge of town and replaced by two faster Mercedes sedans. A sack would be over Bohlendorf's head the whole time. The only person who would talk to him was a Ukrainian Jew who would use the name "Bogdan." The only other language anybody would use was German. A video camera was ready to film Bohlendorf's apology and confession: apology to the Ukrainian people and confession to being an East German spy. In the woods a deep hole was ready, covered with bracken and undergrowth, with a chemical powder, made in Ukraine, stored there to help the body decompose. Passports and air tickets were prepared. They would all drive overnight to Frankfurt and fly out of the country the next morning.

The Mossad hit team was ready.

But Peter still had his doubts. At the Office in Tel Aviv he had argued against killing Bohlendorf, who was a valuable future asset. Beyond that, he had felt he was channeling Moshe. "Egypt is not the threat we think it is," he told Harel. "Nasser doesn't want war with Israel, and even if he did, he's no real military threat. And then there's our guys on trial in Cairo, making us look bad. The last thing we want is another mess in Germany, especially now when they're beginning to pay reparations. We need to keep Germany on Israel's side."

"Listen to the politician," Amnon Sela had said. "Thank you for the analysis, but we have better qualified people for that. All you need to do is your job: plan the hit, and wait for the order. Fortunately we have other people above your pay grade who make the decisions."

"It's just wrong," Peter said to Diana in bed that night. "We're playing God. Too many moving parts. Too much can go wrong. And knowing Harel, he may not even have told the prime minister."

"But you've got no choice, anyway."

That was true, and doubly so. An order was an order, but Harel had sweetened the deal. "Tell me again exactly what he said about Arie," Diana said.

"I told you. He didn't say it in so many words but remember, he was head of Shin Bet for years. He knows domestic security backward. He said, 'This police investigation, it is distracting you from your work here, it needs to be put on the back burner. I could possibly take care of that.' Those were his exact words."

"Possibly? Can he do that?"

"Little Isser? He can do anything."

"If he wants to."

"Exactly. If he wants to."

"But then you'll owe him. He used the words 'back burner'? He'll always have that over you."

"Maybe that's what he wants. That's his specialty. But what else can I do? Arie's my brother. God help me."

"What about that English policeman? He's like a terrier."

"True, but it doesn't work like that. He's just a cog in the wheel. What counts is *proteksia*, who you know. It's the head of Mossad talking to the chief of police. Old Palmach fighters over an orange juice. That kind of stuff. Probably at Dahlia's kiosk."

So Peter had dropped his objections and here he was, at 8:03 P.M. on a chilly moonless night, in the back of a Volkswagen transit van, its tuned-up engine softly throbbing, waiting to glide slowly past a dark vegetable patch and stick a canvas bag over Kurt Bohlendorf's head, which should happen in exactly three minutes.

At that moment Mrs. Bohlendorf emerged from her house with her poodle, surprising the agent watching from across the street. In eight weeks of surveillance she had never come out early. She began to walk in the direction of her husband. Ulrika, the agent's code name, her heart thumping, quickly crossed the street and overtook her. She apologized politely for startling her in the dark, and asked for directions to the train station. Which is the best bus? Anything to stall her. But the poodle was impatient and strained at the leash. Mrs. Bohlendorf apologized, saying Boo-Boo wants to meet his master. He'll meet his maker if he doesn't relax, Ulrika thought. "Or is there a bus all the way to Königswinter?" she asked. She knew her cover was blown, Mrs. Bohlendorf would tell the police about the strange woman who had stopped her and asked stupid questions just when her husband disappeared, but she had to delay her.

"Thank you," Ulrika said. "I'm a bit lost, it's a long way from home," and they both laughed while Boo-Boo urinated against a tree. "What a lovely dog," Ulrike said. "How long have you had him?"

A minute later, four hundred yards away, Bohlendorf turned onto the quiet street, walking briskly, carrying a small kit bag. Behind him a Volkswagen Beetle drove slowly, accelerating as Bohlendorf approached the allotment. The second vehicle, the Volkswagen van, idled by the allotment. Inside, Peter slid open the side door at the precise instant that a man with a mask erupted from behind a tree into Bohlendorf. His force and weight crashed into Bohlendorf's ribs so hard the German gasped for breath. He toppled against the car's chassis, his upper body fell inside the door's opening, a powerful pair of hands wrapped around his head and pulled while Yehuda lifted his feet and pushed. Grabbing the dropped kit bag, Yehuda leapt into the van while Peter forced a sack over Bohlendorf's head. Yehuda snapped hand-cuffs over Bohlendorf's wrists and slid the door shut. It was so quick, the assault so aggressive and shocking, the first sound was Bohlendorf's muted scream in a dank sack.

Within six seconds the van had pulled away from the sidewalk, fol-lowed by the Beetle, and the two cars drove slowly up the street, passing Mrs. Bohlendorf and Ulrika deep in conversation.

Yehuda said, "She made her."

Peter was looking back at the two women. "Yes. She must have come out early."

On the edge of town they swapped the Volkswagens for two Mercedes and sped away. That was the good part.

It was at the farm that the operation fell apart.

Just as the two Mercedes drove up to the farmhouse and the men were bundling the hooded victim out of the car, a boy and a screaming half-naked girl ran out from the trees toward one of the drivers, "Leopard," code-named for his deep acne scars. The girl's scream was cut short when she saw two men dragging a third man in a hood into the house. One hand flew to her mouth, the other covered her chest with her shirt. She looked from the door of the house to her shocked boyfriend, then back to the house en-trance where the door had slammed shut.

Leopard pulled her to him while the boy stared.

The girl sobbed, "Help, please, a snake bit me."

"No it didn't, dumbhead!" the boy shouted. "It just went over your foot."

Within minutes the young couple was tied up in the barn, gagged, their heads covered, trembling with fear, terrified by what they could hear of the excited conversation in German.

"They saw my face," Leopard was saying. "What do we do?"

"Who are they? What are they doing here?" Peter said, returning from the house.

"They were making out in the woods," Yehuda said. "The silly kid saw a snake and ran for it."

"*Scheisse.*" Shit. Peter thumped the barn with his fist. Now what? They had to be out of here by two in the morning to make the first plane out of Frankfurt and they still had to deal with Bohlendorf. It was nine fifteen. His mind raced. Could it be good? The kids could be witnesses that we're Ukrainian. Just leave them tied up till someone finds them? But they both saw Leopard's face. And they heard us speak German. Can't take the risk. Especially if Ulrika's been blown.

Yehuda cut in. "You know what we have to do, right?"

"What?"

"You know."

"No, I don't."

"We can't take any chances." Yehuda pointed with his chin at the barn. His body tensed. "We don't have a choice."

Peter looked at Leopard, who nodded slowly back.

"The wife will describe Ulrika to the police," Yehuda said. "It was dark but they were close. And now these two." He shook his head. "The cops will track our whole journey. No way we can leave them."

Another agent, code-named "Indian" because of his dark skin, nodded slowly too and looked away. "We're screwed," he said.

What would Harel do? Peter walked quickly away from the group, went into the barn, and looked at the boy and girl sagging on the chairs, bound, gagged, and hooded. Poor bastards, he thought. All they wanted was a quickie in the woods, and now look at them. He went back into the house where Bogdan was leaning into Bohlendorf's face, poking him with a knife. It was his job to persuade the Nazi to talk on camera. He was using the information Ulrika had given him from her surveillance: Boo-Boo would die. His wife would die, after she was raped. Read the script on camera. Or else.

Peter's mind was racing, calculating. It's already 9:20, a sleepy small village, there's probably a lovers' lane nearby in the woods. We don't have much time, maybe an hour, before the boy and girl would be missed. This place could be swarming with worried families within the hour.

What would Harel do? What would he want? Peter felt himself becoming breathless. He went outside, back into the barn, looked at the boy and girl. They were both crying.

Outside again. "Well," Yehuda said. "What do we do?" They were all looking at him, the whites of their eyes gleaming in the dim moonlight. Birds tweeted, leaves rustled in the wind.

It's no good thinking of what Harel would do; he isn't here, Peter thought. I am and I'm in charge. Decide now. Lives depend on this, and much more. If they do this and get caught, there would be arrests, kidnap and murder charges, headlines, a diplomatic disaster for Israel at the worst possible time.

Damn. Exactly what he'd warned against.

But one thing he knew for certain.

Hell would freeze over before he killed those two kids.

But if there were witnesses they couldn't kill Bohlendorf either.

A minute passed before Peter spoke, slowly. "Right, this is what we do. Get Bohlendorf back in the car. When we're ready to roll, Yehuda, take the hoods off the kids and loosen their ropes. In such a way that it'll take half an hour to free themselves. Keep them gagged so they can't yell. Got it?"

Yehuda saw this was not a time to argue. Peter was the agent-in-charge. Change of plan.

"Got it," he said.

"Leopard, get everyone into the cars, load up everything, don't leave a trace. Especially the camera gear. We only have minutes. Let's go."

A thought occurred to him. Bohlendorf would still have no idea who they were or why he'd been taken, although with his record he'd make some pretty good guesses. Either way he knows he's cooked. If he could he'd make a run for it. To safety: East Germany.

Minutes later they were all on the road, racing back to Bonn. They wound through the traffic as fast as they could without attracting attention. Near the main train station one car dropped a tightly bound, gagged, and furiously struggling Kurt Bohlendorf deep in a dark alley and sped away. The other car waited nearby while Peter found a pay phone and called his top contact in the defense ministry.

"Günther, sorry if I woke you up. Listen carefully. Surprise, surprise. Adenauer's chief of protocol, Kurt Bohlendorf, is an East German spy. You can find him by the trash cans in the middle of the alley at the corner of Meckenheimerallee and Quantiusstrasse. He fell out with his handlers. Get there now. I'll speak to you tomorrow."

What he didn't say was, he'd talk to him tomorrow from Tel Aviv.

An Office driver brought Peter and Yehuda straight from the airport to Ben Yehuda Street, where they were fielding urgent demands from the foreign ministry and Israel's embassy in Bonn to know what had just happened in their front yard. The German Chancellery was bombarding the Israeli ambassador with furious questions about why Germany's head of protocol was tied up like a chicken in an alley, claiming he had been kidnapped by Israelis pretending to be Ukrainians. The German Defense Ministry insinuated Bohlendorf was an East German spy but had no evidence. What the hell's going on?

"Well, you really screwed that one up," Sela said as they waited in the conference room. "Harel is on his way here. There's a diplomatic shitstorm, and just on the day Egypt announced a trial date for the Aman clowns in Cairo. Well done. Mighty Mossad. Mighty Mouse, more like it."

Peter looked at Yehuda and shook his head. Amnon Sela had been an undistinguished field operative in Paris and Rome, who had nevertheless been promoted to European section chief. "You know, Amnon," Peter said.

"You're so scared I'll take your job. Why is that? Why don't you just relax, for once? When did you start being so afraid? It's boring. You're supposed to support the men in the field, not work against us."

"You're full of it. I'm not working against you, you're . . ."

"Enough," Harel said, tight-faced, closing the door behind him. "Nesher, what happened?"

Yehuda broke in. "Peter made the right decision."

Peter looked at him with a raised eyebrow. Sela would not forgive that. "Sir . . ." Peter began, and gave a blow-by-blow account of the plan and what went wrong. Ten minutes later he concluded, saying, "I had to decide on the spot. I had to avoid a real disaster, and I think I managed to salvage something. And please let me emphasize that I took the decision, it is my responsibility, and mine only."

Yehuda looked the Mossad chief in the eyes and said, "Sir, he's one hundred percent right in what he decided."

"Shut up. I'll decide that," Harel said. "Sela, what do you think?"

"I wasn't there, sir. I can't really comment on what Nesher says here, we need to investigate and find out what happened."

"With all respect, I just told you," Peter said, his lips thin.

"Well," Sela said, "there are a couple of questions I could raise."

"Raise them," Harel said.

"Why wasn't there a backup safe house in case the first was compromised? Why weren't guards on the perimeter to stop those kids approaching? Should the kids have been dealt with differently? Bohlendorf's wife? Why wasn't it planned better so that she would not leave the house and blow Ulrika? The operation was full of holes from the start."

Yehuda glared at him. Peter's face was inscrutable. If only Amnon Sela was as skillful at managing the European operation as he was in office politics.

In the pause, Harel was looking from Peter to Sela, tapping his fingers on the table, nodding to himself, his face softening. "Just before I came in I had a call from General Reinhard Gehlen, who runs the West German security apparatus," Harel said. "He told me to ignore the diplomats, they don't know anything yet. He was full of praise and expressed deep thanks for catching Bohlendorf. He's the most highly placed East German spy they have ever discovered, and he has already confessed. He had access to almost everything that passed through the chancellor's office. Gehlen is an old Nazi, a pragmatic man, his own organization is full of ex-SS and Gestapo, all he cares about is defeating the communists. And I care deeply about cooperation with West Germany. Outing Bohlendorf is quite a feather in Mossad's cap. So let's keep it that way."

Now Sela was inscrutable. Peter and Yehuda didn't react.

"Sela. The best plans fall apart and our job is to pick up the pieces. How you do that defines who you are," Harel continued. "Peter. Yehuda. That's what you did. You salvaged something big, very big, from a mess. We all know what it's like. Shit happens in the field. But let's keep it there. Sela, you'll handle the debriefings. Peter, I'll be waiting for your written report. Now I'm going to tell the Old Man the Germans owe us a big one. Just when we need their help in Egypt. The timing is perfect."

TAMARA and ARIE

NEGEV, ISRAEL

January 1956

———————

It was Arie's nod to the fellowship of man: he hitchhiked home from the desert. He would have taken a bus, but it didn't come. And he didn't have the heart to summon Yaacov; his tank-mates would have crucified him if he'd left the base in a chauffeur-driven sedan.

They had just spent twenty-one days of reserve duty oiling, cleaning, and preparing their M-50 Sherman, the American army warhorse that Israel had picked up cheap after World War Two. They took apart and reassembled its main gun, greasing every part, and tested the secondary gun. They raced across sand dunes at close to thirty miles per hour, backed across ditches, maneuvered at night. Their thinly armored tank was built for speed and mobility, but Arie's 27th Reserve Armored Brigade trained as a strike force that would fight head-to-head with the enemy. It was their second call-up in three months. Somebody somewhere was expecting something.

Dudu, the Iraqi driver, a police sergeant in real life, whined that they would be outgunned and out-armored. "One rocket and we're all dead. It'll cut through us like a knife through butter. This sardine can will split open like a can of beans."

Itamar, the gunner from Jerusalem, didn't help. "We'll fry. It'll be a barbeque in here. That's why the Brits call these things the 'Ronson.' Cos it'll burn like a lighter."

Lucky the Egyptians didn't have any battlefield rockets and, even if they did, they'd shoot each other. For three weeks they laughed at the same old jokes. The food was awful and there wasn't enough of it; the water was warm and tasted of oil. The sun baked them and the night froze them, they could barely sleep inside the tank, their beards itched, they itched more from sunburn, mosquitoes, and sandflies, they despised their commanders, they fought about everything and agreed on only one thing: reserve duty was better than being at home with the kids.

Carmel and Daniel, now five years old, were asleep when Arie returned home in a taxi, which he'd caught in Tel Aviv after his last ride. Seeing his passenger disheveled and crumpled in army fatigues, his hair still caked in sand, the Polish cabdriver had immediately launched into his own plan for the next war, a three-pronged paratrooper push through the Negev into Sinai, with a surprise left hook by armored divisions against Jordan in the east that would continue all the way, God willing, to Iraq, but Arie soon shut him up. "We don't need more generals. Just drive, please."

"What we need," Arie called to Tamara from the shower, watching weeks of desert dust swirl away, "is a highway from Be'er Sheva to Tel Aviv. It would cut the drive time by hours. I should put together a consortium and build it."

"What I want," Tamara came into the bathroom and said, "is a talk." She sat on the toilet, holding a beach towel.

"I don't want a walk, I want to sleep."

"I didn't say walk. I said talk."

"I don't want to talk either. I want to you-know-what and sleep."

"That's what I want to talk about. I have something to tell you."

Arie emerged from the shower, flicking water from his body with his hands. He stood close to Tamara, smiling and stroking her head, holding her hair to the side, pulling her toward him. She stood and handed him the towel. "I'll make tea," she said.

"I'd rather have coffee."

"But then you won't be able to sleep."

"Who wants to sleep?"

Tamara put the kettle on and went to the utility room, where she emptied Arie's kit bag into the laundry basket. A mini sandstorm drifted in with socks, underpants, T-shirts, and other stuff. She rescued a pack of cigarettes and a box of matches, placed them on the shelf, and put his Sten gun up with the hats so that the children could not reach it.

When the kettle whistled she turned the gas off, tiptoed into the twins' room to make sure they were still sleeping, and returned to the kitchen, where she made tea with fresh mint and honey. As she carried it into the living room on a tray with biscuits, she grimaced: the perfect little housewife, fulfilling all her duties.

Arie lounged across the sofa, in shorts and a singlet. His body was divided like a graph, shaded in red by the sun. As she set the tray down he pulled her toward him on the sofa. "Not here," Tamara said, "the children may come in. Eat your biscuit."

"They're fast asleep," Arie said, "and you're my biscuit. With a soft center." He cupped her buttocks, kissing her on the mouth, just as Tamara realized what she had barely noticed written on the cigarette pack: a name and an address. Afterward, as Arie stumbled to bed, Tamara went back to the laundry room and found the pack. She read a name: Rosie, and an address, 81D, Ahad Ha'am, and a time: Tuesday, 3:00 P.M.

That's tomorrow.

Arie was fast asleep, snoring lightly, but no rest came to Tamara. She lay on her back, staring at the whirling ceiling fan, her heart thumping almost as fast. She was angry with Arie, but furious at herself. Why did she put up with this?

Rosie. Tomorrow. Three o'clock.

She clenched her fists. She bit her lip. She felt like seizing Arie by the head and shaking him till it came off. She drummed her feet in frustration but it didn't wake him. She turned and edged as far away as she could, staring at the wall.

Diana didn't understand. Diana came from England, she worked at Mossad, she was trained in deceit. "Just leave him," Diana kept saying, as if there was no question. "He's a cheat, in business and love, he's rude to you, he doesn't appreciate how lucky he is, leave the bugger."

But how could she? She came from Egypt, where to speak against her husband was heresy, to leave him inconceivable. Arie had saved her whole family, rescued them from the camp and set them all up in homes and jobs. He had given them something, a lot, when they'd had nothing.

She could imagine Diana's voice, persistent and strong, "So what? You don't owe him anything. He doesn't love you." But he does, in his own way. "No, he doesn't, all he cares about is money, other women, success, ha ha." But he suffered so much. He's never really recovered. Nobody can imagine what he survived. People froze to death around him. Beaten to death. My God, gassed to death. "Stop making excuses for him. It will only get worse. You deserve better." But the children. He's a wonderful father. I could never take them from him. "Remember what I'm saying, it will only get worse." Worse. Worse. The word echoed in her head, a drumbeat that became a chorus: Worse. Worse. Worse. She wanted to scream. She tossed and turned until finally, she must have drifted away.

And in the morning, it was worse. She could hardly look at Arie. He had been away three weeks and already all he could think of was some skirt. He said he would have a long day catching up on business. I bet he would. He'd said, don't expect me home for dinner. So what else was new?

Tamara hadn't even had a chance to tell him her own news. Now that the twins were five years old, almost six, she was going to think of herself for a change. Her parents always wanted her to go to university. In Cairo it hadn't really been an option. Here in Israel, everything was possible.

She had always wanted to be a lawyer and her news was that she had been accepted into the Tel Aviv School of Law and Economics, starting in September.

But how could she dare be a lawyer, it occurred to her, to help people stand up for themselves, if she couldn't even stand up to her own husband?

At one o'clock, with the twins safely in the hands of Lupita, the babysitter, Tamara took the bus to Tel Aviv, with no clear idea why. She got off at the corner of Allenby and Balfour. As she waited for the traffic to thin, she looked down Allenby and felt a tinge of sadness. So close to Polishuk, where Arie had bought his first present for her, a pair of leather boots. He had been so sweet. She still had them, but the leather gloves and the woolen hat, where were they? Where were those days? What had happened? What had she done wrong?

She dimly remembered that her mother had the hat.

She can keep it. And the gloves too. And the boots. Tamara crossed the road and walked up Balfour all the way to Ahad Ha'am, where she turned right toward number 81. The closer she came, the more her heart raced and her thoughts jumbled. Why was she here? What could she do? What odious compulsion drew her? As each man passed she lowered her hat.

She walked right past the building and by now she was breathless and ashamed. I'm going to keep walking and go to Rothschild Boulevard for a coffee at the kiosk. And a cake. Poppyseed.

Instead she crossed the road and walked back by the house, sticking as much as possible to the shade of the trees. This is madness, she thought. He's driving me crazy. She looked at her watch: 2:20. She glanced up quickly, as if searching for the guilty apartment, and hurried by. It was a whitewashed building on columns, with bushes and neat flowers on either side of the path, and an entrance door with glass panes. Each apartment had its own balcony; some had been closed in, others had plants and chairs. There were four stories, apartment 4D must be on the top. Maybe it has a roof terrace. She hoped the plants blew away in the wind.

Rosie. Single or married? Is she cheating too? What horrible people.

Now she noticed that the steps to the basement of the corner house thirty yards away led to a small café below street level. There were a couple of chairs and tables outside, and more inside. There was a counter with a coffee machine, shelves of books for sale, and at head height, narrow windows that looked onto the street. From the corner seat she could observe the entrance to number 81.

She ordered coffee and carrot cake. Her mind was ablaze. Part of her felt excited. I'm a spy, she thought. What a perfect vantage point. Peter would be proud. At the thought of Peter, her whole being relaxed, for a moment. Then she was flooded with sadness. Why wasn't she enough for Arie? What mistake had she made, what was wrong with her? She felt heat in the corner of her eye, a tear began to form and tickled her, she brushed it roughly away with the back of her fingers. There is nothing wrong with me, nothing at all. There is a lot wrong with Arie. She felt strong, determined, confident as she had not felt for a long time, she would not let Arie dig away the ground beneath her. I am a powerful, beautiful woman, she told herself. But if so, then why am I skulking in a basement, spying on my husband?

"Would you like another cake?" the waitress asked. Tamara looked up with shining eyes.

"Are you all right?"

Tamara swallowed and nodded. "No more cake, thank you, but may I have a glass of water?"

When the waitress sat the glass on her table, Tamara said, "Thank you. Tell me, I was wondering, do the local people come here?" Silly question, of course they do. She wanted to ask, Does Rosie come here, but didn't want to give anything away. Then she thought, what on earth do I have to lose?

"Does Rosie come here?" she asked. Mistake. Now she'll tell a detective: Yes, she asked about the dead woman.

"Rosie? I don't know, I don't know a Rosie. I'd remember that name. It sounds English. Or American."

So she thinks she's too good for the little café.

The closer it came to three o'clock, the lower Tamara slumped in her chair, her hat over her brow. She stared through the window at the entrance to the building, and as people came and went at neighboring tables she didn't glance at them, afraid that the slightest lapse of attention would make her miss him.

The minutes ticked by. Where was he? She knew she must look strange, in her frozen posture. Focusing through the narrow window frame was hurting her eyes. At ten past three she went to the door and looked up and down the street. Men walked by but no Arie.

Was she wrong after all? Was it an old message? It had seemed fresh to her. Was this all a crazy flight of imagination? Was she so jealous that she could fabricate a lover's tryst out of a name and a time? Was she misjudging Arie? How cruel, how stupid she was. A jealous, bored housewife who can't even trust herself, let alone her husband. At three fifteen she thought she could cry with relief.

At three twenty, just as she was getting ready to pay, Yaacov pulled up. Arie stepped out of the car, glanced up and down the street, and hurried to the building's entrance. He looked back to Yaacov, tapped his wristwatch, mouthed something, rang a bell, waited for the door to open, and disappeared.

Tamara, watching in horror, felt herself sinking against the doorframe. The horror turned to disgust, for him, for herself.

"Can I get you some more water?" the waitress said, holding her by the elbow. "Are you sure you're all right?"

Tamara nodded, her eyes wide, and she fell into a chair.

For ten minutes Tamara was unaware of any thought; her mind was blank. She sipped her water and stared at the wall, her head sunken, her spirit broken.

She paid her check in silence. Supporting herself with a hand on the wall, she climbed the steps to street level. In a daze, she turned left to walk back to the bus stop on Allenby Street, but stopped to lean with one hand against a tree. She felt she might vomit. At that moment a woman walked into number 81 with two small children in tow. She called for them. One shouted, "Look, a tortoise!," and the other ran over to examine it, while their smiling mother waited patiently.

Maybe it was the woman's pleasant smile that gave her courage, for without thinking Tamara crossed the road, mumbled "Rosie on the fourth floor" as she passed her, and took the stairs slowly. On the third floor, littered with shoes and schoolbags, with plants in dry earth in cracked pots, she stopped and thought, Oh my God! What am I doing?

She felt herself tremble to the tips of her fingers. She also felt her feet moving, as if on a journey of their own. Up they took her, around a corner, and there she found herself, at the top of the stairs, confronted by apartment 4D. The name plate read Grossberg but she didn't see it. Still in a daze, with all her senses telling her to flee, she knocked on the door, faintly at first and then with fury.

A woman's voice called, "Who is it? Stop banging," and the door opened a fraction. It was on the chain. Tamara could see part of a young woman's head. She had disheveled black hair and small brown eyes, with eyebrows that needed trimming and thin lips. Her shoulders were bare, and bony. "What's the noise?" she said. "Who are you?" American.

Tamara still had no idea what she was doing or what she would say. How did she even get here?

Was she poking through the ashes of a burned-out marriage? What came to mind was a steak burned black.

The thought amused her, and the girl disappointed her. She drew herself straight. "Good afternoon, Rosie. You don't have to hide. Tell my husband," Tamara said, and in that instant she knew she was wearing a beautiful smile, "not to come home for a steak ever again."

She slowly turned, displaying her profile, sashayed to the stairs, looked coyly over her shoulder, and gave a slow wink.

Only when she reached the floor below did she hear the door bang.

She all but ran to the nearest pay phone. "Diana," she shouted, "stop saving the country and meet me at that café around the corner from your office. Oh my God, you'll never believe what just happened!"

"You . . . winked at her?" Diana choked with laughter.

Tamara was howling, everyone was looking at them. Between gasps she said, "Don't come home for a steak. I can't believe I said that. I meant to say, Don't come home late, but it came out as 'steak.' Oh, I could die," and tears of laughter streamed down her cheeks. Diana gripped Tamara's hand. "But why, 'don't come home late?' That's even more stupid. Late? Don't come home ever is more like it."

"It's weird, I feel so good now. I knocked on the door like a lunatic and left like a runway model."

"Because you faced up to her. You freed yourself."

"I went there ashamed and hurt, and I left proud and strong."

"Have you been drinking?"

"Her face," Tamara suddenly remembered and cracked up again. "When I said, 'tell my husband.' Oh, my God, it's too much!"

"What do you think she told Arie?"

"Who knows, but I'm sure I ruined their afternoon."

"I bet he couldn't get it up after that."

"He has a problem at the best of times."

"Really?"

"I wish."

"What was Rosie like?"

"Rosie? You mean, 'that slut.'"

"Yes, the witch."

"Skinny. Ugly. She went white. Her mouth opened like a blowfish."

"She's probably had lots of experience with that," Diana said, winking and leaning across to nudge Tamara with her elbow.

"That's not funny," Tamara said. Her face fell and she went silent.

"I'm sorry. I was joking."

Half a minute went by before Tamara spoke. "What do you think I should do?"

"Really? Leave him or not, you mean?"

"Yes."

"You know I've had a pretty wide experience, in different ways?"

"Yes, of course, so what do you think?"

"I really can't say; it's up to you," Diana said. "If every marriage broke up because of a bit on the side, there wouldn't be many married people left. Sorry if that sounds cruel. But to be honest, we all know about Arie, and he isn't going to change. He's just one of those men who want it all. Money. Power. I mean, look at you. You are a truly beautiful woman, and still he can't keep it in his pants."

"Would you leave Peter if he did that?"

"He never would. But what do I know? He's away for months at a time, it's difficult, dangerous, he can be lonely, scared. Who knows?"

"How well did you know him when you married? I mean, really know him?"

"As in, 'really'?"

"Yes."

"I didn't. We worked together in Europe, that's all. It was intense, but nothing ever happened. Then when I came here I hardly knew anybody and he took me out, and it all just seemed to happen. And now, I couldn't be happier." She touched Tamara's fingers.

Tamara gave a wistful smile, a smile of understanding and, yet, of regret. Could she ever tell Diana about that one moment with Peter? A moment of craziness, and yet of honesty and love, when all her defenses were down, a true, willing surrender. But, so long ago.

Diana went on, "We hardly knew each other at all. He was in a hurry." She hesitated, unsure whether to enter dangerous territory, one place they had never been. She went there. It was time. "You know why?"

Tamara nodded. "I think so."

"It was because of you."

"I know what you're going to say. Please don't say it."

They both knew Peter had loved Tamara, and couldn't have her. But he loved Diana now, and that was what mattered. She looked at Tamara, and said it anyway. "Peter lost you and he didn't want to lose me too."

Moments passed before Tamara said, "He lost me? Did he ever have me? He knew me for two hours."

"Those famous 'two hours.' It was enough for him."

"I know," Tamara said softly.

"I always wondered . . ." Diana paused, and at last made herself ask, "What about you? Was two hours enough for you too?"

Tamara looked down, and now it was she who took Diana's hand. She played with her fingers, touched her wedding ring. "You know, you're so lucky, being with Peter. He's so loving, so kind, so honest . . ."

"His business, Tamara, is to lie."

"You know what I mean. That isn't who he is at home."

"Who knows? Really? Who knows truly about anybody? Their thoughts, their dreams, all we know is what they tell us, and what we see. Who knows what we miss? Sometimes I see the two of you together, and I think, I wonder what Peter is thinking? I wonder if he would rather be with Tamara? Is that really over? I see the way he looks at you, and by the way, the way you look at him. I always remember when he told me about you. We were in a little restaurant in Germany somewhere and he talked about you with such love, and then we laughed so much when he told me that he had only met you once. I was jealous even then. I wished someone would love me in that way. So, Peter? Honest? Of course he is. And yet, there's always something there. In his eye; in my mind; something holding us back. It may all be just my imagination. Or, Tamara, it may be you. And you didn't answer my question. Was two hours enough for you?"

"Oh, Diana, you know there's nothing going on between Peter and me."

"Yes, of course I know. I'm just saying, maybe there should have been. Or could be again." Her eyes locked on Tamara's.

Tamara withdrew her hand. "No. Never. Impossible."

"Sad. But true?" Diana said, with all the burden of her secret world. Working at Mossad destroyed her ability to believe. Faith played no role. Either you knew something for certain, or everything was possible. All options were on the table. Until there was no table. Or no options.

"It's true, Diana. I could never cheat on Arie. With all his faults, he's my husband. There's an Arab proverb: Homes are secret places. He tells me things he would never tell anybody else, that happened to him, but I don't think he's ever told me a complete story. He begins, and then stops. Things that the Nazis did to him. Things that nobody can imagine. But the worst thing for him is what he was forced to do to other people. His conscience is killing him, Diana, that's something you can't know. There's another proverb: He who laughs loudest, hurts most, or if there isn't there should be. The way Arie lives his life, he's a collector. Of businesses, of women, of people, of things, it's all because in the back of his mind he is so angry, with everybody and with himself, so hurt. He knows he could lose everything again. I understand that. We lost everything too, but at least my family wasn't killed. He lost it all. Good, simple things, like his family, giving, loving, all torn from him. Burned out of him. And he was so young. So I hate some of the things he does, I truly hate them and can't live with them, but I can't hate him because I understand him, I know why he is like that. It isn't his fault."

"You don't hate him, but you can hate your life with him."

"Am I crazy? I don't hate my life. I love my children, I love my home, and when Arie is nice, well . . ." She trailed off with a sigh.

They sat back in their chairs, gazed around the café. At last Diana broke the heavy silence. "So what will you do, then?" she asked.

Tamara raised her eyebrows, shrugged her shoulders. "What can I do? He won't change."

"But can you? Is this how you really want to live? I mean, really?"

Tamara shook her head, her eyes darkened, she brushed away a tear. She couldn't say what surged through her mind, the truth she tried to bury. What she really wanted was something she could never have: Peter.

MOSHE

TEL AVIV, ISRAEL

April 1956

———

B arely eight steps were possible in Moshe's living room. He covered them dozens of times before Rachel called out, "For goodness sake, stop pacing. Write the story, already! Do you want some more tea?"

"Quiet. I'm thinking."

Paul Goldman, his relentless editor, was on Moshe's back for the week's column but all Moshe could think of was Tamara and Arie. At first they had all been overcome by Arie's energy and competence, and overlooked his unexplained absences and short temper. But the unhappier Tamara became, the more it hurt Rachel, and Moshe too.

What could they do, though? Talk to Arie? He wouldn't listen. In this strange new country where everyone was reinventing themselves, all the traditions and niceties of relationships in Egypt were lost. Here you didn't gain respect with age but lost it. At the head of the table the virtues of wisdom and knowledge were replaced by money and power, the gentle hand and soft tongue replaced by sharp elbows and a big mouth.

How else could it be, though, in a nervous, scared nation threatened by annihilation at any moment?

Moshe forced himself back to his notes, still pacing. He hadn't found his glasses so he was squinting and the bobbing paper made it harder to read. He was trying to forge a connection between a report in the South

American media and the reality of relations between Israel and its neighbors. The South American report, which had been picked up by the world press, seemed a fantasy to him, manufactured to nurture mistrust and fear. But who planted it, and why? To take Israel and its neighbors to war?

"I've found them," Rachel said, handing Moshe his glasses. "They were in the shopping bag. How did they get there?"

The discovery of his glasses inspired Moshe finally to stop mulling and sit down at the table, where the magic finally happened. Within three cups of tea he had finished his column. "Rachel, listen, it's really good, even if I say so myself."

He cleared his throat and began to read.

"'Readers of this column will know my distrust of all things official. Call me a skeptic . . .'"

"No," said Rachel, "never."

"'. . . yet I distrust all things unofficial too, beginning with what purports to be the Arab war plan for the defeat, occupation, and dissolution of the State of Israel.'"

"What?" Rachel interrupted. "Really?"

"You think I made it up? Wait, let me finish."

"'The current issue of *Vision*, distributed in Latin America, claims Western intelligence agents laid their hands on a top-secret master plan circulating at the highest levels of the Syrian and Egyptian armies.

"'According to this so-called war plan, Israel's end will come with a joint Egyptian-Syrian-Jordanian attack, in which Israel's airfields will be destroyed from the air, allowing Arab ground troops to invade and destroy Israeli towns, starting with Tel Aviv. The harbors in Jaffa and Haifa will be spared, to allow Arab navies to use the port installations after their 'victory. . .'"

"'Victory'? Huh, that sounds like nonsense to me, the Arabs would never . . ."

"Please stop interrupting, will you? Wait for a moment."

"'There will be no air attacks on the holy city of Jerusalem, which instead will be occupied by Jordan's Arab legion. The Arab victors will then declare martial law, Jewish homes will be given to returning Arab refugees, and the Jews housed in concentration camps . . .'"

"What?!"

"'Native-born Israelis will be allowed to remain, and everyone else will be shipped back to where they came from, minus their possessions . . .'"

"Of course. So what's new. What didn't we lose in Cairo?"

"For God's sake, Rachel, you're not helping. Wait till I finish. 'Finally,'" Moshe read on from his column, "'the State of Israel will be incorporated into a new Arab state called Palestine. Does this sound familiar? During the world wars the British, Americans, and Germans all routinely planted fantastic stories in Latin America. They wanted foreign correspondents to pick up the stories, that gave the plants greater credibility when they ended up in *The New York Times*, *Le Monde*, and *The Daily Telegraph*.

"'It seems the dirty-tricks department is still in full swing, but whose? After all, who benefits from this scaremongering?

"'The answer is tiny besieged Israel that wants major powers to sell us weapons to fight off the imagined threat from Egypt and Syria. And listen to Prime Minister Ben-Gurion: 'The only thing that might deter the Egyptian dictator and his allies from war is to supply Israel with arms sufficient for its defense in the air, on the sea, and on land.'

"'The only people who fall for such juvenile manipulation are the members of the reading public, who can be panicked.

"'It is clear that in recent months there has been a terrible increase in fedayeen raids against Israel and retaliation by Israeli fighters. But, people, I have news for you. Israel will not be destroyed. Nor will Egypt. We are destined to live alongside each other forever so we should stop fighting each other.

"'Let me quote the French foreign minister, Christian Pineau, who said last week, 'At the moment, there is conflict between Israel and the Arab countries which bears on a number of precise problems. But the essential one, in my opinion, is the mutual fear on each side that they'll be attacked.'

"'It is true. What will lead somebody to attack first is purely the fear that if they don't, the other side will.

'We hear the drumbeat of war, but it is beaten by monkeys. It is time to set aside the sticks and listen to the sounds of silence.'"

Moshe set his sheet of paper on the desk and sat back with a sigh. "There; done. What do you think?"

"Really?"

"Of course not. Only if you like it."

"Would you like some more tea? I'll make some." Rachel went into the kitchen.

After a minute, Moshe followed her. "That bad, is it?"

"It's just, that, well, you're calling our leaders monkeys."

"So?"

"Well, whose side are you on? You make it sound as if Israel wants war, which nobody does, nobody at all. Monkeys indeed." She set the cups on the table with a much louder bang than she'd intended. "If ours are monkeys, what are theirs?"

"Apes, of course. Look, I keep saying it, and unfortunately it's even more true today than it was three months ago. The leaders of Egypt and Israel are talking themselves into war."

"Still, don't call them monkeys and apes. It's silly. They're just frightened people."

Moshe smiled and went back to his desk. Rachel was always right. Sometimes he wrote things just to make himself feel better, knowing she'd object.

He made a few changes, until the last paragraph read, "We hear the drumbeat of war, but we need the sounds of silence."

That's better, he thought. Good old Rachel. Less strident, and just as true.

DIANA

———

"Y ou want a second round?" Diana teased Peter, who was gasping for breath. She climbed over him, ruffling his hair, and padded to the bathroom. "I'll be right back."

"Take your time," Peter mumbled, "please. And don't say 'second round,'" and then, louder, "You know what that means?"

"Yes, I do. I was joking. But anyway . . ." Back on the bed and kneeling above him, cool and damp from the cold shower, she drew on his back with her nipples and whisked him with her long hair. Her tongue flicked along his side, tickling and teasing. "Do you . . . ?" She stroked his belly and her fingers fluttered beneath him to the valley of his groin.

"No. No . . . please . . ." He shivered.

"With me there's no such word as no. 'Please' works, though." Diana turned him and kissed his lips, pulled on them with hers, as her fingers closed gently around him.

"Please, no. Let me sleep. Second round tomorrow. Next week. Please . . . leave me . . . alone," and Peter was fast asleep.

The next day Diana, trying to focus on the intelligence report, chuckled when she came across the phrase "second round." It meant the anticipated war with Egypt, the second attempt by the Arab world to destroy Israel, but she couldn't help thinking of Peter and his sweet, relaxed face. He slept like a baby, sometimes dribbled like one too, she could do anything to his body and he would never know. He would be leaving on another job in a few days; she wanted to enjoy every moment with him while she could. What else could she do to him? Her mind floated with fantasies until she sighed and went back to the "second round" projections on her desk.

Mossad analysts warned that Egypt could attack Israel in August, fewer than two months away. As she tried to read, two dinner-table voices competed in her head: Moshe cursing the foolishness of it all, and Arie shouting that Israel had to attack Egypt before Egypt attacked Israel. Peter didn't contribute much to dinner-table politics, and nor did his old friend Wolfie, the newly promoted paratroop captain. They were doers, not talkers. All Wolfie said was that if there was going to be a fight, the Jewish state could not afford to lose. The Arabs could lose dozens of times, Israel, only once.

She couldn't focus this morning, and she needed to because there was a meeting in the afternoon when section chiefs would present progress on a plan of deception the Office was cooking. If Israel attacked Egypt, it had to be a surprise. But how to achieve surprise with the media speculating every day when war would erupt, Israeli politicians competing with dire warnings and the Egyptians with bloodier threats?

She knew that's what Peter's trip was about, but it was all he was allowed to tell her, which, instead of calming her, frightened her more. His unit had become the Office's tip of the spear.

When Peter played with the twins, washed them, put them to bed, it was on him that her looks lingered now. His bent head, his perpetual smile, his lips kissing first one warm forehead, and then the other. Remember this, she told herself. Their sweet little hands in his rough mitt. Print this instant in your mind, you love this dear man, nothing will ever happen to him. Yet at the same time she told herself: Stop it! Don't torture yourself. Stop tempting the devil.

She loved to see Peter frying eggs in the kitchen, feeding the twins, encouraging them with one spoon and then another, until he beamed when the plate was empty, accomplishment written across his face. He would catch her smiling at him, and he smiled back as their eyes held, and she would blow him a kiss.

Stay safe, my love.

PETER

BONN, GERMANY, AND PARIS, FRANCE
October 1956

For six years SS-Sturmbannführer Hans-Dieter Braun, alias Doktor Lothar Genscher, code name Daffodil because he grew them, had proven a reliable conduit for false information passed on to German colleagues in Egypt.

The money was good, five hundred American dollars a month, paid into a numbered bank account the Americans had set up for him in Switzerland. All he had to do was pass messages to his old Nazi friends working in Cairo, and sometimes receive them too, and pass them to Willi Stinglwagner, who had proven to be a man of his word, even if he was an American pretending to be German. Nothing had compromised his position in the German Ministry for Nuclear Energy, where Daffodil was now chief scientific adviser to the deputy director-general, but he knew his position there gave credibility to the information he transmitted and received.

All in all he was satisfied with the way things had turned out, and for that he needed to thank that sexy masseuse Veronique who had set him up in Brussels. Whatever happened to her? Who was she, really? Thanks to her trap he had sold his business in Brussels for a good sum, was reunited with his real family in Germany, and in his new job was responsible for some of the most cutting-edge technology in the country, and probably Europe.

Not only that, he thought, swirling the wine around in the glass, sniffing and sipping, but this Alsace Riesling is impeccable: dry, floral, spicy. But there is something . . . what is that, he wondered, residual sugar? Or barrel? He smacked his lips, sniffed the wine. There shouldn't be anything but the acidity . . .

"For Gawd's sake, it's just white wine," Peter said over his shoulder, drawing up a chair. "Swallow it."

Genscher, now back to his real name, "Braun," grimaced. "It's a rather complex wine, Willi. You Americans. What will you have? American champagne?"

"*Exactement*," Peter said, and to the waiter, "Coca-Cola, please."

The meet could not have appeared more casual, yet four agents from the Office had Peter's back. Two sat separately at the bar, another watched the front entry from across the street, and one more covered the back entrance. The latter two had tailed Braun since he'd left his office, to make sure he wasn't being followed. Routine but important precautions, for a public meeting between handler and agent broke every tradecraft rule. But in this case Peter judged trust to be critical, which was why he had chosen such an out-of-the-way spot on the outskirts of Bonn. The more casual the transfer of information, he hoped, the less critical it would appear to Daffodil, and therefore the fewer questions he'd have. This had to be handled with care. Daffodil had to see himself as a partner, not a tool.

"The Middle East is at a dangerous crossroads, which could allow the communists to drive a wedge between the Arabs and the West," Peter began, after their pleasantries. He was pressing on a nerve. The one thing that most united the former Nazi Germany and America was fear of Russia. "Since Nasser nationalized the Suez Canal he's convinced one way or another the Tommies and the Frogs are going to try to get their canal back."

How tiresome, Braun thought, these dated wartime terms. Juvenile. "That's what the Yanks think, is it?"

"That's what we know. And Nasser's canary in the coal mine is little Israel. Every time they fart, Nasser thinks Israel's going to attack and the others will join in."

"Do canaries fart?"

"Ah, funny guy. Good mood? What happened, promotion at work?"

"Maybe."

"Keep climbing the greasy pole, my friend." Peter filed the hint away; where does a chief scientific officer go from there? Braun was deep in his pocket, thanks to money and pussy, which he had well documented, in case he ever needed it. The Nazi was already a star member of Peter's network, promotion would give him even greater access, and it wasn't only Germany's secrets the Office wanted. Braun was Germany's chief liaison with the French Ministry of Science, and that's where the jackpot lay—France's nuclear development. Quite apart from his value tracking Egypt's military progress, thanks to the Nazi web.

That's what Peter cared about today, though. All over Europe and the Middle East, Israeli agents were constructing a house of cards, a web of deception. "What are you drinking today, then?"

Braun had emptied his glass.

"Schloss Vollrads. Highly recommended, but not one of their better years or wines. In fact, overall their quality seems to be in decline. A pity, the label is eight hundred years old."

"Waiter," Peter called. "A Coca-Cola for my friend."

Braun's jaw dropped. Peter roared with laughter and slapped him on the elbow. "Just kidding, Hans-Dieter." He called after the waiter. "Change of order, please. Make that a Pepsi. Joking. Another one of these," he said, tapping the wineglass.

"Ach, you're in a good mood today too."

"Why not? Wall Street's on the rise. But back to business. Listen, put this into the system, as wide a distribution as possible. America does not want a stupid war to break out over the canal. It's true Israel is moving troops in the Negev desert, but what we want the Egyptians to understand, we need them to know, is that none of this is directed against Egypt. It's all against Jordan. There have been so many cross-border raids in the northern Negev by both sides that Israel wants to end it once and for all. We don't want fighting there either, by the way, but that's another issue. The main thing is that Egypt understands it is not being threatened by Israel. As for

Jordan, we'll take care of that, but it's not your concern. Unless you have people next to the king. Do you?"

"No."

"Well, as I said, that's our problem. You just make sure your Nazis, excuse me, German military and scientific advisers, get that, and they pass it on to Egypt's military and government. Got it?"

"Of course, no problem. Any papers, documents, proof?"

"Tomorrow morning you'll get a paper from our business attaché about the Frankfurt Autumn Fair. Go straight to pages forty-eight to fifty-three. On the reverse sides will be five pages of invisible ink. Expose them, read them, eat them. Pass on the information, and give me the names of your people and we'll make sure they get hard copies in Cairo or wherever they are. Okay?"

"Yes. What's in it?"

"Troop movements, armored corps unit numbers, mobile supply dumps. The whole McCoy. Destination: Jordan."

"But, between you and me, why not Egypt?" Braun asked. "Everything I hear from my friends is how weak their army is, beneath the bluster. The rocket program is so far behind schedule it isn't relevant, they've just about given up trying to make a working battlefield rocket. And all those weapons they got from Czechoslovakia, they don't know how to use anything larger than a Kalashnikov. Surely this is the time for Israel to move against Egypt, not Jordan?"

"You're asking me? Above my pay grade, buddy. My guess? They attack Egypt, Russia steps in to save Nasser and Jack Robinson, the Russians have their toehold in the Middle East. Thanks, Israel. Win the battle and lose the war. No, thanks."

"So Russia steps in to save Hussein instead. Same result."

"No, they won't. What for? Who cares about Jordan? Poor, small, not even a real country. Egypt is the prize. The biggest Arab country, leader of the Arab world, in their dreams at least. No, we gotta keep Russia out of Egypt. No way Israel attacks Egypt and opens the door to Russia. We won't let that happen, and anyway, Israel's focused on Jordan to stop the terrorism. That's what this is all about. With those troop movements Israel wants to attack Jordan, not Egypt, that's what Nasser needs to know. He needs to dial back his own troop buildup, not provoke Israel, and stay out of the firing line. We're telling him directly but the confirmation info also has to bubble up from the bottom."

"The bottom?"

"Yes. That's you, baby."

Chin on his chest, arms folded, legs stretched out between the man and woman opposite, Peter dozed as the overnight train from Frankfurt to Paris rolled through the French countryside. His neck was stiff, the carriage was too hot, and the window was stuck shut. His stomach growled. He had chosen the carriage at random, and regretted it as soon as the train left the station when the woman unwrapped her sausage and cucumber sandwich. Her tearing of the bread and knackwurst released a mouthwatering aroma of veal and garlic. She gave her husband his half and together they chewed, sighing with satisfaction. Could he ask for a bite? They even had a flask of steaming coffee, which he could have killed for. But it was the cheese and tomato sandwich that almost did him in. And then, the coup de grâce. He couldn't believe it; who brings dessert on a train ride? Vanilla flan, his favorite. His stomach must be louder than the clattering wheels. He couldn't wait to tell Diana the story, he'd have her in stitches. If only he had remembered to bring something to eat. But it had all been so quick, he had barely made the train.

In Paris an Office driver took Peter straight from the Gare du Nord to the suburb of Sèvres, insisting all the way that they didn't have time to stop for a baguette. By the time guards slid open the wrought-iron gate of the villa in rue Emanuel Girot, Peter had a raging headache and knew that at this time in the telling of his story, Diana would be torn between helpless laughter and the need to baby him.

"And then the prime minister walked into the room," he would tell her, for that is what happened. But that is where the story would end. About what was said, his lips were sealed. However much she tickled him.

He had never been in the same room as them all at the same time: Prime Minister David Ben-Gurion with his crown of puffy white hair, the balding army Chief of Staff Moshe Dayan with his black eye patch and the elegant, gray young man introduced as Defense Ministry Director-General Shimon Peres. And what a room it was. Dark green leather chairs around a gleaming mahogany table. Gilt mirrors and paintings in gilt wooden frames above fruitwood inlaid side tables. Carved wooden chests with silver and bronze candelabra. Floor-to-ceiling windows looking onto a manicured lawn lined by flower beds and a pond with water lilies.

Compare this, he thought, to the dumps where Israel receives foreign dignitaries. Instead of the vast crystal chandelier they had a noisy useless fan. Orange juice, plastic chairs, and instead of landscapes by old masters, a curling photo of Ben-Gurion pinned to the wall.

They were waiting for the British and French participants. He didn't know what the meeting was about, just that it was so secret that the Paris station didn't know about it. He was to hand-carry back to Israel a document too important for the diplomatic pouch. He didn't know the French defense and foreign ministers, but did recognize the pudgy face and round spectacles of Selwyn Lloyd, the British foreign secretary.

Peter, happy to be ejected from the meeting and by now giddy with hunger, found the kitchen to get some food, which was lined up in a delicious array of fruit, sandwiches, and canapés for the guests. But a tall, balding French official pushed him out before he could take a bite: *"Pas maintenant."* Not now. In the corner, two French men in dark suits stood over a woman whose fingers flew over a typewriter, which clattered like a machine gun.

The protocol of the secret plan to attack Egypt, which would become notorious as "the best-documented war plot in modern history," was drawn up on the kitchen table.

And Peter was starving.

The protocol stated that Israel would attack Egypt, whereupon France and Britain would invade too, with the excuse that they needed to "separate the combatants" and protect the Suez Canal. In doing so, their warplanes and warships would support Israel's ground troops, in order to keep the waterway open to international shipping.

It was so secret, and the conspiracy so incriminating, that the British immediately regretted agreeing to Israel's insistence on a written protocol and demanded to destroy all three copies. The next day they burned their own in a fireplace at Downing Street, the prime minister's residence. But the French refused to destroy theirs. And Israel's copy of the proof that it was not breaking international law alone, signed by the representatives of Britain and France, was brought safely to Israel in Ben-Gurion's breast pocket.

Peter's document, hidden inside his copy of *War and Peace,* which he was attempting to wade through on El Al's Lockheed Constellation from Paris to Tel Aviv, was a notarized, photographed copy. He was just the backup to the backup.

But at least he was home for the war.

ARIE

Oh no, I'm sorry. Sorry!" Arie healed Carmel's head with a kiss while Daniel clung to his neck. As he had lifted her the metal barrel of his Sten gun, strapped across his back, had hit Carmel on the temple. He wiped her tears. "Sorry. Sorry!" he said again. "And Daniel, look after your sister," he turned to his son, rubbing his nose with his, an Eskimo kiss. "And your mom."

"How long will you be away this time?" Daniel asked. "Will you be home for my birthday?"

"Mine too!" Carmel shouted.

"You'll be six! I hope so. If not, we'll celebrate when I get back. That way you'll have two birthdays, lucky you. Off you get, then, both of you," and he leaned down so that the twins could slide to the ground.

They held Tamara's legs as she hugged her husband. "Be careful," she whispered into his ear.

"Don't worry, it's just another exercise."

Both knew it wasn't true. Exercises were a brigade, at most a division. This time all the men they knew had been called up, everyone was rushing to their units. They had twenty-four hours to get to the front.

Trucks, Jeeps, buses, all were crammed with men with guns. The roads were clogged. The country was emptying outward until borders would be manned with men and machines of war.

Arie's driver, Yaacov, had been called up to the infantry near Jerusalem, so Moshe, proud of his new driving license and setting aside his opposition to what he called "this useless war," volunteered to drive Arie south to his unit's rendezvous near Ashkelon. Along the way they passed hundreds of hitchhiking soldiers and picked up three. These crowded into the backseat, kit bags and weapons crammed on their knees, their heads barely visible. With all the windows open and muggy air swirling through the car, they could hardly hear themselves talk.

Each junction was a mess of snarled military convoys. The one-hour drive took three, as tank transporters, half-tracks, Jeep convoys were waved through before private cars and buses. South of Ashdod cars and trucks attempting shortcuts were stuck in the sand, to the jeers of Arie's passengers. They were so cheerful they could have been going to a football game, but as they approached their staging areas, and one by one took their leave, the car grew quieter until only Moshe and Arie stared silently at the road ahead.

A mile after the Ashkelon turnoff a beat-up track led east through cornfields into a large dirt enclosure. Clouds of dust and sand, visible from a mile, marked the place where fathers dropped off sons, and buses left empty to pick up more fighters. Beyond them armored half-tracks and tanks with swiveling turrets drove off transporters, hitting the ground with a thump and a grinding of gears, throwing up more dust and pebble spray. Among them soldiers were thumping each other on their backs and striding off to find their rides.

The men of the 27th Reserve Armored Brigade under Colonel Chaim Bar-Lev were gathering to do battle, and by now they knew where they would fight. The Israeli army was far too small to dedicate so many troops and so much equipment to a diversion. The war would not be with Jordan as hinted everywhere, but with Egypt, and the tank brigade would be in the thick of it.

Arie, his buddies Dudu and Itamar, and two new guys checked every nut and bolt on the *Queen of Sheba*, their beloved M-50 Sherman. They ran the engines, warmed up the systems, checked the treads, tied their personal gear to the flanks, drank sweet tea, complained about the rations, and before they could close their eyes to sleep were ordered to move out.

Thirteen tanks, E company, rumbled through the night to take up their deployment position a mile from Egypt's border, marked at this point by a simple wire fence. At four in the morning they hid behind a sand ridge, among hedges of cacti, lined up along a track just large enough to take their eleven-foot wide weapons. The half-moon glinted off the cold metal with a cold bluish light. At the next order the tanks would lurch into motion, cannons and guns loaded, and as far as the crew was concerned, the sooner the better.

Israel was going to war and they were the battering ram.

But as usual, it was hurry up and wait. The crew lounged in the tank's shade, each lost in his thoughts, Arie growing more anxious with each passing hour. He was a tank commander now, the veteran, thirty-two years old, leading his boys, the very thought made him nauseous. Would he pass the test? He'd never fought for real inside a tank. In '48 he'd been infantry. Then he could lie on the ground and gaze at the stars and breathe fresh air and, if he wanted to, he could run and hide. And yes, he had run away, twice. How else do you get out of a stinking war in one piece? But now? Stuck inside a smelly firetrap surrounded by explosives. Couldn't he disappear inside his helmet? Couldn't he just go home to his family? But then, who would defend them? At that instant he hated the Arabs. But no. Not really. You hate someone you know, who has wronged you, someone who has hurt you. But to hate a whole race? For what?

There was trouble at the textile factory in Kiryat Gat, he should be taking care of that. The workers wanted more money. Well, who didn't? And in Tel Aviv, they'd just started construction on five more buildings. Now it was all frozen. Did they lock up the tools? In Haifa, two containers with car parts were stuck in the docks. Every day the port costs grew. Does insurance cover acts of war?

He glanced at Dudu, who was asleep, his helmet half-covering his face, arms crossed. The best gunner, even though he always yelled he couldn't see anything through his dirty glasses. Itamar, in charge of comms, how did he do that with a lisp? Their eyes met. Itamar tried to smile, and failed. He's feeling it worse than I am, Arie thought, clicking his tongue and winking at Itamar. Arie looked at the stars. So bright, so many, so beautiful, always been there, always will be. And we are mere dust, or will be. But not yet. Not yet. At last, his head pressed against metal, sleep took him.

Day one passed, warplanes flew high overhead, they heard distant booms, and news filtered through, over Israel radio and military comms, from passing drivers. Israeli paratroopers had landed at the Mitla Pass, deep inside Egypt, only forty-five miles from the Suez Canal. But they had advanced too far and were caught in vicious fighting with Egyptian commandoes. Other paratrooper and tank units were dashing to link up with them.

Day two and still they had no order to move, even as Israeli troops were reported to be sweeping through the Sinai in a rout of Egyptian forces. The BBC claimed Israeli soldiers had murdered fifty civilians on the Jordan border, in a place called Kfar Kassem. What was that all about?

Day three and still they sweltered by their tanks. They took dumps in the prickly pears. Maybe it'll be all over and they could go home safe and sound. All they did was gossip, doze, and suffer the ramblings of their minds.

You have to hate the enemy or how else can you kill them? Arie wondered again. Or do you kill them just so they won't kill you? Kill or be killed? In the ring he'd as good as beaten Jews to death. He didn't hate them. The opposite, he . . . but no, he stopped himself. He refused to think of it. He didn't hate the Arabs, he didn't know any. The workers came and went, Suleiman made the coffee, strong Turkish with cardamom, but he didn't even know his family name. Abu Shmabu? They were invisible. It can't be right, Arie thought. When he gets back he must make friends with some. After all, it's their country too. Well, not really, not in the same way. It's a Jewish state. Our refuge.

Not like the Nazis, them he knew. Them he had the right to hate. As quickly as images of the huts, the lice, the freezing cold, the whips, and the boots came to him, he expelled them from his mind. Gone. Done. For every Jew he fought in the ring, he wished with all his soul he could have killed a hundred of those jeering, evil, stinking SS guards clapping their hands and stamping their feet. Even the terror at Latrun, fighting for Israel's independence in '48, seemed like paradise after the camps. At least he had a gun, even if he ran out of bullets after an hour. But there was always another magazine lying around, there were so many corpses.

The others said when they first went into battle they felt they could never be killed. Him—he felt like he had come back from the dead.

What a horror show his life had been. Peter didn't have any of that. Lucky him. He'd gotten away, all he knew was how to be on the winning side. It's easy for him to be holier than thou. Sanctimonious son of a bitch. I know about him and Tamara. I'm not stupid.

He opened his fly and pissed on a cactus, watched the pee hit the green plant and slide yellow to the ground. He needed to drink more. Easy to dehydrate, with all this waiting around.

They slept in the sand by their tanks. He closed his eyes and sent love to Carmel and Daniel. He clenched his fists and looked skyward, as if in prayer, but for him, even now, there was no such thing. A bit late for that, after Auschwitz and the death march and the poverty when he arrived in Palestine and then three days of training and the rifle stuck in his hand and the order to go fight. He'd made two good friends, both had also survived the camps, only to die next to him at Latrun. That's when he swore to himself, over their bodies, that this too, he would survive, and nothing would stand in his way, he would stop at nothing to reach the top. The top? Of what? The shit pile? Because that's what it is.

Suddenly the comms went crazy. Booms and crashes of mortars and shells began, close, maybe two miles way. Some from the sea, more from land, the clattering of small-arms fire, like popcorn; what? Half a mile away? And heavy guns too, about a mile, like thunderclaps, their booms rumbled across the desert. But still no order to move. Hours went by, with crackling radio reports that the recon guys were bogged down. Egyptian resistance was fierce from heavily fortified ditches and bunkers. A half-track full of infantry, ours, blew up in a minefield, the fire like a beacon attracted more Egyptian artillery. What happened to the promise the Arabs would collapse and run away? We have dead and wounded. The war had arrived.

And then, the order. The field came alive with men springing like grass-hoppers onto their tanks. Whoops of encouragement, war cries, a roar of en-gines, and Arie felt his mouth go dry, his heart thump like a drum, as he called to his crew and they fell into line, the fourth tank in a convoy of thirteen.

Oh, Tamara, forgive me, I have been bad, I will love only you. He looked up again. Oh, whoever you are, whatever you are, let me go home to my wife and children. Please.

Please.

With Arie fighting in the tanks, Peter and Diana deep in their secret world, and Moshe working round the clock at the newspaper, it was left to Tamara and Rachel to gather all the children into Tamara's spacious home.

Like all the country, they listened to Voice of Israel every minute. Colonel Ariel Sharon's paratroopers had broken the Egyptian defenses at Mitla, but with significant Israeli casualties. An armored brigade had fought all the way down the Red Sea to Sharm el-Sheikh at the tip of Sinai. But most baffling, Britain and France had joined the battle. They were shelling Egyptian forces near Rafah, their planes were bombing military targets in Cairo, and thousands of their soldiers were fighting along the Suez Canal. They were helping Israel. The Egyptian army was on the run everywhere—everywhere except Rafah, where there was heavy fighting.

Tamara gripped Rachel's hand. "That's where Arie is," she said, her voice trembling. "Where is Daddy?" Daniel asked. He'd be six in three days, too old to deceive. "In the war," Tamara said, as calmly as she could. Daniel pouted. "I feel sorry for those bad people from Egypt, then." He kicked the sofa and went to sit cross-legged by the window, staring outside. He didn't stir. The sun fell on his hands, which rested on his bare knees. Twenty minutes later his face was in shadow.

"Come and play," Carmel said.

"No. Not till Daddy comes home."

Sixty miles south of Daniel's lookout post, the *Queen of Sheba* crashed over the debris of an already demolished house and powered through a burning construction yard. The tank behind Arie's poured machine-gun fire into the upper floors of the homes they passed. Mechanized infantry swept through the streets as barefoot and bare-chested Egyptian soldiers fled the battle-field and hid among the houses.

At the edge of the city, the tank column's rapid progress was slowed by volleys of machine-gun bullets that crashed into them. The tank in front stopped dead, to fire a shell at the Egyptian gun position in the lee of a hill. A burst of flame, a rolling ball of black smoke, silence from the hill. Arie passed the hulk of a burning half-track with a charred corpse hanging over the side and, yards away, two more bodies smoldering on the ground. Bitter bile rose to Arie's throat, he suppressed a vomit: Israeli dead. The rattling of automatic fire made him duck into the tank, he saw paint chips flying where bullets hit. He reemerged just as a hand grenade dropped by the loader's hatch, he swatted it away, ducked, and felt the tank shake as the treads absorbed the blast. Would the treads survive? They did, and the *Queen* sped on.

More rounds clanged into the tank, Arie felt a surge of love for the old warhorse. He shouldn't have called the tank a smelly firetrap, it was more like a mobile bomb shelter. Everything the enemy was throwing at them just bounced off, even with its thin armor.

They left Rafah and entered the wider terrain of the sand dunes, better for tanks. Arie peered through his binoculars, half-exposed in his turret, searching for targets, but found none. It appeared all the Egyptians had fled. The line of tanks had become ragged, pressing on to the brigade rendezvous in the dunes north of El Arish. So far, so good. His luck was holding.

And then it all went to shit.

Earlier, a grenade or a lucky bullet had severed the tank's radio antenna, and they had lost comms. They'd been down to visual contact, following clouds of dust, and were falling behind. They were losing more time at a clump of bushes and fallen trees that concealed a gully. Now they were stuck. The tank's front end pointed down into a sandy ditch that gave no purchase, the back end whirled wildly on loose undergrowth. The tank couldn't gain traction, the treads spun uselessly. From the turret, Arie struggled to aim his half-inch machine gun, but with the tank bucking and rolling like a wild horse as the driver revved and braked, forward and reverse, frantic to escape the desert's grip, he could barely hold on to the heavy barrel. It pointed at the sky and at the ground and every which way except the one that mattered.

Two low silhouettes had popped up on the sand dune, and all Arie's nerves focused on the barrel they were aiming, an antitank rocket, steady as the evil eye. Fifty yards. He felt his skin shrink, as if his bones were suddenly too big. He was a sitting duck. "Down!" he yelled, throwing himself into the tank. "Down!" But there was nowhere to go. At that instant the back end found traction and propelled the front up and out of the ditch and the tank righted itself, treads spinning, and roared away.

Too late.

The rocket shot out from a ball of flame and smoke. Its impact was horrendous. It was like a rock fell from a hundred feet on one end of a tin can. The tank was lifted half off the ground and settled again with a crash, hurtling everyone into the metal walls, while shock waves doubled the damage. Hooks, bolts, boxes, and jagged corners smashed into flesh, bone, and skull. The stench of gunpowder, scorched fuel, and blood settled over them. The tank's nickname flashed through Arie's mind: Ronson, because it burned like a lighter. Every inch of Arie was trembling, but mostly he noticed, after the bedlam, the silence. "Dudu?" he said at last. "Itamar?"

"Anyone?"

He wanted to cry. He tapped his body, felt his legs, his balls, his head, and looked at his hands. They were red with blood. From where? He flexed his limbs. Everything worked. The heat was unbearable. Were they burning? Out, out, Fast. The ammo will explode. He pushed against the turret, and air rushed in.

A hand tugged at his foot. Arie leaned down and pulled. "No, don't," Dudu cried, "my leg, it's stuck."

"Itamar," Arie cried, "Itamar." There was no answer. He sucked in air to call out for the rest of his crew but in his panic couldn't remember their names. There was blood in his mouth, he spat it out. "Dudu, quick, out, before we blow."

"I can't, I'm stuck." Dudu was sobbing. "You go." Blood was streaming from his head and his neck. "Mummy," he cried, "Oh, it hurts."

Arie dropped to the floor, feeling for Dudu's leg, his foot. The electricity was gone, it was dark, a sharp beam of bright daylight lit up one corner, by it there was a head half severed from its body. The loader. What the hell's his name? Arie pulled at Dudu's foot and Dudu screamed. It was jammed beneath a steel box, the foot somehow pointing the wrong way behind the metal seat. They smelled escaping fuel and the bitter fumes of fire. He only had moments to get Dudu out. And to save himself. Arie used his knife as a lever but it was too small. He grabbed a rifle and used the butt to lever the box off Dudu's foot. "Now, pull!" he shouted, but Dudu didn't budge, he was in shock. "Pull!" Arie screamed and stabbed Dudu's leg with his knife. Dudu shrieked, "You crazy bastard!" and jerked and his foot was free. The box fell to the floor, and with one movement Arie was above Dudu, his head outside, pulling him with all his might until they both collapsed onto the top of the tank, in the fresh air.

Bullets whizzed and clanged around them, Arie pushed Dudu over the side of the tank and jumped onto the ground beside him, sheltered from the shooters. Facing them was flat, open ground until a low ridge about thirty yards away. Dudu had fallen badly, he must have knocked his face on the way down, his nose was broken. He was spitting blood and panting. Incredibly, he winked. "If you ever . . . have . . . a problem . . . with a parking . . . ticket," he managed through bloody mucus, "let me know."

"Yes, corporal." Arie leaned back against the tank, his heart thumping. They were alone, no comms, just them and, on the other side of the tank, two Egyptians with a rocket launcher and a machine gun. Were there more? Who knew? He'd soon find out, and not in a good way. He felt himself all over. Blood from his ear, and above the eye. Otherwise, good to go. Those bastard Arabs.

I'm not done with them, he thought. Oh, no.

"I'm going to get them," he said to Dudu. "If I don't, they'll get us. And we don't want that, now, do we?" He unlatched a kit bag strapped to the side of the tank and took out his Sten gun and three hand grenades. His pistol was still in his belt holster.

Dudu winked again, his eyes slowly closed, and his head fell back.

Suddenly Arie remembered the ammo. He grabbed Dudu under the arms and pulled him backward, leaving two deep grooves in the sand from his heels, keeping the tank between them and the enemy, until he stumbled onto his back behind the raised ground. He lay Dudu on his side, keeping the hole in his head out of the sand. Dudu was pale and sweating, unconscious but breathing. Arie stuffed a bandage into the wound to stem the blood and taped it in place. There was nothing more he could do for him except pray they'd soon be found.

Now Arie began to crawl, pushing with his feet, belly to the sand, weapon up. He knew the Egyptians wouldn't approach the tank until it blew up, and until then they couldn't know if anybody had survived the rocket and the shooting, even if they'd seen him fall out of the turret. He stayed low, behind the ridge, crawling as long as it hid him. If there were more of them, he was sunk, but if he had stayed where he was, he'd be sunk anyway. He kept crawling, waiting for the tank to explode. But there were no flames, it just sat alone in the desert, a useless smoking iron heap.

The farther he crawled the more the undulating dunes hid him. It was clear now the two Egyptians were alone. They must have got lost or fallen behind, just like him. But instead of fleeing they had stayed to fight. He had flanked them now and, staying low to the ground, sand caking his sweaty face, panting, he wriggled toward them, from their rear.

He had plenty of time to think of Tamara, and the twins, and Auschwitz, and whatever, but he didn't. He felt nothing, saw nothing, heard nothing, thought of nothing. It was like he was crawling through a silent narrowing tunnel. Every fiber of his being focused on killing the enemy before they killed him. He had only one thought, over and over: Here I am again—kill or be killed. The sun beat down on him, he was yellow with sand, his lips were parched, but all he thought was: Kill them.

It was easy. When he saw the tops of their heads he rolled onto his back, pulled out the pin, and threw a grenade twenty yards, a looping high throw like tossing a ball to a child for a simple catch. And then he did it again. One explosion followed the other, muted by the soft sand, like hands clapping. There was no debris, the sand absorbed the blasts.

A low moaning started, which became high-pitched, like a cat wailing at night. It gave Arie the shivers. The wailing got louder, there were cries in Arabic, but it appeared to Arie it was all one voice. He rose to his knees, body bent double, saw nothing, straightened his back. Still nothing. He waited, then slowly stood, his Sten gun at his shoulder, aiming forward as he took one small step after another. He saw first a destroyed leg and then the corpse. The cannon was smashed. The second Egyptian, silent now, eyes wide in terror, was on his side in a pool of blood, holding his bleeding open stomach. He stared at the looming Israeli soldier as Arie slowly approached, his barrel pointing at the man's head. The Arab's mouth began to work but only blood dripped out. Arie stood over him, staring at the defeated man, who was trembling from head to toe, pleading with his eyes. Arie lowered his weapon, extended his hand, pulled the man to a sitting position. The man fell back, began to whine again, to moan, to beg. He pointed to his lips. There was a water canteen nearby, it must have been blown away by the blast but it was intact. Arie picked it up, unscrewed it, and held it to the man's mouth, watching him drink. Arie tore a sleeve off the dead man's jacket and stuffed it into the soldier's stomach wound to stanch the bleeding. The man was whimpering. Arie laid him on his back, arranged his legs, and packed the sand into a pillow. His eyes teared in the blinding sun. Arie took the soldier's cap and covered his eyes from the glare. After all, he thought, he could be me.

All Arie could do was wait for the next Israeli soldiers to show up, and hope it was before the Egyptians. So here he was with his very own prisoner of war. What should he do with him? For a moment he imagined that he himself was the prisoner. What would he have wanted? He laid an encouraging hand on the man's shoulder. After all, they were two soldiers, far from home. He made sure there were no weapons around, and walked back to Dudu, keeping a wary distance from the tank.

Dudu's breathing was labored. A deep gash revealed part of his white skull, which didn't appear broken. He seemed comfortable. Arie felt his pulse. Fast, but not too much. He stood, peered at the horizon. Someone will come along soon. He sat and held Dudu's hand and wondered where his mates were. Would they come back searching for him? No, orders were clear, if anyone falls behind, leave him. This war is all about speed and initiative. The tanks would storm ahead and all he could do was wait and stay calm.

And then he heard a sound. A thin sound, a cat? A call. A voice? Banging, a metallic knocking. He jerked his head toward the tank. Is someone inside? Alive? There were booms and gunshots a distance away, the whine of a plane . . . but—"Itamar?" he yelled. He heard a faint voice, "Help!" Dudu's eyes flickered open, he must have heard him too. Arie took two quick steps toward the tank when flames began to lick from the turret, and smoke seeped through the back. Where the shells were stored. Arie threw himself to the ground.

There was a thunderclap and flames shot into the air, erupting from the turret like a volcano. The heat singed his hair, his eyebrows, the blast of hot air peppered him with pebbles and debris. His face stung.

Arie's jaw twitched as he sat by Dudu, his heart racing. Dudu was unconscious again and didn't know Arie was stroking his head. Arie didn't know it either.

After watching the *Queen of Sheba* burn itself out, with Itamar inside, Arie walked back to his prisoner of war and shot him three times in the head.

DANIEL

RAMAT HASHARON, ISRAEL

November 1956

Daniel wouldn't leave the window to go to bed so Tamara brought the bed to him. She and Rachel collected cushions, pillows, and blankets and made him comfortable in the alcove. When they tucked him in he didn't want a story, only good-night kisses. The first night his twin sister Carmel said she'd sleep with him but after an hour Tamara gathered her in her arms and brought her to her own bed. On the second night Daniel's uncle Ido, only six years older, lay next to him.

"Do you want a story?" Ido said.

"Yes."

"What about?"

"Daddy."

"Yours or mine?"

"Where is yours?"

"I don't know. At work."

"What are they doing?"

"I don't know. Same as Uncle Arie, I suppose. Fighting."

"Does it hurt to die?"

"Only if you die slowly. If you die quickly, then it doesn't hurt."

"If Daddy dies, will he come back home?"

"Silly, of course not. He'll be dead."

The two boys lay on their sides. Daniel put his hand on Ido's shoulder. "What happens when you're dead? I mean, where are you?"

"Heaven, if you're good."

"Daddy's good."

"Of course he is."

"I hope he comes home soon."

"Are you really going to sleep here till he comes home?"

"Yes."

"Why?"

"Because then he'll have to come home, to put me to bed."

Four days into the war Diana left the Office and collected Noah and Ezra, her three-year-olds. They didn't want to go and ran back upstairs. They liked it in Auntie Tamara's house with the garden and their big cousins Ido and Estie, and Daniel and Carmel. And Grandma Rachel had cooked and fussed over them and played all the time. "They're enjoying the war," Tamara said.

"Well, let's hope it's the last one," Diana replied.

"We'll see," Tamara said. "I'm looking forward to my dad's column. Peter says he's one of the few who writes the truth as opposed to wishful thinking."

Moshe's column in *Davar*, the labor party newspaper, had become required reading, the Cassandra whose offbeat analysis often proved painfully prescient. He couldn't wait to write the next one but kept delaying.

"There's too much happening," he told his editor. "It's changing all the time." The papers were full of Israel's brilliant victory and Egypt's humiliation, but Moshe had one key question: What will Israel do with the conquered Sinai Peninsula and the Gaza Strip? The answer didn't take long.

On November 4, after five days of fighting, and under irresistible pressure from Washington, Israel agreed to a cease-fire with Egypt. The same day the United Nations authorized a peacekeeping force to separate the enemies.

Israel, with British and French help, had smashed the Egyptian army in the Sinai; smashed the terrorist network in Gaza; and opened the Straits of Tiran to Israeli shipping. It had achieved its war aims.

But Nasser remained in power and he, too, was able to claim victory, thanks to American threats, which forced Israel, France, and Britain to withdraw their troops from every inch of newly occupied Sinai.

"I've got my opening paragraph," Moshe crowed to Rachel at last, "but that's about all," he added sadly. He read aloud: "'This pointless conflict ended in the worst possible way. Israel thinks its military was 'brilliant,' while Nasser thinks he won the war. The truth is that Israel lost politically what it won militarily, and Egypt won politically what it lost militarily.'" He read it again, more slowly. "Drat. Four adverbs in fifteen words. But maybe the repetition is powerful? Need to work on that last sentence. Still, it's the thought that counts. You like it?"

"I do," Rachel said. "Nobody else will."

"I've got the last line too. Listen: 'Israel and Egypt are both deluding themselves and that will lead to another war and disaster.' You like it?" He turned the radio on to listen to the news. "All I need now is the middle."

Two days later, at three o'clock in the morning, Arie, his forehead bound by a fresh white bandage, his fatigues filthy, slowly turned the key and inched the front door open. Without a sound he placed his kit bag on the floor, reached up, left his Sten gun on the hat stand, and stood in the door of the living room, allowing his eyes to adjust to the moonlight that came in through the glass door to the terrace.

The dim light showed a heap by the window, like a pile of clothes. He tiptoed across the room and found Daniel fast asleep on a bed of pillows. It didn't seem strange to him, nothing did anymore. Arie went down on one knee, slipped his arms beneath his son, and carried him to bed, while Daniel smiled in his sleep and said, "Daddy?"

PART TWO

PETER

MADISON, WISCONSIN

July 1962

———

The best thing about their room was the bed. It was the widest they'd ever seen, and the bounciest—they almost reached the ceiling—and it was high enough for Noah to scare Ezra by sitting on his knees and hanging him over the side, backward. "Get off, get off, ouch, my back!" Ezra yelled.

"Stop that!" Diana shouted, pulling Noah off Ezra, who rolled over and punched Noah on the shoulder. They wrestled each other to the floor, knocking the telephone off the bedside table. "Enough, oh for God's sake, do something!" Diana shouted at Peter, who was sitting on the sofa reading the *Wisconsin State Journal*. "Interesting story from Egypt," he said. "Some new rockets in the Independence Day parade."

"Not your problem anymore, or mine. The boys are the problem. They're out of control. You've got to do something, they don't listen to a word I say. Peter? Peter! Did you hear what I said?"

"What?"

"Oh nothing, I'm going downstairs for a drink."

"You don't drink anymore."

"I'll start again, I've got to get away from this madhouse. Stop it!" This last at Ezra, who had pulled the Gideon Bible from the drawer by the bed and thrown it at Noah. "Ouch," he cried. "It's heavy!"

"We're going to get evicted from the hotel," Diana said. "We'll have to stay with the Wilsons."

Peter pushed himself out of the chair. "I'll come with you, let's get away from the boys for a bit."

"Yes, otherwise I'll give birth right now."

Diana put on her cardigan, which barely closed over her stomach, and they went downstairs to the Hilton café.

As soon as the door closed the boys stopped fighting. "What shall we do now?" Noah said.

"I don't know," Ezra said. "Find Mom and Dad?"

"I know, let's phone Israel. Daniel and Carmel. What time is it there? Will they be sleeping?"

"Let's wake them up."

Noah called the hotel operator to ask how to call Israel and gave her the number. Two minutes later, the phone rang. They looked at it. "Pick it up," Ezra said.

"You pick it up," Noah said.

"No, you."

"You."

"You."

"You're such a baby," Noah said, putting the phone to his ear. "Hello?"

"Hello? Who is this?"

"Auntie Tamara? Hello, it's Ezra," Noah said and pushed the phone into Ezra's face. He slapped it away and ran to the other side of the room.

"I mean, it's Noah. Hello."

"Is anything wrong? Do you know what time it is? It's the middle of the night here. What happened?" Noah heard Tamara say, "Wake up. Arie, wake up. It's America."

"America? America? What? Who?"

"Why are you calling, Noah? What's wrong? Where's Mommy? And Daddy?"

"Nothing's wrong," Noah said. "Can I speak to Carmel or Daniel?"

"No, of course not, they're sleeping. Why did you call?"

"Mummy had triplets."

"What? What did you say?"

"Here, Ezra wants to talk to you." Noah put the phone into Ezra's hand and ran into the bathroom.

"Hello, this is Ezra. Hello, Auntie."

"Triplets? Mummy had triplets? Three babies. Oh my God, Arie, triplets!"

"Not really," Ezra said. "Noah just said it. He's stupid." There was silence on the end of the line.

Finally, Tamara said, "Well, it's good that you called anyway, because I was going to call Peter in the morning. Tell him to call the Office. It's urgent," Tamara said slowly. "Don't forget, it's important. Will you remember? Promise?"

"Okay. Hello, Auntie? Hello."

The phone went dead.

As the taxi turned off the highway and entered a grid of streets named after great Americans, Peter became excited. "There," he pointed from the front passenger seat, as they passed a long low building with a parking garage. "That's where I went to school, Middleton High. And there's the basketball court, I was good!" Diana stroked his neck from behind. Peter loved to talk about his youth in America, but he never talked about his German childhood. "I was on the wrestling team, you must get it from me, boys."

Moments later they found Franklin Avenue, the taxi turned, and Peter and his family, holding hands, walked up the concrete path to ring the bell at number 87.

It looked the same, bay windows with potted plants either side of the green door, just a bigger car in the driveway. Crazy, he thought. Since he'd been here last most of his family had been murdered, he'd fought in three wars, and he had a family of his own, while for these lucky people, time stood still. Maybe the hedge was thicker.

Peter approached with a happy heart. For five years this had been his home. The Wilsons had made him one of theirs, their children had been his siblings, and now Chuck and Bud had children of their own too. He squeezed Ezra's hand. "Behave," he said.

Diana smiled. "Nervous?"

He replied with a tight grin. It had been a long time. What, he'd left for the army in '43 and now it's '62. Nineteen years. And this was his first time back. He regretted that.

Footsteps. A lock turning. And there she was, the woman he'd called Mom, with a smile as wide as Wisconsin. Wearing a brown pantsuit, her hair freshly tinted and curled, Mrs. Wilson looked from Peter to Diana to the boys, shaking her head in wonder, until finally, she could talk. "My, my, my," she said, "how you've grown," and she swept Peter into her arms. "Come in, come in," she kept saying, long after they were all inside.

How she fussed, especially over Diana. "Oh, look at you! Sit down, honey, mustn't get too tired. Another one on the way. I'm so jealous." She brought coffee and juice, and filled a tray with cookies and soda for the boys, who ran upstairs with Mrs. Wilson's granddaughter, Alice. "They're getting on well, friends already, how old are your boys, ten, eleven? They're so sweet." Doubt was written across Diana's face.

"Nearly ten. They're . . . unpredictable," Peter said. From upstairs there was a sound of crashing and a yell, and then silence.

A minute later Diana said, "They're too quiet."

"Don't worry, honey," Mrs. Wilson said. "Alice is a bit older than them, she can take care of herself. Believe me, she's one tough cookie."

"She'll need to be, with those two," Peter said. He looked around the familiar room, the same brown fluffy carpet, the same stained sofa, the side table with the new big box of a TV, local landscapes in dark wooden frames on the wall, the piano crowded with silver-framed family photographs. He picked up one of three boys grinning with baseball bats over their shoulders and showed it to Diana. "Here, look, me with Bud and Chuck. I was the pitcher." He looked up, appearing wistful. "Mrs. Wilson, you haven't changed one bit."

She threw her head back with a guffaw. "And the world is flat. Still, thank you. And please, call me Vera. It's lonely here, to be honest. It was kind of you to phone when Mr. Wilson was sick. It meant a lot to him."

Her husband had passed away three years earlier. Her two sons and their families lived far away, one in Taos, New Mexico, and one in St. Louis, Missouri. It was lucky that Alice liked to visit, a real handful for her parents, though, a mind of her own, that girl. Twelve years old going on twenty, mind you, nothing new, she used to be eight going on fifteen.

As Peter set the photo back on the piano, Mrs. Wilson said, with a fond smile, "You still have your father's watch, I see. That's nice."

"He never takes it off," Diana said.

Mrs. Wilson sighed, looking at a photo of her husband. "But tell me about yourself, you wrote you're on a one-month vacation traveling around America? Isn't it a bit too much for you, Diana? How far along are you?"

"Seven months."

"Peter, don't let Diana carry a thing. Where are you going? The Grand Canyon, you wrote? Las Vegas, of course. And you've been in America for three years. So much to tell me!"

"Yes, we've been studying, a bit late in life but better late than never. I got study leave from work, did a bachelor's in political science at NYU and Diana . . ."

"I did mine in psychology at City College . . ."

"Not that it helps with the boys," Peter cut in.

"Or with you, frankly."

Peter headed her off. "It sounds like the twins and Alice should get on like a house on fire."

"Well, Alice is what? Two, three years older, she's a young woman compared to them," Mrs. Wilson said. "Let them stay little boys as long as possible, believe you me."

Diana groaned. "Oh, no, don't say that, I wish they'd grow up."

"I heard that," Ezra said, peering around the door. "Daddy, I just remembered. Auntie Tamara said you should phone the office. It's urgent."

"What? When?"

"This morning. No, yesterday. Or was it the day before?"

"Urgent? And you just told me now. Thank you very much."

"Urgent?" Mrs. Wilson said. "Oh, dear, I do hope nothing is wrong. Would you like to use my telephone?"

"Thank you, yes, please, I'll call collect."

Vera showed Peter and Diana to the den, its walls covered in baseball pennants and team shirts, and went upstairs to check on the children.

"The office?" Diana said after Peter placed the call.

"That's what he said. There's only one office for me. Office. Capital O."

"What do they want?"

"Urgent? We'll find out in a moment. But they've left us alone for three years. Three-and-a-half. What can 'urgent' mean? Only that they want me to do something. Maybe you'll have to go to the Grand Canyon without me."

"Without you? Just me and the boys? Are you insane? Shoot me now."

The call went straight through to the deputy operations chief. Diana heard only Peter's end of the conversation, but watched his face grow grimmer.

"You asked me to call? When? I'm on vacation. The boss himself said it? Do I have a choice? Can you tell me anything about it? I understand. Well, all right, it'll take me a few days, I'm in the Midwest. Good-bye."

Diana watched Peter slowly place the receiver in the holder and stare at it. After a few seconds she said, "Well?"

He sighed and sat on the edge of the desk. "Look. We've paid for all the tickets. You may as well go on with the boys. Have some fun. Me, it looks like duty calls. Something's up and they want me back. At least they waited till we finished our exams."

"Duty calls? Didn't you give it all up?"

"Yes. Well. Sort of . . ."

They'd discussed many times what else they could do after they finished their degrees, even staying in America. But it always came down to the same issue: If they didn't stay in Israel, then who would? What had all the struggle been for? The country was only fourteen years old. Of course it was hard. There were no luxuries. America was a land of plenty, but so what? Did it really matter how big your car was and how many you had? How many bathrooms does a house need? Living in peace and quiet was a blessing, but if the price of that was closing our minds to the lives of family and friends back home, then how could we be happy? We would just be selfish and blind. That wasn't happiness, that was ignorance. Round and round they had gone, always the same thoughts, but ultimately, it came down to the struggle. Israel was involved in a life-and-death struggle that would determine the security and future of the Jewish people, and they needed to be part of the fight. They had skills the country needed, their boys would fight too. God knows they were getting enough practice at home. Friends always said they prayed that their children would not need to fight in a war. Who were they kidding? Only when Israel made peace with the Arabs would the country be safe, and the Arabs would never accept the existence of Israel. So if they were condemned to a future of struggle, why not just stay in America? Who needs it? What kind of future was that for their children? Round and round they went, chewing the same cud.

What awaited them in Tel Aviv? Prices had gone up, they weren't even sure they could rent in the center of Tel Aviv anymore. Arie had offered to help, but Peter swore he'd never take a penny from his crooked brother. "He's considered a respectable businessman," Diana would say, over and over, he's becoming one of Israel's wealthiest men. He must be doing something right, he isn't crooked, he just knows how to work the system. Peter didn't care. "He has nothing in his mind but money, and I want no part of it."

All Diana could do was close her eyes and give a deep sigh, retreat inside. That's how it always ended. He was as stubborn as a mule. But a loyal, loving mule, and she loved him for it.

Their discussions, which sometimes became arguments, and then fights, had been about the future. Now, the future had arrived.

"Diana." Peter took his wife's hand. He forced himself to look into her eyes. "I just don't know what to do, but it's decision time." He placed his hands on her stomach, felt the roundness, felt for a baby elbow or foot. "What's best for all of us? I could find work here somewhere. Easily. But I just don't know what the point would be."

"Maybe the point would be it's time to think of ourselves and our children. The best place for a good life. And soon there'll be another one of us." She placed her hand on his and pressed it on her navel. "Pushing hard. Must be another boy."

"God forbid."

They laughed. "But, really," Diana said. "What shall we do?"

"I just don't know. Look, I said on the phone I'd go back, so let's go back. I'll see what they want from me, and we'll take it from there. I can always come back here."

"I don't buy the 'What's best for the Jewish state' anymore. What I want to know is, What's best for us? What's best for our children? England? America? Israel?"

"But what does that mean? Best? An easy life? America, then. A life with meaning? Israel."

Diana said with a smile, "A life with neither? England."

"Well, either way, the vacation's over. Let's go home and see what happens."

They stayed for dinner, roast chicken and fries, but then said they had to go, not west to Vegas and the Canyon, but back to New York to pack and return to Israel. If she could get on the plane at seven months' pregnant, Diana pointed out. She'd need a very loose coat.

"It just means that we'll come back and see you again on our next trip West," Peter said.

"I do hope so, and not in another nineteen years," Vera said, serving the last slice of carrot cake with the coffee and cream. "But you never really said what you do. The office called you back? It must be very important if they call you back from America. Can't someone else do it while you're on vacation? Mr. Wilson always made sure there was another consultant on call to service his clients. Something always pops up in insurance, you know."

"Yes, they didn't say what, exactly. Still, never mind, we had a good run, can't sneeze at three years in America."

"No, indeed. But what do you do? If the boys ask me, and they will, you know."

"Foreign ministry. Protocol and liaison with the diplomatic corps. Involves a bit of travel sometimes. But they were kind enough to allow me three years study leave, to get a second wind in my life, so to speak, so I can hardly let them down now."

"Oh, of course not. Well, it sounds like a very good job."

When Peter and Diana called the boys and rose to leave, Vera had tears in her eyes. "I hope you come back," she said, gripping Peter. "You were such a lovely little boy, lost and lonely, and now look at you, I'm so very proud of you." She paused. "And I'm so sorry about your family, you know that. I read the stories and I always thought of your parents and brother and sisters. How lucky you are to have your brother."

Peter kissed her on the cheek. "You must come and visit us in Israel one day."

"Oh, I'm a bit old for that, but . . ."

"I'll come," Alice cut in. "Ezra and Noah said I can stay with them, can I go, Grandma?"

"You'll have to ask your parents, my dear."

"But they'll say no, they always do."

"And does that ever stop you?"

"I'll see you in Israel," Alice said with a bright laugh, and kissed each boy on the cheek. They blushed bright crimson and said "Yuck" and wiped their cheeks. Everybody laughed.

"Bye-bye," Alice waved as the taxi pulled away. "See you in Israel. I promise."

PETER

Not only couldn't they decide whether to stay in Israel, they couldn't even agree on where to live while they decided. Mossad only footed two weeks in a hotel. After that, Peter wanted to rent an apartment in Tel Aviv, while Diana wanted to accept Tamara's offer to stay in her new house.

Arie had bought four dunams, an acre, on the neglected clifftop near Herzliya and among the ragged cacti and dunes had built what he claimed was the biggest home in Israel. One day, he said, this would be prime real estate. Ten miles north of Tel Aviv, it had infinite views over the Mediterranean with its breathtaking sunsets, there was a huge yard for the kids to play in, and parking for half a dozen cars. There were two other, much smaller homes nearby.

"It's crazy," Tamara had told Diana. "It's megalomania. But it's also beautiful. The weirdest thing is that we have two maids and a gardener who live in the *ma'abara* slum in Nof Yam. It's almost next door. That's where I used to live. And now I live in this villa that's big enough for half the slum to live in. Please come and stay, there's plenty of room. There's a good school close by and Yaacov drives the kids there and back."

For Peter, that was the final straw. "Absolutely not. Are you crazy? A chauffeur for the twins? Who do you think we are? I know Arie thinks he's Louis the Fourteenth, but Tamara, what does she think about all this?"

"She loves it. Who wouldn't? Get off your high horse, Peter. And anyway, she's amazing. She's a human rights lawyer now, so she's helping those poor people in the *ma'abara*, not just getting upset. You think it helps them if we live in two rooms on the third floor with no elevator when I'm about to give birth? Do you know how heavy the groceries are?"

"We'll find a ground-floor flat. I just don't want charity from my brother."

"Oh, come off it. You're not in competition. Ah! That's it, isn't it? You don't want him to think he's winning? Just because he's got more money. You don't want him to think . . ."

"Don't be ridiculous. It's not about money. We live in different worlds, and his pays more, that doesn't worry me. It's just that . . . well, his values are so messed up, I don't want any part of it."

Diana continued the argument, but Peter wasn't listening. He had drifted off into his usual inner confusion in which he hated what Arie did but understood why he did it. He could never find the right words. It emerged as criticism, anger, and jealousy, but that wasn't what he felt. Who was he, who had had it so easy, to criticize, compared to his younger brother, who had had it so hard? On the other hand you don't excuse a murderer because he had a bad childhood. Anyway, Arie wasn't really evil, he just played the system to get stinking rich. Why did he resent that so much? Was it purer in Israel to be poor? Should the rich apologize? Those values were just as messed up as Arie's, only different.

"Maybe we should just go live in America after all," he said.

"What? Did you hear what I've been saying? What's wrong with you?"

"Sorry. I drifted off. What?"

"That's it. I can't take this. Look, we're moving in with Tamara. I mean, think about it. We get a small flat in Tel Aviv, you're not even home, you're off in Europe somewhere . . ."

"Who says I'm going anywhere?"

". . . and I have a baby all alone as per usual. No help. What's better? That? Or staying with Arie and Tamara, family who love me, and daily help, and the boys playing with their cousins, lots of space. Come on, Peter, it's obvious. If you just stop obsessing about your brother, we can have a lovely time. And then when you come back from wherever you're going, we'll find our own place, in good time, without the stress of rushing around now to find a little place before you leave."

"You seem to have decided I'm going back to the Office. All I'm going to do is see what they want. Then we'll see."

"Oh, sure. You're going to say no to Little Isser. That'll be the day. Anyway, I've decided. We're moving in with Arie and Tamara, and, in case you don't know, we're very grateful for their offer, and I want you to say thank you to Arie."

Before that penance, Peter had to perform another chore in Tel Aviv, and for that he dressed in his finest khaki pants and short-sleeved khaki shirt. His only nod to three years in America were the soft brown tassel loafers, which drew titters as he waited in the café by the new Mossad headquarters off King Saul Boulevard. He stared at the Office entrance, a nondescript door between a bank and some shops, in the rundown lobby of an eight-floor building. There was no indication the door was bomb-proof.

After three minutes it opened and there was Gingie, her arms open, with a huge grin. "Welcome home. When's the baby due?"

They hugged, patting each other's backs. "In seven weeks," Peter said. "Can't wait."

"Good luck with that. They have plans for you."

"I'm going to be at the birth. I swore to Diana."

"I hope you had your fingers crossed then. They want you on the top floor right away."

Gingie shut the door behind him with the dull clang of reinforced steel. "Consider that a metaphor," she said. "The door just slammed on you."

"Cute."

As the elevator climbed, Peter felt a rush of anxiety. What did they want from him? What would he say? Diana had left it up to him. So that he could take the blame?

"First floor, Communications," Gingie counted. "Second and third floors, Research and Development." A low whine of machine and metal coils. "Fourth floor, Analysts and Planning. Fifth, you lot. Sixth . . ."

"Yes, yes, Gingie. How are you? I'd like to say it's good to be back, but . . ."

"Eighth and top floor," Gingie interrupted. "Directors. The elevator, and the buck, stops here."

"Unless there's a screwup. Then the shit flows right down to the first floor."

"Nothing's changed. And that's why you're here."

Isser Harel was where he most liked to be, in the field, overseeing an op in Europe. Where? Do you need to know? No. But when his secretary, Dvora, showed Peter into Harel's office, he found another legendary figure of the shadows. Short and barrel-chested, like Harel, but a lot more frightening, Rafi Eitan, Mossad's deputy operations chief, watched Peter enter with a wary eye. He waved him to a chair.

It was the first time Peter had seen Eitan since his triumph of capturing Adolf Eichmann, Hitler's architect of the Final Solution. When Eichmann was abducted from a Buenos Aires street, it was Eitan who seized his head in the getaway vehicle. On the other hand he let Doctor Mengele, the Auschwitz Angel of Death, get away, saying that his capture could jeopardize the even more important kidnapping of Eichmann. That was two years ago. Whatever Mossad got up to, success or failure, it seemed that the legendary Eitan was all over it. Eitan's reputation was second to none in Mossad, which made him one of the world's most effective spies. That made his offer all the more compelling.

"You will work directly with me," he began as if issuing an order. "On a specific mission. Long-term. Risky. Promotion. I know you're just back from America, congratulations on your degree. I know you must have other options and you're probably considering them. Probably in America. So? Are you in or out?"

Peter tried not to, but he had to laugh. It came out as a snigger. Eitan didn't move a muscle. His stare was unwavering.

"Rafi, how long have we known each other?" Peter said. "How about a word of greeting maybe? How's Diana? Something?"

"You need time to think?"

"All right, if that's the way it is. We're having a baby. I want to be there at the birth. I want to spend more time at home with Diana. Yes, you're right as usual, we're thinking of moving to America. I do have some options there . . ."

"So your answer is?"

Peter looked past Eitan's shoulder, he considered the boss's spartan room, the simple wooden desk, not one ornament. He hadn't even been offered a glass of water. What a difference. His lowly college professor's study suite in New York would swallow this office several times. His suite had a liquor cabinet as well-stocked as a hotel bar. Oil paintings hung on the wall, the deep leather sofa was covered with Colombian rugs, there was a wall of books and a big color television.

Israel didn't even have TV.

But he and Diana had chewed this over interminably. What's life really all about? At this point, their children. Where do we want to raise them? With what values? And after all, how many watches can we wear? How big does a kitchen have to be? Do we really need a car? Diana had said he should decide. May as well be now.

Peter stretched out his hand to Israel's top spy.

"My answer is, yes. I'm in. But in what?"

TAMARA and DIANA, PETER and ARIE

T he cabbie was so excited to pull in to the circular driveway of such a mansion that he leaned on the horn as if summoning a flock of servants. "Whose palace is this, Nebuchadnezzar?"

Three fully grown and freshly planted palm trees lined either side of the cobblestoned entry. An ancient olive tree topped a new hill with patchy grass. Water dripped over a rock into an empty fishpond.

"My brother," Peter said, "and this is his Hanging Garden of Babylon."

"Well, lucky him—and you. Does he need a driver?"

"I'm sure he has several. How much do I owe you?"

"Can I double the fare?"

"Sure, if he pays. Unfortunately, I'm paying. Can I have a reduction?"

"You're in a good mood. I would be too if I had a brother like that. Mine's in jail."

"What for?"

"He says he didn't do it."

"Well, my brother did do it. That's how he got this place."

There was a shriek from the house. Tamara was at the door, arms wide, sweeping up Ezra and Noah with a cry of welcome.

"Boys, come back and get your bags," called Diana.

"Don't tell me the poor lads have to carry their own bags!" the cabbie shouted as he drove away. "What is this country coming to?"

Peter shook his head and picked up two shoulder bags, two suitcases, and some packages, which fell as he walked through the door.

"My God, this is beautiful," Diana said, as she entered the kitchen, "it's huge." At the double sink she looked through a large picture window onto the lawn that stretched to the cliff. Beyond it lay the Mediterranean Sea, blue and bright to the horizon, its waves whipped white by the wind.

"Awful wear and tear, so close to the sea. All that salt in the air," Peter said. "Everything will rust."

"Don't be so miserable," Diana said.

"I'm joking." Peter put his arms around Tamara and kissed her on both cheeks. "Tamara, thank you so much for letting us stay. You're saving us."

"No, you're saving me. I hardly ever see Arie, and Daniel and Carmel can't wait to see Ezra and Noah. They'll be home from school soon. It'll be such fun, all the twins living together. Here, let's do the tour and I'll show you to your rooms."

The twins carried their bags, bounced on their beds, and explored the house until they all met again on the terrace for orange juice.

"It's amazing," Diana said. "Such an enormous garden."

"Not forever, though. You know Arie, he thinks ahead," Tamara said. "The land wasn't very expensive, most people don't like to be by the sea, but he says that will change. He says the location is the best in Israel, even if people don't know it yet. He built the house on one dunam, and he says in a few years he'll build houses on the other three dunams and sell them. That way the profit will pay for our home and a lot more. We'll have got all this for nothing."

"You have to laugh," Peter said, pouring more juice. "The man is extraordinary."

They heard a car crunch up on the gravel, a slamming door, footsteps tapping across the Swedish oak floor, and Arie appeared through the kitchen door, his arms wide. He hugged them all, holding on to Peter for the longest time. "Welcome, brother. I want you to stay for as long as you like. Diana, you'll have your baby here, it'll give us such pleasure, right, Tamara?"

He laid his arm around her shoulder and pulled her to him, kissing her forehead. She smiled at them. "Yes. Yes, it would. And we can help with the boys."

Arie poured himself some orange juice, and brought out a bottle. "Vodka, anyone?" he said, adding a healthy tot to his juice.

"Before lunch?" Peter said.

"Don't you start as well. So what do you think?" he said, throwing his arms wide. "The house that Peugeot built."

"Peugeot? It's such a good business?"

"That and more. The whole car business is booming and we have a finger in every pie. Spare parts. Road construction. Traffic lights. Even radios. I'm putting one in each car I sell, I've done a deal with a new Japanese company called Sony, they make cheap transistor radios. We're putting them in our cars. We're going to be the agent for all their products in Israel, Greece, Cyprus, and Turkey."

"What about construction?" Peter asked.

"That too. A different company though. Remember Natanel, from Herzliya city hall? He's running it for me. It's incredible. Israel's population has trebled in fourteen years. There's never been a country like it. Everyone needs a home and we're building them. It isn't even our money, it's from the bank. As long as we pay back the interest, we're printing money."

"You've done so well," Diana said. "How many people are working for you now?"

Arie laughed. "Let's see, how many fingers do you have? Full-time? Two hundred and eighty-five in Dimona, in the textile factory, another seventy-three at Feather Products. Most of the construction work is done on contract or day work. Cars and related, another two hundred or so, and growing quickly. Food products, with the grocery chain we're setting up, maybe another hundred so far. I'd say all in all pushing a thousand, without construction, with two areas of rapid growth built in."

"And then there's my law practice," Tamara said with mock pride. "I have an assistant and two clients."

That afternoon Peter and Diana unpacked their bags. As they tried a siesta, Peter shifted and sighed, turned and moaned.

"What is it?" Diana said. "What's on your mind?"

"Oh, nothing."

"Come on, tell me," Diana said, sitting up against the wall. "I can't sleep either, I'm too excited. There's so much going on in our lives right now."

"Well, if you must know, it's Arie. He's hardly seen us in three years, but he didn't ask one question about America. Not one. It's all about him. Always was, always will be."

"Oh, don't be silly. Tamara must have told him everything. He was just happy to see us, and he's proud of what he's done. He has a right to be. Let's talk about something else. You still don't know what the Office wants?"

"I have another meeting tonight. With Rafi Eitan. One bit of good news though. The promotion comes with a pay raise. Five percent for the job and five percent for my academic grade. Ten percent."

"Oh good," Diana giggled, and pulled him close. "We'll be able to afford a bigger flat. Maybe as big as this bedroom. Come on, don't look so glum. Laugh." She tickled him under the arms and opened his trousers to tickle his tummy. She kissed him too, and took his hand and placed it inside her T-shirt, and rubbed her big belly against him.

"We can't," Peter said. "Look at you, you're about to burst. I'll crush the baby."

"Oh, Peter dear, use your imagination." She crouched and wagged her tail.

PETER

Later that afternoon Yaacov drove Arie and Peter to their different meetings in town. It was a mostly silent ride, each lost in his thoughts. Arie was guarded about who he was seeing, and what time he'd be home. And Peter was just as guarded, saying only he had to meet his boss at the office.

Peter's first meeting turned out to be not with Eitan but with Amnon Sela, his nemesis, the European Section Chief. Sela couldn't have been more cordial though, congratulating Peter on his degree, inquiring about America, Diana, the twins, making Peter wonder what the catch was: Keep your friends close, keep your enemies closer? Sela made two coffees and put out a saucer of cookies while filling in the background, starting with Cairo's Revolution Day shocker.

"Egypt's new rockets put the fear of God into our leaders. Complete surprise. Where were we? Don't ask. It's the Nazis back up to their usual tricks. Harel wants them stopped once and for all, and at last Ben-Gurion is on board. It's going to get rough. Why are you smiling?"

"Just that I guessed it."

"The lovey-dovey approach with Germany didn't work, Adenauer refused to rein in the German scientists in Egypt. So we have the green light to get rid of them. No German scientists, no Egyptian rockets. Not to mince words, we are going to speak the only language that works with those murdering scum Nazis, their own language—threats and elimination. Yitzhak Shamir's crew in Paris are experts at that. With some help, of course. Not from you though."

He paused, to let it all sink in, waiting for the obvious response from Peter.

"So where do I fit in?"

"Good question. Come with me. Rafi is waiting for you."

When Peter returned to the villa, it was dark. He tiptoed in and found Diana fast asleep, lying on her side with his pillow supporting her belly. He sighed as he gazed at her. It isn't fair, he thought, on her or the boys. But how could he say no? Rafi Eitan had anticipated every reaction and objection so that he was helpless, like a fly in a spider's web. It was good to be on his side though. Rafi and Harel were the best, and they had chosen him to work with them on this crazy coup. A career person would do well to hitch himself to their wagon. Really, how could he say no?

But would Diana see it that way?'

He had to leave in two days.

He lay on his back in the dark, savoring a slight sea breeze from the open window, trying to make sense of the story Eitan had told. It beggared belief. The bottom line was that Adolf Hitler's top Gestapo commando, an SS-Colonel, the toughest, most feared fighter of the Nazi Special Forces, had been recruited by Mossad. He was the first port of refuge for Nazis on the run in Europe, he protected them, and now he was an Israeli agent. What a breakthrough! And Isser Harel and Rafi Eitan wanted him, Peter Nesher, to run him. And to make sure he wasn't a double agent. Because if he was for real, the Nazi scientists, if they could be made to fear for their lives, would fly to the colonel like bees to honey. Or like dogs to shit. And we can pick them off one by one.

He perspired at the thought. Because if he wasn't for real, the commando colonel could probably kill him with one hand.

A car drove up, its door clicked shut. Peter jumped to the window and saw Arie in a pool of light checking his watch. His own showed three thirty. Up to his usual tricks, then.

Peter tiptoed down to meet his brother and found him in the kitchen, pouring a beer.

Arie looked up with a start, almost spilling his drink. "Oh! You'll give me a heart attack, creeping up like that."

"You thought I was Tamara?"

"She's asleep. I hope. One for you?" Arie said, holding out the bottle.

"Sure." Peter filled his glass and gestured with it to the table. "Sit? Talk?"

Arie shrugged. He'd rather sleep, but all right.

Peter walked to the staircase door and closed it. "Don't want to wake anyone," he said.

"What makes me think I'm about to get a lecture," Arie said.

"Why, is there a reason?"

"From you, always. Or have you changed?" He stood at the window, looking into the night. "How about going outside, it's warm tonight and there's a nice breeze."

The brothers refilled their glasses and strolled to the end of the garden. It merged with the public footpath, which led past ferns and rocks to the cliff itself. There they stood as close to the edge as they dared. Below them was a hundred-foot drop onto the rocks and sandy beach of Herzliya, with the dark sea glimmering in the moonlight. They looked up at the galaxies, the fluffy streak of the Milky Way. The calm and the silence were so complete they could almost touch them.

Arie joined Peter on a flat rock they used as a bench. The only sounds were the rippling waves, collapsing onto the sand as they always had and would. Approaching the horizon, the moon was ready to bow out.

There was no lecture. Instead, Peter took Arie's hand in his and held it, possibly for the first time in their adult lives. He stretched his legs, put one foot over the other. The moment stretched into a minute, of contemplation, their thoughts turning inward. Until Peter turned to Arie. They'd never really talked about their parents or their sisters. It was too painful, too mysterious, too hard. A story with a pleasant enough beginning, no middle, and a horrific end. "In the camps," Peter asked at last, "did you ever look up at the sky like this?"

Arie withdrew his hand. "Don't ruin the moment."

After a few seconds Peter said, "Arie, it's 1962, it's been over seventeen years."

The waves lapped and the silence grew. Finally, Arie said, "Peter, it's never over."

There was so much more Peter wanted to ask. Arie had never said a word, not even about his last moments with Mama and Pappi, Renata and Ruth.

Peter had also wanted to tell Arie that he was leaving in two days, to thank him for looking after his family, to ask him to take care of Diana and the new baby. Again he would miss the birth of his child. He wanted to . . .

But Arie stood and walked away, calling over his shoulder, "Come on. It's late."

At eight o'clock Peter walked the two sets of twins to school, sinking into sand where the sidewalk ran out, telling them not to throw stones, and warning Ezra and Noah that when they came home he would not be there. "Back in a few weeks," he said, knowing it could well be much longer.

At the corner, Ezra said, "That's it, Dad, don't come closer." In case he didn't get the message, Noah said, "Say good-bye here." Peter laughed. He remembered, with a pang of conscience, how his parents had embarrassed him in front of his friends. Not that he had many in Germany, he was the only Jew in his class. He'd have died if his parents had come to the school gate.

"It's fine," he said. "I'll see you to the gate."

"No," they both yelled in terror.

"Just kidding. Here, give me a hug. Two hugs and I'll bring presents." Even that wasn't enough. They pressed their bodies against his in puny imitations of an embrace and ran off with Carmel and Daniel, shouting, "see you when you get back, Dad."

He took his time walking back to his brother's home. It was another sunny day with a deep blue sky, a blessed day. He felt satisfaction course through his veins and a glow in his cheeks. I know why I feel so good, he thought. I'm going away with two children and when I come home, I'll have three. In just a few weeks. He felt a surge of gratitude to Diana, of love, of completeness. He was lucky to have her, to have the boys, to be home, to have it all. Yes, he had made the right decision to stay in Israel.

When he reached home Diana was lying in a deck chair facing the sea, her legs in the lap of Tamara, who was stroking and kneading her feet. Her oily toes glistened in the sun. The friends looked up at him, and smiled in a dreamy way. The scene looked comfortable, reassuring, safe.

Diana's hands rested on her belly and her eyes fluttered shut. "I feel sleepy," she whispered.

As Peter gazed at her, with a pensive smile, Tamara said, "Don't worry, Peter. She's in good hands."

PETER

O tto Skorzeny had Willi Stinglwagner hooting with laughter. "I've re-cruited a few people in my time," he boomed in his cavernous voice, "but nothing like this. It was so bad it had to be on purpose. It was either incredibly clever or incredibly stupid."

"Well, it worked," Peter, alias Willi, said, "so please give us the benefit of the doubt."

The scar-faced Gestapo hatchet man turned out to be an excellent ra-conteur with a taste for the best cognac, which he drank prodigiously.

Fittingly, he said, he was in a bar when Mossad initiated the double honey trap. "They wanted a foursome!" he roared.

On a need-to-know basis Peter had not been told how Mossad recruited Skorzeny, whose account now seemed fanciful to him, but he had to admit it was a hilarious story.

A young German couple had just been robbed of all their papers and money and ended up in a bar in Madrid, where Skorzeny was having a drink with his much younger wife, Ilse von Finckenstein, the niece of Hitler's finance minister. After a few drinks she invited the distraught but charming couple to spend the night at her home. There they had a few more drinks and a lot of laughs, but just when things were getting hot and heavy, Skorzeny pulled out a gun, saying calmly, "I know who you are, and I know why you're here. You are Mossad, and you've come to kill me."

At this point Peter was laughing so hard he couldn't hold his glass anymore. "You're making it up," he gasped.

"I swear it on the Führer's life."

"He's already dead. Isn't he?"

"If I told you I'd have to kill you," Skorzeny said. "But let me go on. So the man said, 'You're half right. We're from Mossad, but if we'd come to kill you, you'd have been dead weeks ago.'"

"Probably true," Peter said.

"Yes. Either that, or they would have been dead." Skorzeny raised an eyebrow, and his glass. "Prost."

"Cheers."

Peter was learning what an entertaining dinner companion and host Skorzeny was, but he was still the Nazi who crash-landed a glider on an Italian mountaintop to rescue the former dictator Benito Mussolini; who led his special forces behind American lines, dressed in American uniforms, harassing and killing Allied troops. He may be charming, but he was also six foot four of muscle; he would be a formidable opponent. Peter's conclusion was that if Rafi Eitan was wrong about him he, Peter Nesher, expectant father, was a dead man.

He'd soon find out. The next day one of the German scientists in Egypt who wanted Skorzeny's protection would arrive in Munich—Heinz Krug, who ran an Egyptian front company that shipped vital parts to the scientists. He was near the top of Mossad's hit list. It was a perfect setup. With one proviso.

Was Skorzeny for real? Would he really kill his own people? Why would he? What was his reason for turning? Money? He was already a rich man with an import-export business in Madrid that was his cover to help fleeing Nazis. All of a sudden he loved the Jews after helping kill tens of thousands in Hungary? Not a chance. Yet Rafi Eitan, of all people, trusted him, for now at least.

Eitan wanted Krug killed as a warning to the rest of the scientists that they faced the same fate if they didn't leave Egypt immediately.

They were already scared to death. Mossad had mailed them letter bombs and sent threatening letters to their wives and children. The Germans had hired bodyguards in Cairo and traveled in packs; the luster of high wages and high living was dimming. But still they toiled in Factory 333, developing ballistic missiles to attack the Jewish state. So Mossad decided to turn the screws.

The next day Skorzeny met Krug at Gabelsbergerstrasse 35. Half the block was a construction site. "An attempt at humor, my friend," Skorzeny said. "To put you at your ease. This is the site of the new Egyptian Museum."

Krug didn't smile. Instead his eyes darted every which way, and his lips were tight. "Relax," Skorzeny said. "I have experience in these matters. You will not be harmed."

"My wife got a letter just yesterday from those damn Jews. They're going to kill me, I know it."

"They won't touch you, believe me." Krug got into the Mercedes and Skorzeny pulled away from the building site. There was already a fine layer of dust on the shiny black car. "We'll go somewhere safe to talk, a nice beer garden in the forest. There are two bodyguards in the car behind, they'll follow us everywhere. Your worries are over. You didn't tell anyone you're meeting me?"

"No, of course not."

"You're sure? Not even your wife? Nobody knows?"

"Nobody."

Skorzeny was a fast driver, hard to follow as he wove through the morning traffic, but in the Audi behind, Peter stayed on his tail. Next to him was Boris, a small-arms expert, who kept his eyes on the car ahead and didn't say a word.

Boris had only one duty. In the forest, when Skorzeny took out his revolver to shoot Krug, as planned, he should discreetly cover Skorzeny. If Skorzeny even looked at Peter the wrong way, he should shoot him dead.

But they needn't have worried. Skorzeny even had a good line, which Peter quoted in his operations report as an example of the character of the man. As the four of them walked through the trees, and Krug wondered where the beer garden was, Skorzeny said, "You know I said I won't let the Jews hurt you?"

"Yes. I appreciate that."

"Well, it's true. They won't. I will."

He slid out his silenced pistol and shot Krug in the back of the head, which sent him crashing into a tree, leaving blood on the bark. He confirmed the kill with a bullet to the heart.

They rolled Krug into the hole waiting for him and poured acid over him. After twenty minutes they poured lime over the remains to ward off sniffing dogs and wild animals. They covered him with earth, leaves, and branches and carried a heavy log so that there would be no drag marks and laid it on top.

They were panting now; it had been hard work. Peter was bent double, hands on knees, drawing big breaths, Boris was leaning against a tree, wiping his brow with the back of his hand.

Otto Skorzeny pulled on his black leather gloves and stood ramrod straight. "Right," he said. "Let's go find that beer garden."

A Löwenbräu with the Nazi killer was the last thing Peter wanted. He was unnerved by a spasm of hatred and distaste for the man. It was the leather gloves that had done it. He had noticed with all the Nazis he had the misfortune to work with: they all wore leather gloves. It must be some sort of last nod to their glory days. They felt no shame or sorrow. They didn't regret what they had done; they only regretted that they had lost the war.

Still wary, Peter kept three steps behind Skorzeny as they followed the narrow track back to the cars. Now that the deed was done he wanted nothing more than to leave Germany. He didn't have much time.

Krug would be reported as missing within hours. He needed to use that time to put as much distance as possible between himself and Otto Skorzeny.

But although the standard follow-up to an assassination was to fly straight back to Israel, Mossad was moving fast, and Peter had more work to do.

So they decided to keep him in Germany.

A decision he would regret forever.

DIANA

TEL AVIV, ISRAEL

October 1962

———————

Doctor Max Shilanski was in a hurry to get to Haifa for Yom Kippur with his parents. But his patient had only dilated five centimeters, and he couldn't hand her over to a colleague because they'd all left already to be at home for the holiest day of them all, the Day of Atonement.

Diana Nesher had been pushing and screaming on and off for seven hours. She was sweating, her face was scarlet, and she was yelling in English, a language Doctor Shilanski didn't speak. But while languages differed, mothers didn't. What else could she be yelling but "Baby, come already!"

The contraction passed with no more dilation. Diana was moaning and cursing Peter for being a man and not having to go through this agony. If men did this there would be no procreation, the species would be extinct in a generation. And good riddance, if this was what it took. And where was he, anyway? Peter, get your ass back here! "Aaaaarrrggghh!" she yelled, this time not in agony but in frustration.

Nurse Hannah ran back into the room to find Diana desperate for water. Hannah supported her so she could drink until Diana fell back with a gasp. "How long?" she managed to ask.

"It's been seven hours," the nurse said.

"I mean, how much longer?"

"Soon, my dear. It'll get easier."

"That's easy for you to say. Oh!" Another contraction, longer even, more screaming. With dilation at six centimeters, Diana asked as the nurse mopped her brow, "How do you know it gets easier? Have you had any babies?"

"Seven."

"Oh my God," Diana said, "how could you? Aaaaarrrggghhh!"

"Push, push, that's it, push now."

Baby wasn't quite ready yet.

In the waiting room Tamara peered at each nurse that emerged from the obstetrics department. When one walked by with a bundle under her arm she sat up but it was just some laundry. Arie kept looking at his watch. "I'll have to go soon," he said, "baby or no baby."

"Business?"

"Yes."

"Business right before Yom Kippur?"

"No rest for the wicked."

"You said it."

"I'll see you at home, then. I'll be with the children."

Diana's children, Noah and Ezra, were at the house, with Tamara's parents, who were babysitting them and their cousins, nine-year-old Carmel and Daniel. Tamara telephoned them each hour on the hour to keep them informed. If Tamara was anxious for the delivery, her parents couldn't wait for the birth either. "These are the worst behaved children I've ever met," Rachel complained. "They don't listen to a word I say. Now they're playing by the cliff. It's a wonder they don't fall off."

"Don't push them," Tamara said.

"I can't promise. How is Diana doing?"

"I don't know. They're not very communicative here, everyone wants to go home and Diana is holding them up. Anyway . . . wait a minute, here comes the doctor." She held the phone away from her lips while Rachel strained to hear.

Doctor Shilanski tapped along the corridor toward her, unbuttoning his white coat with one hand, carrying a small case in the other. He looked relieved; his replacement had just arrived.

"It's a girl. Healthy, 3.2 kilos. Just in time for Yom Kippur."

Tamara shrieked into the telephone. "Did you hear that, Ima? A girl, healthy." And to the doctor: "And Diana?"

"Who?"

"The mother."

"Fast asleep. Everything is hunky-dory. The nurse will take over from here. I suggest you go home before the roads close. There's nothing more to be done here now."

Tamara could hardly talk with excitement but called Gingie at the Office. "It's a girl. 3.2 kilos. Mommy and baby are fine. You'll tell Peter?"

"Of course, right away. That's wonderful news. Thank you for calling, Tamara. *Tsom Kal*." Easy fast. The traditional Yom Kippur wish when Jews prayed and fasted for twenty-four hours. The whole country shut down for the day. Nobody worked, every shop and business was closed, cars were not allowed on the road.

It wasn't until the next day's telexed message drop routinely rerouted through an Office diamond company in Antwerp that Peter heard. "Healthy girl. Congratulations."

At first he was confused, he didn't recognize the secret code until he realized, No! It isn't code, it's his baby! A girl! A second message followed, an apparent afterthought: "Mother doing well." In his hotel room he walked to and fro, smacking a fist into his palm, grinning at himself in the mirror, until he could burst with delight. He had to force himself not to break protocol and call home. He went downstairs to the hotel bar and despite the early hour ordered a glass of German Sekt, cheaper than French champagne.

He'd done it! They'd wanted a girl, and now they had one. Perfect. Two boys and a girl. If only he could have been there. And his parents, and Renata and Ruth. He glanced at his watch, Pappi's watch. The silver frame was dull and the leather strap, which he couldn't bring himself to change, was faded and worn. Its presence, its weight, gave Pappi shape, preserved the hope that somewhere his father could still be alive, and one day he could finally give the watch back. The watch told more than the time, it told the truth; he hoped.

One day. Well anyway, the children have grandparents in Britain, they'd be visiting soon. With his elbows on the polished wooden bar, viewing himself in the mirror with the empty room behind him, and savoring the bubbly, he ran through names for a girl. He'd always liked Kim. Or Yasmine. How about Cornelia? He wasn't very good at this. Or Veronique, or Karla? No, that wasn't funny, that part of Diana's life was over. Should she even continue on the Office desk? Would she want to stay at home? They'd need another bedroom. They'd have to get a bigger apartment. Oh, how about Hagar, that's a beautiful name for a beautiful girl.

He made a face in the mirror. Why bother? Diana will decide, she always does. And then he remembered he shouldn't be drinking. It was Yom Kippur.

He strolled along the banks of the sparkling River Rhine, killing time until his meeting with Lothar Genscher, of the ministry for nuclear energy. Men and women ran by in their athletics shorts. A young father cooed in his baby's ear. Soon that could be me, Peter thought with a grin. He pictured his baby in Diana's arms, tiny lips clamped to her mother's nipple, Diana's eyes closed in bliss, kissing the baby's head. But this idyllic image soon turned to what Genscher had told him in their last meeting, one reason he had to stay longer in Germany. As his mind turned from breast milk to terror, he snorted: Crazy. The two sides of Peter Nesher.

Israel already knew that the Egyptians were developing a surface-to-surface missile with a warhead containing radioactive waste that could pollute entire regions of Israel. Genscher's shock, however, was that the Egyptians, or rather their German scientists, wanted to use highly enriched uranium from Dutch or West German centrifuges to build an atomic bomb.

After receiving documentary evidence from Genscher, Peter had another task: to travel to Freiburg on the Swiss-German border to take charge of an Office team that was tailing a target. The idea was to take it down a notch. They wouldn't kill the scientist, who was in Egypt, but they would terrify his daughter until she demanded he come home. This should snowball until all the scientists, understanding that even Otto Skorzeny couldn't keep them safe, would leave Egypt and put an end to the Egyptian's weapons program. That was the plan.

And the quicker, the better. All he really wanted was to get back to Diana and the children.

Diana was dozing and the baby was back in its crib, yet she could still feel its weight on her chest. She was a perfect fit, her head lay on her breast, her tiny feet reached Diana's tummy, her little hands rested on Diana's face. Most of all Diana loved the warmth of her sigh, like a whisper, when she pulled away from the nipple, and the thought made Diana sigh too. She lay on her back with a drowsy smile. After Yom Kippur the twins would come to meet their sister.

She felt warm between the legs, and that warmth made her feel warm all over, and complete and joyful at the miracle that had emerged from her womb. She was still half-asleep and felt the warmth on her hand and it was only when she brought her hand from beneath the sheets that she realized the warm ooze was blood. With her other hand she felt her thighs and the damp that had spread to the sheets. Her heart began to race as she called for the nurse. She looked around: the other five beds were empty. She called again and after a minute a young nurse came in with a smile. "What is it, sweetie?"

"Where is Hannah?" Diana said.

"Oh, she'll be home by now. I'm on duty. I'm Nurse Nastasiya. What is it?"

"I think I'm bleeding."

"That's normal, let me see." She lifted the sheet and blanket. "Yes, it's fine, I'll change you." She dropped the soiled pad into a bin, washed Diana with a damp cloth and put in a fresh pad. "There, clean and fresh. Would you like a drink?"

Diana shook her head. "I'm sleepy. Can I see my baby?"

"Not yet, he's sleeping . . ."

"She," Diana murmured.

"Yes, she's sleeping, I'll bring her back in three hours, you try to rest now." But Diana was already drifting away.

Until a sharp pain pierced her sleep, it cut into her stomach like a knife. She woke with a start and put her hands to her tummy. Now it was aching, like a bruise. She didn't want to call the nurse, but it scared her. If only there were other women in the ward. She felt alone and afraid. After five minutes she called the nurse. After two more minutes she called again, and then again.

"Sorry," Nastasiya said as she finally hurried in, "we had an issue at the other end of the ward. I'm here alone, Yom Kippur, you know. What is it?"

Diana's voice was faint and unclear. "My stomach hurts, it's a sharp pain and then an ache."

"It's the last of the placenta, the uterus, all normal, here, have a drink, no need to worry. Try to sleep."

"I was asleep, but it hurts. It hurts right now."

"I can give you a painkiller but it's better not to." She patted Diana's wrist to reassure her.

Diana shifted in the bed and wiped her brow. "I feel a bit clammy."

"You do look a bit pale. But really, there's nothing to worry about . . ."

"Aren't I supposed to look glowing and healthy?" Diana said, catching her breath. "I feel terrible. And my stomach hurts a lot."

"Well, you need to rest, let's wait and see if it goes away. If it doesn't, I can give you a painkiller. Here, drink if you feel like it." She left a glass of water at Diana's bedside and her footsteps became fainter.

Diana lay back, breathing heavily, trying not to panic. She should ask to see the doctor. She couldn't call Tamara, it was Yom Kippur and she wouldn't answer the phone. Nobody was working in the whole country, except presumably the most junior staff in hospitals and the like. Nurse Nastasiya doesn't seem to know much. How old is she, twelve? A painkiller and a glass of water. How many years of medical training does it take to come up with that?

She tried to sleep but sensed that warm ooze between her legs again. She felt blood. And now she felt woozy, as if the room was spinning. She closed her eyes but it was worse. She opened them and the room steadied but now she felt breathless. Something wrong? Or just panic? She wanted to call the nurse but didn't want to be a nuisance, obviously she has a lot on her plate. And what does she know, anyway?

She thought of Peter. His grin and wide eyes when he would see their tiny daughter, her hand the size of his thumb. He would kiss the baby and lie down next to them and she would sleep with her hand on his cheek, as she always did, and he would sleep with his hand on her stomach, as he always did.

She felt her strength ebbing, her breaths were short and rasping. She called for the nurse. She could barely hear herself.

"I feel awful," Diana said, when the nurse finally appeared. "Do I have a fever?"

"No, you're just warm from sleep."

"No. There's something wrong. Please, can I see the doctor?"

"He's very busy. He'll be doing his round in the morning. No need before that, everything is fine." The nurse patted Diana's hand. "You're fine, really, just very tired. It's natural."

"I'm worried. Do I have a temperature?"

"I'll check if you like. But there's really no need. Let me see." She put the back of her hand on Diana's forehead and withdrew it with a start. "You're burning," she said. She took a thermometer from her gown. "Put this under your tongue."

She left the room and came back with two pills and more water. "The doctor says to take these and he'll come by as soon as he can. Don't worry, dear, everything is all right. He's just a bit busy right now, he's the only doctor here today."

Diana was white and sweating. Nastasiya began to change the pad, and the towel she had put beneath her. Both were soaked in blood.

Nurse Nastasiya took Diana's pulse. Her lips tightened. "Very slow," she muttered. She took her temperature, Diana saw concern on her face.

"What is it?" she whispered, gripping the nurse's wrist. "My stomach is really bad, it hurts a lot."

She wiped her brow. The sweat was cold. She was dizzy and closed her eyes and felt worse, everything was spinning. She began to panic. Where's the damn doctor? She felt blood between her legs, the whole bed was wet.

"Nurse. Nurse. What's wrong?" Her face was as white as the sheet. "I need a doctor." She tried to shout, "Now!"

But the nurse was already running down the corridor, yelling, "Doctor, Doctor."

"Peter, Peter." The words barely passed Diana's lips. An unbearable sadness weighed upon her, she sank into the sheets, into a void, her fingers searching for her baby. Come little baby, what is your name, I have milk for you. What's happening to me? Peter, come to me, where are you, I need you, now . . .

The tapping of rapid footsteps, a face, a man's face, peering at her. A sharp pain in her arm, an injection. Everything blurred, Diana's eyelids fluttered and closed, she sighed, her lips curled with the beginning of a smile.

Bonn airport was closest but there was a quicker, direct connection from Frankfurt, an hour forty drive away in the rented Mercedes, which should get him there in time, if he raced. An Office contact met him with his flight ticket, and to return his car, which saved Peter another twenty minutes, and an El Al official raced him through VIP check-in straight to the aircraft. As he entered the plane the steps pulled back and the door closed.

From receiving the message a hundred miles away to takeoff it took two and a half hours. Couldn't be quicker, he thought smugly. He hadn't even checked out of his hotel room, that would be taken care of. Lucky he always carried his passport. The message from the Office was to return home instantly, and he'd taken them at their word. They had bought him a business-class ticket too, things were looking up.

But what was the hurry? Was it to get him back to Israel or out of Germany? If it was to leave Germany, then something must have gone wrong somewhere and he had to get out before he was arrested. But what? Maybe it wasn't only to do with him but a related operation?

And if it was to get back to Israel, why? Skorzeny? Must be something to do with him. He's not a person who can be handled. Diana would have never shaken his hand. She'd have shot him.

No complaints though, this way he'd get to see his baby sooner.

He fell asleep, playing with names for his little girl, and woke only with the loud clapping that greeted each successful landing in the Holy Land. Why did passengers always do that? He never joined in. Was it such a surprise the pilot landed the plane? Nobody ever applauded him for doing his job.

As Peter walked down the airplane steps he saw a familiar face from the Office, a young woman who worked in the reception area. That's strange, he thought, but knew better than to ask her what was going on. She wouldn't know anyway. She had been sent to fetch him, that's all she would know.

They drove in an airport car from the plane straight to the VIP lounge. Why here? This was not good. He felt his heartbeat. Wary now, he followed the woman past the sofas and chairs, where a politician he recognized was drinking coffee with a group of people, probably reporters, leaning forward with notebooks in their hands.

He followed the young woman into a small room, and stopped in confusion, as she said, "I'll be outside," and closed the door.

Waiting for him were Arie and Tamara, her eyes red and swollen. She held a handkerchief in her hand. Arie looked like a ghost.

Peter went cold and felt he would vomit.

"What is it?" he said.

"What is it?" he said again, when they didn't answer.

Arie's face crumpled. He stepped forward and took Peter into his arms. "I'm sorry, Peter. I'm so sorry."

"But what is it, tell me, is it my baby, what's wrong?"

Tamara burst into tears. "No, Peter," she said. "It's Diana. Diana died."

Peter froze. Not a muscle twitched, not an eyebrow rose, he didn't blink. Slowly his eyes met Arie's, who fought to compose himself. Peter didn't feel Tamara's arms around him, he heard nothing, he didn't know that he was drinking water from a glass. He didn't know that he had lowered himself onto the sofa and was lying on his back, eyes fixed on nothing, breathing deeply and loudly.

"Peter. Peter?" Arie said.

Peter's heart thudded, harder and faster, the beat in his head got louder and rattled his skull, like a howl. He tried to stand but fell back. All he said was, "No, no."

A doctor sedated Peter with an injection and they took him home.

Waves broke against a seawall, again and again, throwing up a plume of spray, which turned black. A river rose and rose and filled a canyon until it became a dam that burst, carrying with it houses and cars and people flailing and struggling against rapids breaking against huge rocks. Men struggled to breathe, little dots, they sucked in air and called for help as they went under. A baby screamed and that was too much.

Peter started awake in the dark, panting. There was breathing next to him. He didn't understand and felt with his arm but the sleeping figure came awake and it was Arie. "Peter, Peter, are you okay?" He took Peter's arm and shook it.

"Is it true?"

"Yes, Peter. I'm so sorry, it is."

"Do the boys know?"

"No, they don't. We thought we should wait till you were home. We'll tell them if you like. Tamara will."

"No. No. I will. But what happened? Oh, God. They said she was fine."

"I don't understand much, the doctors will tell you. There was internal bleeding, a huge amount, and I think they didn't realize in time. Of course, they'll never admit it. She went into shock, and then cardiac arrest. And it was Yom Kippur, a skeleton staff, they didn't react quickly enough. They tried electric shock but it didn't work. That's what I understood. I may be wrong."

"You mean they could have saved her?"

"I don't know. I don't want to say that. What time is it?" He took his watch from the side table. "Six o'clock. You slept eight hours."

"Why are you in my bed, anyway?"

"In case the boys came in and you didn't know they didn't know."

The brothers fell silent. Peter tried to void his mind, but Diana filled him. Everything in the room held her. Light streaming through the curtains lit her bottles and brushes on the night stand, her dress draped over the chair, white with a blue trim, her glasses on an open book, a pile of shoes. He could never get her to put them away.

They had only been in this bedroom for a couple of months, but already it was soaked with her presence. He felt small and alone. He should stay in bed. He should get up. And then: "The baby. Where's the baby?"

"In the hospital. It's all been so quick."

Peter stood slowly. "You undressed me?"

"Of course. We put you to bed. How do you feel?"

Peter looked at him and shook his head.

"Sorry," Arie said.

"I want to see her. Diana. Where is she? I want to see Diana." A sob welled into his throat and his eyes filled.

There was a commotion and running footsteps and the door flew open. "Daddy, let's go and get Mummy and the baby. Are they coming home today?" Noah and Ezra fell onto the bed, pulling Peter down with them, already fighting. Noah had Ezra around the neck and Ezra was kicking and squirming and pulling Peter by the arm. "Come on, Dad, you're on my side."

"Uncle Arie, you're with me!" Noah shouted.

"No, I have to go downstairs." Arie gently closed the door.

In the kitchen, Tamara looked at him. He shrugged. Their children came in and sat silently, without touching their orange juice. Her mother, Rachel, came in, disheveled and bent. "Moshe had to go to the paper," she said. They had stayed over since the news.

Upstairs the bedroom had gone silent.

They heard the door open, slow light steps, and the boys' door closed after them. They looked upstairs, and at each other.

If they were two lines on a graph, this was where time and emptiness crossed.

Ten minutes later they heard Peter go into the boys' room, and after a few minutes more the three of them came down the stairs, holding hands.

Carmel and Daniel didn't know where to look, or what to do. The adults couldn't meet each other's eyes. They all stood in the living room, looking lost, as if they needed an introduction. Carmel moved first. She went to Noah, whispered in his ear, and put her arms around him, and Daniel followed with Ezra. They moved closer until the cousins were all embracing, one body with many arms.

Peter had to look away: my parents and sisters were murdered, my cousins, aunts and uncles too, and now my wife is gone. He rubbed at his eyes as Arie put an arm around his shoulder.

Peter broke the silence. "We'd like to go to the hospital. To collect our baby." His voice trailed off. "And see Diana one more time."

Tamara and Arie exchanged glances. The boys too? They're only eight years old. "Of course," Tamara said. "We'll take you there."

"I'll drive," Arie said.

At Ichilov hospital Arie took care of the formalities until an orderly appeared in the waiting room and took Peter and his sons, accompanied by Arie and Tamara, to the morgue. It was only as their hollow steps echoed in the long basement corridor that Peter had second thoughts. Should the boys really see their mother laid out on a slab? He could hardly bear it, how could they? What was best? He didn't know. What would Diana have said? That, he did know.

He stopped, putting his hands on the boys' shoulders. "I know," he said. "Do you want to see the baby? Before me?"

"Yes, yes."

"All right, lucky you! Arie, would you and Tamara mind taking the boys to the ward, and I'll be up there very soon? I think that's probably best."

"I think so too," Tamara said. "Much better. Come on, boys, let's go find your little sister. I think we can take her home today."

Home. The word was a wound. Peter put his hand to his heart, and Tamara understood: How empty had that word become.

"Thank you. I'll be right along." Peter tried to keep it light, for the boys' sake. "Think of a name for your sister," he called after them as their footsteps faded.

"All right, let's go," he said to the orderly, and turned away from his children, to find his wife in the bare white room.

Her eyes and mouth were closed, her skin was pale as alabaster, her chest was still. She looked composed, arranged, as if waiting for the kiss of life. Her hair glowed copper beneath the dim bulb. A green hospital sheet covered her from ankles to shoulders, which were bare: a delicate marble carving with cold white feet. On her throat lay her silver name chain: Diana, the Roman goddess of childbirth. From her big toe hung a paper disc with the number b274.

Peter gazed at the frozen features of his beautiful wife, his rapid breathing the only sound, until finally he kissed Diana's icy lips and sank to his knees in despair.

BABY

Three days later, on Friday the twenty-sixth, Arie's twins Daniel and Carmel were twelve years old, but there was no party. Two days after that Noah and Ezra were nine, and they missed out too. The family came together not to celebrate but to sit shiva, the seven days of mourning.

Peter's baby entered a silent house. Tamara held her whenever she was awake, fed her milk from a bottle, and did everything but surround her with joy. She worried about that. Would the poor little child have enough love? Who would look after her when she went back to work? Tamara's law firm had allowed her a month to help at home, but then what? She worried about Peter, who slept most of the time. Would he have to change his job? His Mossad boss, Isser Harel, had visited the shiva twice and told Peter to take all the time he needed, but what else could he say? She didn't know exactly what work Peter did, but he couldn't leave the country for months at a time anymore. He was a widower now with three small children; his life would have to change. But could he do that? He was a man of contradictions. Peter was gentle and considerate but he was intimidating too; hard and calculating. What had Harel meant when he said Israel was a safer place because of Peter. Why? What did he really do at Mossad?

Anyway, his work would have to change.

When Arie had offered him a job Peter had scoffed. "What can I do for you?" he had said. "I'm no businessman."

"You'll learn," Arie replied. "It's time you made some real money."

"But what could I do? I'm not a lawyer or an accountant. What do I know?"

"That's not the point. I buy lawyers and accountants. What I need most are smart people I can trust. You can join me in the head office, I'll put you at the top of one of my companies. You bring integrity, I know how much they value you at the Office, you earned that. You have no idea how much I need you."

"It's too soon to talk about it, Arie. But thanks, I'll think about it."

That evening, the day after the shiva ended, the four twins wanted to make a joint announcement. While Hadassah, the maid, cleared away the dinner dishes, Daniel asked for silence, and waited for everyone to settle down. Peter sat on a sofa with Tamara and Arie, Moshe and Rachel sat on the other one, Ido and Estie sat on cushions on the floor, and the baby slept in her bassinet, which Tamara carried with her everywhere.

"Shut up," Noah said to Ezra, "stop pushing."

"You shut up," Ezra replied.

Carmel pushed them both. "Sssshh."

Daniel stood by the crib, looking down at the infant girl and played with her hand. He's looking more and more like his father, Peter thought. He's got Arie's broad shoulders. He's twelve, bar mitzvah next year, he'll be a strong young man.

While the baby yawned and stretched, Daniel said, "Everybody, it's time the baby had a name, and we have decided what it is." He looked around as if expecting applause.

"What?" Peter said with his first smile in eight days. "You decided?"

"Yes, all of us together. Noah said that at the hospital you told him and Ezra to think of a name for the baby. So we did."

"That's true," Peter said, nodding at everyone. "I did. But that doesn't mean I'll agree."

"You have to," Noah said. "Whose baby is it?"

"Mine."

"Ours," Ezra said.

"The parents decide," Tamara said, and flushed at her blunder. "I mean . . . do you have a name, Peter?"

"No. We didn't talk about it."

"Well, we have a name, don't we?" Daniel said, and the cousins said in a chorus, "Yes."

"All right," Peter said. This was so sweet of them. "What is it?"

"Diana."

The air seemed to suck out from the room. "Diana," Peter murmured. Diana. His eyes stung, he told himself, Do not cry. But still a tear escaped.

Little Diana's deep brown eyes, wide and unwavering, were fixed on his, and he could have sworn they were smiling.

PETER

Far out, a sheet of rain dappled the sea. Clouds were thinning, announc-
ing another glorious spring day, releasing the sweet jasmine Peter loved
so much. On his balcony, as leaves rustled in the breeze, he breathed in
deeply, holding little Diana tightly to his chest. Snug inside her pink blanket, she breathed quietly, her lips forming a perfect heart. Peter drew the
bottle from her mouth and went back inside, lost in thought.

There was an eruption from the kitchen, running, yelling, doors slamming, and the boys were gone for the day.

The bell rang. He sipped his coffee, gathered up Diana's bags, and went
to the door. "Good morning, Rachel," he greeted Tamara's mother. "Here
she is. She has eaten, I just changed her diaper, she'll probably sleep for an
hour. She likes the new toy." It was a red wooden ball on the end of a stick
and something inside made the noise of shaken rice. He rattled it by Diana's
head, but Rachel grabbed his hand. "Don't wake her! What time, four
o'clock? Will you collect her or shall I bring her?"

"I don't know, I'll let you know. Today is decision day."

Peter locked the door, and fell on the sofa. He looked at his watch and
stared out the window. He had to leave in an hour. A bird fluttered onto
the flower box, strutted along the edge, jutted its head to and fro, and lifted

off. He went to the bathroom and ran the shower. The water was cold but he hardly noticed. What to do?

He'd been working with Arie for two months and was bored out of his mind. He just couldn't get excited about flowcharts, asset and debit columns, and union negotiations. His instinct with a whining clerk was a two-knuckle stab in the throat and if that didn't shut him up, then an elbow to the temple. Still, it kept him at home with the children and paid exactly double his government salary. Now Arie had said his apprenticeship was over and he should take the reins of the new plastics company, a sector set to explode, using techniques developed in West German laboratories adapted to Middle Eastern conditions. There wasn't a single thing we use, Arie said, that couldn't be manufactured in plastic. Cheaper, more durable, easier to clean, available in any color, flexible, waterproof, doesn't corrode, strong; in short, the miracle product of our age. Plastic outdoor furniture, plastic indoor everything, Arie said, there's the future. Israel's economy is booming. Per capita income is 820 dollars, the highest in this part of the Middle East. Grow with it! One in twenty-five owns a car. "You'll get a company Peugeot. A 404 sedan!"

But set against that was a bizarre twist at the Office. His tragedy at home had saved him from the catastrophe at work.

The operation he had been set to take over in Freiburg had turned into one of Mossad's greatest fiascoes, and ended Isser Harel's career. Ben-Gurion had forced him to resign.

Instead of collapsing with fear, the German scientist's daughter they had threatened had gone straight to the police, who arrested the Mossad spies. Harel's entire black program of threats and murder buttressed by lies to the media had been blown wide open, to the fury of the prime minister, who was most concerned with maintaining West Germany's secret flow of weapons to Israel, and cementing relations with the German government. Try doing that while Mossad was murdering German civilians.

Harel's replacement, General Meir Amit, who doubled as the head of military intelligence, wanted a Mossad veteran to take over a key new unit, someone he already knew and everyone trusted: Peter Nesher.

But was he playing hard to get? The idea that he preferred to run a plastics company and look after his daughter had to be a negotiating ploy.

"What does he really want?" Amit asked his new colleagues. "Ask him," Yehuda Shur, the muscleman analyst turned field agent turned head of training, said. "He'll tell you, you won't find a straighter arrow than Nesher, or smarter. But remember, his wife just died. One of ours. In her time she was an excellent field agent. She died after giving birth. Six months ago."

"And since then he's been working with his brother?"

"It took him a couple of months to get back on his feet. But since then, yes."

"I know him, Arie Nesher. A piece of work. He'll throw money at Peter to keep him."

"Yes," Yehuda said. "But if there's one person that money can't buy, it's Peter Nesher."

"All right. Get him in here."

Major-General Amit still had to get used to the idea that outside the army people didn't salute every order. So by the time Peter arrived, three days later, Amit's first words were, "Where were you?"

"At home with my daughter. And at work." He felt no need to apologize. But no need to be rude either. "And how are you settling in?"

Amit stared at him. Settling in? Who cared? In the army it wasn't relevant. All that mattered was the job you did. These prima donnas needed their feathers trimmed.

"How do you think I settled in? The first thing I found on my desk was a letter signed by the top Mossad agents in Europe complaining about everything, especially me. Then four of the senior people here resign because Harel's gone. And now I hear you're selling plastic garden chairs while we're fighting for Israel's survival."

"It's tough, but someone has to do it. Sell garden chairs, I mean."

Amit had to smile. He had read Peter's file and it confirmed everything he had already heard. Nesher was an intelligence man through and through, with a brief but successful military background; a meticulous planner who, in the field, improvised brilliantly; thorough, imaginative, and reliable; admired by his colleagues, recommended by Ben-Gurion himself. He needed this man. He changed his tack.

"You liked Harel?"

"We all did. I admired him. He was good to me."

"But?"

"Is there a but?"

"Don't be cagey with me, Nesher."

"So be specific. What do you want to know?"

"I want to know what the next move is with the German scientists you were involved with. You're the expert on Nazis, what should we do? Killing them is out."

"Personally, sir, I never thought it was in. That was the policy, so we did it, but now that it's been abandoned, I do think there is another way, which I always thought was the better one . . ."

"Carry on."

They were sitting now in the corner suite around the coffee table, drinking Botz, the thick Israeli coffee that translates as "mud." The new director general of Mossad had told his secretary to hold all non-urgent calls except from the prime minister's office, and had suppressed a smile while Nesher phoned Rachel to say he'd be late picking up Diana.

Morality didn't concern Amit, so they moved past that controversy with an acknowledgment that Nazi vermin could be useful too. Peter's elimination of two of them was described and welcomed. The tradecraft, the running of the agents, was routine. The role of Veronique and Karla interested Amit as precursors of the honey trap. He knew that the agent Diana Greenberg had become Peter's wife, and now had died. Peter's disagreement with, but ultimate acceptance of, Harel's intimidation and murder program was understood and the program's effectiveness assessed, and the prime minister's anger explained.

"Harel tried to scare the German scientists into leaving, but there's another way, which I argued in the beginning. For most of them it isn't about being Nazis or fighting Jews or helping Nasser, most of them were simply enticed with high salaries to do work they loved and couldn't do anywhere else. As simple as that. So they moved to Cairo. They're more like high-level economic migrants. All we need to do is find a way to offer them even more money, but above all challenging and interesting work, and they'll come home. That's all. The German government should help with funds and projects."

"That would free up a lot of our resources too," Amit added as he made notes. "We need to focus on new areas, and that's what I want to talk to you about. But first I have to know if you're in or out."

Peter laughed. The phrase rang a bell. "The last time someone said that to me was Rafi Eitan, when I finished my studies in the U.S. What, eight months ago? He wanted to know whether I'd come back to the Office. And that's where I am again today."

He fell silent. He was wrong. That was not where he was today.

Then, he and Diana had had to decide what kind of a life they would lead together. Now he had to decide what kind of a life he would live alone.

Everything was different. He was forty years old and lonely. The best part of his life was over. What woman wants a morose man with three children and no money? He physically ached for Diana, he became nauseous when he dwelt on her. When he lay awake at night he felt like going to the hospital with a pistol. The doctors had denied all responsibility, they had hidden together behind a smokescreen of jargon, but he had rejected Arie's offer of a lawyer. Would it bring her back? It was over. Move on. That's what Diana would have wanted: a loving home for her children, not a bitter, unhappy father torturing himself over how to make those bastards pay.

Rachel was an angel. She had stepped in, changed her whole life, and looked after little Diana every day. And Tamara . . . well; Tamara. His brother's wife.

Don't go there.

"Well?" he heard.

Peter snapped back. To the corner office with windows facing the boulevard, framed photographs of fighter jets swooping low over Tel Aviv and tanks bursting through clouds of sand, a picture of Amit's mentor, Moshe Dayan, a finger rubbing behind his black eye patch over a crooked smile.

"Well?" Amit repeated. "In or out?"

"Can I be frank, sir?"

"Of course. That's what I want, your reputation precedes you."

Peter sighed. He didn't like to bring this up, but he had to. "It's about my personal circumstances. It shouldn't count, but it does."

"Of course, it always does. It must."

"Yes. Well. Right now I'm relying on family help, my sister-in-law's mother . . ." He stopped. He hated this. "I'm sorry, this has nothing to do with you. The fact is, on my salary here, I just couldn't afford the help I need at home. I have three children with no mother. The hours, all day and night, traveling away from home for weeks at a time . . ."

"Nesher. Stop right there. Look, I'm new here, but the army, Mossad, we're all in this world together. We help each other, we're a family. Whatever you need to make this work, you'll get. Frankly, we need you. The threats against Israel have entered a new stage. Economically and militarily we have never been in such a strong and stable position. But our enemies are stronger too. They are uniting under Nasser. They'll finish Hitler's job if they get half a chance. Our job is to think ahead and that's where we need you. The local Arabs, the so-called 'Palestinians,' are organizing, saboteurs are attacking across our borders almost daily, from Jordan, Syria, Gaza, pinpricks so far but they will become a more serious threat. I am forming a new unit to deal precisely with their activities abroad. Shin Bet and Aman will deal with them at home, I want you to be in charge of all anti-Palestinian activities outside Israel. Of course there will be considerable overlap, and I want you also to coordinate all domestic and foreign activities. It's a big job, and it is also the job of the future. You will be a department head. It prepares you for a senior executive role in Mossad. You will travel less. It's a significant promotion that comes with a significant salary increase, and there are ways to bump that up too. You will have more money than you need to care for your children. A lot more. I want you, Peter. We need you."

Amit laid a hand on Peter's shoulder. "The business of plastic chairs will take care of itself. Israel's security will not."

ARIE and TAMARA

TEL AVIV, ISRAEL

January 1964

It all blew up with a short gossip item on page nineteen of *The Jerusalem Post*'s weekend edition. The gossip column, a popular weekly feature, listed who was seen where and with whom, and sucked up to politicians, businessmen, and artists, praising their speeches and promoting their performances. Ido, keen to improve his English, read it every Friday. Moshe hated the column because its puerile tittle-tattle had many more readers than his consequential political analysis in *Davar*; he claimed it was just a way for the page editor to get free concert tickets and access to society parties.

"Look, Dad," Ido called across the room. "Is this true about Arie?"

"Everything's true about your brother-in-law," Moshe said, without looking up from his newspaper.

"This better not be, though."

"What do you mean? Read it out loud. We'll see if my English is good enough."

In heavily accented English, rumbling his Rs and lengthening his vowels, Ido read: "Tel Aviv society's worst-kept secret was on open display at the Cameri Theatre Wednesday night when business big shot Arie Nesher left in the intermission with longtime 'very close friend' swimsuit designer

Gila Goldfarb. They emerged hand in hand, apparently too impatient to wait for the end of Sammy Gronemann's smash hit *The King and the Cobbler*."

Ido looked over at Moshe, whose face was as set as the Sphinx.

"Very close friend," Ido said. "Is that true, Dad? Holding hands?"

"Don't tell Tamara," Moshe said.

But Tamara already knew. Three women she rarely heard from couldn't wait to tell her: "You must feel awful." "Everyone's talking about it." "Poor you."

"What a bastard," the fourth caller, Cindy, from her law firm, said. "I didn't see it myself, Rafi Kabiljo told me. His wife told him."

So he was with that bitch again Wednesday, after he'd sworn it was over. And he hadn't come home last night. He'll be home tonight, though, for the Sabbath meal; he never misses that, his so-called "family time."

Well, we'll see about that.

The ball of fire sank beneath the sea, the sky was ablaze in streaks of orange and crimson. Arie's face glowed in its reflection, and the bouquets of red and yellow roses he held in each hand seemed like a celebration of the heavens. They should. They cost a fortune because they were out of season and imported, but they were an investment. Thank God that garbage was in the English-language *Post*, which hardly anybody read. It was possible that Tamara had not heard about it. Possible but unlikely. He'd find out any moment. He looked up again at the fiery sky, which seemed to blazon a warning. Help me, God.

The setting sun and the first stars heralded the start of the Sabbath, the day of rest. He sensed he wouldn't be getting much of that.

But where was everyone? He put the flowers in the sink, and peered around the door into the dining room. He went out onto the terrace, walked down to the pool, back to the house, calling, "Tamara? Carmel? Daniel?" Were they hiding? Was it a birthday surprise? It wasn't his birthday. He went into their bedroom with a sinking feeling. Don't tell me she's gone. He looked into Tamara's closet. Her clothes were still there, everything was in order. Her toothbrush was in the bathroom.

So where are they? What about dinner? He was starving.

As the oldest female present, Rachel lit the two candles while welcoming the Sabbath with prayer. In Arie's absence, Moshe laid his hands on the forehead of each child and prayed for the Lord's blessing. He recited the kiddush prayer and blessed the wine, and everybody sipped from a full cup signifying joy and overflowing bounty. Tamara broke the challah bread into pieces, sprinkled each with salt, passed portions to everyone at the table, and they got down to the serious business: matzo ball soup followed by roast chicken, roast potatoes, minutely chopped salad, and, as no Rachel meal would be complete without it, a plate of hummus with pine nuts and mushrooms.

Daniel and Carmel, who were fourteen now, kept asking, "Where's Daddy?" Ido and Estie, eighteen and twenty years old, respectively, and both on weekend leave from the army, exchanged glances and wondered how their sister would answer. Tamara didn't. All she thought, as the Sabbath meal progressed, the warmest, most intimate family moment of the week, was, That bastard!

How dare he?

How long could she put up with this? He would never change, so what was the point of waiting? At work she defended women with abusive husbands, while at home her own husband abused her emotionally every day. Did he really think money and comfort made up for it? Obviously he did. Well, it didn't. Not anymore. And all his nonsense about loving her and needing her, all rubbish. He's just afraid, he needs the security of a little wife at home while he runs after every moneygrubbing trollop in town, and God knows there are plenty of them. She knew the truth about Goldfarb, she was no "special" friend, if she was special, so was the secretary and the secretary's secretary.

There's something manic in his philandering. What's he trying to prove? Well, who cares, it's too late now, she couldn't take it anymore. Throwing out his clothes had been comic relief, she had cackled like a witch. But then she had thrown herself onto the bed and wept.

It took Arie a few minutes to realize that yes, Tamara's clothes were still in the closet, but where were his? His cupboard was bare. His drawers, empty. He went back into the bathroom and saw Tamara's toothbrush. But where was his?

He ran along the corridor to the east wing and opened the door to the guest suite. The bitch! His clothes were strewn around the bed and the room. He didn't know he had so many, he was ankle-deep in trousers, shirts, vests and jackets. His shoes were everywhere, and yes, there was his toothbrush on the floor. He pulled back; there was broken glass: his tooth mug. She must have been in a frenzy.

So she'd seen that *Jerusalem Post* story after all. He'd find out what miserable bastard wrote that and wring his neck. People just can't mind their own business.

The phone rang. At last, where were they? He didn't mean to hurt her, it all seemed beyond him, he just could not control his restlessness. Tamara must understand, he loved her, he loved his family, he didn't want it to be this way. She must see reason. He sat on the edge of the bed and slowly picked up the phone, hoping his voice would tremble.

"Tamara?" he said.

"Arie?"

"Gila? You're calling me at home? Are you crazy?"

She was sobbing. "Arie, my husband left me. What shall we do?"

"We?" Arie jerked the handset away from his ear, looked at it in dismay, and hung up. He stood and kicked the bed.

At Moshe and Rachel's, Tamara tried to evict Arie from her thoughts, to savor the family's Sabbath meal, the festive, leisurely highlight of their week. But there was no escape: the conversation was all about men and women. It started when Ezra asked his aunt Estie what she did in the army and she replied, "I make the coffee." She said at the Kirya, army HQ in Tel Aviv, girls were secretaries. "If I'm really good," she said, "and make really good coffee, and lots of it, I could get promoted and then I get to make the tea. That's a complicated balance of tea with mint and sugar, while coffee is just black and strong. But only the best girls get promoted."

"You're joking, I hope," Tamara said.

"Not by much. And the way the officers talk, it's like a school playground. They're married men, you'd never know."

Arie fits right in, Tamara thought.

"What do you mean?" Rachel said.

"Oh, the things they say. Leaning over you, putting their arms around you, you know . . ."

"No, I don't," Tamara said, although she did. She could just imagine Arie pawing and leering at the girls in his office. And who knew what he got up to when he toured the factories and shop floors; Big Boss in his suit and tie, with a pocketful of cash. "What do they do?" she said.

"Nothing they don't do outside the army too," Ido said, holding a chicken wing up to his mouth. Tamara looked at him sharply: Does he mean Arie? Everybody must know about the story in the *Post*, but they're too polite, or scared, to mention it. It was humiliating. That bastard! "What about you, Ido?" she asked her brother, wanting to change the subject. "How is the Makim course going?"

"Hard. Really hard. But I love it. It's made for me." The Golani squad leaders course was the stepping-stone to being an officer, Ido's ambition. Wolfie, now an infantry colonel, was keeping an eye on Ido's progress but despite Arie's request to his childhood friend, Wolfie had refused to put in a good word for Ido. "If he isn't good enough to be an officer he'll be a danger to his men. If he is good enough, he'll make it on his own. Anyway, from what I hear, he's excellent officer material."

At eighteen, Ido, cropped black hair, muscular, tanned, handsome, looked the part. He was the tallest in the family, and his army training made him the fittest. He had moved smoothly from straight A's at high school to top recruit in basic training. Moshe had written a column headed "The New Israeli" and in it had boasted, "I needn't look far to see the future of the Jews, and how different it is from our past. The future sits on the other side of the breakfast table."

Tamara had been furious. "What about his sister? She isn't the future? She doesn't exist for you?"

"That's not what I meant," Moshe said. "But it's different, you know. She's a girl." Oh, how quickly he had tried to make amends. "I mean . . ."

Too late. Tamara's summary was: "You can take the Egyptian out of Egypt, but you can't take the misogynist out of the Egyptian."

That had made Estie laugh. "I don't mind, Tamara. You think the *yekkes* are any different? In the army the girls are all just pretty faces."

Now at dinner Moshe asked, "Has anybody gone too far with you? Those officers, they think they're God."

"Depends what you mean, too far," Estie said. "I can tell you this: All the girls talk about it, and the problem is, because they're officers, there's nobody to complain to."

Tamara felt her eyes well up, she glanced around, and dabbed at them with her napkin. It was painful to hear this, it was a nasty reminder how ordinary Arie really was: just another man who could get away with anything because there was no one to stop him. Men with power were untouchable, and she was just as guilty as all the other women who didn't stand up for themselves. Girls in the army at least had the excuse of being young and naïve—what was her excuse? She was just another weak, abused woman, and it had to stop. She frowned with determination. Throwing him out of their bedroom was just the start.

"Yes," Moshe said. "Because who judges them? Other officers. And they're all the same."

"No, they aren't," Ido said. "At HQ maybe they have too much time on their hands. In the field, nobody's got time to mess about. Or energy. Pass me the potatoes, please."

"Amazing," Rachel said. "There's seven of us around the table, it's full of food, and Ido has eaten half of it by himself."

"Pass the chicken too," Ido said. "I have to keep growing."

"But where's Dad?" Carmel said.

At the very mention of him Tamara's blood rose, anger surged through her, she'd show him. All the faces at the table turned to her. Her children, their cousins, her parents, family time around the Sabbath table, with the best silverware, a clean white linen over the challah bread, glowing candles. Was this the moment to say what was in her heart, to tear their lives apart? She hesitated, torn between her anger, her humiliation, and saying something she may regret forever.

"Well?" Carmel said.

At last she said, attempting a smile, "I'm sorry. Daddy's at home, he was busy this evening. You'll see him later."

CARMEL and ARIE

TEL AVIV, ISRAEL

April 1964

Carmel received a letter from America. The red, brown, and blue fifteen-cent Montgomery Blair stamp thrilled her, it would be a new one for her collection. But who did she know in America? She checked again that it really was her name on the envelope, and turned it over and over. She found a knife, worked it beneath the flap, and slit the envelope open neatly to preserve the stamp.

> *Dear Carmel,*
>
> *You don't know me but I hope that we can become pen pals. My grand-parents adopted your uncle, Peter Berg, when he was a boy in America. I heard a lot of stories about "the little Jewish boy" and now he is an important man in your government. I would love to know about you and your life and your country. I don't even know if your English is good enough to read this, but it is certainly better than my Jewish, ha ha . . .*

Alice Wilson explained that in a letter to her grandmother Peter had suggested she write because she and Carmel were almost the same age. She hoped it was all right. Alice wrote about her junior high school, the neat boy who lived opposite, Gadi Bronson, and her life in Taos, New Mexico. She loved to ski, hike in the mountains, swim in the lakes, although the water was icy cold, and her favorite television programs were *The Dick Van Dyke Show, Gunsmoke,* and *Walt Disney Presents.*

Carmel was excited to have an American friend and wrote back immediately in the best English she could. The news that she couldn't watch the television programs because Israel didn't have TV both amused and horrified Alice, who replied that her greatest ambition now was to visit Israel, for a country without television must be a very special place. What did Carmel do all day?

Carmel couldn't wait to see her parents. "Daddy, can Alice come and stay with us?"

"Of course," Arie said. "Maybe when she's a bit older, it's a long way to come alone. In the meantime you could work harder at English. Would you like a private teacher? I can get someone from the office. Maybe you can go to America one day. You can run my New York office."

"Really? I didn't know you had one."

"I don't, but by the time you're old enough, I will. That's going to be the biggest market. Bigger than Europe."

"Can I, really? I could leave school, go there soon . . ."

Arie laughed. "Not so fast. School, army, university, marriage, babies, there's a lot to do in life. Let's just start with English lessons, that's important. More important than German. Which reminds me, I must go, I'm meeting Peter for lunch."

"Tell him thank you for introducing me to Alice. I haven't seen Peter for ages."

"I will." He kissed her on the forehead and each cheek and went to the car, where Yaacov was waiting to drive him to town.

"Where to, boss?"

"Dizengoff Street. Keton. Lunch with Peter."

"Ha. Good luck."

"I'll need it."

It was a silent drive. He was getting fed up with Peter. Tamara always complained that he judged her and criticized her, which he didn't. But Peter did to him. He never stopped playing the older brother. Who needs this? What did Peter want to talk about this time? He could guess, the same old story: "Tamara, she deserves better." What does he know; they hadn't had sex for three months. "Spend more time with the children. Grow up. Life is about more than money." Oh yes?

The only thing he looked forward to was the chicken soup with kreplach. And the apple strudel with vanilla ice cream.

Keton was a landmark, a restaurant older than the state, that began as a kiosk serving ice cream and watermelon and was now famed for its chicken schnitzel and potato salad, as well as stuff from the shtetl he wouldn't touch, like *ptcha* and *kishke*.

They met at the door at 12:30. "Two *yekkes*," Arie said, taking Peter's hand. "The only two punctual Israelis."

"Have you booked?" Sara, the owner, said, as she always did, indicating the empty restaurant. Peter laughed, as usual. "Please try to squeeze us in." On purpose he led the way to a corner table. He knew Arie loved to sit by the window or outside on the sidewalk where people could see him and he could greet them with his regal wave. The mogul with the big cigar. Peter preferred the anonymity of a table by the wall. "Look," he said, nudging Arie. "The heavy man with the hat who just sat down outside? Igael Tumarkin. The artist."

"I just bought one of his sculptures. For the office lobby. He thinks a lot of himself."

"You mean it was expensive."

"Any luck with the ladies?" Arie asked, but regretted it; it was a clear segue to Tamara.

"Not as much as you," Peter replied, inspecting the menu. "Actually, that's a sore point."

"Why? Sounds interesting."

"Believe me, it isn't."

"Try me." Arie hoped to distract Peter from his sermon of the day. But Peter trod lightly: He was glad Carmel was happy with her new pen pal. Things were quiet at work. Little Diana liked to dance but every time she tried the hora she spun and fell over. The sweetest thing. After they ordered apple strudel and Peter started on Noah and Ezra's schoolwork, Arie had to interrupt.

"Sorry, Peter, not that your boys' Torah classes don't fascinate me, but you said there was something you wanted to talk about?"

Peter took a long drink of his beer and set it down with a sigh.

"Actually, yes. You're in trouble."

"So what's new?"

"No. I mean real trouble."

Now what? Arie thought. Loans due? Interest. Banks. Debt repayments. Surely he doesn't know about Miriam. "Why? What do you mean?"

"A journalist is working on an old police case."

"So?"

"The Schwartz file, the guy they found near the Yarkon River."

"Him? That was ten years ago. And it had nothing to do with me. Not that anybody knows, anyway. It was an accident. I don't have anything to worry about."

"I'm not so sure. He found that English policeman, Ludlow, who Harel closed down. He's retired now, lives in Ashdod, and he's got a big mouth."

Arie leaned forward, stretched his arms, cracked his knuckles. He scanned the restaurant, which was filling up. Three people had joined Tumarkin, artist types.

"Ludlow told him the top floor closed the case," Peter continued. "He knows there's a Mossad connection."

"So isn't that the end of the road for him, then?"

"No. It just makes it a better story."

"What can happen?"

"Worst case? He writes a dramatic story, they reopen the murder investigation, and you're the main suspect."

Arie's lips tightened. "Could they?"

"Depends what he learns. You were seen arguing with Schwartz. Your sister-in-law Diana asked for his police file. Ludlow found out. Harel got the police chief to close the file."

"Well, he can't interview Diana."

"Lucky you."

"That's not what I meant. But why does he care so much? It happened a decade ago."

"I don't know. Cold murder case? Police cover-up? Mossad?" Peter watched two couples sit at tables nearby. He lowered his voice further. "The name of the millionaire Arie Nesher comes up. It's a good story for a young up-and-comer trying to make a name for himself."

"What's his name?"

"Yoram Shemesh."

"You said he's young? How young?"

"Nineteen."

"What? Nineteen?" Arie wrote the name on a napkin, then tore it up. No records. "That's all? Why isn't he in the army?"

"He got some kind of deferment. Unfit to serve."

"I bet he is," Arie said. "Who is he writing this rubbish for?"

"He's a freelancer. *HaOlam HaZeh* is interested."

"That left-wing rag."

He's cool as a cucumber, Peter thought, but hard. All he wants to do is fight back. Never underestimate him. "You know the editor, Uri Avnery; a police cover-up is right up his street."

"I'll get someone to do a story on the kid, get him before he gets me. If he avoided army service, let's get him on that. Did he lie to get out of serving? Is he a pacifist, a conscientious objector? Maybe he's got a police record himself? How close is he to publishing something? I've got a couple of big deals going through, bad publicity could rock the boat."

"Don't be stupid, Arie. If you plant a story against him, he'll find out it came from you and that will make it worse. It's probably better at this stage to lie low, don't draw attention to yourself." That'll be the day. Lying low was not his brother's forte. "There's something else," Peter said.

"Don't tell me it gets worse. What?"

"About something else. About Tamara."

"Oh, for God's sake, there's enough on my mind right now," Arie hissed, hitting the table with the palm of his hand. The young couple two tables away looked up at the bang. "Mind your own business."

"You talking to me or them?" Peter said, pulling back slowly from the table, his calculating eye's fixed on his brother's. Arie's burst of anger faced Peter's cold appraisal, for with one phrase from Arie, they both understood their fight was in the open: Tamara was Peter's business, and always had been.

Peter finally asked the question whose answer he already knew. "The letter I gave you, years ago, before you married her, for Tamara. You never gave it to her, did you."

"What letter?"

"You know very well. When we first met Tamara, and I went away on a job, I gave you a letter for her, asking her to wait for me. You didn't give it to her, did you?"

"What? When? Fifteen years ago? I don't know what you're talking about."

"You have a very selective memory, don't you." Peter said.

Arie shifted in his chair, folded his arms. "It's true, I block some things out," Arie said. "That's how I carry on. But a letter for Tamara? No, never happened."

PETER and ARIE

TEL AVIV AND PARIS

May 1964

————

The Paris station was Mossad's largest in Europe but Mahmoud al-Faradis would speak only to Peter Nesher. "If anybody else turns up, I leave," he warned the station chief.

Peter had recruited the Egyptian army officer, code-named Nile, during his years sabotaging Nasser's rocket program, and earned his confidence by keeping every promise he had ever made. When Nile's infant son needed surgery for his polio Peter had even arranged a private clinic in Paris, as well as, to relieve Nile's understandable stress, a tall blonde. A camera lens concealed in the hotel room's ceiling lamp had recorded their grunts and groans, but that was routine.

Nile was a useful source of information, and when he switched from the army to the Mukhabarat, Egypt's General Intelligence Directorate, he became a gold mine. Because his new area of responsibility was the same as Peter's, only the opposite. His job was to help the Arabs of Palestine. Peter's was to stop them.

Now in Paris to meet leaders of the nascent Palestine Liberation Organization, Nile had obtained their first plan of attacks against Israel's water carrier, as well as against Israeli targets in Europe.

Places. Times. Methods. Names.

An intelligence coup, for Nesher's eyes only, in return for fifty thousand American dollars wired to the Swiss bank account Peter had set up for Nile years earlier. Peter needed to fly to Paris immediately.

"It's just one night," he told Rachel, "maybe less. I'll try to come back the same day." The trip was poor timing for Peter. Diana, one-and-a-half now, could manage an hour at Gan Dahlia, Dahlia's play-school, but then bawled for her father, couldn't be consoled, and had to be taken home. He was hoping she would learn to enjoy the other children and would stay longer, maybe the whole morning, to give Rachel a break. Dahlia said she would adjust with time. But Peter was worried he didn't have time, that Rachel would give up her job of mothering his daughter. What then? She also cooked lunch for the boys. Was it becoming too much for her? He paid her well, but if she stopped, and he couldn't blame her if she did, who would look after his children?

He wasn't much of a dad, but what else could he do? Fate had been more than unkind. He loosened his seat belt, pushed back his seat, and closed his eyes. Six hours to Paris.

He tried to sleep, thought of his children, and then . . . oh, Diana. A low groan escaped his throat. It had been a year and seven months. Every day when he held his daughter, played with her, kissed her, he thought of Diana. He always would. Poor little Diana, with no mother. Poor little Peter, with no wife.

He woke up thinking of Nile. Fifty thousand was way too much. He'd get him down to ten, with the promise that they'd buy a lot more information. Nile wouldn't be happy, he needed money to pay his son's hospital bills, fund his gambling addiction, and support the wife he couldn't abide who managed their villa in Cairo and their horse farm outside Alexandria. But lately Nile had shown signs of independence, as if he thought his new job gave him the upper hand. If Nile didn't agree to ten thousand, it may be time to use the photographs, although somebody else should play bad cop. It wouldn't go down well in Cairo that the tall blonde was a man.

A few hours in Paris should be enough. The station chief was ready, three rings of security, with a twist. Everything was arranged for Nile to meet Peter in the Café des Sports in Saint-Sulpice, except that when the hour came and Nile entered the café, an agent brushed against him at the door and told him to leave and go straight to the Bar de la Nuit in the parallel street.

Peter was waiting alone in the corner. Two elderly men at the bar dipped almond biscuits in their coffee and cognac, watching soccer on a small television set high on the wall. Behind the shiny wooden counter a stout lady in spectacles dried beer glasses. At a window table a young couple held hands over a plate of cheeses. Good people. Peter had helped oversee their training course.

Even though he hadn't met Nile in six months, Peter wanted to get this over as quickly as possible. He hoped to make the evening flight back to Tel Aviv, to be at home in the morning when Diana went to play-school. He felt the good-bye ritual gave her confidence and it was important that she feel good there. He really couldn't afford to lose Rachel, she was a safe port in the storm. He had to sort his life out.

Peter stood when Nile approached and indicated the chair. He greeted him with a German-accented Arabic salutation, to which Nile replied in German, *"Grüss Gott."* Their usual friendly sparring. Nile placed his leather attaché case at his feet and before he sat ordered a double cognac. Peter raised an eyebrow and continued in English. "What's that? Celebrating? Drowning your sorrows? Plucking up courage?"

"None of those," Nile said. "Just trying to get through the day."

After inquiring about the health of his son and his other children, and the well-being of his wife, Peter broke the news, in a low voice, that he could only pay ten thousand dollars, and even that only when the Office had analyzed the documents and agreed they were worthwhile: "To be paid in the usual way." He was surprised by Nile's quick agreement.

"Is something wrong?" Peter asked. A bead of sweat on Nile's hairline glistened in the electric light. Was Nile's hand shaking? Peter glanced around the room, met the eyes of the woman at the window table.

"Do you have the papers?" Peter said.

"Yes, I do." Nile hesitated, leaned forward and reached into the attaché case beneath the table. His hand searched in the case. Peter tensed. Three feet away the young man pushed his chair back while the woman flicked the safety catch of the gun in her purse.

At that moment in Tel Aviv, Arie shook the hand of Yoram Shemesh. "I heard you were a young journalist," Arie said, "but, to be honest, you look as if you should be in middle school." He was thin and frail. He looked as if he could do with a good meal.

"People say that. I feel a lot older though. Nice office."

"Thank you. Follow me, this is the lobby. Tea? Coffee? Water?"

"Nothing. This sculpture—Tumarkin, yes?"

"You have a good eye," Arie said as he passed the reception desk. "Tammy, a coffee for me please, and some lemon water." At the end of the corridor he held his office door open for the young man.

Shemesh crossed to the window. "Quite a view."

"Sit down. Here," Arie said, indicating the suite of sofas around a coffee table. The journalist set down his backpack and took in the office: a large wooden bookcase with few books but sculptures in bronze and clay. On the wall hung paintings and framed photographs of Israel, Bedouin rugs were scattered around the wood floor, and the desk was piled with papers and files. A second sitting area by the corner windows.

"This may be the largest office I've ever been in," Shemesh said.

"How can I help you?" Arie said, throwing out his arms. "I understand you want to write a flattering profile of Israel's leading businessman." His smile was not returned. Shemesh seemed lost for words. Arie waited, accepting a coffee from his secretary.

"Well?" Arie said.

At last, Shemesh asked, "Why did you agree to see me? You have a reputation for avoiding the press."

Arie shrugged. "Why not? Times change. Every businessman could do with some good publicity. I have nothing to hide. Fire away."

Shemesh took out his notebook, his pen hovered. Avoiding Arie's eye, he said, "I probably should have said earlier, but it's not exactly a business profile I'm working on."

"Oh, really? Then why did you ask to interview a businessman?"

Shemesh blushed. The silence was becoming awkward. "Well?" Arie said.

He blurted it out. "I'm writing a report about a police murder case and I was told you may have done it. Or rather, you may be a suspect. Or you were. Once." He tried to look at Arie but couldn't.

"What? Done what? What are you talking about?"

The young journalist's face creased, almost in pain. He's plucking up courage, Arie thought, and became almost impatient: Come on, out with it, how much do you know? He waited.

Finally: "Did you know a man called Hans Schwartz?"

That took Arie by surprise. "No, I don't. I didn't. Who is he?"

"You may have known him as Yonathan Schwartz. Or Yoni."

"Ah," Arie said. "Yonathan Schwartz. Now that rings a bell. Let me see, now." All he wanted from this meeting, the reason he'd agreed to see the journalist, was to find out how closely that English policeman had linked him to Schwartz. Did the police know they'd met the night he died? Had they been seen together? Did this young man know everything the police knew, or just some of it? "Why do you ask? What about this man?"

"You knew him then?"

Arie exhaled. "I certainly know the name. But you're going back a long time. I'm not sure I can remember much. Why don't you help me, why do you think I know him? And what if I do?"

"As I said, the police think you murdered him."

"Oh. Do they? Why would they think that? And if they do, why don't they arrest me?"

"You're very calm?"

"Am I? How should I react to such a ludicrous claim coming from no-where, or rather, coming from the mouth of . . . how can I say this po-litely . . . you. You come into my office for an innocent interview and then you accuse me of . . ."

"Not me. The police."

"When am I supposed to have committed this murder?"

"Ten years ago."

Arie laughed. "Well, I didn't kill anybody ten years ago, or any other time. Why do they think I did? And why are you writing about it now, after all this time?"

He could see the journalist was nervous. He gripped his pen tight, he was beating his foot. Arie poured him a glass of water. "What is it?" he said. "Are you all right?"

Yoram Shemesh took a long drink, and a deep breath. "The police report," he began with a shaky voice, that became firmer, "shows that Yonathan Schwartz was found with his head crushed. They found blood nearby and footmarks of at least two people. The marks in the grass and earth were over each other, deep, in a small area, as if there had been a struggle. So they believe there was a fight and Yonathan Schwartz either fell or was beaten." He studied Arie's reaction.

"Anything else?"

"Yes. The police know Yonathan Schwartz argued with a man the same day in a Dizengoff café. They say that man was you. Is that true?"

"So they think I killed him."

"They wanted to interview you, but they were told to drop the case."

"I suppose because it was a stupid thing to believe."

"No. The policeman investigating you was very angry to be pulled off the case. It was hushed up."

"Hushed up? Who by? And how do you know?"

"I spoke to the policeman. He told me himself. He said there was only one suspect. You. He also said you knew Yonathan Schwartz from the war. That you were in the same concentration camp."

The faintest shiver went through Arie. So they know that. And what else?

"And?" he said.

"I don't know. I was hoping you'd tell me."

"Tell you what? That I knew this man and killed him?"

"Did you know him?"

"Yes, I did, I remember now."

Shemesh went silent. He managed to control his features. He swallowed, before asking. "Do you have a number on your arm?"

Now Arie was surprised. "Yes, I do."

"May I see it?"

"No."

Shemesh fell silent again. Arie said, "This man, Yonathan Schwartz, you say he died ten years ago. It was so long ago, why do you care about him? Or do you care about me, for some reason? You want to write a story claiming that I, Arie Nesher, am a killer? Why? Based on what? An old police report?"

"One that was hushed up by Mossad. The policeman told me he complained officially at the time. Somebody in Mossad asked for the file, and later the investigation was closed down. That Mossad person was your sister-in-law, but she doesn't work there anymore. The policeman told me. I have her name and I will find her."

"What is her name?"

"Diana Nesher."

"You'll have a hard time interviewing her."

"Why?"

"She's dead."

"Oh. You went that far to cover your tracks."

The silence hung heavy, and grew heavier. "I'm sorry, I didn't mean it, I shouldn't have said that."

Arie rose. "Get out." Close to forty, he was still a powerful man. "I'm going to put that down to the stupidity of youth. If you weren't a child I'd kick your ass. And to save your time investigating another imagined murder, Diana died in childbirth. Now get the hell out of my office."

"I'm sorry, Mister Nesher. That just came out." He stood. "I didn't mean it, really. It was stupid of me, I apologize. I'm sorry she died in childbirth, I had no idea. Please, you said something, I really need to know more. You said you knew Yonathan Schwartz, I'd like to ask you about him. Please. Can we sit down again? I'm sorry."

Arie was holding the door open, pointing the way out. He hesitated. He's just a stupid kid but he could do real damage with this report. It was a sexy story. Murder. Cover-up. Mossad. Arie Nesher.

"Why? Why do you care so much about how that man Yonathan Schwartz died ten years ago?"

"Hans Schwartz. He changed it to Yoni. You see—he was my father."

"Ah. I see." Arie's heart thumped. That's why he won't give up—he never will. He stepped back into the room and closed the door. "I'm sorry about your father. I mean, what happened to him." What to say? What to do? What could he give the boy that would shut him up? "Coffee now?"

"No, thank you. May I sit?"

Arie poured two glasses of water and gave one to Yoram. He drained his own and poured another. He walked to the wall, adjusted a painting. "Never stays straight, that one. Always annoys me." Finally he sat down, and pulled his chair closer to Yoram. "Important to keep hydrated," he said, gesturing with his glass to Yoram's. Yoram drank.

"So after your father died, you grew up with your mother?"

"No. I didn't know her, she died when I was a year old. In a displaced persons camp in Germany. Tuberculosis."

"She was a survivor too?"

"Yes. My parents met after the war, I was born nine months later in the DP camp. A quick romance."

"Yes. There was a lot of that in those days. So your father brought you up, then he died, when you were, what? Nine? What happened to you then?"

"I don't have any relatives. Everybody died in the camps. I was in a home, I hated it. I left when I was fourteen, I've been alone since then."

"Supporting yourself?"

"Yes."

"What about the army?"

"I have diabetes. And asthma."

"I see. That's quite a story. And you're just nineteen."

"Yes."

"Are you really a journalist?"

"No, sir. Sorry. I'd like to be one day."

"How do you support yourself then?"

"I work in a kiosk. On Gordon Street."

Arie picked up Yoram's pen, his notebook, and looked at him with a thin smile. "So what's this all about then? Looking for your father's . . . so-called killer?"

Yoram looked as if he would cry. Finally he said, "It didn't start like that. I found a newspaper cutting that I must have kept from the time, it mentioned my father having an argument with a concentration camp survivor who knew him in Auschwitz. So I went to the police to find him—the other survivor. They could only tell me about Mister Ludlow, and he told me about you . . ." He looked down. "And all the rest."

He sucked in air, tried to compose himself. "I wanted to find someone who knew my father in Auschwitz. Who could tell me about him there. Did you know him in Auschwitz? Can you tell me about him? What he was like? Where he came from? Because I know so little about him, and I never had anybody else."

His eyes filled with tears. "Where do I come from? I don't know who I am."

Arie was touched. He laid a hand on the boy's arm, patted it. He felt a sudden kinship, as if their stories, their lives, were intertwined, and in a way they were. Everything the boy wanted to know was what he had spent so long trying to forget. Yet what if someone could tell him what happened to his own father? And mother. And sisters. Wouldn't he do anything to find out? Did he owe it to them all to tell this lost boy what he knew?

There was another long silence as Arie filled the glasses again until the jug was drained. "I did meet your father," he said at last, offering the boy a glass. "I didn't know him well. I can tell you a little about him, but this is not the place to talk of such things."

Yoram wiped his eyes again. He shivered. "It would mean so much to me."

"To me too," Arie said. "But not here. Why don't you come to my home, we can talk there. Tomorrow? Take the 90 bus, it stops a ten-minute walk from the house. Come for dinner. Seven o'clock."

In the Bar de la Nuit in Saint-Sulpice, a very strange kind of history was made that day.

Everything was wrong about Nile's movement. Instead of picking up his attaché case to take out a document, he leaned down and stretched his arm into the case. Instead of looking down to choose the right papers, he looked up at Peter. He kept that posture a shade too long.

Peter's neck hair stood, his balls shrank, he shot a look at his backup.

The man took two quick steps forward, the woman aimed her gun, still hidden in the purse. A roar came from the television at a missed goal, one of the old men slapped the counter.

There was a blur of motion. Still seated, Nile whipped a gun into Peter's face.

Peter saw nothing but the small round hole of his death, every movement a single jerky frame in a film. He saw Nile's finger tighten on the trigger, he threw himself to the side, his hand shot out to grab the gun, but too late.

Nile squeezed the trigger a foot from Peter's face. It clicked like a clucking tongue. Nothing happened. The gun had jammed. In that instant the Mossad agent, already aiming at Nile's chest, pulled her trigger. Another click. Nothing happened. It was impossible, but her gun jammed too. Before the other agent could reach Nile, Peter had grabbed his gun hand, twisted it up and round and pulled the gun from his grasp. Now the pistol was in Peter's hand.

Nile's mouth fell open but he was quick to react. He pushed past the agent and ran from the café. Outside, two covering agents, not knowing what happened but seeing Nile's panic, ran after him.

Inside, Peter fell back into his chair, his heart hammering like that of a sprinter. The woman was dazed, she looked up and down, from her purse to Peter, from Peter to her purse. What just happened? The male agent rushed to the door but there was nothing to do but get Peter to a safe place.

The bartender was still looking down into the sink as she scrubbed the beer glasses; the men at the bar, with their backs to Peter, were transfixed by the game.

It was so quick it was as if nothing had happened.

But it went down in Mossad history as the Day the Guns Jammed.

For Peter, it was the day he got his life back.

The near assassination of a Mossad department chief was an epic failure that led to weeks of deconstruction. Why had Nile turned? How was the veteran Peter Nesher fooled into a trap? Why didn't the security rings work? And of course, the big one, who to blame?

But on the flight home, Peter, facing what he knew would be a brutal debriefing, and shaken by his near death, had only one thought on his mind: If he had been killed, who would look after the children? Diana wasn't yet two, Ezra and Noah were eleven. Rachel was a lifesaver, but they needed a mother. And he needed a wife.

As he lay back in his seat, legs stretched out, arms folded, drowsy, his thoughts tumbled over each other. He had been given a second chance at life. He needed to share it with someone. Diana would have wanted that. But who? Arie was always introducing him to women and he'd gone out with some. He'd liked Vardit, they had been together a month, but she was honest: she didn't want to inherit three children. So that was that. Michal? She liked him. But she kept trying to communicate with the spirits, with Diana. It was freakish. Then there was . . .

Peter was asleep and woke suddenly with her name on his lips. Did he say it aloud?

Tamara. Oh, Tamara. He had dreamt of her. Her damp hair, her sweet lips. While he was married to Diana he had pushed that part of Tamara from his mind. She played many parts: sister-in-law, friend, his wife's best friend, the cook, the mother, the human rights lawyer. But that part of her he most wanted, their one moment together, he pushed from his mind. They had been so young and it had been so brief, but oh, what would he give to make love to her again. In a way, he had lived a lie. Had she? Now that he had been reprieved, was this a second chance?

But what was he thinking? His brother's wife?

Tamara's marriage to Arie had long been a sham, they had separate bedrooms. He always had at least one woman on the side, and Tamara knew it. They stayed together for the children. How old were they now? Fourteen. In four years their twins would be soldiers, they would leave home.

He had to face himself, he had to talk to Tamara. Did she feel the same? Was he imagining it all, were these just the crazy thoughts of a vulnerable lonely man?

The gun's muzzle again, a round blackness, in his face. Click. Click. Two guns jammed. At the same time. God must be rocking with laughter.

The stewardess was shaking his shoulder. "Buckle up, sir. We land in Tel Aviv in fifteen minutes."

Before he could turn the key in the door, Rachel opened it. Behind her, the boys were playing on the floor with a friend, some kind of board game, colored pieces were piled in front of each player. Monopoly? They hardly looked up.

"How was the trip?" Rachel asked.

"Oh, fine," Peter answered. "Just another day at the office."

The next night, dinner was a strained affair. Arie never explained properly to Tamara why he had invited this strange young man, but she was polite, even as the twins couldn't leave the table fast enough. And as Hadassah, the maid, cleared the plates, Arie said to Tamara that he and Yoram would go to the study to talk.

Was he offering him a job? Why would he bring him home? Tamara didn't wonder too long. "I have some files to work through," she said. "I'll be on the back terrace, it's a beautiful evening."

Arie led Yoram into his study. It had a high ceiling and a wall covered with landscapes by Israeli artists. A floor-to-ceiling glass wall looked out onto the back garden. "Not bad," Yoram said. "This room is twice as big as my home." He walked slowly along the shelves of antiquities: oil lamps, glass bowls, cracked and repaired, clay vases, what looked like a painted cat's head, long and pointed. "Roman artifacts, very undervalued," Arie said. "You can buy these things for a song although they're thousands of years old. They'll be worth a fortune one day. But the best thing is the view, look. Oh, it's dark!"

The window looked past the terrace to the sea, which was a dark mass sparkling from the stars' reflection. "That's the only thing those bastards couldn't take from us," Arie said, "the sky. Sit down."

Outside, the air was still. As Tamara read by the electric light, the overhead fan kept the mosquitoes away; its whirr reduced the low tones she heard through the open study window to a muddy murmur, so at odds with the evening calm.

". . . and the face of the Russian soldier who looked at us through the wire," Arie was saying. "He vomited. I had no idea until then how disgusting I must have been. At that moment, just when I knew I'd live, that I had survived, I saw myself through his eyes. Diseased. Disgusting. At least I was standing. There were hundreds who didn't have the strength, pulling themselves along the icy ground, like worms."

Yoram broke in. "And my father? He was there? Please tell me about him."

Arie stiffened. What had touched him about this earnest child? Their related suffering? Did the boy's pain touch his own, that he had never been able to confront? Was Yoram's father just the trigger, the conduit? Arie spoke in a monotone, as if distancing himself from his own thoughts. He told of the boarded-up freight train that crossed Europe for days, transporting him and his parents and sisters, crammed inside a stinking cattle car with their neighbors, with no food or water or toilets, no air, no room to sit, boiling during the day, freezing at night, coughing and spitting. The floor sodden with urine and excrement. The bright, clean world sliding by through a crack in the wood. A quarter of them died before they even reached Auschwitz.

There was something riveting, relentless, about his tone that made Tamara strain to understand her husband's words through the window. She laid her papers aside. She caught only occasional words, like "Auschwitz" and "train," until she realized she should turn off the fan. When the whirring stopped and she moved closer to stand with her back to the open window, she could hear every word. She was transfixed. She had never heard Arie talk like this. Never. Not only what he said but how he said it. It was as if he could hardly believe his own words.

Who was this boy? Why was Arie telling him all this? And then she heard Arie say, "Your father and I had the same job for months. It was supposed to be an easy job." Arie paused, considering Yoram. "You really want to hear this?" A grimace passed for a smile.

"Yes, I do," Yoram said. This was what he had come for. He had not dared to interrupt, but he had to know about his father.

Tamara's heart sped as she listened; the twinkling stars, the gentle silence outside, made this stolen moment all the more horrifying, and tears ran down her cheeks.

"The guards packed the Jews into the gas chambers so tightly that when it was over and the doors were opened, the corpses stayed upright, like naked clay figures. Holding hands. Hugging. Their faces were the worst. Distended, mouths open. Dead but standing. Standing on babies. There was no room to fall down.

"We had to handle the bodies. The Nazis took everything of value. They smashed the teeth to take the gold fillings. Our job, your father and me . . . our job was to search body cavities for valuables."

Tamara dug her fist into her mouth to stop from crying out.

"Do you know what I mean?" Arie said.

Yoram nodded, and then shook his head. "No."

"We had to stick our fingers into the mouths, noses, the rectums, the vaginas of the bodies. Feeling for diamonds, money. There were piles of corpses and we had to work through every one. We dragged them, stacked them, burned them. We didn't smell the stink anymore. But that wasn't the worst of it. The worst was the insult, the constant Nazi insult, to the corpses, to ourselves, to the Jews. I swore that if I lived through it, nobody would insult me ever again. All we wanted was to stay alive ourselves for as long as possible. Your father. And me.

"I did that for about half a year. I met up with your father again months later, when I had a special position due to sports. I'll be honest with you, your father didn't like me then, nobody did, but I did anything I could to survive. Anything. I'm not proud. But I live with myself." His voice trailed off so Tamara could barely make it out. "I do my best."

Tamara shuddered and wiped her eyes with the back of her hand. What pitiful agony was held in those words: I do my best. He has suffered so much for so long. He was only a child when he'd entered hell, not much older than their own children, Carmel and Daniel. She leaned against the wall; she felt she may faint.

"Your father must have been the same," Tamara heard Arie say after a while. "We hated ourselves. We hated the world that didn't help. We even hated our rescuers for seeing us in our filth. And ever since then, we held it all inside. Because if we said what happened, everybody else would hate us too. There could be no forgiveness. Your father and I, we were not close, nobody was, but we understood each other. Everything can be taken from you, everything and everybody. We were fighting for our lives. We could die at any moment, everybody was the enemy."

And they still are, Tamara thought. You're still fighting to survive, terrified to lose it all, everyone is still your enemy. Everyone? She trembled. Is that what I am to you? Even partially? Only now she truly grasped the man she married fourteen years ago.

TAMARA and PETER

TEL AVIV, ISRAEL

August 1964

———————

T amara wept that night, her pillow became damp. Was she just another kind of guard who had taken away Arie's freedom? Did he hate
her for it?

Should she go to his bed? Twice she threw back the cover to go to him,
twice she pulled it back again. She had loved him, once. Could she again?
This tortured soul, barely hanging on, her husband, the father of her
children, he needed her, even if he didn't know it.

But what did she need?

If Arie was haunted and driven by the evil of the camps, tortured still,
did that give him the right to torture her today? I am not my husband's
keeper, she said to herself, nor his victim.

Or was she being selfish, did that make her a bad wife to a troubled
man? Shouldn't she help him overcome his torment rather than punish him
for it?

She stared at the dark, her hands lay on her belly. Whatever the reasons,
and they would never change, he was a terrible husband, always cheating, he
was the selfish one. All he did was work and chase other women. Money?
She didn't want a penny of it. She was thirty-three and beautiful. She
wanted love, and it was time.

Should she leave Arie? The thought that had been so painful now seemed to comfort her. At the edge of her pain she felt a thrilling promise, akin to a bird spreading its wings on a branch, set to soar. She turned onto her side and at last began to drift away, hugging her second pillow like a lover.

In the morning the phone rang. It was Peter.

They met in his new apartment, still in the same house where long ago they had made love, where she had been seduced, nay overcome, by the pleasure in his eyes. Today his home had two bedrooms and a narrow balcony, where they now sat in white plastic chairs made by Arie's company, drank sugared lemon juice, and wanted to hold hands. The first chords of "Love Me Do" rang out on the radio.

"The Beatles?" Tamara said with mock horror. "You're a government servant. Are you allowed to listen to such subversive drivel?"

Peter laughed. "Can you believe it? Golda banning the Beatles? A threat to the country's youth?"

"The government says they have no artistic merit. They could cause mass hysteria and disorder among young people. Like Cliff Richard did last year." She threw her head back with a guffaw. "Wish I'd been at his concert!"

Peter thought, that's exactly what Diana would have said.

"Is that what you're working on?" Peter said. "Protecting the human rights of young women to throw their bras at four long-haired men on stage?"

"Not exactly; it couldn't be more different. I'm working on two Arab cases. I'm helping a sweet young woman who was raped and then had to run away from her family because her father and brothers want to kill her for bringing shame to the family. She's in hiding and I'm trying to find her a more permanent shelter. And there's another case, a man whose son wants to study in America. The man is the imam of a mosque, I can't say where, and he was told by Shin Bet his son would only get travel papers if he, as the leader of the mosque, informed on his community. He refused, so Shin Bet jailed his son on some trumped-up charge. America or jail? What a choice. But instead of becoming a snitch, the imam came to our office, and I have the case. It's outrageous."

"But necessary, they do it all the time," Peter said. "It's their best weapon. As soon as an Arab wants something, they make him give something in return. Especially information." He stopped himself. Coercion was the most effective domestic weapon. Jews were being attacked on all the borders and Shin Bet's fear was that the Arabs living inside the state would join the Arab struggle led from outside.

"But that's blackmail," Tamara said. "Of course we need to know what is going on in our own country, but not by exploiting an innocent prayer leader and his son. The boy is in jail for no reason and his father will become an informer. And one day his village will find out and he'll be an outcast. We're ruining their lives, only to make ours marginally better." She stabbed Peter with her finger. "And it's illegal."

"Ouch. No, it isn't, not under the martial law that applies to the Arabs."

"Oh, so it's official blackmail. Two laws, one for them and one for us. That's a slippery slope. What kind of a country are we?"

"One that is always under threat from outside, and we don't want to be threatened from inside too. That's the kind of country. There's a price to pay for being the only Jewish state, surrounded by Arab enemies."

"If that price makes us like them, then what's the point?"

"So that we can live safely somewhere?"

"But why do the Arabs have to suffer for it? We should make them equal partners, then they won't threaten us."

"But Tamara, as long as they do threaten us, we have to defend ourselves, and that means removing the threat, not being surprised by it. We must know what they're planning. Information is power."

"Peter, that imam isn't even allowed to leave his village to travel anywhere without permission from us, no Arabs are. And before we give them permission, we blackmail them."

"Tamara." He drew out her name, and drew out the words that followed, as if this was a lesson she would be tested on. "There are seven hundred and fifty thousand Arabs inside Israel—" He cut himself off. Tamara was red in the face, drumming the floor with her heel, forcing herself not to interrupt. This was not going the way he had hoped.

Nor was it for her. "You're sounding very pompous, you and I are on completely opposite ends of the spectrum. In your job . . ."

"Please, Tamara, enough. Why didn't you specialize in real estate law, or commercial law?" he said. "Much more lucrative."

"No, thanks. Shin Bet is bad enough, but those fields would put me up against sharks like Arie. I'd rather win some cases."

Peter laughed. "I see what you mean. How is Arie?"

After ten seconds, in which Tamara rolled her eyes and sighed, clearly struggling, he said, "I see."

"Exactly."

"Anything in particular?"

"How long do you have?"

"How long do you need?"

"How much do you want to hear? About your own brother?"

"You think there's something I don't already know?"

Tamara sniggered. "At some point we have to stop asking questions and say something. Don't you think?"

"Do you?"

They laughed and chinked glasses.

"So?" Peter said. "Tell me."

On the balcony above them a woman hanging laundry chatted with her neighbor, who was folding hers. Across the courtyard a woman raised her voice to be heard over piano music. A man's deep voice boomed between the buildings, so that Peter had to lean forward to hear what Tamara was saying, for as she talked about Arie, her voice became low and hesitant. On the hour the news on Israel radio interrupted everyone. What bad news was there now?

Peter was only half-listening to Tamara, his face close to hers. His attention was more on Tamara's lips and the teasing tip of her tongue. Her hair was swept up tightly into a bun, and her face, half in shade, sad but fervent, was fully revealed. Drops of perspiration glinted in the valley of her throat. In the muggy heat her dress rode up her legs and clung to her thighs, her breasts billowed over the low-cut top, and all Peter could think of was to put his hands on her bare legs and at last kiss her on her luscious mouth.

But . . . his brother's wife?

"Why now?" he heard himself saying, after Tamara's complaints about her husband appeared to have run dry. "Arie has always been like this, has anything special happened recently?"

Tamara hung her head, as if exhausted by the weight of it all. He wanted to take her in his hands, pull her to him, raise her mouth, so close, to his.

"No, nothing new. I told him to stop seeing Batia or Sharon or whoever it is, or I'd leave him, but how many times have I said that? He promises, he swears, he apologizes, and then goes right back to them." She sighed in exasperation. "There's nothing new, it's just too much of the same. I've seen the future, if you like, and it's just like the present, and the past. And I can't take it anymore. It's not what I want." She looked into Peter's eyes, as if she didn't need to say the rest.

In the same instant Peter's heart leapt and fell. He yearned to hold her, but couldn't hurt Arie, even though Arie hurt her.

A sense of unfairness surged through him, a feeling of hopelessness that hit him in the pit of the stomach. Just as he straightened, pulling away from Tamara, forcing himself from temptation, forcing himself to listen, a name startled him. Tamara had changed the subject. "Yoram Schwartz? Schwartz's son?" he said.

"Yes, he changed his name to Shemesh. Arie and his father were in Auschwitz together. That's the point. He came to dinner and that's when I heard it all. Through the window. Arie doesn't know I heard him."

Now a different set of nerves was on edge. Every scenario raced through Peter's mind, and none were good.

"How did they meet?"

"The boy said he was a journalist, just to get to meet him. Arie liked him, and now he wants to pay to send him to school. He's given him a part-time job too. He's had a terrible life, Arie seems to feel something special for him. Anyway, he's helping him get on his feet."

"He's given him a job?"

"Part-time, while he studies, yes, and he's been to our home for dinner. That's what's so hard about Arie. Every time I hate him he does something wonderful that makes me think I must be wrong, that I should give him another chance."

Peter went silent. Everything was wrong about this. Arie, the snake, must sense trouble in the lad, and felt threatened, so in the time-honored way, Arie was keeping his friends close, but his enemy closer.

And Peter knew, when Arie had an enemy, anything could happen. Arie killed the boy's father, Peter was sure of it. What would he do to the son? What does the son know? And what does Tamara know of all this?

"I'm sorry," he said. "What did you say?"

"I said I'd better be going. It's getting late, I'm tiring you, you drifted away."

He shook his head. "No. Yes. I did, I'm sorry, I thought of something."

"My fault. I talk too much."

"Not possible."

She stood slowly, as if waiting to be stopped. She smoothed her dress, worked her feet into her sandals, taking her time, drained her glass of water, put it back on the table.

At the door he laid his hands on her shoulders and she must have sensed a change in his touch, a question, because she slowly turned, with downcast eyes. His hands found hers and for a moment they stood, at the edge of mankind's oldest question. Their eyes met, their fingers entwined, their hearts raced.

Until one word came between them. "Arie," Tamara whispered. She felt the shudder of Peter's sigh in his hands.

As Tamara's wooden sandals tapped down the stairs, like a ticking clock, Peter groaned. Go after her, he told himself. Now. This is it.

PETER

TEL AVIV, ISRAEL

September 1964

Mahmoud al-Faradis and Arie. The two names tumbled through Peter's mind. He closed the file he was reading and stared at the wall. His team's unanimous conclusion was that Nile, who had nearly killed him, had to be killed himself. In this new conflict they all knew was just beginning, Palestinians needed a warning of what would happen if they crossed a Mossad agent.

And now they had found him, in Paris.

Israeli agents had long known of an emerging leader of the Palestinian cause, a planner of terrorist attacks against Israel. He called himself Abu Ammar but was better known as Yasser Arafat, though even that wasn't his real name. Mossad helpers routinely tracked Arafat in Paris as he recruited fighters among exiled Palestinians; their names were collected and passed to Shin Bet. Their families back home were identified, and blackmail candidates noted for future coercion.

Several months after the attempted murder Arafat had met two men in the café of the Gare du Nord. To the agents' surprise, one of them was Nile. He was back in town. Nile was now being tailed around the clock, and Mossad's top floor had to decide: Should Nile live or die? Peter pushed for a decision—they had to act quickly.

It was hard to focus. His brother imposed himself upon every thought, demanding attention. Act quickly with Nile? With Arie too? Harm an agent? Would Arie harm the boy Yoram and make things worse? Live or die? Would Yoram, despite Arie's help, pursue the murder file against Arie?

Peter couldn't get Arie out of his mind.

Did Yoram believe Arie killed his father? What would he do? He visits the house. Could Tamara or her children be in danger?

Nile and Arie. Peter stood and moved slowly around the conference room, the only office large enough to contain him, where he could pace and find complete silence to think. He had approved the plan to eliminate Nile, now it was up to his boss Amit. But what was his plan with Arie? The more he thought about his brother the angrier he became.

Nile had failed to take his life, but Arie was destroying it.

He destroyed everything he touched, while enriching himself in every way.

Tamara. If only, he thought. If only he'd gone after her on the stairs. That was the moment, and he had missed it. He had hesitated, and she had left. Instead of rushing after her he had watched from the balcony as she walked along the path and disappeared behind the trees.

He sat down heavily at the table and poured himself a glass of water. He must get a grip. There was too much going on. Killing Nile. Confronting Arie. Tamara.

He had to act, on every front, and now.

He drained the glass, phoned Arie's office, hailed a taxi, and rode straight to the tower building under construction at the end of Herzl Street. Arie had rented new office space on the ninth and tenth floors, and was reviewing the building's progress with the owners.

He's a megalomaniac, Peter was thinking as the building came into view. In addition to new offices Arie had also offered to rent the entire thirty-sixth floor as a residence, which would give him the highest floor of the tallest building in the Middle East, with a view of the Mediterranean to the west and on a clear day, to the hills of Jerusalem in the east. His palace in the sky.

Israel's largest city would be at Arie's feet. How fitting. Peter hoped the owners would decline the offer.

He found Arie just as he was ending the tour, shaking hands with Moshe Meir, one of the three brothers building the tower. "What a pity," Peter couldn't resist saying. "Everyone loved the old building here, the first Hebrew high school, a beautiful Ottoman design. Pity it was demolished to make way for this . . ." He glanced at the tower emerging from the earth. ". . . this . . . building."

"Progress, brother," Arie said with a winner's chuckle and a wink to Moshe. He put his arm around Peter's shoulder and guided him to his car. "Change of plan, I'm sorry. I need to get back to my office. We can talk there."

Peter looked at his watch. He had an hour and a quarter before the meeting with Meir Amit, when he hoped to get the green light to eliminate Nile. He'd have to get to the point with Arie straightaway. But with Yaacov driving, it had to wait. They barely talked in the car, even though it had been a month or more since they had last spoken. Children fine? That's good. Ido in the army, outstanding soldier, making us all proud.

By the time they reached Arie's office, Peter could contain himself no longer. He had no time and there was too much on his mind, infuriating him.

"This young man, Yoram Shemesh. You've hired him? Why? You're playing with fire, Arie, and that risks me too."

"What? Slow down, brother. No it doesn't."

"Yes, it does. I got that police case suppressed, remember? I brought Mossad into a civil murder investigation and got it quashed. If it gets reopened, I'll be in the firing line."

"No, you won't."

"I will. I should never have helped you. And now you think you're so clever, putting your arms around this man, hiring him, paying for his studies . . ."

Arie flushed. "Who told you? Tamara?"

"Why hire him?"

"What does it matter? If I said I felt sorry for him, I just wanted to help him, you wouldn't believe it anyway."

"That's true enough. Anyway, it's too late now. They had a direct line to you, through Gingie and Tamara, and if they reopen the file, they'll find it. And then me. What a mess you've gotten us into."

"Pipe down, Peter, and don't get so excited . . ."

Barely controlling his voice, Peter launched into a tirade against his brother. It poured out. His selfishness. His arrogance. His false values. How he treated Tamara. His . . .

"Ah, so that's it. Now we're getting somewhere," Arie said. "Tamara. That's what this is all about. That's what it's always about. I wondered why you were getting so hot under the collar. This isn't about Schwartz, it's about Tamara."

"Don't be ridiculous . . ."

"You don't be ridiculous. And let me tell you something. There's no danger from Yoram Shemesh. He won't reopen the file. He can't."

"He can, he only has to . . ."

"He can't. I'll tell you why. Because the police don't have the file."

"Of course they do. Just because it was ten years ago doesn't mean anything, their files go back to the twenties."

"Not the Schwartz case. Not anymore." Arie took out two keys and went to his safe, cemented into the floor beneath his desk. He pulled out a faded olive green file with black print and writing in red and blue on the cover. He flipped through it.

"Because here it is. The police file." He dropped it on the desk with a flourish. "They have nothing on me, on you, on the case. It's all here. I got it a week ago." Peter picked it up and leafed through sheets of handwritten notes, a typed report of a dozen pages, interview transcripts, and an envelope of photographs.

He shook his head in disbelief. "You stole it?"

"I didn't."

"Who did?"

Arie sat behind the desk, leaned back with his arms outstretched, tapping his fingers. How Peter wanted to wipe that smug grin off his face.

"Let's just say an old friend repaid a debt."

"Are you crazy?" Peter almost shouted, then hissed, eyeing the door, "this is a serious crime. Stealing police property. Interfering with an investigation. God knows what else."

"Better than a trumped-up murder charge. Anyway, you can talk, with all the stuff you get up to." He put the file back into the safe and locked it. "I saved my soldier's life in a tank once, he's now a police detective, and he paid me back by saving me from potential embarrassment. That's all, I . . ."

"Arie, you're insane. Potential embarrassment? More like a genuine murder charge. You're just digging a deeper hole for yourself. We're done. I didn't hear any of this, I don't know about it, this conversation never took place. I have to go."

"Oh, come on. Don't play the innocent. I know why you're getting so angry. This is about you and Tamara . . ."

"This is not about Tamara, you damn fool."

"Yes, it is. I may not be the best husband, but she's my wife, and always will be, so you stay away."

Peter turned from the door, each step toward Arie a little firmer, each word more deliberate. "She's not your property. The way you treat her, she should have left you years ago."

"Then why didn't she? Because she loves me. Me, Peter. Me."

"But you don't love her. All you do is cheat. On her, in business, on everyone. And she deserves better . . ."

"Better? You? Stay away from my wife, Peter. I'm warning you."

"You're warning me? Of what? You think I'm Yonathan Schwartz? You're going to smash my head with a rock?" Now Peter was a meter from Arie, the vein throbbing at his temple. "Or do you get somebody else to do your dirty work these days?"

His heart was pumping, his mind racing, yet oddly focused. Mahmoud al-Faradis. Arie. Guns, death, fear. His brother was big, strong, fearsome, but with the thrust of a knuckle he could immobilize Arie before Arie even raised a fist. Instead, Peter stepped back. "Get a grip, Arie. You're threatening your own brother?"

"Stay out of my marriage, Peter. Stay away from my wife. Don't push me."

Peter forced himself to stay calm. If he spoke up now there was no going back. It was one thing to call Arie a bad husband; quite another to announce himself as a rival; to confirm Arie's fears. Keep him guessing. His breathing calmed, his training took over. If you make an enemy, don't let him know it.

Anyway, it isn't up to Arie, or me, he thought, it's up to Tamara. Who does she want? Truly?

MOSHE

TEL AVIV, ISRAEL

October 1964

———

Moshe thumped the final key and called out "Done!" to the walls of his living room. The headline always came to him last, when he had finished writing the column: "Murder in the City of Light"—*Yes!* He liked the "Light" reference: it was ironic, it played off how dark the story was.

When Mahmoud al-Faradis was shot dead by the cheese stall of the Rue de la Gaîté market in Montparnasse, French tabloids called it payback for gambling debts, a cover story the French police put out.

But Moshe had two solid sources for the real story behind the murder of the Egyptian army officer. The man on the motorcycle, his face hidden by goggles and a helmet, who shot al-Faradis three times in the head and raced away along Avenue du Maine, was a hit man for a rival Palestinian group fighting Yasser Arafat's new Palestine Liberation Organization. Moshe's third paragraph quoted an Israeli intelligence source: "The Palestinians are organizing against Israel but already they kill each other. It's a sign of how fragmented and weak they really are, despite all their empty threats."

Peter chuckled the next day when he read the newspaper. He must remember to congratulate Moshe on his "scoop." And also the guys on the information desk who had planted the false story that Moshe had picked up. There was nobody better than Mossad at planting disinformation and sowing discord. Moshe's inaccurate column would be picked up by the international media, translated into Arabic, and pretty soon the so-called Palestinians really would be killing each other.

"You shouted 'Done.' What's done?" Tamara said as she entered Moshe's living room, laden with groceries. She kissed her father on the forehead at the dining table where he worked, and carried the bags to the kitchen, calling out, "Ima."

"Your mother's out, she had to go to school to talk with the principal about Peter's boys. More trouble. It's all getting a bit much."

"What is it this time?" Tamara said from the door.

"Don't know."

Tamara returned minutes later with two glasses of mint tea. "What's done?" she asked again.

"Oh, my next column, let's not talk about that now. I wanted to ask you something. About Arie."

"Not that again. Please, Abba, don't ask."

"What again?"

"Us. Me. Him."

"What about you? Is everything all right? I wanted to ask you about his business. I read he's investing even more heavily in industry and construction in development towns, and expanding his garages and service stations. I want you to tell him not to invest so much. I think the economy is going to stop booming and slow down dramatically . . ."

"It isn't his money," Tamara interrupted. "It never is, it's investors, bank loans . . . and anyway, he's interested in politics, he thinks investment in these places will help him climb inside Mapai. He's thinking of his future, maybe Parliament. God help Israel."

Moshe laughed. "Prime Minister Arie Nesher. At least he gets things done. But as for the economy, he has to pay interest, and eventually pay back the loans. My next column will be about the recession around the corner. It's been too good here, too long. And it isn't based on production, that's what I've been researching." He stirred two sugars into the tea. "The boom is based on German reparations money flooding the country, American aid, Israel bonds, it's all smoke and mirrors, it can't last. Arie may be one of the richest men in Israel, but he's also by far the most overextended. His debts vastly exceed his assets. I've been studying it. He needs to retrench before the recession hits."

"Well, he'll be here soon, tell him yourself, you think he listens to me?"

"He should, if he's so rich then so are you, and you're a smart lawyer, of course he should listen to you."

"Well that's hard because we rarely talk. Anyway, so why do you think the economy is about to collapse?"

"Not collapse, but the prime minister's advisers tell me Eshkol will have to rein in spending. People will have to make do with less. He'll give a big speech soon on the economy. So this is what will happen, this is my next column: Money becomes tighter, businesses which depend on loans can't pay the interest and collapse, people lose jobs, and at the same time immigration is slowing, fewer Jews come to live here, while others leave because it's too hard, so there's less demand for housing, less demand for goods, more businesses collapse, more people lose jobs, and finally people here will have to live on what they make and not on what they borrow. Two of Arie's biggest businesses, transport and construction, will be hit hardest."

"But why should all that happen?" Tamara asked. "The government wants more people here, not fewer. And they need homes." But was Arie in trouble? Maybe that explained his foul mood lately.

"I told you, we're living in a fool's paradise. The government needs to reduce spending and increase productivity. Anyway look, what do I know, I just write a column, but I tell you, Arie needs to be careful, he's been riding a wave and it's hitting the rocks. I like that!" He wrote the phrase in his notebook.

A car drew up outside and the door slammed.

"Well, tell him yourself, here he is."

The engine was still running when Arie entered the apartment. He looked around. "It's about time you moved to a larger place, Moshe. I'll see what I can do."

"Ah, the perfect opening for me," Moshe said. "No thanks, Arie, I'll stay right here where I can afford it. And if I were you I'd take another look at my finances."

"Why, what's wrong with your finances?"

"Funny guy. I meant yours."

"What do you mean? Things were never better. Darling," he said, turning to Tamara, "I can't stay after all, Yaacov is waiting to take me to a meeting, I just wanted to say hello to your parents. Moshe, how are you, apart from giving me financial advice, which I think you're not exactly qualified to do, no disrespect intended."

"None taken."

"What kind of meeting?" Tamara asked again.

"Business of course. Moshe, don't worry, everything's on the up. The country's exports are close to a billion US dollars, Israel is barely sixteen years old and already we're about fifteenth in the world in per capita GNP, we're producing most of what we eat. In short, stop pissing in the tent."

"Yes, all true, but we're spending way too much on the military, more than ten percent of the budget, inflation is rising every year . . ."

Tamara interrupted. "Another business meeting? Who with this time? Batia? Naomi? . . ."

"Enough!" Arie raised his voice so that Moshe looked up sharply. "I told you this morning, you're fantasizing, there's no one else, it's all in your head." He all but shouted the last word and emphasized it with a fist.

Tamara almost hissed. "Not in front of Abba. Go, then. Go to her, whichever one it is. Don't come back." Her body tensed, she felt the muscle in her arm. Oh, how she'd like to slap him. "Go on, get out."

Arie shook his head, as if in disbelief. "I'll come home as soon as I can."

She slammed the door after him, muttering to herself, "Yes, at four in the morning."

When she turned, Moshe was staring at his notes.

"Sorry, Abba," Tamara said quietly.

After a moment he said, "I am too," and held out his hand. Tamara took it and sat down heavily next to him. They sipped their tea, until Moshe dared break the silence.

"How bad is it?"

Seconds passed. Tamara's shoulders trembled. She squeezed her father's hand until it hurt, and a tear fell from her eye. And then another, and another, until she was sobbing in Moshe's arms, while he stroked her head, wishing he could find the right words to comfort his daughter. How long could she bear that man?

Rachel entered the room but before she could react he shushed her with a finger to his lips. Arie, he mouthed.

After a final sob that turned into a grunt of frustration, Tamara slipped away from her father's arms and hit the table in vexation. "Look at me," she said, half to herself, drying her cheeks and trying to laugh. "My job is to help people look after themselves. But I can't help myself."

"What can you do, that's life," her mother called, striding across the room, opening a package. "Here, have some cake, it's Egyptian cinnamon, Peter's girlfriend Etti made it. What a cook, it's delicious. Have a slice, you'll feel a lot better, my dear."

PETER

TEL AVIV, ISRAEL
November 1965

M ossad's new deputy head of special operations waited impatiently for the room to settle down, until all eyes were on Peter Nesher, glaring from the head of the laminated conference table. They knew him as a legendary field agent and saw his frustration. For Nesher had swapped the back streets for the boardroom, the pistol for the pen.

He shifted uncomfortably, in his third meeting of the day. "I'll start with the good news: the last of the German scientists are leaving Egypt, to work in Europe at about double the money. But the bad news is we're losing the intelligence stream from those Germans just as Nasser is ratcheting up his threats against us." Peter scanned the familiar faces around the table, feeling he was on the wrong side.

"To make it worse, when Wolfgang Lotz was captured in March we lost the best source of information in Egypt we ever had, and the same in Syria in January when Eli Cohen was caught. Our two best assets, lost within six weeks of each other, thanks to Russian radio monitoring equipment. Together, that may be the biggest blow we've ever suffered, just when it's clear we're heading for another war and information is critical. In the north, the shelling from Syria means that thousands of our children spend days, weeks, sleeping in bomb shelters, while the new threat from Palestinian terrorists, based in Syria and Jordan, threatens those same communities with ground attacks every day. Too many of our citizens live in fear."

Peter could have added that a week earlier he had visited his friends Wolfie and Mayan on their kibbutz near the Sea of Galilee. Their five-year-old daughter Sophia hummed herself to sleep with the sound of a siren, and earlier when Peter's son Ezra had picked up an overlooked case of cucumbers in a field, Sophia had almost screamed, Don't touch it! It may be a bomb!

He heard himself continue. "The next round is approaching fast. We cannot overestimate the Arabs' thirst for revenge. However, as usual, our colleagues over at military intelligence disagree. Aman believes there is no chance of war with Egypt until '69 or '70, while Moscow prefers to keep the pot boiling, with no real war. But our own analysis shows that war is inevitable, and soon. Our task is to prove it."

Next came forty-five minutes of reports by section heads on the covert war—assassination, sabotage, paramilitary operations and psychological warfare—until Peter Nesher wrapped up the meeting with a deep sigh. He missed the action, but what could he do?

He had dodged the issue as long as he could, until Gingie and Tamara had forced him to face the obvious: Peter wasn't Israel's only secret agent, and right now his children needed him more than his country.

His twins had become too much for Rachel to handle, Noah and Ezra had grown into the original dreadful duo. When they weren't fighting each other, they fought with other boys at school, while at home they were morose, uncommunicative, and rude. Only when they played with their little sister, Diana, did their gentle souls emerge. They bathed and fed her and took turns telling her bedtime stories. Rachel told Tamara, Tamara told Gingie, and finally Peter got the message: Stop going away all the time. His twins were sweet but wild. It was three years since Diana had died, and at twelve years old they needed a parent at home—they needed their dad.

Although frustrated behind a desk, Peter had to admit that as a dad he was like a fish in water. At weekends he swam with his sons in the Mediterranean, took them for ice cream at Montana at the port, played football in HaYarkon Park, and in the apartment they wrestled, which he now understood was really just a boy's way to cuddle. There were no more vexed calls from the school's principal.

His boys reminded him so much of their mother that he shuddered at the shallow nature of his affair with Ayelet, who he had been seeing on and off for half a year. When he ended it, she had merely shrugged, picked up her jacket, said, "Go to hell," and walked out. He had watched the door close behind her and knew Ayelet would never cross his mind again.

It was his brother's wife who occupied that space. Even though he rarely saw Tamara, at birthdays and bar mitzvahs for the most part, he couldn't get her out of his head; seeing her left him empty and alone. He had loved Diana deeply, yet even when she was alive and Tamara was her closest friend, he had felt an unseemly attraction for Tamara that unsettled him. Forbidden then, forbidden now. Oddly, it was Arie's anger with him that gave him most encouragement. If he's so angry, there must be something to be angry about.

When the family had last gathered, three weeks earlier, to celebrate the birthday of his twins, the only jarring notes were the frosty looks between Tamara and Arie. It seemed the more cars in their driveway, the grander their home, the more modern their furnishings, with old master paintings, imported rugs, and ornate sets of china, the more distant the couple became. They barely acknowledged each other. It at once saddened Peter and almost gave him encouragement. But what to do? It was hopeless.

And then she approached him. For the wrong reason, he thought, but it was a start.

She asked to meet him on a park bench, overlooking the sea by the new Hilton hotel, at seven o'clock in the evening. The sun, nearing the horizon, sparkled on the crystal water, which lapped onto the beach below them. Peter, early as always, stood as Tamara approached.

"You're the last polite man in Israel," Tamara said with a smile and a kiss on the cheek. "Or the first, I'm not sure which."

"It's the German in me," Peter replied. "Here, I brought some orange juice."

"Fresh?"

"Of course."

They sipped quietly, sitting on the bench, facing the sea, the sun warming their faces. Tamara sighed, and Peter stole a glance. She brushed his cheek with her fingers. "You need to shave."

His heart leapt, until he remembered why she wanted to meet.

"You said it's about work," he said.

"Sorry, but yes," she said, nodding. "I have a new client, and he said some things that made me think you may be involved."

"Me? Involved? In what?"

"Can you keep a secret?"

Peter laughed. "Me? Never."

Tamara smiled. "I'll take that as a yes. Do you know the name Mahmoud al-Faradis? He was murdered in Paris a year ago."

"No. Why?" A puzzled look.

"His brother came to me asking for help. He has a strange story. I can't go into it all with you, you know, client privilege, but it's the old story, Shin Bet is blackmailing him, they're threatening to deport him from his home, make him live in another town, they're refusing him a permit to take his wife to the hospital nearby, but instead of becoming an informer, he wants to fight them."

"So."

"Well, he says his brother was killed by Mossad."

"Okay."

"Peter, I know you too well."

"What?"

"I mean you're being monosyllabic. That means you're not being honest."

Peter laughed aloud and took Tamara's hand. "I love that you know me so well. Is that my giveaway sign? I'll have to find some longer words." His face crinkled in delight and he laughed again. "I'll never play poker with you."

"So, do you know anything about it?" she said, pulling her hand from his.

"No, I told you, I don't. Why do you ask?"

"He mentioned a name that his brother gave him once, somebody his brother said that if ever something happened to him, he should contact this person."

"To say what?"

"He didn't say. I think it was just to find out the truth. Whatever that is."

"So what was the name?"

"A funny one. A German name. That's why I thought of you." She took out a piece of paper and read the name. "Willi Stinglwagner."

"Never heard of him."

"Mahmoud al-Faradis told his brother, my client, that this man was a Mossad agent working in Europe, a German, or more likely an Israeli. That's all I know. And . . . so . . . guess who I thought of."

"Your brother-in-law."

"Exactly."

"And you want help with the Shin Bet, to get them to leave your client alone."

"You're so quick."

"Did you tell your client you knew someone in Mossad?"

"Of course not."

"You're sure."

"Of course I'm sure."

"Tamara, it's very important you keep it that way."

Peter stared out to sea, at the golden ball settling at water's end, half hidden in clouds. A minute went by as he worked the odds. What were the chances that an Israeli Arab, brother of a Palestinian terrorist, could know that he was Stinglwagner? Why had he approached, of all the lawyers in Israel, his sister-in law? Chance? Peter didn't believe in chance. But if they knew his identity they could reach him directly, they wouldn't need to go through Tamara. In fact, they'd avoid her, rather than widen the circle. So maybe it was a coincidence after all. And why wait a year? Anyway, what would they want from him? Revenge, to kill him? To send him a message? He sucked his lip. For none of that would they need Tamara. Or to open a back channel? He swiveled his head. Could they be following her? Who? Why?

No, he decided. Nobody could know who Stinglwagner really was. And

going through Tamara was too complicated, too iffy. This must be a coincidence. But he would take no chances, he needed to find out who Tamara's
client was, have Shin Bet pick him up again, do what they do best, and find
out what the hell was going on. Gingie would take care of that.

"So," Tamara finally said, "a penny for your thoughts. Did I hit a nerve?
Do you want to tell me what you're thinking?"

"No, I don't. I can tell you something else I'm thinking, though."

"Yes, Peter?"

Jarred by his own words, as if he had challenged himself to speak up,
Peter studied the sea. He watched the orange-tipped waves roll gently
landward, until he found his hand reaching for Tamara's. He held it in silence, felt its warmth, felt her fingers curling around his in response, knowing he could not stop now. There would never be the perfect time. And he
had wasted too much of it already. Peter caressed Tamara's fingers until at
last he turned toward her, hope pounding in his heart.

ARIE

TEL AVIV, ISRAEL
December 1966

A rie surveyed the tin roofs of Neve Tzedek, a low sprawl beneath him that stretched almost to the sea, an island of poverty in the midst of Tel Aviv's building boom. I should buy out the Yemenites and Moroccans there, he thought, and build. He examined their crumbling roofs and dense alleys. It's so close to the sea, that land is a gold mine, and it's on my doorstep.

On clear days, which was most of them, the view from his new offices stretched north past the power station at Sde Dov to Netanya and south to the hill of Jaffa and the cross of the church whose name he could never remember. He congratulated himself: It's the best view in Israel, not bad for a boy from . . . He paused. A sense of irritation disturbed him, as it did each time he looked out. Why hadn't he rented higher floors? The view is much better from up there. He still had the option for a residence on the top floor of the tower, but the municipality was claiming the building had no residential license, only commercial. Well, he'd deal with that. Why else had he been cozying up to the mayor and paying off half his staff?

He turned as his secretary, Sharon, knocked and opened the door. "Your ten o'clock," she said. "Larry Larone."

Arie managed a smile and pointed to the white leather sofa. "Larry! Sit down, please. How are you?" Larone was the uncle of his daughter's American pen pal, Alice. The girl wanted to come and work on a kibbutz next Easter for a few months, and Larone had used that slim connection to meet the Israeli tycoon and pitch a truly off-the-wall business proposition. And yet, Arie had been intrigued. "Any luck at the dig?" Arie asked. His English was good, with an accent more staccato German than slurred Hebrew.

The Texan, tall and thin with a carefully trimmed goatee, walked right by Arie to the double window, as did most visitors. "Oh my Lord," he said, "what a view! And look at Jaffa for Heaven's sake, there's St. Peter's, the beacon for pilgrims to the Holy Land. And the hill of Jaffa, where Saint Peter raised Tabitha from the dead. And to think, you gaze upon this holy sight every day of your life. You are indeed blessed, Arie, even if you don't believe a word of it."

He shouted with laughter—Heh!—and slapped Arie on the shoulder: "Let yourself be guided by the Lord, Jesus Christ, our Savior, and all will be granted to men of faith."

"Thank you," Arie said. "I will try. But in the meantime, any luck at the dig?"

"The well, you mean. We're not there yet. But have faith, for the Lord guideth us. Not to green pastures, but to black gold." Another loud Heh! "But seriously my friend, I need to know, did you decide, will you invest? Can you improve your offer?"

Arie poured a glass of water and reached across to the oilman, who in return gave him a colorful brochure. Arie could not decide whether Larry really was a devout Christian who truly believed the Bible pointed to vast oil reserves beneath the Holy Land, or a con artist.

Apart from salt and a few chemicals in the Dead Sea, Israel had no known mineral wealth. Yet with half the Arab world growing rich from oil, it made no sense that there was no oil or gas buried beneath Israel. Why would it stop at Israel's border, a line in the sand?

Arie was deeply invested in transport, from building roads to selling and servicing cars, so the logical next step was to provide the fuel for the engines. Finding oil would be the master coup. But could he really trust this Bible-thumping, God-fearing evangelical Texan with the strange leather boots and silver string tie who had wrung a drilling concession from the government based on ancient biblical prophecy? Here it was at the head of the prospectus, in large bold blue type: *"And of Asher he said, Let Asher be blessed with children; let him be acceptable to his brethren, and let him dip his foot in oil* (Deuteronomy 33:24)."

The Texan's company was drilling near Haifa, in the Carmel mountains, part of a region known in the Bible as the "foot of Asher." "Oh praise the Lord!" Larry had shouted, "the Lord keeps his promise. Trust in the Lord for His word is Truth!"

So far the wells were dry. But the Bible was explicit. Referring to the land given to the twelve tribes of Israel, it stated that oil would be found where Asher's foot met Joseph's head. "Well, maybe not explicit, but more or less," Larone had said. "It's implied that where the two lands meet, that's where it is. That's where we're digging, we've found signs of hydrocarbons. We're reaching the Jurassic crest." All man has to do is believe, dig, and wait for the gusher.

And all this man, Arie Nesher, had to do was finance the wait. One million dollars would last a long time.

Not a chance, Arie had said. After all, what if the Bible was referring not to crude oil but to olive oil? For the region was blanketed with olive trees and always had been. His offer: three hundred thousand for 51 percent of the company. It was worth a gamble, he thought, and what Larry didn't know was that he was covering his bet by backing an Israeli company that was searching for gas offshore.

After twenty minutes, Arie walked the Texan back to the elevator through his offices, pointing out company names fixed in bronze to each cluster of doors: his empire, renamed Feather Holdings. "Textiles, construction, automobiles, a chain of grocery stores, another chain of pharmacies, an insurance company, and more. We're a conglomerate now."

"So why so mean?" Larone said. "Make it eight hundred thousand, I could never persuade my partners to sell 51 percent for three hundred Gs." They stopped by the kitchen, a recess with water and a coffee machine.

"I shouldn't have boasted about my company," Arie said. "Listen, it isn't only about money. With me you get contacts, *proteksia*, I can get things done, smooth things over with the mayors, the party, even the police if necessary. Think of me not only as a business partner but as a facilitator, consultant, analyst. The best there is. That's who you're bringing into the company."

When the elevator door closed on Larone, who promised to work on his partners, Arie returned to the coffeemaker and waited for the water to boil. He needed a moment. He had presented himself as the dynamic, successful businessman, image was everything, but that wasn't how he felt. With all the buzz around him in the media, and his employees bustling in the corridor and others with their heads down at their desks, he still felt a cold sweat. All was not well with the business. Insurance and pharmacies were performing well, but they were the sectors with the least investment and external financing. Every other sphere was struggling to remain in the black while construction and automobiles, where he was most leveraged, were hemorrhaging money. His business plan was that his earnings grow to pay his debt, but instead his earnings were falling. His next meeting in an hour was at Bank Leumi, which was threatening to call in two separate loans. He needed to sell assets to pay the debts, and quickly, but the economy was drying up. Foreign investment had slowed, government financing was disappearing, immigration was down, so was demand for housing, cars, everything. He felt like banging his cup on the table. Moshe had warned of this a year earlier. He should have listened to the old coot. The economy was in free fall and he was going down with it.

The oil and gas investments—should he do them? However bad the situation today, he still needed to build for tomorrow. He was on a bicycle that needed forward motion or it would crash. Borrow, buy, consolidate, profit, sell. That had worked so far, and for it to continue to work, to build more wealth, he needed to invest in the future while divesting some of the failing businesses. But again, back to the same problem: who will buy? Nobody can get financing.

It seemed for Israel, after eighteen years of statehood, the party was over. The economy was a game of musical chairs and he was left without one. Arie felt ill. He was way overextended. But he couldn't admit it or the sharks would lunge. His only way forward was to invest more, bluff, and extend the terms of his bank loans. After all, the banks knew if he went under they would lose their money too. This was a time for strong nerves and no false steps. Business as usual. He nodded at his chief accountant and smiled as heartily as he could at the personnel manager.

On the way back to his office Arie stopped at Sharon's desk, sipping his coffee. "How is it going, the presents?" Arie asked.

The first day of Hanukah was a week away, December 18, in the Jewish calendar the 24th of Kislev, 5726. Sharon had brought presents for everybody on Arie's list, from his own children to his parents-in-law, Tamara's siblings Ido and Estie, as well as Peter and his children. All but one.

"I don't know what to get Tamara," Sharon said. "I think you should pick something yourself, really, it's too personal."

"Don't worry, buy her some jewelry, she likes earrings."

"I bought her earrings last year. Or rather, you did."

"So a bracelet, then. Or a necklace."

"Or both?"

"Better still, yes, both."

"With matching earrings? A ring? A set? Diamonds?"

Arie gritted his teeth and nodded.

As he walked to his office and slammed the door, she looked after him, shaking her head.

TAMARA and PETER

TEL AVIV, ISRAEL

December 1966

Tamara froze at the foot of the ficus tree, half stripped of leaves by the winter chill. She didn't move a muscle, barely drew a breath. Above her, maybe five feet, a white bird with an S-curved neck watched immobile from a jutting limb. It was large with a long yellow bill, sharp like a dagger, and thin black legs. It's an egret, she thought, it must be lost. It should be on the migration route, in the Hula Valley. What is it doing here?

She was bewitched by the dazzling white-feathered beauty, so noble, so close she felt she could touch it, until she realized she could ask the same question of herself. What was she doing here? She looked up at Peter's apartment. Was she lost too? But her head movement, as she turned back to the bird, startled it, and with a flap of its mighty wings, so close she felt the shifting air, the egret soared, to seek its flock.

She should leave too, she thought, this is madness. She belonged with her family.

But the family was changing. The twins were sixteen and seemed to prefer the homes of their friends. Ever since Peter had asked to meet, alone, secretly, she had been racked with doubt. She lay awake at night, questioning every part of her life, but especially Arie, who rarely slept at her side. How long had he been cheating on her? Forever. And everybody knew. If she was her own client she would have advised herself to leave her husband years ago. And now here she was, doing the same thing as him. Or about to. She looked up again at Peter's balcony, at the pants and shirts drying on the line, a bicycle's handlebars visible above the brick wall, the ugly square air conditioner sticking out like a wart.

She remained in the tree's shade, absorbing the grace of the diminishing bird as its white body vanished among puffs of gray cloud. She looked around, over her shoulder. Is anybody watching, does anybody know me? All she had to do was walk the final few steps to the building's entrance and climb the stairs into Peter's arms. But with a sinking feeling she thought, I can't, I truly can't. Despite everything, this is so wrong.

Upstairs, there was nothing more Peter could do but wait, and hope Tamara would come. He had changed the sheets, smoothed the pillows, collected the pile of shoes and sandals that littered the entrance and stuffed them beneath the hall table. He had taken all the toys and skates and dropped them in the children's room. He had dusted the surfaces and re-arranged everything that moved. The boys were at school and wouldn't be home till two o'clock, while Rachel would pick up little Diana from kin-dergarten at midday and take her to her own home. He had four hours. But where was Tamara?

Resisting the temptation to look out of the balcony every ten seconds, Peter poured a glass of lemon juice from the jug he had prepared for Ta-mara and sprawled across the sofa, resting his head on a cushion, his feet draped over the end. He closed his eyes, trying to control his breathing, but his mind kept turning to what would happen when Tamara knocked on the door. If she did. Would she? He placed his hand on his heart, felt its rapid beat; I could be on a stakeout, waiting for a target to leave the building. No, I'm never this nervous at work.

How long had he wanted Tamara? He didn't dare answer, even to him-self, he didn't dare consider that all the nine years he had been married with Diana he had loved someone else. It wasn't even true, even to think it was disloyal and false. And yet . . . they had only come together because Arie had got in first with Tamara. There. Said it. He quickly banished the thought, but here it was again. Oh, Tamara.

Will she come? But what about Arie? His own brother.

Peter pushed that thought away too. He wouldn't let him ruin it. He wanted to strip away all pretense, all borders, and finally, after all these years, let the chips fall where they may. For once he had to be true to himself.

But where was she? He went to the balcony. He looked to the left and to the right, peered along the path through the trees. No sign of Tamara. He felt nauseous.

So did Tamara, who was now at the door, her hand raised to knock, but slowly she let it fall to her side, her heart thumping.

This is madness, she thought again. What if Arie found out? He would go crazy. Yes, she knew Peter had loved her, since they'd first met, that is what he told her on the park bench, that he had always loved her, that Diana had been his love too, his true love, but she, Tamara, had always been the one, the one he had lost. What made it worse was that his words were honey to her soul, they stirred her heart. She had held his hand tighter and tighter and when he had poured out his love, at the end, when he had asked if she would come to see him, and he had said they could no longer deny themselves, she had answered with one word, the one simple word that threatened everything she had and who she was. She answered, so quietly he could hardly hear, or believe what he heard, she answered with one daring, dangerous, deceitful word: Yes.

Peter looked at the clock. It was ten past ten, she was ten minutes late. That's nothing, he thought. Maybe she couldn't find a taxi, maybe it broke down, anything could be delaying her. At a quarter past a sense of desperation came over him. If she doesn't come now, she isn't coming. He had given her his heart, and she had rejected it. He could never offer it again. He had made his play, and he had lost. He couldn't blame her. Life in a mansion with one of Israel's richest men, even if it was a lousy marriage, was better than living with him in a messy two-bedroom apartment with three kids. What did he really have to offer? He must have been crazy, all these years of longing and frustration. Get real, Peter. The dream is over.

At ten sixteen there was a tap on the door.

Twice he had hidden Diana's photograph in a drawer, and twice he had taken it out again. In the end he had left her where she always was, presiding over the room from her silver frame, in the middle of the sideboard.

He knew she'd approve.

When he heard the tap on the door Peter couldn't help glancing at Diana. He felt a shiver. Was it delight? Regret? Or anticipation? Or dread at his next move, one that could destroy his family and hers? Maybe it would be smarter not to answer the door.

He moved slowly, adjusting his belt, running his hand through his hair.

On the other side of the door, Tamara was thinking, maybe he isn't here. Maybe he forgot. She was ready to turn and flee. The flying egret flashed through her mind as the door opened and there was Peter. She thought, he looks so serious.

He closed the door behind her and watched. Silently she took off her jacket and draped it over a chair. She wore a white high-collared blouse with a tight gray skirt, as if she was going to her law office. Keeping up the pretense, a step toward deceit. She turned and hesitated. Uncertainty, tension: What did a good woman do? A good woman about to become a bad woman.

Peter gazed into her eyes, as if he was amazed she had come. With good reason, she thought, yet she found herself leaning toward him, until, as one, they moved into each other. Peter embraced her, and she rested comfortably against him and in this way they stood, silent, snug, her chest against his thin shirt, his against her flimsy blouse, each feeling the other's pounding heart, their touch and tightness saying more than words ever could.

And then, at last, Peter's lips found hers, and her sweet softness, yielding all the promise and hopes of the years, surrendered with a passion that grew with every passing second. Fifteen years of longing sweetened every sense until Peter felt giddy and had to steady himself with an arm on the entrance table.

Tamara held him, and smiled. She took him by the hand and turned, as if to say, Come with me.

In the bedroom, standing, they kissed more, passion and impatience now overwhelming them. Peter's hands rose to Tamara's breasts and one by one he unfastened the buttons on her blouse, while she opened his belt. Their lips still joined, Peter pulled off his shirt and held her against him, unclasping her bra. At last their lips parted and he looked down and gently kissed each breast, sinking to his knees, as if worshipping her, while Tamara threw her head back in ecstasy. She could barely breathe as his lips brushed her belly, his tongue flickering against her, his hands cupping her breasts. She tore off her skirt.

Looking up, Peter peeled down her panties. Tamara stepped out of her shoes and stood naked before him. She had never felt so beautiful, so proud, so majestic, like a noble egret settling its wings. It seemed to her now that this was where she belonged. With this man, who had loved her quietly, truly, with no reward, for so long. She took him by the hand, raised him to his feet, and opened his pants. They kissed again, harder now, urgently, he caressing her, from her shoulders to the small of her back, her skin warm and soft, and then, grateful, every nerve of his body awake, lower and lower until he clasped her bottom with both hands and pulled her against him, and she felt his hardness against her belly. Shivering with pleasure, she leaned back, away from him, and looking down, with no shame, pulled his shorts over his erection and down to his feet.

She held him, her head on his shoulder, chest to chest, hip to hip. In the far distance a warning sounded in Peter's mind, only to be silenced by the rapture building inside him. Tamara's body was at once firm and soft, empty of guile and full of promise. Peter tensed to pick her up but Tamara placed a finger on his lips as if to quiet him, and with the slightest pressure on his shoulder turned him around, inspecting him. His muscled, lean body, his chest fluffy and dark with hair, his buttocks slim and . . . She trailed her fingers across his scars and murmured, "You are a fighting man." These were their first words.

Her finger rested on a mottled purple patch below his right hip. "What is this from? And this?" A wine-red indentation in the shoulder, the width of a finger.

"A burn. A bullet. One German. One Arab. From another life."

Tamara completed the rotation, a little smile on her lips. She brought her mouth to his chest, and toyed with one nipple, and then the other. But

Peter couldn't wait. He had a sense of time evaporating, he wanted her, needed her, now.

"My body may have a fault or two, but you, Tamara, you are perfect," he whispered as he moved her to the bed. Lying by her he trailed his fingers along every ebb and flow of her, silken and thrilling, kissed her eyes and her throat all the way down to her thighs, wondering and exploring every inch of her flesh, until he found her very center, her revealed core, and there he lingered.

She trembled at his touch, rousing and insistent, her eyes clenched, her hands balled into fists. Her breath came in loud gasps until she arched, rocked, and finally shuddered to rest in his arms.

He could hardly believe it. Tamara . . . he overflowed with tenderness toward her. Everything that didn't make sense before now did. He gently entered her as the words slipped from his mouth: "I love you."

Tamara sighed and shifted to receive him, gripping him with her arms and legs. She breathed words he couldn't hear, but when he put his ear to her lips he heard what he longed for: "Peter. I love you too."

He hadn't loved a woman since Diana, and Tamara hadn't loved a man for a decade. They were like two drifting branches that reached the waterfall together, and swept over entangled and dripping, crashing into the cauldron below. She fell off the bed, he pulled her back and took her from behind, she collapsed and he pulled her on top, he couldn't get deep enough and she couldn't get enough of him. She came first, then he did, then they rested, gasping and laughing, and did it again.

Spent, they fell silent, lying back against the headboard, holding hands. With a deep sigh Tamara slipped down and laid her head on Peter's chest, her long hair sprawled across him. He rearranged her locks so that they lay by her shoulder, and he stroked her neck. She was hot and sweaty, and every few seconds her body shook, squeezing out every last gram of pleasure. Her mind was blank, her hand quiet on Peter's groin.

And then came the reckoning. Tamara took long gulps of lemon juice while Peter smoked half a cigarette before they spoke. "Now what?" he said.

"You do have a way with words," Tamara said. She added, "Nobody must know. This is our secret."

And then, "Let's not think about it. Enjoy the Now." For right now, Arie did not exist for her.

He did for Peter. His thoughts were a jumble, but uppermost was jealousy. How could Arie have been so lucky for so long, to have such a beautiful, sexy, glorious wife? And he doesn't even love her. He sighed. Although he inhabited a secret world, he could not lead a secret affair with Tamara. In the end they'd be found out anyway. Better to take the initiative. She must divorce Arie and marry him. For all they knew, Arie would be happy to divorce Tamara; their marriage had long been a sham. The problem with Arie would not be his nonexistent love for Tamara, but his pride.

Under Tamara's warm touch his brother receded, he felt himself growing hard again. They kissed, she gripped his buttocks as he held her by the waist, he wanted to make love to her forever, he didn't want to come. But he did, loudly, and fell asleep in her arms, while she dozed with a smile on her face.

Tamara could not remember when she last felt so relaxed, so deeply content, so full. She rested her hand between her legs. Moist, so deeply sated. She drifted in and out of sleep, trying to prolong the moment, the joy of holding Peter's naked body. As he breathed, long, deep, safe breaths, she fought her own sleep, wanting to enjoy the feel of him, the beating of his heart, the powerful arms and legs, like a big strong baby in her arms, his chest rising and falling, his breath tickling her cheeks, his sweet smell of sweaty pleasure. She never wanted to leave this bed, she wanted this moment to last forever.

"Oh!" Rachel caught her breath and closed the bedroom door.

Tamara shot upright. She looked at Peter, at the door, back to Peter. "Peter!" She jabbed him, shook him. "Peter."

He stirred, groaned.

"Peter, Peter!"

"Yes, my love?" His hand searched, fell onto her belly. He snuggled against her. "What time is it?"

She glanced at her watch. "Twelve thirty."

"Lots of time. Come back to sleep." He shifted, settled, and slept. "Peter!" Tamara jabbed him again. "Wake up. I think someone's here."

Peter tensed, and in an instant was on his feet, with his finger to his lips. He whispered, "Why?"

"I think someone opened the door. And closed it."

Peter slipped into his shorts and pants, pulled on his shirt. He padded to the door, strained to hear, took a deep breath, and pulled it open. He heard sounds in the kitchen, tiptoed there. Diana was sitting on the floor, looking up at him. "Daddy, I don't feel good. I miss Mummy."

"Mummy?" he said, bending down. He looked up at Rachel. "What happened?"

Rachel could not look him in the eyes. Her lips began to move but no sound emerged. At last she managed, "Tea?"

"No, thank you." She saw us. He took some biscuits from the cupboard and put them on a plate. "Here, darling," he said, putting the plate on the floor by Diana. "Was she crying at school again?" he asked Rachel.

She nodded, her eyes everywhere but on him.

He picked Diana up and held her close, whispering into her ear, soothing her. But she struggled to get out of his arms, to reach the biscuits.

Peter walked back to the bedroom and closed the door, looking grim.

"What is it?" Tamara was sitting on the bed, dressed, holding her hand to her throat, her eyes wide. "Who is it?"

He wouldn't mention Diana crying for her mummy. It would be too hurtful. He tried to smile but failed. "Well, some secret. We're busted."

"Who is it?"

"Your mother."

Tamara's face went from white to red. This couldn't be happening. Her mother! She had no idea what to feel. Or say.

"Whatever happens," she said finally, "after giving birth, this was the best moment of my life. Thank you, Peter."

"So formal. This is just the beginning. Anyway, what do you mean, whatever happens? We need to hold hands, go out there, and face your mother."

"No. Oh, God no! Not yet!"

"Well, she's out there. We can't hide in here."

"We can. We can. Get under the bed, I'll get in the closet."

"Good thinking. Maybe she'll leave and forget all about it," Peter said.

"Yes, yes. She has a horrible memory."

"We can just deny it. Deny is always the best response. She can't prove anything. No photographs."

"I have to talk to her," Tamara said, standing up.

Rachel called through the door, her voice more quavering than usual, "I'll go then, Peter, put Diana to bed. Bye-bye."

Tamara flew through the door. "Ima, wait, don't go."

Peter sat on the bed and sighed, torn between Tamara and the thought of poor little Diana. How could he make her understand that they all missed her mother, but they had to get on with their lives, they could never bring her back?

He looked at the door, feeling sheepish. Best let Tamara handle her mother.

And then he thought, wait. I'm forty-two years old, I'm deputy head of the Special Operations Division of the Israeli Secret Service, and I don't have to be afraid of Auntie Rachel.

RACHEL, MOSHE, and ARIE

TEL AVIV, ISRAEL

December 1966

For the first time ever, Rachel missed her bus stop; she only realized
when the driver turned on the radio news, which startled her from her
reverie. But then she welcomed the extra time as she walked home before
seeing Moshe.

At first she had been bewildered by the sight of Tamara and Peter sleeping in bed together. Were they sick? Then she had seen their clothes on the
floor, their underwear even, which had all but sent her into shock. She had
closed the door as quietly as she could, and backed away as if in a trance.
She had wanted to leave immediately but couldn't leave Diana alone, so she
had made tea while she thought what to do. Her hand had trembled so
much she thought she would spill the water as she poured. What did she
just see? What did it mean? And then Tamara had caught her by the arm at
the door, and sworn her to secrecy. It was true that Peter was a most charming man, and Arie was a terrible husband. And this was Israel, not Egypt,
she wasn't stupid, she knew what went on. But still—brothers. This could
only end badly. Very badly.

And shouldn't she tell Moshe? She had never kept a secret from him in
her life, nor he from her. Maybe it was best to stay out of it. As she turned
the last corner and walked to her building, she still hadn't decided. *Ya Allah!*

She stopped in her tracks. Arie's car was at the door. Did he know? Why had he come?

She hurried home, to hear Moshe's raised voice. When he was excited he almost shouted, it was his way. She heard "Russia" and "stupid people."

"Hello, Rachel," Arie said, kissing her on the cheek and taking her bag. "Save me from Moshe."

"Save us all from the government!" Moshe shouted. "Really, it's true," he continued where he had left off, barely acknowledging his wife. "Every time the army attacks Syria or Jordan in retaliation for a terrorist attack, the truth is we provoked it. I'm telling you, our government wants war."

"Every time?" Arie said. "Oh, come on. Why would we want war? We want peace, to grow the economy, it's in terrible shape, that's what we want."

"That's what you want. What Eshkol and Meir and all those other blockheads care about is more land, and an excuse to take it. We send a tractor into a demilitarized zone, the Syrians shoot at it, we bomb their gun position, and so it goes. Each time—"

"Is that what you're going to write? How do you know? We want peace. You're like a propagandist for—"

"Me? All I want is for people to know the truth. And the truth is—"

"The truth is terrorists are crossing into our country, killing our farmers, mortaring the kibbutzim, laying land mines in the fields, and we have to stop them. That's the truth."

"That's what the government wants you to think. You're a sheep, you believe everything they say."

"And what every other journalist thinks and writes. Why should you know better . . . ?"

"I'm making some tea, would anyone like some?" Rachel put in when she could, with a higher-pitched voice than usual. She retreated to the kitchen, heaving a sigh. How could she look Arie in the eyes again? She knew now she couldn't tell Moshe, knowing him he would blurt it out. But what was Arie doing here, talking politics with Moshe, or rather, arguing? Even in the kitchen she heard every word.

Moshe was beating the table: "In Samua last month, that Jordanian village, we killed fourteen Jordanian soldiers, we blew up at least fifty houses, and why? Because three of our boys died when they hit a land mine in the Hebron hills. Now the Jordanian army is on alert. Don't you see, one thing leads to another, we never miss an opportunity to create bigger clashes, and soon we'll have a war crashing down on us. It's my duty to write about it. All you do is read the hacks who spout the government line."

"Where do you get your information from? The Arabs? The Russians? You're playing right into their hands. You're helping them."

"Me, are you crazy? My own son, Ido, is in the infantry, a captain, they're the ones who cross the borders at night. Do you think I want to help the enemy? I want him to come home in one piece, we can't sleep we're so afraid for him."

"How is Ido?" Arie said, his voice softening as it always did when he talked about Tamara's little brother. "Does he come home at weekends?"

"When he can. If he does, all he does is sleep. He doesn't tell us anything, and he shouldn't. We write about what we know, but there's much more we don't know. We're in a low-level war that will explode, mark my words."

"Give Ido my love. He's a real fighter."

"And Estie. Two children in the army, God help me. She's in intelligence. Arie," Moshe said, placing his hand on Arie's forearm across the table. "Believe me, when I write about Israel, I write only the truth, for their sake. All I want is for them to come home safely. I want peace. And then maybe, your children will not have to fight. I hope not."

"Me too, Moshe. Tamara and I pray for Ido and Estie, they are the best of the best. How old are they now?"

"Ido is twenty. And Estie is twenty-two. She signed on for three more years, she's an officer too."

Rachel brought in the tea, and some biscuits. "We ran out, Arie, this is the best I can do."

"Thank you, Rachel," Arie said, looking down. "I do love to visit."

Moshe sensed something. "And we love to see you. But you never said why you came, I just went on and on. Because I'm writing a column on this. Forgive me. Is anything wrong, can I help?"

"Well, there is something I wanted to talk to you about, apart from war and peace."

Rachel froze. She didn't want to hear this. How long had this all been going on for? Tamara had said it was just once. She didn't know what to believe. "I'll just clean up in the kitchen," she said. She went to close the door but couldn't help herself and left it ajar, listening, her heart aflutter.

"Tamara," Arie said.

Rachel's heart sank. She felt the blood draining from her face.

"I can't really talk to her about this. Or anybody. It's strange really, everybody I meet wants something from me: money, a job, an introduction, advice, help, it's always give, give give."

Moshe began to say, well, you have so much more than anybody else, what's wrong with giving, but stopped himself. Arie never spoke like this. He should listen, not comment.

At the door, Rachel strained to hear. Her hand shook. Was this the end of her daughter's marriage?

Arie went on: "And yet the people closest to me, who I love most: you, Rachel, my brother, Tamara, you never ask for anything."

Moshe nodded gravely, arms folded, waiting.

"What I'm trying to say," Arie went on, "in a very roundabout way, is that I don't have so much to give anymore, and I can't talk about it to Tamara, or really, anyone." He came to a halt.

Moshe put in, "Is business that bad?"

"You were the only one who warned me, everybody else was pushing me to invest in this and that, and only you warned me of the recession around the corner. I remember you telling me it was all smoke and mirrors, that I was far too heavily invested when I should be hedging my bets. Anyway, you were right and everybody else was wrong." Again, he halted suddenly.

Rachel quietly closed the door. Thank God that's all it's about. Maybe it really was just once and would never happen again.

Moshe prompted him. "And?"

"Well," Arie said with a short laugh. "Nothing really. I guess I'm just looking for sympathy. And for someone with their finger to the wind. What do you think will happen now? I'm trying to sell the grocery chain but there are no buyers. No foreign investment either. And frankly, between you and me, servicing the loans is killing me. If one of the banks calls in a loan, and word gets out, and investors panic, which they would, there could be a landslide, an avalanche."

"But just last week *Maariv* ran a story on you and your new investments in mining."

"It's all a bluff. Putting a brave face on it all. I told them about potential investments, not actual money on the table. I may have blurred it a bit. As you said yourself, smoke and mirrors. There's another strike in Kiryat Gat in the textile factory, and that could spread to my other plants. Car sales? In the toilet. Construction? No loans to build; we've halted three large projects in the middle but we still have to service the debt. The pharmacies? Too many of them. Electronics? Nobody's buying, taxes are too high. Believe it or not, the only real growth area is chicken featherbeds. They're huge in Romania."

They both laughed.

"I missed my vocation," Moshe said. "But seriously, you know that for the first time since the founding of the state, more Jews are leaving than coming?"

"No, is that so? Why?"

"It's just too hard for many people. The recession. People won't come if they can't work."

"It means business won't pick up anytime soon."

"Exactly. The only way there'll be more business is if there's a war. And going back to where we began, it's coming."

Arie nodded. "Well, I refuse to hope that war will save me. When I think of Ido, I'd rather go under."

Moshe studied him. You know, he thought, I think he just may mean it.

IDO

———————

The order was to take one alive, information now being more critical than deterrence. That meant hand-to-hand combat, so the burliest fighters of the 3rd Company of the 12th battalion were up front. Leading the squad was Captain Ido, brother of Tamara, son of Moshe.

Family was important to Ido; early on he had taken heat from other soldiers for being a rare Mizrahi among mostly Ashkenazi kibbutzniks. The dark-skinned, black-haired exception among the tousle-haired, weather-beaten Europeans. Behind his back they called him Kushi, which meant Blackie.

But they didn't have to go to a bar with him; they only had to trust him with their lives. And now, to a man, they did. Stay close to Ido, was the word, he'll get you home again. After a dozen missions across the border they competed to buy him drinks.

Clouds half obscured the silver sliver of moon that glinted weakly on the dark waters of the Sea of Galilee. On the eastern shore, on the slopes of the Syrian Golan Heights, the rock escarpment which loomed seventeen hundred feet above the lake, the squad suffered through their third freezing night, camouflaged among the trees and shrubs above kibbutz Ein Gev. Lying in ambush, four soldiers turned the infiltrator route into a kill zone for the Fatah terrorists that intel reported would creep down from the Heights to lay land mines along the border patrol road. Four more soldiers hid higher up, dug in among the rocks so that when the surviving Arabs turned and fled, they would run right into them. One would be spared, bound, blindfolded, and taken for interrogation. The main question: How much are the Syrians helping you? Israel needed to know whether the weekly raids by Fatah, the fighting arm of the newly formed Palestine Liberation Organization, were merely a local irritation, or part of a larger plan. Was Syria's goal simply to farm the demilitarized areas or was it preparing for all-out war on the Jewish state? What Ido couldn't know was that one of the people who most needed the information was his brother-in-law, Peter Nesher.

All night the soldiers maintained total silence, the dark scented by groves of eucalyptus trees. They lay in two semicircles, communicating only by touching feet and pointing. To urinate they rolled over, avoiding leaves. In the all but moonless night they saw only shadows of shadows, every distant hoot or bird tweet could signal the coming enemy.

Ido's focus was constant. And it was Ido, highest up the hill, closest to the enemy, who heard them first. He glanced beneath the leather flap covering his watch face. 02.15. At last.

First, a cracking twig, murmurs, light footsteps. Then, so close he heard labored breathing. Reflected moonlight pierced the gloom, glinting off a swinging wristwatch between the outline of two trees. He figured three or four Arabs, treading softly, right into the ambush.

Along the line, one soldier's foot connected with another, fingers pointed. Painted faces rose from the damp earth, Uzi semiautomatics at the men's shoulders.

Three silhouettes loomed in the dark, menacing, outlined like hunchbacks. They're carrying backpacks with land mines. Ido let them pass, fifteen meters away. He wondered, for the briefest moment, which one would live. Who chose him to see his family again, one day, while the others would die here and now? A spasm of fear gripped him, would it all go wrong, was this his night to die? It passed as quickly as it came; he knew fear was greatest before the first bullet was fired. Who won't return? Who'll be wounded? Not me. Never me. Someone else. But if so, why not me? Who says I'm special?

Focus! It's just another mission.

He had five seconds, the time for them to enter the kill zone. Two would die, one would bolt in panic, vulnerable, and five to ten seconds after the first shots were fired the terrorist would run into the arms of his men, who would seize him alive. That was his plan anyway.

Ido rose silently to one knee. He was trembling. He welcomed it, he needed it, he knew it wasn't the lack of fear that would keep him alive, but fear itself. Fear was good. The familiar fury built inside him, as if he must kill to avenge his own death. Twigs and leaves stuck from the webbing of his steel helmet above his blackened face. He saw the identifying white lines on the back of his men's helmets rise slowly with him. He breathed a short prayer.

Four guns fired simultaneously, in short bursts, then again, and again, raking the trail, there was yelling, screams, the thud of bodies falling, dogs barking far away, heavy feet pounding the earth, a call in Arabic for mercy followed by a single gunshot, and another, and Hebrew shouting, and the third man burst through the bushes, thrashing with his arms, firing wildly as he fled back the way he had come.

And then it all went to shit. There was a second group. As two of his men tackled the fleeing gunman's legs and the third grabbed his weapon, yanked it from his hand and smashed him on the head, more yelling came from above Ido, the pounding of feet, and more Fatah fighters popped out of the dark, spreading into the bushes and jumping through them. They're not running away, they're fighting, Ido thought before he reacted. How many are there? He would never let them take back their man. Or shoot his men while they struggled with the prisoner. He spun behind the tree for cover and as an Arab ran by he dropped him with one shot to the head and finished him with another. He crouched, saw running shadows, aimed higher, fired three short bursts, two more, saw one man fall, bullets slammed into the tree by him, a branch fell catching him in the eye, stinging him, he raked the area with fire and saw a second shadow fall, he fired another burst toward the sound of feet thumping and crashing through some ferns. Ido rolled over and over to switch position, find new cover behind a rock, but all fell silent and as quickly as that it was over. His men were shouting, the barking dogs were louder, but all he heard was his own rapid rasping breath. He slumped against a rock. He was dripping with sweat and his eye stung.

When his heartbeat calmed he called out his number. One! The answer came: Two! Then, Three! and so on, all accounted for, not a scratch.

A groan came from the trail, a plea in Arabic.

Switch positions, Ido called. We wait for light.

His men blindfolded and muffled their captive, hid in secondary ambush positions in case of more Fatah infiltrators, and waited for the first rays of dawn.

The night was punctuated by the groans of a second Arab, wounded and abandoned on the trail, his calls for water and for his mother growing weaker, but Ido refused to approach until he could see him clearly. He wouldn't let himself be surprised by a knife or a gun. As the sky began to clear over the Heights, and the first hint of light gleamed on the wounded enemy, Ido finally crawled over, made sure he was unarmed and helpless, and called the medic to dress his wound.

The wounded Arab had a hole in his chest with an exit wound the size of a hand above the shoulder blade, and another hole in his stomach. He had lost a lot of blood, he was pale and weak, and was chattering with cold. Sergeant Eli, husky and bearded, wanted to finish him off. "Our orders are one prisoner. Now we've got two, this bastard's extra, and he's dying anyway. Put a bullet in his head and let's go."

Ido glared at his men. They avoided his eyes. Eli was stamping his feet, trying to circulate the blood. They were all freezing, they needed to get back to camp before daylight. "We have orders to bring in one," Eli said again. "We have two, so one of them's gonna get it right now." Eli glared at the wounded Arab, who looked blankly at the bodies of his comrades, their faces now covered by leaves. Before the fight Ido had wondered who decided which Arab would live or die. Now he knew. It wasn't God, nothing so grand. It was him, a twenty-one-year-old army captain who had that power. The blindfolded prisoner, the first one, a powerfully built man, stood with his head slumped, his arms handcuffed behind his back, a soldier on either side gripping his arms.

The sky was lightening with rose streaks above the Golan Heights. Dawn pinked Eli's angry eyes.

"Eli, you're a great soldier," Ido said at last. "But you'd make a lousy prisoner. Because if you touch this wounded man, or the other guy, it's a war crime and I'll make damn sure you go to jail. So shut the hell up. Yoram, get out the stretcher."

"I'll be damned if I'll carry him," Eli said, and it was clear from the way they stepped back that his mates agreed. "Finish him off," two more muttered.

Ido stepped between them and the prisoner. "You do what I say. Get the stretcher out. Put him on it."

Ido understood his men. If it was the other way around the Arabs would have cut the tongues out of the Jews and slit their throats slowly, one by one. He knew it, his men knew it, and most of all, the wounded Arab knew it. He begged for mercy, babbling in pain and shock.

The soldiers stood among the trees, damp and cold. Their blood was up, but Ido was cold and calm. The men's only responsibility was to follow orders and kill the enemy. His responsibility was greater: to protect his men and fulfill the mission. To do this he had to get them and their prisoner back to base before daylight. Where did committing a war crime fit in? Nowhere, as far as he was concerned. But he had to keep the peace among his men. Their lives were in each other's hands, their first loyalty was not to Israel or the general or a rule book, but to each other.

Ido decided. He pulled at the first prisoner's arms and ordered, "Free his hands. He's a big bugger, let him carry his mate." Eli shrugged and turned away. So be it.

Thirty minutes later the eight soldiers and their two prisoners dragged their feet into the base beside the kibbutz. Before the first debrief, Ido delivered the wounded prisoner to the clinic, where a medic cut off the Arab's shirt and got to work. He soon called for a surgeon. But the long exposure to the icy night, the massive loss of blood, and the jolting and shaking of his journey had sapped the unconscious Fatah fighter so much that after two hours the doctor gave up and pronounced him dead.

THE FAMILY

———

Rachel had still not told Moshe about Tamara and Peter, and the deceit was killing her. To make it worse, while babysitting Diana Rachel sometimes found herself in Peter's apartment, where, against all her instincts, she couldn't resist looking for signs of her daughter. Almost sick with guilt, she searched in drawers, careful not to disturb the clothes. She peered under the bed for any discarded items. She didn't want to be nosy but she couldn't help herself, for this wasn't only about two people, it was about two families, her whole family circle, her little world, that Tamara and Peter could bring crashing down.

Rachel would stand in Peter's bedroom, staring at the bed, feeling miserable and helpless. She knew Arie would find out one day, and there would be hell to pay. She should tell Moshe, she could not bear this alone.

She was right about one thing. Peter and Tamara were in love and his modest bedroom was their lovers' den. In Tamara's phrase, here pleasure united with truth. Their truth. Honesty was another matter, for they still could not bear to tell her husband, his brother.

As for Arie, who had barely touched Tamara in months, all his energies went into saving his empire while not losing face. In his struggle to stave off the banks, find investors, and sell declining assets, image was everything. If rivals smelled blood, he was finished. So he hosted business dinners at the Hilton hotel, paraded his new Peugeots, and attended gala events, always giving the most generous donation. He was helping build the new children's wing of Ichilov Hospital, all with his company's dwindling funds.

Only at home did he slump morosely in a corner, as he did now, avoiding conversation. When your best business bet is a loony Christian using the Bible as a treasure map, he thought, you must be in trouble.

It was Moshe's sixty-fifth birthday and the family was gathering in Arie and Tamara's reception room. Peter, a colorful box under his arm, greeted Tamara with a peck on the cheek and added his present to the pile on the sideboard. Rachel fussed over the long dining table, adjusting napkins and straightening knives and forks.

Upstairs was a special guest. Tamara's daughter, Carmel, was lying on her bed with Alice, her pen pal who had finally fulfilled her dream and come from America to work on a kibbutz. Carmel was showing photographs of a hike with friends by the salt waters of the Dead Sea, where they floated on their backs. Everything excited Alice, especially the idea of visiting the Christian holy places in Jerusalem, Bethlehem, Nazareth, and the Sea of Galilee.

"I've never been to any of them," Carmel said, feeling slightly guilty. "But I think you can't see them in Jerusalem, they're on the Jordan side. Same with Bethlehem."

"Well, I have an American passport, I can just cross over."

"Don't tell my parents then, they'll say they're responsible for you and it's too dangerous."

"Nonsense. I can't come all the way from America and not see where Jesus was born and crucified. I'll go by myself."

"Would you really, go by yourself?"

"Of course. I'm seventeen. Or I can join a tour group. Anyway, who's that?" She pointed to a photo of a boy chasing Carmel out of the water. "He's cute!"

"Oh, he's stupid," Carmel said. "He splashed me in the Dead Sea. I got salt in my eyes and it stung like anything."

"Did he lick it clean?" Alice launched herself into the air, laughing. "Just joking. He does look cute though," she said, taking the photo again. "What's his name?"

"Reuven. You wouldn't like him. He's full of himself, chases all the girls."

"Including you, in the photo anyway. Did he catch you?"

Carmel blushed. Alice laughed with delight. "He did, didn't he! Come on, tell me. Everything. What did you do? With him? What? Tell me?"

"No, I can't."

"Of course you can."

"I can't."

"Why? Is it rude?"

"Stop it, you're embarrassing me! What about you, have you got a boyfriend?"

Alice raised her eyebrow, turned her shoulder, winked over it. She laughed. "Oh, one or two. But they're just boys. From school. I can't wait to go to the kibbutz. I've heard so much about them. Is it true boys and girls shower together?"

"Until the age of ten. I think. Or twelve."

"And they sleep in the same room?"

Carmel shrieked. "Not at our age! Still, you'll love it there, it's very different, free and easy."

"Hmmm, I'm so looking forward. You have a lovely family."

"You think so? Sometimes I'm not so sure. Everyone's coming this evening for Granddaddy's birthday. Even Ido, if he can get special permission."

"Ido?"

"My uncle. But he's like a big brother. He's only four years older than me. He's in the army and he needs a pass to come home. He hasn't been home for a month, so I hope he comes. You'll like him. He's special."

"In what way?"

"You'll see. If he wasn't my uncle . . . put it this way, all my friends are in love with him."

"In that case, I can't wait. Let's hope he comes."

Downstairs Peter, Moshe, and Arie were solving Israel's problems. "All the signs are that Syria and Egypt don't want war, and precisely for that reason I'm suspicious," Peter was saying. "When all the security agencies agree on something, and the government agrees too, well, that naturally makes me doubt them. Anyway, we're prepared for anything, and that's the way . . ."

"I agree," Moshe interrupted. "Except that Israel isn't sitting innocently by, we're stoking the fire, by—"

"We all read that column you wrote," Arie put in. "And everyone denied it. When you wrote that Israel was deliberately provoking the Jordanians so that we can go in and kill them—"

"That isn't what I wrote. I said we want more land and—"

"The government spokesman asked you to apologize," Arie said.

"No way. I—"

"It's all lies—"

"Let him finish, Arie, stop interrupting. Moshe, why do you still believe Israel is provoking the Arabs? Why should we? And Arie, let him speak for once."

"Thank you Peter, very kind. It is my birthday after all. Ben-Gurion said, and I quote, more or less, 'We are interested in peace based on the status quo, but if the Arabs force us to fight perhaps the status quo will change.'" Moshe paused to let the words sink in. "Perhaps. Perhaps," Moshe emphasized. "In fact, we do want to change the status quo and that's why we want a fight. But we can't start the fight. So we provoke the other side. Ah, Peter, meet our young guest, I believe you knew her when she was a little girl."

"Alice?" Peter said, spreading his arms as Alice and Carmel entered the room with smiles as wide as their faces. "Look at you, a young woman, beautiful." She let him hug her. "My parents send you hugs and lots of love," she said, "and they made sure I would thank you for helping organize my visit to Israel. So thank you so much," and she made a little curtsy that charmed the entire room.

"I do believe that's the first time anyone has ever curtsied in Israel," Peter said. "How are your parents? And your grandmother Vera?"

But before Alice could answer, the bell rang, and they heard Rachel call out, "Ido!" followed by, "Oh, God in heaven, what happened?"

A dismissive chuckle from the entrance. "It's nothing, it looks worse than it is, really, nothing."

Everybody pushed toward the door and there stood Ido, every inch the Israeli fighter, in olive-green fatigues, brown boots, and beret, his Uzi submachine gun over his shoulder. He was the tallest in the room, the broadest, sun-bronzed, unshaven. His smile creased his face and made his eye patch rise.

"What have you done?" Rachel said again, almost in tears. "What happened to your eye?"

"Really, nothing, I promise," he answered as he greeted everyone with a hug. "A scratch in the eye, it's bloodshot, I have to rest it."

"It makes you look even more of a rogue than usual," Arie said, and held him tight. Over Arie's shoulder Ido saw Alice. "And who do we have here?" Ido said in English. "I'm getting a hug from everybody else, what about you? You must be Alice, yes? I've heard so much about you, but I thought you were younger."

"I'm nearly eighteen."

Ido pulled the rifle strap over his shoulder, unclipped the magazine, and placed the gun high up on a ledge over the door. Alice couldn't take her eyes off him. He unbuttoned the top of his shirt, revealing an olive T-shirt. "I'm home!" he shouted. "Thank God!"

He pulled Moshe into a bear hug. "Happy birthday, Dad, I'll get you a present tomorrow."

"You are my present," Moshe said, his head crunched against Ido's shoulder. Tamara looked with pride at her little brother. "Just do me a favor," Ido called out. "No war stories. It's Dad's party, let's celebrate." He looked around. "Where's Estie?"

"Your sister couldn't get away," Peter said. "She's on duty tonight."

Over dinner Ido was forced to explain how he hurt his eye. "Training accident," he said, involuntarily glancing at Peter, as if he would know the truth. By now Ido understood the general area of Peter's work, and appreciated his brother-in-law's silent strength even more: he was understated, a man who didn't have to prove a thing. In the army Ido had met men like him, all very senior officers.

Later, after Moshe had unwrapped his presents and made a little speech, Carmel, Alice, and Ido drifted into the garden, where Ido offered Alice a sip of his beer. "Hey," he said, "I said a sip, not to finish it."

She exhaled loudly and wiped her lips. "Not cold enough," she said.

Carmel made a face. "I hate beer," she said.

Alice laughed. "Me too. But at home everybody drinks."

"Do your parents know?"

"Of course not. If they knew half the things I do they'd never let me leave the house." Her smile lingered on Ido as she said this.

Carmel smirked. "I think I'll get an orange juice. By the way," she added helpfully, "Ido, Alice wants to know if boys and girls sleep in the same room on the kibbutz."

"Only the lucky ones," Ido said.

Alice threw her head back and laughed.

"I told you," Carmel said as she walked away.

"She told you what?" Ido asked Alice.

"Oh, nothing."

Ido shrugged and turned to lean on the fence, looking at the sky. Alice joined him. They stood in silence, their shoulders almost touching. "It's beautiful here, isn't it," Ido said after a few moments.

Alice sighed. "It is." The Milky Way glowed softly above them. "There, you see," Ido said, pointing. "That's Orion, you see the three stars almost together? That's the belt. And there, northeast of it, that's Gemini, and that very bright star . . ."

Alice laughed. "Why is it that whenever a boy and a girl look at the night sky the boy tells the girl what she's looking at? Girls never tell the boy."

"Because girls don't know?"

"Don't they?"

"Do you?"

"Actually, no, I don't. But the boys don't know either, they just like to show off."

Ido laughed out loud. "Well, I do. Know them I mean. We use the sky for night navigation."

Alice fell silent. She had never met a boy like Ido in Taos. She wanted to ask about the army. What it was like, had he ever killed someone, but she felt they were silly questions. Instead, she asked where he lived when he was in the army. "You mean, where is my base?" he said. "Actually it's very near the kibbutz you'll be on. My base is near the Kinneret, what you call the Sea of Galilee, and your kibbutz, Ashdot Yaacov, is just a mile or two south."

"Really? Could I see you there?" She bit her lip. She should have waited for him to ask.

"If I'm really, really lucky."

Alice smiled and whispered, "I think you're the lucky type."

Ido smiled too, and edged closer, his hand grazing hers on the wooden fence. They gazed at the sky and Ido said, "There's Ursa Major."

She nudged him with her elbow. "Everybody knows Ursa Major."

After a while he said, "When do you go to the kibbutz?"

"In two days."

"So you're right then, I am lucky. That's when I go back to base. If you like, we can travel together."

Alice smiled in the dark and didn't answer right away. She had to catch her breath. When she did she pointed into the sky and said, "Look, there's Cupid."

"Cupid? What's that? Is there a constellation by that name?"

"If not, there should be." Alice said, brushing Ido's hand.

PETER and TAMARA

TEL AVIV, ISRAEL
April 15, 1967

———————

S trictly speaking it wasn't Peter's business. His job included collecting intelligence on Palestinians as well as the ability and intentions of Syria, Egypt, Jordan, and Lebanon to wage war on Israel: to monitor Israel's immediate neighbors.

But the way Israel was handling the growing number of attacks in the north worried him; it seemed the bigger question was not what the Arabs were planning but Israel's intentions. It really seemed Moshe could be right: the military appeared to be provoking the Syrians, and now they had gone too far. A week earlier, two Israeli armored tractors had begun working near the Syrian border, the Syrians had opened fire with tanks, the Israelis returned fire, then the air forces got involved and by the end of the day Israel had shot down six Syrian warplanes, including one near Damascus, sixty miles inside Syria.

The media played it up as Israel's greatest military success in a decade, the politicians competed for credit, but for Peter it rang alarm bells. Syria would have to respond. The Soviet Union would back its client. So might Egypt, even though the assessment was that Egypt didn't want to fight yet. Jordan may get dragged in. What would America do? Where was this heading?

Peter's most immediate concern though was not the international chess-board or even Israel's survival, but Alice. He had promised her parents that he would look after her and now there she was, working and studying on a kibbutz that was on the edge of a potential war zone. Terrorists were striking twice a week, laying land mines on roads, under a bridge, attacking railroads, water towers, pipelines, shooting at farmers in fields, all within three miles of his ward. Should he send Alice back to America, or at least bring her back to Tel Aviv, out of harm's way?

He had asked Tamara and she had responded with a laugh. "I don't think she'll listen to you," she had said. "Ido told me that he's smitten. The two of them seem to have started quite a romance. He visits her on the kibbutz whenever he can, and, to make matters worse, or better, she has her own room."

"That isn't funny. I'm responsible for her. Ido better be careful."

"You can trust him. He has a heart of gold."

"Yes, and he also has a . . . well, I won't say it. He's twenty-one, a soldier. I'd say I know what's on his mind."

"Well, whatever it is, it's too late now."

"But she's only seventeen."

"Seventeen is the new twenty-five."

Peter pulled Tamara to him, unzipping her skirt. He had to be back at the Office in an hour. "Well, moving right along, what is the new forty-four?"

"Hmmm. In your case, twenty-six?"

"And you, what is the new—how old are you, anyway?"

"Let's just say, I am the new me."

"Amen to that."

"Which brings us to Arie," Tamara said.

"No, it doesn't. It brings me to you." Peter had reached Tamara's last item of frilly clothing, but she was already pulling it down.

Their arrangement was that Peter would never call Tamara anywhere, neither at home nor at the office. She could only call him at home between 8:30 and 9:00 in the morning, when he was alone, or on a phone number which, in a land with a years-long waiting list for telephones, he was able to change every month. They were sure they were covering their tracks; after all, she was a lawyer and he was a spy. But they were also wise enough to know that in the history of infidelity, nobody ever got away with it. Eventually they would be discovered, and already there was a weak link: Rachel. Peter had joked that if he was on a job, he'd eliminate the risk factor. Not funny, Tamara said. Or a neighbor could notice Tamara coming and going, even though she hid beneath a large hat. Or some family member would notice one tender glance too many, a pointed meeting of their eyes. At a certain point, Peter had warned, subconsciously they may even want to be discovered.

"So maybe it's time to tell Arie," he said, propped up on the pillows. He blew smoke from the corner of his mouth, away from Tamara. She was lying against him, one hand resting on his belly. "What do you think?" he continued. "I can't bear this lying any longer. Anyway, he'll find out one day, it's much better if he finds out from us."

She responded with a sigh and the tiniest shake of her head.

"Well?" Peter said. "I love you, I always have, one way or another. It's time to live together, come on, what do you say?" He stubbed out his cigarette and turned to face her. "And please decide now, I have to leave in ten minutes."

"Oh, no pressure, then."

"Exactly."

"I don't know. Maybe we should leave things the way they are for now. I'm so happy with you. Why upset the cart? Can't we just go on like this?"

"I don't want a fight with Arie either, but it'll come sooner or later. It's better to control the battleground, so to speak. I'll have to tell him. I'll call him."

"No," Tamara cried in alarm. "No, not yet. Peter, think about it, where will we live? Here? And my children, they'll live here with us? Where will they sleep, in the kitchen? Or they'll stay with Arie? I couldn't bear that. Divorce Arie? He'll fight us, Peter, he'll take my children away . . ."

"They're fifteen, Tamara. They're adults, almost. They can stay where they are and you can see them every day. Tamara, please, just think about it, it's time to decide. We can't go on forever hiding like this, this isn't a life, we have to come out into the open. Be happy. Man and wife. Tamara, say you'll do this. If Arie finds out first, it will get truly ugly. We have to go to him, not the other way around."

Tamara glanced at her watch. "Peter, you must go. I can't say yes or no now, I need time to think about it."

"Think about it? That's all I've been doing, I need you, Tamara, I love you, I want to live with you."

Tamara sighed heavily, her breasts rose and fell, Peter kissed one and then the other. He stood and silently drew on his clothes. At the door he hesitated, contemplating his lover half-covered by the rumpled sheets. "So now it's up to you, Tamara. Call me."

He left, leaving her staring at the door.

Peter walked the last mile to work, struggling to focus on the hard-nosed questions waiting for him at Mossad. How to halt the slide to war? His job was to provide the politicians with information, not decide what to do with it. But what if you don't trust the politicians? He heard raised voices, cars honking, and along Dizengoff Street came hundreds of people, a dozen abreast, holding up the traffic. Men protesting against unemployment. They needn't worry, he thought, they'd get called up soon enough, they'd earn money in the reserves.

But his thoughts kept returning to Tamara. He stopped for a coffee, it didn't matter if he was five minutes late, after all, he was heading the meeting. He needed time to think more about her. He could still feel Tamara's kisses, her warmth and softness, her body rocking against him. Yet . . . she didn't appear ready to bite the bullet. Did she even want to leave Arie? He couldn't tell. He thought she wanted to, but would she? Right now she had the best of both worlds, living a chaste life in luxury as well as a passionate secret life: who wouldn't want that to continue?

And why should he get into a fight with Arie? As it was they hardly spoke, they were both too busy, the only time they met was at birthdays, the family was the wrong age-group for funerals and weddings. Not for divorce though. Should he have it out with Arie? His younger brother. He didn't often think of his parents, it was all too long ago, too hard; distant, yet too painful to bear. Now the thought of them sent a chill through him: they gave their lives for their children, and here am I, about to take my brother's wife. I will destroy the family they died to save.

He drained his coffee, examined the mud that remained; watched the traffic and the passing people and the shadows of the ficus leaves shifting in the breeze. A part of his spirit rebelled. Don't be romantic: Mama and Pappi didn't die to save his life. They died for no good reason, only because they were murdered, that's all. He didn't need to carry this guilt forever. On the other hand, they did give him up, send him away, endured the pain of losing their eldest son to save his life. Yes, that they did. He couldn't begin to imagine what that must have been like for them. And then he realized, yes, he could understand. When he disappeared from their lives, when his father waved good-bye at the station, he was fourteen years old. Exactly the same age as his own two sons today. It would be like sending Ezra and Noah away, knowing he may never see them again, to save them. And if he could only save one, which would it be? How could a parent choose? And yet that was exactly what his own parents had done. They had chosen him. What courage it took, what pain it caused them.

And this is how he repaid them.

And Arie, who he left behind with an empty promise to bring him to America. Arie, condemned to five years of concentration camps, so painful that he never spoke about it. And this is Arie's reward, to be betrayed by his own brother?

Oh Tamara, what price our love?

PETER and ALICE

When Robyn Wilson had warned him on the phone that her daughter Alice was a stubborn child, Peter had to chuckle: she's no child. That girl is all woman, and parents are always the last to see it. He wondered if he'd be the same with Diana in ten years. That made him miss the operative word—stubborn.

He had called Alice's mother to give her a progress report on her daughter but also to hint that peaceful Israel could be approaching more turbulent times. He had wondered whether she would feel more comfortable if Alice returned home earlier than planned.

"Oh, thank you for letting us know, but we got a letter from Alice yesterday saying how quiet it is there and how much she enjoys working on the kibbutz. She's been to the Sea of Galilee and even Capernaum where St. Peter lived and Jesus preached. She's met a nice boy too so, knowing her, nothing will move her. Have you met him? His name is Ido."

"Yes, he's my nephew."

"Oh, that's nice, then."

"He's a soldier."

"A soldier?" Her voice wilted.

"An officer."

"Oh. Well, I'm sure that's fine, then."

Sure, Peter thought, she's in safe hands, like the sun rises in the west. A pretty seventeen-year-old girl with a handsome twenty-one-year-old army captain. He had better speak to Ido fast.

Amikam, his Office driver, had been at the wheel two hours when the Beit Shean Road winding east dropped steeply through hairpin bends to join the Jordan valley road to Tiberias. They followed the river that formed the Jordanian border, past the green fields and grazing pastures of Kibbutz Ashdot Yaacov where Alice was working. No time to stop yet though, that treat was for later, his meeting was in an hour at the northern end of the lake.

He leafed through his notes. Although Mossad's brief was to operate against Israel's enemies outside its borders, that blurred when those external enemies operated inside Israel. Some of the Palestinian infiltrators were disguised Syrian regular soldiers; worse, Moscow was pushing Syria to be more belligerent. Mossad believed Moscow was playing the long game. The more Syria confronted Israel, the more Syria would need the support of Russia. And what Russia most wanted was a dependent state in the Middle East, an Arab pawn in the Cold War.

When Israel's French-made Dassault warplanes shot down the six Soviet MIGs flown by Syrian pilots it was a slap in the face of the communists. A victory of West over East. Moscow warned Jerusalem about "possible consequences" of more confrontations with Syria.

Which made it clearer than ever that if war erupted, Israel needed to strike first, or the Soviet-backed armies of Syria, Egypt, and possibly Jordan could overwhelm tiny Israel, which had only reluctant American support.

Israel's dilemma was that America insisted it have a good reason, some Arab provocation, to strike first. That was what Peter needed to discuss with agents in the north, before a defense ministry briefing he was to give the next day in Tel Aviv with the head of Mossad, Meir Amit.

Amit wanted ammunition to prove that Israel could not afford to wait. So far, Peter didn't have it. Nor did he understand why Amit wanted it: Did Israel want war, or did Israel want to avoid war?

If that was a tricky question, it was just a tease for his next mission that would require a much more delicate touch: to persuade a love-struck seventeen-year-old girl to go home, or at least to come back with him to Tel Aviv. For now he was more convinced than ever that Alice Wilson was in the wrong place at the wrong time. In the afternoon meetings guards had brought him a shackled Palestinian fighter. He had been captured inside Israel in an army ambush weeks earlier, and told interrogators that his final instructions before crossing into Israel had been given by a Syrian army officer and a Russian adviser.

The fuse was burning. Israel had to act.

He had to act quickly with Alice too. Half the terrorist attacks came through Jordan, the border of which was a few hundred yards from the fields of her kibbutz. His American ward was most definitely in harm's way.

The only problem was she was in love, and she wasn't too shy to say so. He discovered that when he tracked her down to her bare room in the volunteers' quarters. There was little more than a table, the wooden chair he sat on, and the single bed where she lay studying Hebrew. She was delighted to see him but quickly added that Ido could come at any moment and if he did, she asked with a blush, would Peter mind leaving them alone for a while?

Yes, he would mind, definitely, but he was so taken aback by the girl's brazenness that he could only say, "How often does Ido come here? After all, he's in the army." Maybe he should have a word with Ido's commanding officer, get him confined to base.

"Not often, he can't get away from his base. He said maybe he could come today."

"You had a good drive up with him?"

"Yes. We took the bus."

"How was that?"

"We held hands." She giggled. Anything else? he wondered.

"I'm trying to learn the Hebrew alphabet, but it's so hard. These letters are crazy, all squiggles and dots." Alice rolled her eyes as she held up her exercise book. "I'm on letter *daled*. After a week I'm four letters into the alphabet. Pathetic! But I like working in the bananas. Look," she said, flexing her biceps, "I'm a farmer now."

He wondered how best to phrase his demand, though he knew it was doomed. "Alice, I know you like it here, but there have been so many terrorist attacks around here lately, and shells from Syria, there's a buildup of military just in the last week, anything could happen, so I think, Alice, it would be better if you left here for a while and came back with me to Tel Aviv. Just for a bit, Alice. You can come back as soon as it's quiet again." His sad smile showed he felt for her, but regretfully there was no choice.

Her body drooped, her eyes reddened, her lips quivered. "I thought you just came to say hello."

"I did. That too. But, also to bring you back to town. Just until it's safe. I'm responsible for you, Alice, I promised your parents." Such a pity, such a lovely, spirited girl. She looked so disappointed, but it was for her own good. She would understand.

"Well, I'm not coming, forget it. No way. Not a chance. I don't care what you say. I love it here. And I love Ido. I won't leave him. If all these families can stay here with their little children, I can stay here too. If it's safe for them, it's safe for me. I'm not coming. I'll tell my parents myself."

For an instant Peter felt like grabbing her by the arm and dragging her to the car. But with her set jaw, her wild eyes, and shaking her little fists, he suddenly saw who Alice reminded him of: Diana, at her most stubborn. That's exactly what his wife would have said. He was facing a teenage Diana with an American accent. He wished he had known Diana when she was seventeen. He wished she hadn't died so young, just thirty-four. Twice this girl's age. He stared at Alice.

"What?" she said.

"I was just wondering what I'll say to your mother."

"Don't say anything. Nothing has happened, don't make an issue of something that may never happen."

Wise words, he thought. Seventeen, going on thirty. Lucky Ido.

On cue, there was a light tap on the door, and in he walked, in olive fatigues. Ido's face lit up in surprise. "Peter. Fantastic. What are you doing here?" He crossed the room in two steps and fell onto the bed next to Alice, went to take her hand but thought better of it.

Peter smiled. He didn't miss a thing. "How's the army?" he said.

Ido glanced briefly at Alice. "Fine. Quiet."

330 I MARTIN FLETCHER

Peter nodded. Good for Ido, no need to boast. At the briefing he had been told the name of the squad leader who had caught the terrorist and protected a wounded prisoner. It had filled him with pride in the new generation, though he hadn't revealed that Ido was his nephew. Now he thought, Ido deserves this sweet girl. He's a soldier, anything could happen, at any time. And frankly, she deserves him. He contemplated them for a moment. "I'm going to find a room," Peter said, "I'll stay over for the night. I leave early for Tel Aviv. Will you still be here in, say, an hour?" He'd give them that.

"No, I have to get right back. I just dropped by to see if Alice needed anything. Hebrew lessons, you know?"

"Yes, I know. Alice, what's the fifth letter of the alphabet, what comes after *daled*?"

"Hey, I don't know. I guess I'm about to find out." She took Ido's hand and winked at Peter.

He winked back, and wished he hadn't. "I'll be back in an hour," he said, closing the door.

A lot can happen in an hour, but it didn't. As they kissed, sitting back against the wall, Ido applied gentle pressure on Alice's shoulders, until they were lying on the bed. He managed to open Alice's shirt, his hands found her bra clasp, but she wriggled away. "Please don't," she whispered. He kissed her throat with open lips and darting tongue, making her shiver. "Just this," he murmured, slipping his hand beneath her bra, cupping her firm warm breast and hard little nipple. "Don't worry, just this," he repeated as she settled against him, returning his kisses.

"I could stay like this forever," Ido sighed in Alice's ear, his warm breath tickling her so that she giggled and pulled away. "Me too," she said, "but you're tickling me. Look, feel this." She raised her head and blew gently into his ear. "Mmm, good," he said, sliding his fingers into the waistband of her jeans, excited by the firmness of her curves. She pulled his hand away. He probed for minutes, now at her side, now at the base of her spine, gaining an inch here, half an inch there, pressing against her on the lumpy single bed. "There's something sticking into me," she said, moving away.

"It isn't me!" Ido shouted with a laugh.

"No, feel this, it's a lump in the mattress, at night I have to arrange my-self around it."

"Let me," Ido said, and punched and poked until the lump had gone, the clump of fiber now evenly distributed. "That's better," Alice laughed, spreading herself across the bed. "My hero, come here."

"Oh, no," he said sharply, looking at his watch. "I have to get back to base." He adjusted his pants and tucked in his shirt. "I'm not really sup-posed to be away."

"To be continued."

"I can't wait. I'll come back soon." Clasping her buttocks, he kissed her until they could barely breathe, and left.

But Ido did not see Alice again soon. That same night his brigade was ordered south, where army intelligence showed Egypt was building up its forces in the Sinai Peninsula.

PETER and ARIE

———————

The reason nobody understood what Egypt's president was planning was because Nasser himself had no idea; he was swept along by events, and so was Israel.

Incited by Soviet claims that Israel was amassing troops on Syria's border, and the Syrian president's panicked reaction to the shooting down of his six MIGs, Nasser made a historic miscalculation: he expelled the three and a half thousand peacekeepers of the United Nations Emergency Force who since the 1956 war had acted as a buffer between Egypt and Israel. Worse, to relieve supposed Israeli pressure on Syria's border, and hoping to satisfy his Soviet mentors, Nasser ordered troops and tanks into Sinai to distract Israel's attention from Syria.

In days, six hundred Egyptian tanks and fifty thousand men were massed in the sweltering desert dunes within miles of Israel's almost open border. Arab radio broadcasts rejoiced in the imminent slaughter of the Jews.

The boys had just gone to bed when Peter got the call to return to Mossad headquarters ASAP. He didn't get back home for four all-but-sleepless-nights.

That first night at the Office Meir Amit outlined to his section heads their urgent challenge. "Until now," Amit said, "we thought Nasser was bluffing. But now it looks like the lunatic really thinks he is the leader of the Arab world, and he may attack us. We know his military capability is limited, and he has overreached himself. Our military has a plan which will work. Our challenge now is diplomatic and tactical, and in some sense it is contradictory. We need to advise the government on the optimal moment to attack Egypt, while considering another key question, how to keep America on our side. That is what the prime minister needs from us."

Peter broke the momentary silence. "The army wants to attack now, the sooner the better. The prime minister wants to wait until we have American approval, however long it takes. We need to find the balance. Correct?"

"Exactly," Amit said. "It puts us in great danger. We know that the Egyptian army has attack plans of their own. We need to let the enemy build up on our border until the world understands we have no choice, but we also have to attack first. It's extremely delicate and complex. We call this an anticipatory counteroffensive. It's all about the timing. The generals only care about annihilating the Egyptian army. But Eshkol also cares about who will support us the day after. Nobody wants another Suez, where we won the battle and lost the war."

But as Peter's team mined their agents and sources, it seemed that armed conflict may not be inevitable. As politicians bickered and the military blustered, the intelligence agencies struggled to come up with proof that Nasser really wanted war.

By the next afternoon, a secret source in the Egyptian operations room had delivered his army's battle orders showing the Egyptian divisions in Sinai were drawing up for defense, not offense. Radio communications monitored by Israeli signals intelligence confirmed this, as did reports from elite reconnaissance units of the Israeli army on the ground in Egypt's Sinai desert, among them, Captain Ido Nesher.

The recommendation of Peter's section then was not to rush to judgment, there was still an opportunity to avoid armed conflict. But the next evening they were overtaken by events.

Damascus had mobilized fifty battalions, Iraq sent army brigades closer to Jordan's border: next stop could be Israel. The governments of Kuwait, Yemen, and Algeria announced they were ready to send planes and men to help Egypt and Syria. Egypt was still pouring men across the Suez Canal into Sinai, and Syria continued to pour cannon fire into Israel's northern settlements.

If Nasser was bluffing, it was one hell of a bluff. Under furious pressure from the army, the Israeli government decided it could not risk a surprise attack by the Arabs and took a decisive step: a general mobilization of reserves. Every half hour radio announcers read out code names of units being called up: Silver Lining, Wedding March, Gates of Salvation, Peace and Greetings, and more. Electricians downed their tools, grocers closed their stores, teachers walked out of class as the citizen army of Israel rushed home to swap slacks and shirts for army fatigues, kiss their spouses and children good-bye, grab their guns, and gather at their preplanned collection points.

Once mobilized, little Israel could not afford to stay mobilized for long. It had to attack or stand down before the economy came to a standstill. The pressure was on.

Then it got worse.

Declaring that "No Israeli ship will ever navigate it again," President Nasser closed the waters of the Straits of Tiran, Israel's southern lifeline, its gateway to Asia and Africa. Jerusalem had long considered any move to block the Red Sea a *causus belli*.

The public was frightened, the borders seemed to be closing in, there was a sense of suffocation. Israel could not let it stand, but its leaders were riven by doubt.

The word was that Ben-Gurion, in his desert refuge, believed Israel could not win. General Harkabi at the Defense Ministry feared even if Israel won, ten thousand could die. America was more optimistic. The CIA station chief in Tel Aviv assessed Israel could defeat any combination of Arab armies in six to ten days. But Washington let it be known that if Israel attacked first, and without good reason, America could support Egypt.

With the public losing confidence in their prime minister, Eshkol's military adviser besieged Mossad with calls. The prime minister was under pressure to resign and had to know: Should the general mobilization become total mobilization for war, or the opposite, should the reserves stand down and go home? War or peace? He needed information on Arab intentions, *now*.

With the country on the edge of total war, the government in chaos, and still no clear conclusion after four straight days of frenzy in the Office, Peter took a break and walked home, sucking in fresh air, giddy from fatigue. He hadn't seen Tamara in a week, and he missed her. He hadn't even been able to take her calls, the pressure was unprecedented. He had never felt such a weight of responsibility for the lives of his family and his countrymen. The gloom in the city further weighed on him. In cafés people argued and cursed, pausing only to listen to the hourly radio news. Newspapers reported there were two kinds of craven types: those hoarding food and those fleeing the country. Passing a group of elderly men around two tables, he overheard snippets: "Isn't it hard enough here already, I can't afford sugar in the coffee, for this I survived." A different voice said, "And now there's another war. Like a hole in the head I need this crazy place."

Peter would have paused to listen more if he had the energy, but all he wanted was to hurry home and sleep. He needed six hours, and then he'd go back to work. At seven o'clock in the morning he needed to give a report to Amit on the plans of the Palestinians in the Gaza Strip, who were manning positions abandoned by the UNEF troops; he had three agents among them. Peter's Palestinian report was a small contribution to the bigger issue: If there was war, would it be just with Egypt or Syria? Or both? With or without Jordan, the Palestinians, Lebanon, Iraq? Amit would present Mossad's analysis to the prime minister in Jerusalem at ten o'clock.

Meanwhile rumors were leaking from the defense ministry in Tel Aviv that something was up with the chief of staff. Was Yitzhak Rabin really having a nervous breakdown, was the stress too great for him? If this warrior couldn't take it, how could the country? It seemed inconceivable, but could Israel lose?

Could Israel face annihilation? Could the whole glorious adventure be doomed, after only nineteen years? Arab armies mobbing the streets of Jerusalem, Tel Aviv, Haifa, Ashdod? Cutting the throats of his children? Raping the women? As he approached his apartment building in the early evening Peter shook his head. Get a grip. Get some sleep. It'll all look different at dawn. Or rather, when he had to get up, at two o'clock at night.

Diana was at Rachel's, and Noah and Ezra were at the youth movement clubhouse where they spent hours every day with their friends. He wrote a note telling them not to wake him up, stuck it onto the fridge, always the twins' first port of call, set his alarm and had a long cold shower. That freshened him enough to put on shorts and a T-shirt and sit on the narrow balcony to enjoy the air and listen to the radio. He'd hear the news and then go to bed.

Within a minute a familiar bulky figure came striding through the trees, looking up to his apartment. Peter waved. "Arie," he called out, "what brings you here, you're lucky I'm home. Come up." He was glad to see him, he hadn't seen his brother in weeks. He poured some juice from the fridge, scanning the small apartment for signs of Tamara. Arie's heavy footsteps took the stairs two at a time. "What's up with him," Peter wondered, and quickly found out.

Arie was shouting even as he entered the room, drowning out the radio. He went straight to Peter and pushed him with two hands, so that Peter stumbled against the table. "You *ben zonah*! You son of a whore!" he yelled, waving his fist into Peter's face, "you're screwing my wife!"

Peter stepped to the side to gain some space. "Orange juice?" he offered.

"I know all about it!" Arie shouted. "How long's it been going on? Behind my back. You bastard, I'll . . ."

"First of all, don't swear at me and, second, don't talk about Tamara like that." He was playing for time, he should have told Arie first, he knew it, but now it was too late.

"How long have you been screwing her!"

"Don't talk like that. It's complicated, you know it is. I . . ."

Arie moved fast, faster than Peter anticipated, and landed a blow on Peter's head that spun him around and against a chair, so hard that he almost lost his balance. Before he could gather himself Arie hit him again with full force in the stomach and again on the chin, almost lifting him off the floor. Peter fell back dazed onto the sofa, desperately collecting himself, and as Arie went to grab his head Peter slipped to the side and from a lying position caught Arie with a kick in the groin that doubled him over, shocking his breath away. Arie gasped in pain as Peter pulled himself up and landed a hefty kick on Arie's ass that toppled him onto the floor. He lay there, holding his balls, groaning and cursing. Peter stood above him, panting, holding his jaw with one hand, wiping sweat from his brow with the other.

Arie tried to force words past the groans. "That was . . . a pussy . . . kick."

Peter fought to gain his breath. "Consider yourself lucky. You could be dead." A flush of guilt swept Peter. Between loyalty to his brother and love for Tamara he had chosen love. Of course he had. Loyalty is for the past. Love is for the future.

"You bastard," Arie said. "My own brother. After all I've done for you."

"You haven't done shit for me. I never let you."

"I offered."

Peter sat heavily on a chair, holding his chin. "I don't want anything from you."

"Except my wife."

"Some marriage. How many women have you got on the side?"

"That's my business. Stay away from her. I'm warning you." As the threat hung in the air, the calm voice of the radio announcer broke through, reading a list of unit call-up codes to mobilize more reserves. Like all of Israel, they froze. A monotone: "Morning Dew. Early Winter. Red Rose. . . ."

"Red Rose. That's me," Arie said, speaking with a kind of wonder. "That's my brigade." He tried to stand but couldn't. He kneeled on the floor, doubled over, his groin throbbing. "You think if I didn't have such big balls it wouldn't hurt so much?"

"Probably."

"Next time it'll be the other way around. I promise you, Peter, if I'm getting my ass blown off in Sinai and you're here doing Tamara, I'll kill you. I'll drive my tank right up your ass."

"Fighting words. Keep it for the Arabs. Arie, come on, let's talk like grown-ups." He hadn't planned it this way but at least it was in the open at last. "Tamara and . . ."

"I don't want to hear it. I have to go. Peter, listen to me. Leave her alone, or so help me God, I don't care if you're my brother, I'll finish you." Gripping the door frame, his last words were, "You understand me? I love Tamara and she's mine."

Peter was torn. Between: She's yours? You don't own her. And: You're going to war, again? Let me hug you.

Peter ran after Arie and stopped him at the top of the stairs, pulling him into an embrace. "Arie, good luck, my brother, stay safe."

Arie held him off with a look of contempt and ran down the stairs. Over the clatter of shoes, Peter heard the shout, "Go to hell."

TAMARA

TEL AVIV, ISRAEL

May 23, 1967

Tamara pounded through the streets, sweating in the dry heat, her heart pumping. She felt like throwing away her jacket, it was too heavy and hot. She kept looking over her shoulder but every taxi was full; men were rushing home to get their guns or racing to their units. Arie's driver had been called up days ago, and there were no buses, they were all transporting soldiers. She passed women digging ditches in the gardens of their apartment buildings, and elderly men mixing concrete to block up windows against shrapnel. Across the road a woman clung to her uniformed man as his friends shouted at him to get into the truck. Men bent by their cars painting headlights blue. Ahead of her a man stood back, surveyed his handiwork, put the paint into the trunk, and climbed behind the wheel. She ran up and asked if by any chance he was going to Herzliya.

"No, Haifa, I'm in the navy."

Tamara looked around with wild eyes and said, "Good luck then, sir," and turned away.

"But it's on the way. Jump in, I'll take you."

"Oh, really, that's so kind of you. My husband has been called up and I have to say good-bye."

"My wife said good-bye," he said. "Three years ago."

Tamara looked at him in alarm, but he laughed. "A joke," he said.

"Oh, good, I was worried."

"A man can wish, can't he?"

"You're joking again?"

"What else is there to do? I'm forty-nine, one year to go and I could have got out of it, instead I'm going to be sick for the next month."

"You're in the navy and you get seasick?"

"From the food, my dear. And I'm the cook."

Tamara smiled, for the first time since Arie had bullied the truth out of her that morning. He had shaken her, raised his hand, shouted, threatened her, and in the end she admitted it: she was sleeping with Peter. She thought he would hit her but instead he had backed away, red with fury, and rushed out of the house. When she stopped shaking she phoned Peter at the office to warn him, but he had left for a walk. She couldn't leave a message, he had always told her not to, so she had gone to work in Tel Aviv. And then Arie had called her, as if he had forgotten their fight. He told her he had to join the brigade, he wanted to kiss her good-bye, in case there really was a war.

"Thank you for the ride," she said. "I couldn't bear not kissing him," she said, knowing despite everything it was the truth.

"Well, he's a lucky man. Don't worry, sweetie, I'll get you home in twenty minutes."

But by the time she got home, Arie had left. At forty-three, he was still a tank platoon commander, he had to prepare the equipment and get tanks assigned, preferably before the crews arrived. And this wasn't another exercise, the Arabs were coming, again. His third war, the third time only luck and God would stand between him and death, if you don't include the Holocaust.

Tamara stood in the hall staring at the envelope she found on the side-table. She turned it over in her hand, images from that morning flooding back. We had a huge fight, she thought, maybe the worst ever, and now he's gone to war. He must be furious, she failed him, and oh God, what if something happens to him? She didn't even say good-bye. The last he saw, she was cursing him, crying. With trembling fingers she opened the envelope and slid out the Hebrew note:

Tamara,

You broke my heart. You cheated with my own brother. I saw him today, we had a fight. All a man wants in war is to come home again. Now I wonder, do I even have a home? I could not wait any longer so I can't even say good-bye. So be it. I may not have been the best husband but you'll never know how hard I tried.

Your Arie

The note took her breath away, tears came to her eyes. She sat miserably against the cushions on the sofa, drawing her legs up beneath her. What did you expect, she thought, a love letter? So Arie had a fight with Peter. A real fight? Fists? Or an argument? She could only call Peter in the evening. They knew one day they would have to have it out with Arie, and now it had come to pass, but at the worst possible time. What had she done to him? A soldier has to have a home to come back to, a reason to lay his life on the line. What would Arie be fighting for? His country, yes. His family? She hoped so. He loves Carmel and Daniel so much, he's a wonderful father. She felt sick in the stomach.

So much had happened since they all met—what? Seventeen years ago. What a mistake. She should have waited for Peter. But she was so young, so desperate in the refugee camp, and so afraid that Peter had made her pregnant and left her. She had been so impressed by Arie's room. Hot water! And his old car. She shook her head in disbelief. Now look at this house, it's a mansion, two new cars in the driveway, another in the garage. But so what? She walked to the end of the garden and stared at the horizon, where the sun hung steady, reassuring, the constant in the clear blue sky. She sighed. How she longed to live with Peter. Her reverie was broken by the clanging of the telephone. She ran into the house. Peter? Arie? She hesitated before picking it up, catching her breath. "Hello?" she said at last. There was a scratching sound, beeps and a woman's voice. "Tamara, Tamara, is that you?" American accent.

"Yes."

"Tamara, this is Mrs. Wilson from Taos, in America, Alice's mother."

"Oh, yes, Mrs. Wilson, of course, how are you, is everything all right?"

"That's what I wanted to ask you. We're hearing terrible things. It's no place for a young girl, I want Alice to come home immediately. I couldn't get a call through to her kibbutz. It's near the border with Syria. I asked her to come home before but she wouldn't. Now she must. Can you tell her? Are you in touch with her? Hello? Hello?"

Tamara laid a hand on her heart, she hadn't realized how much stress she was under. She didn't know who she wanted to hear from most, Peter or Arie.

"Mrs. Wilson, I can try to get a call through to her but it's very difficult at the moment, the lines are busy all the time because of the situation. I'll try to tell her though."

"Please, it's dangerous . . ."

After five more minutes telling Tamara she had to hang up because the phone call was so expensive, Mrs. Wilson hung up, just as Carmel came in.

"I don't think so," Carmel said, when her mother told her what Mrs. Wilson wanted. "I got a letter from Alice this morning. If there's a war she volunteered to work as a hospital assistant. She said that on her kibbutz a hundred and twenty men have been called up, out of a hundred and eighty. Can you imagine? All the women afraid for their men. So she feels she has to do something too. And, Mummy, I also want to do something. So as from tomorrow, it's all organized, I can leave school early, I'm the new mailman."

Tears sprang into Tamara's eyes as she hugged her daughter. Such a darling, soon this child too will be a soldier. With all her heart and soul, Tamara hoped there would be no more war. When Carmel, still in her mother's arms, asked why she was crying, Tamara said, when she could, "for so many things, my sweet little Carmi, for so many things."

ARIE, IDO, and ALICE

SINAI, EGYPT, AND ASHDOT YAACOV, ISRAEL

June 1, 1967

———————

The tank column idled as the gunner of the lead tank attached a metal cable to an armored personnel carrier that had sunk to its axle in the sand. A dozen infantry, their faces swathed in khaki bandannas, caked in sweat and dust, jeered their driver, who gave them the finger. It was the hottest day so far, ninety-six degrees, and they itched and stank. The infantry captain jumped onto the tank to confer with its commander. Both wore helmets and dust goggles, their faces grimy, but their eyes lit up. "Ido!" "Arie!"

The brothers-in-law slapped each other's shoulders, bumped helmets. "Hurry up and wait, the usual," Arie complained. "We've had two singers, one dance troupe, and half-a-dozen pep talks, all we want is to get it over with. What do you think? We'll get a chance to screw 'em?"

"Who knows?" Ido said. "Eshkol can't decide, half the cabinet wants to get rid of him. Maybe Dayan will come in, at least as defense minister. Watch out for that. If he does, it's a go. But I tell you something, it won't be easy, at least, not where we were."

"What do you mean, where you were?"

"Over there," Ido said, raising his chin toward Egypt. "Five days. Recon."

"Inside? Where was that?"

"Near Um Cataf. The Germans helped set it up for the Egyptians in the Fifties. Minefields, pillboxes, trenches, barbed wire for miles, thousands of the bastards, They're waiting for us. We'd do better to go round it."

"What did you see?"

"Not for your ears, my brother."

"Where are you heading to now?"

"Back up north. The Golan."

"Aha. I heard about your 'up north.' How is Alice? I wish I was twenty again. You did the deed?"

"Not for your ears, my brother!"

Arie laughed, then looked down sharply, pointing to his earpiece as it came to life. The stuck half-track lurched out of its desert trap onto firmer ground and the gunner ran back with the cable. Arie spoke into his mouthpiece and tapped Ido on the shoulder: "Stay safe, brother." Ido jumped to the ground. As Arie's Sherman tank swung forward in a billow of smoke and sand, his heart clenched at the sudden thought of Tamara. It isn't over, no way. He saluted her little brother, and his tank column rolled south, toward the enemy.

Facing Israel across the border now was a massive force of seven Egyptian army divisions, a hundred and twenty thousand soldiers. Two thousand tanks. Nine thousand antitank guns. Arie's mission, if war erupted, was a dash south across flat ground, wiping out any opposition, and then a swing east to join a night assault on Abu Agheila, the key junction dominating the main north–south road in Sinai. He who controlled Abu Agheila controlled Sinai.

Israel's assault force was led by a barrel-chested thirty-eight-year-old brigadier, the youngest in the army, Ariel Sharon. He was a controversial hero of the 1956 war who had dropped his paratroopers behind enemy lines, with heavy casualties. His vastly outnumbered division today would rely on a series of overlapping attacks on four fronts to surprise the Egyptians and crush them. Surveying his own platoon of middle-aged reservists Arie couldn't help thinking, despite his bravado with Ido: let's hope it never happens.

Ido, back in the north now, thinking of Alice and his own affairs, prayed it would. God, let it happen, me and Alice, he muttered as he marched through the kibbutz to Alice's room. It was two o'clock, siesta time, he had the whole afternoon off, after twenty straight days of operations. He hadn't seen Alice in almost six weeks—when his reconnaissance unit was launched, they fell off the radar.

He had warned her that he couldn't be in contact. He hoped she understood.

But when he knocked on her door, there was no answer. He peered inside. Empty. Oh, no. He hadn't been able to tell her he was back, the only phone on the kibbutz was always busy. A tall blond boy walked by, he must be a foreign volunteer. "Hey," Ido called. "Have you seen Alice?"

"No, I think she may be in Haifa. Or Zefat. A group went to work in the hospitals. In case there's war."

Ido's heart sank. He had counted on seeing her. Every night he had kept up a silent conversation with her image. Alice's cheeky grin, her sweet lips, to say nothing of her body's promise, had sustained him through the desert, hiking through the icy nights, hiding in the sweltering day, peering through binoculars for hours, every passing shepherd boy or camel herder spelling possible disaster. Yet all the time, part of him was smiling, knowing Alice was waiting.

Now what?

"Do you know when Alice will be back?" the volunteer called to an English girl.

"Soon. She's at the first aid class."

"Oh, she's back then?"

"Yes, they came back from Haifa yesterday, they were in Rambam Hospital."

Ido's heart leapt: there is a God. "Thank you," he said, searching the lawn for shade where he could wait. The sun was high, the air in the Jordan valley was leaden. Flowers must be wilting; he certainly was.

"I'll wait inside," he said aloud, "it's too hot."

The only comfortable place in Alice's room was the bed, so Ido stashed his Uzi beneath it, unlaced his brown combat boots, took off his shirt, and lay in his combat trousers and white T-shirt, head cradled in his hands, looking at the ceiling. His metal dog tag hung from his neck. He sighed happily. The sleepless nights in the desert, the long drives, the muggy heat, soon did their work. He loosened his pants, his eyes closed, and in minutes Ido was fast asleep.

That's how Alice found him. She opened the door and there he was at last, the boy, the man, who had made the passing of time so painful. Finally he had come. How sweet he looked, such long eyelashes, his face so relaxed, his gentle breaths, black hair from his brown chest poking over his white vest. How far she had come, she thought, so quickly. From tenth-grade football games in Taos, New Mexico, to Israel's Jordan valley on the brink of war, with a beautiful man in her room, and a submachine gun under her bed. Thank God Mom's not here.

Her pink-walled bedroom with her crocheted throw and collection of stuffed rabbits sitting against the pillows, her life-sized poster of Elvis bent double stamping his foot and strumming his guitar, it all seemed from another lifetime. She had argued with her mother on the phone, tried to explain how happy she was in Israel, denied the danger, refused to return home. She hadn't said it, but it was because of Ido, and now here he was, all hers. She backed out of the room and quietly closed the door, not wanting to wake him. She looked around the lawn, wondering where she could wait. She could lie in the shade of that tree. Or drink a soda in the dining room. Or visit one of the girls. Or go over her notes from the first aid class. Or . . . or . . . do what she really wanted to do.

She gently pushed the door open, closed it quietly behind her, locked it, and stood by the bed, gazing with love at her sleeping soldier. A yearning as old as time came over her, the fear of losing her man in war before she fully knew him. She had a gift for him, and he for her. All this she felt, barely knowing it. Hesitating only a moment, Alice slipped off her shoes, and her shirt, stopping with her hands inside her waistband. Should she take off her pants? She didn't dare. She lay beside Ido on the bed. Half of her was hanging over the side, so she snuggled against him.

She was unsure what to do with her arm and finally laid it on his. In the hot muggy room, sleep overtook her too, until she felt a stirring at her side. Ido was turning, discovering her, his eyes opened in delight, until he closed them again, as if asleep, now facing her. Each lying on their side, their faces close, they both pretended to sleep. Their breath mingled, Alice hoped she didn't smell of milk. Ido sighed, his hand moved and found Alice's hip, and rested there. Alice responded, edging closer. A moment passed until Ido, sleeping of course, moved his hand to rest gently on Alice's breast. The tenderness of the moment swept over her.

Eyes still closed, she raised her lips to his and found them. Rested, aroused, Ido pulled her to him, in an instant their bodies wove around each other like twine, his legs through hers, her arms around him, their mouths as one. During all the classes on how to treat wounded soldiers, Alice had prayed Ido would never be one of them, but swore if he was she would always care for him. She felt an overwhelming urge to keep him safe, to never let go. He rose to an elbow, pulled off his T-shirt, he was so muscled, his skin sleek, his body hard. He pulled off her bra, his hands were at her waist, pulling off her pants, she helped him unbutton his own, his underpants came off, and hers. She was naked now, and so was he. She raked him with her fingers, felt him hard against her belly, he was heavy upon her, stroking her everywhere, kissing her wildly, touching her, pushing into her. "Gently," she whispered, "please, slowly, it hurts. Inside, it hurts."

Ido rose to his elbows, brushed her hair from her face, kissed her eyes and her nose and her mouth. "Have you done this before?" he whispered.

"No," she whispered back. "But I want to. Now, with you. I love you. But, please, slowly, don't hurt me." Alice held his hard buttocks, pulling him in while holding him off.

"I won't, I won't, I love you too," his voice rising in ecstasy. She shifted beneath him, her legs wider than they'd ever been, she strained against him, trying to make it easier, but it hurt. Her eyes were squeezed so tight her face contorted, she felt herself being opened, being filled, it stung, it hurt, oh it hurt, but his kisses sweetened her, and her lips clamped onto his so that he shouted out and she relaxed, her mouth relaxed, she kissed him gently, her body relaxed. She moved with him, welcoming him, her legs felt free and wrapped around him, and they moved together as Ido kissed Alice's throat, taking her, until she felt his whole body shudder again and again, he groaned and groaned, collapsed on her, and rolled over onto his back, glistening. She lay by him, in shock and joy.

"God," Ido gasped, while Alice lay with her eyes closed, in a trance, her heart leaping, bounding like a doe in a field of flowers. Every nerve tingled, every sense was piqued. She brushed her nipples, they were hard as diamonds. Ido lay his head on her chest and suckled at her breast. She cried, and he held her, both sighing with satisfaction. She felt warmth on the inside of her thigh and knew it was blood, and was glad.

They made love again, and this time it was slow and tender, at first. Alice was confused when Ido slid down the bed and kissed her toes and brushed his tongue along the inside of her leg to the velvety top and stayed there, exploring, probing, but she allowed herself to be transported, clinging to his head with one hand, clinging with the other to the bed frame, her body arching higher and higher until she exploded, jerking and shaking, and finally collapsed, laughing hysterically.

Later she walked him to the kibbutz gate, where he would hitchhike back to base. She held his hand with both of hers, and chatted gaily. But the closer they came to the road the more subdued she became. "Can you come back tomorrow?" she asked.

"I'd come back tonight if I could, but I can't. Yes, I'll come tomorrow but . . ." He sighed. "Who knows what will happen tomorrow? We're all just waiting for the order."

"Do you know where you'll go?"

He squeezed her hand. "It'll be up there somewhere," he said, looking toward the looming Golan Heights. Shade crept up the escarpment as the sun sank in the west, behind the mountain of Gilboa, where King Saul fell in battle with the Philistines. "The Syrians can see half of Israel from the Golan. We must take the Heights, and it won't be easy. Uphill all the way." As if in confirmation, they heard distant booms. "Very steep. They're well dug in, it'll be bloody. But we'll do it."

Alice pulled Ido against a tree and rested her head on his chest. He leaned into her, his thigh between her legs, his rifle over his shoulder. "I love you," he said.

"I love you too," Alice murmured, and pulled back so that she could look him in the eyes. "But I want to say something to you." He smiled and raised his eyebrows. "I want to say," she went on, hesitating, "it's sort of a confession, I told you that you are the only person I ever made love to. I want to say that I didn't lose something, my virginity, I found something, you. And I am glad that if you do go to war, that you will have me to think of, and you will know that I will always be here, waiting for you, however long it takes. Because I love you, Ido, and I always will. And I ask only one thing in return."

"Of course, my darling, anything. What?"

She smiled and kissed him. "Don't tell my mother."

He burst out laughing. "I promise." How funny she was, yet so sincere, how beautiful, how American. No Israeli girl would have said what she just did. All he wanted right now was to take her back to her room and do it all over again. He felt he should say something in return, but what? She looks like she'll cry. "Don't be sad," he said, "I'll be back, I promise. It'll all be over in a few days, we'll kick their ass."

"Kill them all, and come home to me."

Ido shook his head slowly, his eyes distant. "No. It isn't like that. We train and go on missions, but when it comes to it, all we really want is to go home. I'll do everything I have to do, and more, but if I'm really, really lucky I won't have to kill anyone. Who, after all? They're not so different from us, they're just people. I bet right now some poor Ahmed up there is kissing his girl, just like I am, hoping he'll get back in one piece too. No, I'm not looking forward to this. We're all just doing what we're told to do, isn't that the story of every soldier in every war? I just want to get it over with. If there's no more war, I guess it's worthwhile. Me? All I want is to stop them from shooting at us. At you."

Alice knew she loved him, now she knew he was worth loving. She clung to him until he whispered he'd better go, and she clung to him all the way to the road. There, too quickly, a pickup truck stopped. Ido climbed into the back and saluted Alice, who looked after him and kept waving until the truck faded into the long dark road.

TAMARA and MOSHE

TEL AVIV, ISRAEL

June 3, 1967

———————

The waiting was the worst. The country crept, hanging its head. The Holocaust and the terrible price of the war of liberation hung over the people. They trembled, hoarded food, and listened to the radio news with dread: Arab leaders called for the annihilation of Israel, boasted of Arab strength—they had more soldiers, more warplanes, more tanks, more guns, more of everything and all was aimed at the slaughter of the two million Jews of Israel.

Egypt declared a mutual defense pact with Jordan and sent it two commando brigades; Iraq joined the pact and sent more commando brigades and tanks, while its president swore, "No Jewish survivors." Syria moved four infantry brigades to Israel's Golan border, promising "a battle of annihilation."

"They'd kill every last one of us if they could," Moshe was saying, "but we have the ultimate weapon—we're small and alone. Our weakness is our strength." Moshe repeated the phrase, savoring it.

"Is that your column today?" Tamara asked, stacking weeks' worth of eggs, cooking oil, rice, cans of vegetables, candles. She didn't consider herself a hoarder, but with her children and Peter's in the house, and her parents, she had to stock up for the war.

"Yes. I spoke to Peter, he told me something interesting. Egypt was all set to surprise us last week. Their plan was to attack our airfields, destroy our planes before we had time to react, bomb the runways, our ports, and at the same time invade with tanks to cut our country in two. Without our air force, we'd be helpless."

Tamara looked up, holding bags of rice. "So why didn't they?"

"Russia stopped them. I don't know why."

"Peter said that?"

"Yes. He's in a position to know."

"I thought Russia wanted them to attack us?"

"Who knows what's really going on?"

"Is it true that making Moshe Dayan defense minister means there will definitely be war?"

"Of course. Why else do it? We have to attack, there's a limit to how long we can call up the reserves."

The soldiers' frustration was no secret. Army camps were like summer picnic areas, with families bringing sandwiches, soup, fridge-loads of food for the fighters. Women played chamber music, barbers offered free haircuts, children played paddleball as if they were at the beach—anything to relieve the strain of the long wait.

Daniel and Carmel also clamored to visit their dad, but Tamara was torn. Arie's parting note had been like a dagger, and after Peter had told her about the fight, she didn't know what to think. How she must have hurt Arie. Yet he had hurt her for fifteen years and even now probably still had a mistress in some Tel Aviv apartment.

In their one phone call since he had been called up, Arie had sounded beaten. It was their first real talk, beyond children and the house, for months. He sounded so needy. And when he said good-bye, Tamara had said, I love you. How could she not? Her husband, her children's father, was going to war and he was troubled. What else could she say? she asked herself now. Did she mean it? Did he mean it too, when he said the same? After all, he was sleeping by his tank in the desert, soon to kill or be killed. For any man, a time for reckoning, and Arie had more to reckon with than most. But who else was he calling for sympathy? How many other women? All she knew for certain was that Arie was in pain, so was Peter, and so was she.

Their fight had exposed all she had denied or concealed: their failing marriage, her love for Peter, the need to choose. Arie had to choose between his wife or his lovers. She had to choose between Arie or Peter. Peter had to choose how long he could wait for her. They could not all keep hurting each other, hiding and cheating. Had her mother told her father? She must have.

"It's complicated," Tamara said to herself, unaware she was speaking aloud. "No it isn't," Moshe said without looking up. "With 'weakness is our strength,' I mean, that gives us a motivation Arab soldiers just don't have."

Tamara sighed. "That isn't what I meant. Life, Father. Life is complicated. Do you know what I mean?"

Now Moshe did raise his head. He had been waiting for an opening for weeks. "I think I may know what you mean. Tamara, my child, yes, it's complicated. How can I help you?"

Tamara's eyes became misty and she kissed the crown of his head. "You can't, Daddy. You can't."

PETER

With most of the outer windows dark, an observer could think it was just another early night for the workers of Mossad. But in the inner rooms of the Office, hidden from the street, lights were ablaze, years of work were coming to a climax.

Peter finished reading a cable and sighed with satisfaction. War was coming, and the Egyptians didn't have one rocket worth firing. Most couldn't even be launched, and those that could were inaccurate and couldn't carry a payload. Much of his early career had been dedicated to just this goal—eliminating the rocket threat at time of war. He handed it back to Gingie with a short smile. "What's next?" he said, dismissing a decade of danger. "What else is there?"

"I hate to tempt the gods," she said, handing him another sheaf of cables, "but it's all looking good."

The government had dithered for weeks, weighing if and when it should attack Egypt. But the wavering had one critical benefit: it told the Arabs Israel was afraid of war.

It confused their patron too. Peter nodded in approval as he read a cable intercepted from the Russian ambassador in Tel Aviv to Moscow estimating that any Israeli attack was at least two weeks away. The British ambassador's intercepted report said fifteen days.

Peter's smug smile was interrupted by a long, loud yawn. He hadn't left the Office in two days, managing his agents, who were spreading the lie that Israel was not ready to strike.

He read another cable summary. Chatter on Egyptian army comms was all about preparations to counter Israel's opening move, which would be a massive attack on the ground. Egyptian forces had about fifteen days to get ready.

In fact, in eight hours Israel would launch a massive air attack. At 07.50 the next morning, Monday, June 5, Israel would go to war.

Gingie sat down heavily across from Peter. "I'm exhausted," she said. "So are you. Our work is done. It's eleven o'clock. Go home."

"You go home."

"I think I will. But you should too. At least for a few hours."

He shrugged. "You're right. I'll get some sleep. I'll be back by seven thirty."

"Me too. But I'm not leaving till you leave. I don't trust you."

Arm in arm the two friends left the building, to be driven home in a Mossad car. "You first," Gingie said, "where shall we drop you off, your dump or the palace? I mean, your apartment or Tamara's place?"

"Drive north, I'll decide on the way."

The dark, deserted streets slid by, the sliver of moon cast the merest of shadows through the trees that lined the boulevards. It was the calm before all hell would break loose, when the fate of Israel would be decided.

Peter tried, but failed, to shrug away the thought that had bedeviled him for days. It was unworthy, evil, but he couldn't shake it off. He didn't mean it, he didn't want it, the thought horrified and dirtied him, but he couldn't help himself. All his thoughts of Tamara led him to the same vile place: wouldn't it be simpler if Arie was killed in his tank? He commanded his mind to stop going there, that foul stinking corner of his soul. He did not want that. Yet how much easier things would be. His fight with Arie was just on hold, hostage to the war, but when Arie came home in one piece, as God willing he would, the day of reckoning must come.

Peter sighed and unfolded his arms. He pinched the wheel and wound his watch, and felt a weight upon him: how unworthy he had proven of his father's trust. How painful for his parents' memory that their sons should fall out over a woman.

He couldn't bring himself to go to Tamara's now, even though his children were sleeping there. He'd hardly seen Tamara since Arie had been called up two weeks earlier. He was too busy and she said it seemed too deceitful. As soon as the war was over they'd have to deal with Arie, come what may.

"The dump," he said. "I mean, my place."

ARIE

At 07:45, with Egyptian pilots on coffee break, their command staff stuck in Cairo traffic, and their Sinai command's radio frequencies partially jammed, four Israeli Mystère fighter-bombers hugged the ground over southern Israel, engines flaming, jet stream shimmering. They flew so low that Arie flinched, he swiveled his head so fast his helmet slipped over his eyes. As he adjusted it, another rumble from the north and four Israeli Mirages thundered by, skimming the dunes, so low Arie could count their missiles.

This must be it, at last. A tremor went through the men. They had been on red alert since first light, tank engines idling, systems warmed, radio silence. Needing no order, they climbed into their tanks, ready to move. The young gunner at tank eight waved and cheered after the warplanes, but most moved deliberately, lost in thought. If the eighteen-year-old conscripts were exhilarated at the prospect of drawing their first blood, all these family men wanted was to get through the coming slaughter and go home. But first they needed to protect it.

At 08:00 a siren pierced the radio silence, startling everyone, and the code, "Red Flag, Red Flag." Nothing fully prepares for the shock: War.

Two helicopters clattered overhead as the four tanks of Platoon 2, D company roared from the eucalyptus groves onto the track south. A hundred yards to the left, more tanks appeared through the trees, ripping up the potato fields, while behind them APCs chased them with squads of infantry sitting in rows. Arie, like all the commanders, stood tall in the turret, a warrior at war, and he felt the power of the mighty killing machine course through his body. He held out his hand. No, it wasn't shaking. Twice that morning he had found himself trembling, from anticipation more than fear, or so he told himself. He was by now a veteran of death. He raised his fingers to his lips and kissed his wedding ring.

The massive war machines kept a rough formation, spread over a mile, five deep. Plunging forward, Arie felt the heat of raw power, the thrill of battle, a thrill also at what this mighty force stood for: victim no more. He had survived the Holocaust, barely able to walk, and grown into a fighter: in the War of Independence, then in the Suez war; now he was again at the tip of the Jewish spear: this would be their war to end all wars. As for Peter . . . No. Not now, he ordered himself. First of all, stay alive.

The radio crackled with the commander's call to arms: "God is with us, for Israel." Arie's skin prickled, he flagged that he understood, and he ducked into the command cupola. They had entered the sands of Egypt. Death could come at any instant, a bullet, a missile, a mine, a freak accident. With a tight grimace, Arie glanced at the sky: God, don't forget, I'm on your side.

Tamara heard the same siren, as did every citizen and soldier of Israel. She gathered the children and her parents and ran to the bomb shelter, where nervous neighbors collected around the radio. Would the Arabs bomb Tel Aviv? Ashkelon and Ashdod were farther south, closer to Egypt, would they be hit first? At 9:00 instead of the news the Hebrew announcer read in a flat voice a list of coded mobilization orders: No information here. Later someone tuned to the BBC, and Rachel went white. For weeks the nation had trembled with fear, threatened with another Holocaust, and now there was no escape. The Egyptians were already bombing the towns of Israel, destroying the army, they had shot down 124 Israeli planes and that was just their opening shot. The BBC quoted Arab boasts: Jihad was triumphing, the Jews would be slaughtered. An Arab speaker turned to Radio Cairo and translated in a trembling voice: "We are drowning the

Zionist cowards in our hellfire. Now, Jews, you will see how your cowards die."

Tamara pulled Carmel into her bosom as if she would be safe there, and glared at Rachel, who had begun to sob. "Calm down," Moshe said. "Everyone calm down," he said again. "What else would the Arabs say? I don't believe a word of it. Let's wait and see, there is a long way to go."

But it wasn't long. Within an hour the BBC had changed its tune. It was the other way around. The Israelis were smashing the Egyptian forces, destroying their air force on the ground. No official word from Israel, but the BBC reported that in the first hour Israel had destroyed the Egyptian air force and had won complete control of the skies. The announcers struggled to believe it: almost before it started the Jews had all but won the war.

But on the ground, there was still a long way to go. Arie's platoon fell in with the mad dash south, led by General Israel Tal's northern armored brigade. Over rough tracks that linked villages, through crushed vegetable patches, past terrified donkeys and cattle. Arie's four M-50 Shermans made quick progress in the wake of the havoc wreaked by Tal's tanks. His machine gunner fired blindly into copses and thickets, a cloud of dust announced their progress from afar. A tank shell obliterated a barricade of bricks and wood that had blocked the road, but still no sign of the enemy.

Only in the fields approaching Khan Younis to the west did they catch up with the war. They saw men running through destroyed houses, followed immediately by the pings of bullets bouncing off their armor. They rode on, speed of the essence, along tracks cleared of land mines. His brigade was to rendezvous in El Arish, thirty miles south, then swing east with General Tal's Steel Division to link up with General Ariel Sharon and destroy the Egyptians at Abu Ageila. This would open the gateway to the Suez Canal, and certain defeat for Egypt. If it worked.

Around a bend the road narrowed between clusters of houses on either side. Perfect ambush spot. Arie's stomach clenched. This isn't right. Was he on the wrong road? He glanced down at his map, but it was too late for that. His company had fanned out, three tanks were right behind him. Nothing left but to barrel through. Swinging the machine gun, he laid down protective fire at the right side and then the left. They were abreast of the houses now, his body braced for the shock of a shell, but they were through; he felt his bowels tighten. They passed burning wrecks, Arab prisoners, an old man pulling a reluctant donkey by a rope. Medics worked on wounded Israeli soldiers lying in rows by the track, while behind them, pillars of smoke rose over the dunes. Arie slowed, knowing battle was close, his skin crawling with tension. He was almost relieved when the order came: "Advance southeast, enemy at six hundred meters, engage and destroy."

"Follow me, boys," Arie called on his radio, and Levi the driver sped forward. The hull of a Soviet T-34 appeared backward from behind a dune, reversing from some threat, only to position itself right in Arie's line of fire, an opening gift from the God of war. "Straight ahead gunner!" Arie shouted. The cannon roared and the Egyptian tank shook in a ball of flame and black smoke. Soldiers leapt out, one on fire. Levi edged past, and within a minute the Sherman was looming over a trench with dozens of Egyptian soldiers. With his cannon pointing straight at them, they threw down their weapons and fled for their lives.

Israeli and Egyptian tanks clashed in a ferocious battle over two square miles. The Israelis pressed forward, machine-gunning soldiers in ditches, crushing barbed wire a dozen meters thick, outgunning the Egyptian tanks with speed and accuracy. They were vastly outnumbered by the Egyptian brigade but with Israeli fighter planes swooping through the uncontested skies, strafing and bombing, the Egyptian force was obliterated.

There was a ten-minute respite in their seats for Arie's men, surrounded by burning tanks and wounded or abandoned Egyptian soldiers wandering the desert. Arie was soaked in sweat; he gulped water from his flask. Then his orders were changed. Instead of continuing south to the rendezvous at El Arish, his platoon was ordered west into Rafah, a crowded, sprawling town at the southern end of the Gaza Strip. Something's changed, Arie thought, high command told us we'd keep out of Gaza. We're doing too well, it must have gone to their heads.

Out of the desert it looked like a different planet. They passed lush vegetable fields, stands of trees, fences of twigs and branches with sand on one side and dark earth on the other. Didn't I pass here in '56, Arie wondered.

Are we fighting for the same land? I almost died then, and now I'll be lucky to get through this again. He thought of his son and daughter, safe with Tamara. In three years they'd be in the army. Would Daniel be in a tank in the same shit desert? No way, the boy would be a cook, he'd make sure of that. Carmel will be in intelligence, safe in army HQ in Tel Aviv. This is madness.

The radio crackled with shouting and explosions from the field and panicked appeals for help, answered by the calm, stern voice of the colonel. Paratroopers were in trouble in Rafah, they needed support. Arie's tanks were ordered to avoid the refugee camps, stay on the main road, evade the enemy, head due west, and find the trapped soldiers around the blue mosque on the crossroads of the main Gaza north-south road. Quick.

Arie guided his force of four tanks from high inside the command cupola, forcing his way deeper into the packed Arab town. Progress was too slow. Between the low houses he saw an Israeli armored personnel carrier racing the same way, but he couldn't get his tank onto the fast road. The roads he was on narrowed and curved, crossed each other and went off at tangents, they were entering a warren, due west toward the sea was what looked like a school, a clinic, crowded homes. Arie tried to go around, he swung to the left but was blocked by a row of buildings.

Now there was the staccato of shooting, paint chips flew from his tank, bullets pinged off the armor, and then: and then a red flash from ahead and the tank behind him rocked on its tracks, a direct hit from a missile. To escape the line of sight, Arie roared up an alley, crushing homes of wood and tin. Each time they swung the cannon's barrel it knocked the corner of a building. There were more Egyptians ahead. "Shoot!" Arie shouted, and the cannon fired a shell blindly, to clear the way. "Left!" Arie yelled, swinging the machine gun at the rooftops from where Arab fighters were pouring fire into his tank. He was alone, separated from his column, he was sweating, his heart pounding, struggling not to panic. "Back up," he shouted to the driver, and then repeated it, quieter, trying to project calm. The tank stopped with a jolt and went into fast reverse, tracks digging into the dirt. "Hula 1," he said into the radio, identifying himself. "We're trapped, separated, trying to find the main road."

The radio responded, "Hula 1, your position?"

"I don't fucking know," he shouted, regretting it immediately. "I don't know," he tried again as calmly as he could. He flew to the side, banging his shoulder as the driver tried to make a sharp turn. He saw an Arab rush from the side and throw a hand grenade, and ducked. The grenade bounced off the turret. More Arabs appeared between shacks with guns, there was a flash and a boom as another grenade exploded by the cupola, muted by his headphones, on the roofs he saw a dozen men firing at him. Levi couldn't make the turn, but down an alley he saw open land. He made a dash for it, engine roaring. The tank hit rubble and veered on one track like a sailboat racing into the wind, finding purchase on piles of concrete and bricks.

And then, Arie's heart all but stopped. An Egyptian T-54 blocked the alley, its turret swung round, its barrel found them from fifty yards. "Fire," Arie yelled, "now!" His gunner had seen the target and swung the turret but the barrel smashed into a wall. The driver reversed to free the cannon, just as the Egyptian fired. Not again, Arie's brain screamed. There was a blinding flash of light inside the hull, the tank rocked on its axle, a direct hit, Arie's head smashed into the metal cupola base, he smelled the stink of burning oil. "Out boys, out!" Arie yelled, jerking the cupola open. He leapt to the ground, rolled away and jammed against the wall of a house. Chaim the gunner joined him; they fired their Uzis from their hips as they ran.

Behind them the explosion shot a blast of heat and smoke up the alley, shrapnel hit Chaim in the head and back and Arie, who had just turned to see who else made it, was hit in the shoulder and face. Bullets whizzed by, ricocheted off the walls, dug into the earth at their feet. Wiping blood from their faces they ran low and fast, but to where? The alley was narrow and straight, Arabs at both ends and on the roofs.

TAMARA

At the words "The news from Kol Israel," Tamara and Rachel ran to the radio in the living room, where Peter's children Noah and Ezra were already gathered. On the hour every hour Israel came to a standstill for the latest from the fronts. From fear they had moved to joy as every bulletin brought news of another advance. Noah sat, head down, crayon poised over the map he had drawn of Israel, on which he colored every bit of newly conquered territory with the blue and white of Israel.

Jerusalem was theirs after two thousand years; the West Bank was falling, Ramallah, Nablus, Hebron, town after town; Jordan was begging for a cease-fire.

Sinai was occupied, Israel's army stood on the Suez Canal; Egypt's air force was destroyed, its army demolished; with no military to defend Cairo, Nasser too called for a cease-fire.

Moshe phoned from the newspaper—Syria is next. Noah whooped: "The Golan Heights. Damascus. I may as well color it in now."

"Shush," Rachel reprimanded him. "The Adelsons."

That same morning they had heard the cry of anguish from their neighbor Ida Adelson when she answered the knock on her door. Her husband Yossi had fallen in the battle for Bir Gafkafa. All across Israel hundreds of families were broken by similar news; hospitals were overflowing with the wounded.

"We should hear from Arie soon," Tamara said, gripping her mother's hand. "If the fighting in Sinai is over and we're sitting on the canal, he'll call. If anyone can find a phone, it's Arie."

In the evening Alice telephoned from Rambam Hospital in Haifa. "I heard from Ido," she said. "A friend of his came to the hospital to visit someone and brought a note. He said he's having a quiet war, they're still waiting for orders."

"Thank God," Tamara said. "God willing they'll never come. How are you? Your parents called twice, I told them not to worry, you are safe and well."

"Safe but not so well. I can't believe how naïve I was."

"What are you doing?"

"Whatever I can. Writing letters for the poor boys, cleaning them everywhere, holding their hands. Helping families who visit. It's horrible, so much crying. There's no room, they're lying in the corridors, the doctors and nurses never sleep, there is so much to do, so many to help. I hope Ido never gets any orders to go anywhere."

"You sound very tired," Tamara said, "can you get any rest?"

"I go to bed, but I can't sleep. Tamara, there's so many of them, they're all so young. Everywhere it smells of blood. Some of them, all you can see are their eyes, they're burned all over. When I met Ido he seemed so strong, a god, now I realize . . . it's awful, I never imagined . . . I love him, I hope . . ." She began to weep, and the line went dead.

Tamara told Rachel, whose eyes filled. Please God, they prayed, bring Arie and Ido home safely. No more war.

PETER

Peter stared out of the open window, sucking in air, with each breath feeling a part of his self ebb away: Arie, my brother, the last of our tribe. How could he tell his children?

Behind him Gingie stood, head bowed, holding the report. She placed it gently on his desk. "There's still hope," she said.

Peter sat back at his desk, turned the folder over in his hand. Mossad was responsible for intelligence activity outside Israel, and Gaza was still outside Israel. It was a military matter but Mossad was kept informed; a formality. Gingie had spotted the name in a Gaza situation report.

He would have to tell Tamara. He felt his heart with his hand, he was palpitating. Reading his thoughts, Gingie said, "Don't tell Tamara. Not yet. There's nothing to say, wait till you have something concrete."

Concrete. What a hard word.

"What else do we know?" Peter said, almost in a whisper.

"MIA. Missing in Action. Only what's in the report, and what I got out of his commander, who doesn't know much yet." Gingie kept it formal, it would be easier that way, for both of them. Her heart went out to her old friend. "They found the tank, it was still smoking. The crew got caught in a narrow alley and couldn't fight their way out. There were dozens of Arabs at either end. We found two bodies inside the tank, burned but they've been identified by their ID tags. The names of the two missing crewmen are Chaim Peled and Arie Nesher. There was blood twenty yards from the tank in the alley, two separate tracks so they were both wounded. There were Uzi shell casings along the alley for another thirty yards and then no more, so they got that far. But where the shell casings ended, there was no significant extra blood, so they didn't die there. It seems they were wounded. The shell count looks as if they didn't have any spare magazines and quickly ran out of ammunition. Our troops have flooded the area, a day went by before they began looking." She added softly, "If he's captured, they'll find him."

"One thing about Arie, he's a fighter and a survivor."

"That's two things."

"Two things, then." Peter put his head on the desk, his hands in his pocket, as if folding into himself. After a moment he looked up at Gingie. "How long to Rafah? Three hours? But who knows, it could be a whole day getting past the convoys."

"Oh no, you're not going. What good would it do? You'd get in the way."

"I could get a plane. The war's over down there, we're just mopping up. The brass will be going down, I can hitch a ride. Gingie, arrange it."

"No, Peter, no, the army and Shin Bet are all over it, what good would it do for you to go? We need you here."

Peter bit his lip. Arie Nesher, MIA. Better than KIA, killed in action. His foulest imagination had conceived of such a thing, he cursed himself for ever allowing such evil to pollute his mind. Mama, Pappi, Renata, and Ruth, all gone, and now Arie. Maybe Arie. He sat up, steeling himself.

He drummed his fingers on the desk, stood, walked to the window, his lips tight. "Give me the report again."

Gingie handed it to him. "What are you thinking? You were drumming your fingers. And I know that look."

"I'm thinking," he said slowly, drawing out the words, "that this is a job for me. For us. Bear with me, I think I have something. Listen. If he was dead we'd have found his body by now. If he's alive, he's been captured. The Egyptians wouldn't take him, they're running for their lives, he's wounded and would slow them down. So somebody else must have him. Who? I'll tell you who. Fatah in Rafah. The Palestinians were building a strong cell there, we have most of their names, they would have been fighting our troops too. I think—there's a strong chance anyway—that Fatah captured him. And the other guy, Peled. My money is on Fatah holding them as hostages. He's being held in a house somewhere. Down a well, who knows. Now that we've occupied Rafah and Gaza the Fatah men want to get out. Two Israeli hostages are their ticket to anywhere."

"If they wanted to get out they could just put down their guns and run, like everyone else."

"Maybe. Maybe they want to be heroes, make a name for themselves. Or maybe they're in trouble with the Egyptians too. Maybe they can't leave their families."

"Whatever, what can you do about it? If that's all true, we wait until Fatah gets in touch."

"And what happens to Arie in the meantime? And Peled? Torture? Or they die of their wounds? Or Fatah decide to kill them anyway? And if the army does find them, they're not very subtle. They'll go in guns blazing and kill everyone, including my brother. No. I think I could help. I know some of the Fatah names. And addresses. Gingie, get me on a chopper. Now."

He fingered his silver watch, rubbed the leather strap. Don't worry, Pappi, I'll find him. If he's alive.

IDO

———————

Above the rocky plain and fertile slopes, the snowcapped summit of Mount Hermon loomed over the plateau, a battleground for thousands of years. Below the plains stretched the Sea of Galilee and Israel's Hula valley, for years sitting ducks for Syrian guns.

Ido slumped against the bullet-pocked wall of a bunker, panting, his mouth hung open. Each breath brought the smell of blood, gunpowder, burning fuel, and sweat. He licked his parched lips, his fingers fumbled at his belt to unclasp the water bottle. A medic did it for him and dribbled water into his mouth. "Slowly," he said, pulling open Ido's shirt. "Where are you hit?"

"I'm not. I just can't move. I'm dead on my feet."

"So rest." The medic moved to David next to him. "Leave me," the soldier said, "there's much more badly wounded."

"Where are you hit," the medic said.

"It's nothing, just a little blood."

"But where?"

The soldier pointed to his stomach. "Here, a bullet. Go to Yehuda, he's more urgent." He nodded toward the next soldier in the row, whose head was covered in blood.

"You're in the next ambulance," the medic said to David. "It may not look like much but who knows what damage the bullet did inside." He moved to Yehuda, wiped his face, bound his forehead and his ear. "You're fine," he said, "it looks worse than it is. Wait here." He moved to the next man, and the next, while Ido licked his lips, his eyes closed, trying to shut out the carnage.

The medics had fought with the second wave of soldiers, picking their way through the dead, some blown to bits by land mines, others ripped by machine-gun bullets and hand grenades, blood and broken bones marking the infantry's costly, stubborn progress up the hill. The Syrian bunkers and trenches were still smoking from the Israeli grenades. Syrian corpses lay by the Israeli dead where they had fought with fists, knives, and rifle butts. The wounded groaned, some screamed for help. An ambulance left with some, another came for more.

Ido opened his eyes and rolled to his side. He steadied himself with one hand, the other still grasping his weapon. With a mighty exhalation and effort, he rose to his knees, and then, leaning against the concrete bunker, he stood, bent double, gasping for breath. Finally he straightened and surveyed the hill of death. Earlier, it seemed from another age, he had forced himself to look into the staring remaining eye of Baruch, who had carried the heavy machine gun. The top of his head was missing, a shell must have sheared it off, scalped him. How did this happen? Baruch, a mountain of a man who carried the heavy gun like a toothpick. A medic had come, Ido thought that maybe he thinks he's alive, after all, and will take his pulse. Instead, the medic covered Baruch's face with a jacket.

One by one his friends were killed at his side. He couldn't even help the wounded, the order was to climb up and up, forward and forward, officers first. Over the barbed wire, shooting into trenches, man-to-man, more barbed wire, more trenches, more enemy, then the bunkers, firing into the slits, dropping in hand grenades, no surrender, no prisoners.

Ido teetered, and vomited. He crouched, retching and spitting. A medic splashed water into his face. "I'm okay," Ido said, "a bit dizzy."

"Sit down, that's an order."

Ido lay on the ground, his eyes closed. "Ido," Yehuda said, scratching the bandage around his head, "Ido, you hear me?" He shook him hard. "Stay with me. Ido? Stay with me! Medic!" he yelled, "over here, quickly!"

Ido's eyes flickered. "Stop shouting, you're making it worse. Give me water. Maybe a drip. I'm just dehydrated."

In the dark, half-tracks drove the Golani fighters back to base, while fresh soldiers occupied the Syrian bunker complex that was now in Israeli hands. It was the same all across the Golan Heights. Burning tanks, smashed Jeeps, crashed warplanes, broken bodies, and a promise that never again would Syrian artillery terrorize Israeli civilians working the valley fields. But the price was high, very high.

TAMARA

On the same day, at four twenty-five in the afternoon, Daniel answered a knock on the door. It was the wartime nightmare that united all Israelis: two strangers in uniform. Daniel took a step back. "Is your mother home?" the woman said.

Daniel couldn't answer. He tried, his mouth opened, but no sound emerged. He opened the door wider and gestured for them to come in. The man, an officer, said, "Are you the son of Arie Nesher?"

Daniel nodded, tears sprung.

"Please get your mother, is she at home?"

Daniel called in a flat voice from the foot of the stairs, "Ima. Tamara. Someone here to see you." Rachel came out of the next room, saw the officers, and tottered against the wall. She began to wail. The female officer took her arm and guided her to the sofa. "We don't know anything for sure, we're just here to keep you informed, maybe there is nothing wrong."

"Then why are you here?" Rachel said, her body shuddering. "What has happened?"

From the landing Tamara called out, "Coming." As she descended the stairs she noticed the uniformed officers and halted. Her hand flew to her mouth, with the other she grabbed the banister. Her legs buckled, but she held herself upright, as the officer looked up. "Mrs. Nesher, please do not be alarmed," the man said in a soft but firm voice. "We do not have any-thing to report, but we do have to inform you that your husband is missing, the army is searching for him . . ."

"Missing? What do you mean, missing? Is he all right?"

"Please come and sit down. We don't know yet. We are sorry to frighten you . . ."

Tamara interrupted. "How long has he been missing?"

"Four days."

"Four days!"

"Yes, I'd like to tell you of the circumstances, and what we are doing. If you have any questions at all, of any kind, I'm at the end of the phone on this number, anytime, day and night. My name is Ariel, and this is Captain Shulamit. She is a psychologist and can stay here with you if you like. Everybody is looking for your husband, Mrs. Nesher, with God's help we will find him."

"But what do you mean missing? What happened?"

Captain Ariel of the K'tzin Ha'ir, the city's military liaison office, told her what he knew, while Rachel quietly sobbed.

Daniel's eyes were blank. He had gone back eleven years, to the little boy sleeping by the window, refusing to move until his father came home from the war. It had become a family joke and Daniel always retorted: "But it worked." Now he moved behind Tamara and stroked her head. "Abba is all right, Mummy," he said in a thin voice that betrayed him. "I know it. I just know it. He's coming home. I promise. I'll wait for him at the win-dow."

Tamara burst into tears.

As soon as the officers left, promising to phone with every bit of infor-mation, she phoned Peter, he would know what to do. He could find out more than what the army was telling her. She collected herself, she had to be calm. There was no answer on his direct line, so she called back and asked the desk if she could speak to him. Gingie took the call, sounding uncertain. Peter had told her not to say anything, he hoped they'd find Arie before Tamara needed to worry.

"Tamara, how are you?"

"I'm looking for Peter, is he there?"

"No, not right now, I think he's out in the field."

"I have to speak to him. It's urgent. Oh Gingie, Arie is missing. Missing in action. What can I do?" She sobbed, collected herself. "I'm sorry. But I just heard. Maybe Peter knows something. Maybe he can do something. I must speak to him. Where is he, Gingie?"

"Peter is in Gaza, Tamara. He's looking for Arie."

IDO and ALICE

---

*A*ize bardak,*" what a mess, Ido said to his sergeant, Avinoam, trying to
park the Jeep. Ziv Hospital's parking lot swarmed with men in uniform, families carrying baskets of food, ambulances weaving through, si-
rens wailing. Exhausted nurses in green smocks and doctors in white coats
leaned against pillars and sat on patches of grass or brick walls, smoking
silently with vacant stares.

The emergency room was even worse and the corridors, smelling of dis-
infectant and blood, almost impassable. Wounded soldiers lay on stretchers
on the floor with drips in their arms, parents knelt at their sides, tannoys
kept up a din of announcements, calls for doctors, and appeals for quiet.

"This is where they bring the wounded?" Ido muttered, "I'd rather be on
the Golan. Well, maybe not."

"Maybe not," Avinoam said. "Hey, there's David."

From the middle of a row of beds they saw David waving. Their combat
boots clattered on the tiles as they went to him. Ido kissed him on the
head. David had been the joker of the unit, now he just looked tired and
used up. "So what's the story?" Ido said.

"Nothing. I'm fine. I'm lucky, the bullet missed everything . . ."

"Well, it hit you," Avinoam said.

"But it missed all the vital organs. They took it out this morning, just has to heal, I'll have a hole the size of a fingertip, otherwise, I'm great."

"Good to hear," Ido said, sitting on the side of the bed. "Where are the others?"

"I don't know, I haven't seen anyone. It's bedlam, but the doctors, nurses, the volunteers, they're all amazing. You think we had it tough. They have to look after us." He tried to laugh but contorted in pain. At the mention of volunteers Ido felt a pang of regret: what a pity that Alice was in Haifa's Rambam Hospital, he didn't know when he would be released, when he would see her next.

"It won't hurt for long," Avinoam tried to reassure David, resting his hand on his arm. They fell silent, looking around the ward. The wounded soldiers most needed sleep but distraught families crowded around their beds. A nurse drew a curtain around one soldier and ushered his parents out. Another nurse wheeled in a trolley. They heard a single shout. "Uunh!" the mother gasped, as if it was she in pain, and fell onto the next bed. The soldier in it, his head and chest swathed in bandages, shifted to make room. "Sit down," they heard him say. "Your boy is in good hands."

The ward fell silent for the radio news: A spectacular victory. The country trebled its size. The world applauds the plucky Jewish state. Ido said, "Let's hope the cease-fire holds, it started at 4:30."

"Yeah. I can't go through that again," Avinoam said.

"Let the world rejoice," Ido said, "but it's not the way I feel." They counted the names of their dead buddies, it was inconceivable how many there were. Just in one battle, at Tel Faher, of twenty-five Israeli infantrymen, the Syrians killed twenty-one. So many funerals to attend, families to comfort. A gloomy silence fell over them, with Ido and Avinoam sitting on either side of David, holding his hands. "Well," Ido stood at last with a sigh, "let's go find the other lucky ones." In their new world, a bullet in the stomach or shrapnel in the head counted as lucky. "Come on, Avinoam. How many of our guys are here, David, do you know?"

"No idea. Most of the wounded went to Rambam. There must be a list somewhere."

"You're kidding. Maybe in a week. Okay, gotta go, we'll be back. Anything you need? Shall we call your family? You want to send a letter?"

"That's okay, they have volunteers here, they do all that. There was a pretty Yemenite chick from Rosh Pinna here last night, big lips, she held my hand for an hour." He smiled at the memory. "I wouldn't let go. I kept trying to pull her hand under the sheets."

They burst out laughing. "No, don't, it hurts," David cried. "But I tell you what, that was one strong girl, I couldn't get her hand past my knee."

"You're kidding, right?"

"Tonight I'll have better luck."

"There's nothing wrong with you," Ido said. "We're off, we'll see who else we find."

"Thanks for coming, guys, really. I mean it." He looked away.

"Is that a tear?" Avinoam said. "Don't be a baby."

"Piss off."

"Okay, he's officially healed," Ido said. "Take care, my friend, see you very soon."

"Yes, Captain. I'd salute but I never learned how."

David followed them with his eyes. Lucky bastards, he thought. He edged down in the bed to relieve the pressure on his stomach. He hadn't even known he'd been shot, it must have come sideways through the flak jacket, he had felt an impact but thought a stone had somehow jumped up, he'd kept jumping from bush to rock, weaving and firing, and only when he lay behind a boulder to catch his breath did he see the blood, and the pain set in. It was Avinoam who fell next to him and bound the wound. He should have thanked him just now, he wished he had, but he couldn't find the words. Instead they had just held hands.

Ido led the way, scanning each ward as they passed, on the left and right, searching for wounded comrades. They found Jojo surrounded by his family who lived nearby in Kyriat Shmona, a town of mostly Moroccan immigrants. His neck was in a brace, his left arm in a sling, and his stomach and chest bandaged. He had been shot three times, but the greatest pain was the sprained ankle. He should have rested it but couldn't, he had hobbled and fought for an hour. Now it was the size of a football.

Across the noisy corridor was Yoram, the medic who interrupted his studies in England to rescue Israel. He'd go back to school with a leg missing below the knee from land mine shrapnel. His eyes were swollen from tears.

After two hours they emerged into the fresh air and slumped on a wall with exhausted medics and volunteers. For ten minutes they found no words that matched their thoughts.

Watching an ambulance load a burn victim for the drive to Haifa's Rambam Hospital, Ido broke the silence with a dull monotone. "At least we won."

"Some victory."

"Shit." Ido stamped a foot, as if extinguishing a cigarette stub. "Now, what? All I want to do is go home."

"Me too."

"They'll keep me here till last," Ido sighed. "The men go home first, officers clean up."

They sat with slumped shoulders, watching the bustle around them. At the entrance to the hospital soldiers who could walk stood with drips in their arms, snacking, chatting. Ido stood. "Come on, let's get back to base, they may need us."

They walked past another burn case being maneuvered into an ambulance and climbed into the Jeep. Avinoam twisted around, with his arm around the back of Ido's seat as he backed out, while Ido stared into the distance. He felt depressed, and relieved, but above all, in this moment, he just felt lonely as hell.

There was a knock on the window. He looked up, and started. Her long brown hair was pulled up beneath a scarf, her eyes were wide with surprise, her mouth was open with delight, she was walking backward as the Jeep moved, holding onto the roof. "Avinoam, stop," Ido shouted. He leapt out. "Alice! Oh Alice!"

"Ido, it is you!"

She leapt onto him, wrapped her legs around his waist so that he staggered back against the Jeep. She was laughing and planting kisses all over his face. Her three friends stood in surprise.

When he disengaged from her lips and she slid off him Ido could barely speak through his smile. "Alice, oh God, I'm so happy to see you. What are you doing here? I thought you were in Haifa."

"I was, but now they've sent us here." She nodded over her shoulder at her friends. "We've come to help."

Ido smiled at them, a boy and two girls, foreign-looking. "We're all volunteers from kibbutzim. We met in Rambam. Oh, Ido, thank God you are safe." She tapped his shoulders, his arms, his chest, his legs. "You are, aren't you? You're not hurt?"

"No, no, we're just checking on our mates." He took her hand and pulled her aside. "Let me look at you. It's only been a week since I saw you. What, eight days? It seems like a year." He hugged her again, stroked her hair, and her face, and kissed each eye. "God, I miss you, I need you. How was it? In Rambam?"

"It was everything. It was horrible, it was wonderful, it was sad, but in a weird way. Boys with terrible wounds, but alive. Nobody knew what to feel. So we just helped. I wrote letters, I held their hands, I helped families find their men. I felt emotions I never knew existed. We have so much to talk about. But who cares about me. You? What happened to you?"

"Let's not talk about it. Not yet. It was terrible. At least we won." He clasped her to him, his breath tickled her neck, his chest rose and fell against her breast. He stared into the distance, seeing nothing at all, clinging to her thin frame as if to a sapling in a storm. She felt him tremble and shudder and held him tightly, wanting to comfort him, while tears rolled down her cheeks. She had seen boys with terrible wounds, but knew now not all wounds can be seen.

At last they unfolded and returned to her friends. The volunteers were crowded around Avinoam, tall with black curls, big-chested, in combat boots and uniform, his Uzi strapped to his shoulder, a pistol in his belt. His eyes had their old sparkle. He looked at Ido with a smirk. "Meet Birgitte," he said. "She's from Denmark."

PETER and ARIE

RAFAH, GAZA
June 10, 1967

Ido had found Alice, but Peter was still searching for Arie. The only news, which had not yet been officially announced, was the worst: Chaim Peled, KIA. The soldier who had escaped the tank with Arie Nesher had been found buried in a trash heap, shot, battered, with a slit throat.

The ambulance helicopter with Peter aboard followed the coast south until Gaza where it cut east, fast and low, to land in the newly occupied Arab town of Khan Younis, deliver medical supplies, and pick up more wounded. All the pilots knew was that the morose passenger they dropped off was a senior Mossad official. From the landing pad he rode in an armored personnel carrier to brigade headquarters in a Rafah schoolyard. Rows of APCs and Jeeps were lined up before the bullet-pocked white building, while soldiers maintained a perimeter around the four corners of the complex. Snipers on rooftops surveyed the area with binoculars, tanks blocked the streets, paratroopers piled their equipment for redeployment.

Peter hurried to the commander's office, past an inner courtyard where lines of handcuffed Arab men sat in rows, heads bowed under the beating sun, waiting to be summoned by Shin Bet interrogators.

"Peter Nesher!" Colonel Uri sprung from behind his desk. "I didn't know it was you coming. Why Mossad's interest?"

"It's been a long time," Peter said, extending his hand. "And Mossad isn't interested, I should make that clear. I am. Arie Nesher is my brother."

The Colonel, unshaven and weary, looked hard at Peter, nodding with pursed lips. "I see. The Arie Nesher."

Peter handed him a folder. "Here are the files of seven members of Fatah, they all live in Rafah, terrorists. I have a hunch they may know where he is, they may even be holding him."

Uri went to the door and called out, "Get Ben-Tsion." He turned to Peter. "He's the Shin Bet chief down here, he'll pick them up, if they're still here. Most of the men have run."

Peter paced, explaining his logic to the colonel, who didn't dismiss the idea. "You have to understand," the officer said when Peter finished, "this is our number one priority. We've had patrols out every minute, all day and night, looking for him. Shin Bet too. Those Arabs waiting outside? They're from the area where he went missing, that's why they're here. Someone must have seen something. We're on it, Peter. And I'll be straight with you. You being here makes me very uncomfortable. The other poor sod's family couldn't come here, you're pulling rank. I understand, I'd probably do the same. But I don't want anyone here to know he's your brother. Just say Mossad has its reasons."

Peter nodded. He would have said the same. But he didn't give a hoot what anyone said, he'd turn Gaza upside down to find Arie.

Ben-Tsion entered, a short gruff man with cropped iron-gray hair. He ignored Peter. The colonel didn't waste words. "Arie Nesher, the MIA. Our friend here from Mossad thinks these people are worth checking on," Uri said. "You'll see why in the folder." The Shin Bet agent took it without a word, glanced at Peter, and left.

"He's a good man, Peter, but he has his hands full, to put it mildly."

"Don't worry, I'm used to it. They're all like that."

Colonel Uri chuckled, as a lieutenant rushed in. "Sir, they may have found the MIA. Comms from Gimmel patrol, a mile northeast of the refugee camp along the old railroad track." The colonel glanced at Peter and back at the officer. "What do we know?"

"Just that. There is a contact now."

"A firefight?"

"Not clear. Just that first word."

"Get backup there right away. If they're not needed they can return but get them moving."

"Yes, sir." The lieutenant ran out the door.

Peter raised an eyebrow. "You stay here," Uri said. "No disrespect, Peter, but this is army. We're handling it. Nothing you can do. But your timing, as always, is impeccable."

Peter's jaw clenched, but again, he knew the colonel was right. All the soldiers would need was more soldiers, not some civilian getting in the way.

He swallowed hard. "Are you going?" he said. The colonel hesitated. The area was calm and this was the biggest operation of the day. An Israeli life was at stake. And he hated the thought, but it was Arie Nesher, the tycoon. What the hell was he doing in a tank? Couldn't he buy his way out of serving?

"All right, let's go," he said. "But don't say anything, don't do anything. We may need you to identify him if necessary. I hope it isn't. Come."

They raced out of the compound, dust flying: two APCs loaded with the paratroopers delayed from their mission north, led by two Jeeps, with the colonel and Peter in one, medics and their supplies in the other. An ambulance would follow.

When they found the patrol, guarding a single old man in a torn shirt sitting on the railroad track, the colonel cursed. "What the hell is this?" he demanded. "What's the story here?"

When he came back to the Jeep he told Peter, "There was a language issue. The old man kept saying '*jesh, yehud,*' which is about all the Arabic our boys know—army, Jew—but now a Moroccan soldier turned up, he's translating. And this could be it, Peter. The old man says he has an Israeli soldier in his house. That he's been hiding him."

"Since when?"

"Five days. It fits. He says the soldier burst into his home at night, bleeding heavily from the head. His neighbors would have killed him, but I guess he's one of the good ones, he hid him. He couldn't get away to find a patrol until now because he was scared. He says it isn't looking good for the soldier. Infection, he's delirious. So he took the risk."

"Is this too good to be true? A trap? I mean, if he's delirious, making noise, the neighbors would have heard him," Peter said.

"I'm thinking that too. But we have to check. Of course that'll compromise the old man. The neighbors will know he helped the Jew."

"One step at a time. Let's go."

The man refused to get in an Israeli Jeep in case the neighbors saw him, so the Jeeps and APC's followed him as he hobbled, twenty yards ahead. Progress was slow. He looked over his shoulder many times, as if he'd changed his mind and was hoping the Jews had gone.

"Hurry up," Peter muttered. "He's a good man though," he said. "We'll have to look after him."

"If it isn't a trap."

"Yes. What will you do when you get there?"

"Depends on the location. If it's a narrow alley, in the middle of the refugee camp, we have a problem. And they're all narrow, it's like a maze."

They bumped along in silence. The homes became smaller and crowded, sewage ran down the dirt track and gathered in ditches. It stank, flies buzzed in the jeep. The army had kept out of the refugee camp, one of the largest in the Gaza Strip. It had no strategic value, so there was no reason to risk patrols when every alley and rooftop could hide a dozen fighters who could shoot and disappear in seconds.

When the old man stopped and pointed, a paratroop officer approached him with the translator. The convoy halted behind them. Children stopped playing in the alleys to gawk and their mothers ran out, gathered them up, and scuttled away. Faces appeared in windows, women in scarves pulled back, their places taken by men. It was noon, the sun glared at them, glinting in dark pools of wastewater. Peter wiped the sweat from his face.

"Well, it's about as bad as it gets," Uri said. "It couldn't be narrower. And it's long too." He looked down the alley, at Peter, down the alley again. "Are you thinking what I'm thinking?" Uri said. "About how we should handle this?"

"You mean I go in? Yes, it makes sense. I can identify him. And alone, in case it's an ambush."

"You don't have to. You shouldn't even be here."

"But I am. And I will."

Peter's face was set and grim as he stepped from the Jeep. "Wait until we see the APC blocking the other end of the alley," the colonel said. "We'll place groups of three in every side alley. If the shit hits the fan we'll be with you in less than ten seconds."

Peter snorted. "A lot can happen in ten seconds. Give me a weapon, at least." Uri took an Uzi from a soldier to add to Peter's own pistol. He handed it to him, with two fresh magazines.

One APC with a dozen paratroopers backed up, looking for a way to reach the far end of the lane. Minutes later it appeared, oddly foreshortened. It loomed over the wretched homes. The street was quiet, no children, no faces at the window, everyone hiding.

"Okay, good luck, Peter."

Peter nodded and gripped the old man by the arm. They made an odd couple, picking their way past dirty puddles and scrap, the hobbling old Arab and the Israeli with a pistol in his belt, an Uzi in his hands.

Peter knew he was taking a big risk but there was no other way. After all, plenty of Arabs speak Hebrew. They could have taken an Israeli uniform from a corpse and put it on one of their fighters, to entice more Israelis to their death. Only he could immediately identify his brother, and there was no point risking anybody else.

The old man's hands were trembling. Maybe terrorists had forced him to approach the Israelis, Peter thought, either that or he was a brave and good man. He'd soon find out, the hard way.

They crept along the alley, which was silent as the grave. Peter's eyes scanned each hut, his Uzi following his gaze. Damn. He should have taken grenades. He'd love to have one in his hand right now.

Looking left, his skin prickled. Three Israeli soldiers were kneeling twenty yards down the alley, ready to sprint forward at the first gunshot. He'd feel better if they were at his shoulder, but that could alarm the people holding Arie, if he was here. They could shoot him and run. Better this way.

Seconds later the Arab stopped. "*Whooa hina,*" he said, "Here it is." Peter pulled the man closer, scanning the silent alley, the menacing roofs. He gestured at the hut, his Uzi in the man's back.

The old Arab nodded and saying something in a soothing voice in Arabic, he pushed open the door. It creaked and hung ajar, a harsh line of light cutting the darkness. Peter pushed him in and took a step, waiting for his eyes to adjust. He made out an old woman cowering against a wall, protecting two little children who were pressed into her long skirts. She pointed with her chin toward another door at the head of a narrow, dark corridor separating two more rooms. Sleeping rooms? That's not right. Why so many? As Peter stared into the gloom, his neck hairs rose.

He prodded the old man, motioned with his Uzi for him to lead the way, but when the Arab glanced at his wife and hesitated, there was a scraping sound. A door opening? One of the rooms? It was too dark to see. Peter leapt to the side, grabbed the man, held him tight to his chest, he'd take the first bullet. He reached back and kicked the entrance door open farther, but it gave no more light. He signaled to the woman to get out. She shook her head and sank to her knees against the wall, still gripping her children. What's she afraid of? Him, somebody else? He shouldn't take a chance, he should get out now. But what if it was Arie? If they had him? They'd shoot him if they knew they'd been rumbled. No choice. Move. Fast.

Peter pushed the man forward so that he stumbled into the corridor. Step for step behind him, Peter yanked open one door, Uzi at his shoulder, finger tight on the trigger, he scanned the room. Nothing. He whirled round, opened the other room, and pushed the old man in first. It all happened in a flash, there was no room for failure. At his feet there was a blur of motion and a squeal.

A fat shape with a long thin tail, a rat, bigger and darker than any he'd ever seen, brushed against him, followed by two more. He lashed out with his foot, catching one square in the gut, lifting it feet into the air where it hit the wall. It fell to the ground, its feet scrabbling, and raced out of the door into the street.

Peter's heart thudded against his ribs. He fought for breath. The area was clear.

The old Arab watched him wordlessly from inside the room. He shrugged and nodded at the wall dividing them from the first room. Peter nodded, picked up a gaslight for the man to light and carry.

The Arab led the way, the flickering light playing on the walls as he opened the door. The stench was overwhelming, a smell that you could feel. The Arab pulled aside a pile of mattresses to reveal a man, motionless, on his back, arms folded on his chest, legs crossed. Peter shivered. That's how Arie used to sleep, as if in a coffin, when they'd shared a room. The Arab moved the light closer, it reflected off the whites of the eyes, and Peter saw, through the clotted blood on the head and face, it was his brother, with staring blank eyes.

Arie's face and head were covered in sores, and he was trembling. His chin was slick with drool, his teeth chattered, he lay in his own waste. Peter stared, then burst out of the room and into the alley, shouting at Uri, "It's him, it's okay, come!" Two medics raced forward, with a squad of paratroopers. Peter ran back into the room, calling "Thank you, thank you" to the old couple.

"Arie," he said, kneeling by him. "It's over, you're safe; it's me, Peter." He raised his brother's filthy hand to his lips and kissed it, but there was no response in Arie's eyes. "Arie, Arie?" His forehead was burning, his pulse was racing. Peter turned away and felt his stomach churn.

PETER, ARIE, and TAMARA

TEL HASHOMER HOSPITAL, TEL AVIV

June 14, 1967

A Voice of Israel interviewer was struggling to moderate a radio shout-fest on what to do with Israel's newly conquered territories. An academic's "Give it back in return for peace" was drowned out by a rabbi's triumphant "The kingdom of Israel is restored to its glory," while a parliament member yelled, "Annex all of it!" a decibel louder than the columnist's "The age of empire is over, colonialism is dead." They only agreed on two things: A war between the Jews was more likely than another war with the Arabs; and Jerusalem: the miracle of a united Jerusalem would never be undone.

From this day, the radio journalist said, Shavuot, the feast of the harvest and the day that commemorates the giving of the Torah to Moses, Jews can again visit the Western Wall, all that remained of the Jewish temple destroyed two thousand years ago by the Roman emperor Nero. Already by midafternoon, 250,000 Jews had entered the gates of Jerusalem's walled Old City, in Jewish hands for the first time in two millennia, to worship and wonder. Inspired by the glory of the victory, the interviewer waxed poetic.

From Sharm el-Sheikh at the scorching southern tip of the Sinai Peninsula in the south, he pronounced, to the frozen white summit of Mount Hermon in the north, and all of biblical Judea and Samaria in between, all had been conquered by Jewish warriors. Every goal had been achieved, and much more. The Straits of Tiran and the Red Sea were open. Israel occupied Sinai and sat on the Suez Canal. Jordan lost half its kingdom. Syria lost the Golan Heights. The Arab armies were smashed, their air forces and their pride crushed. Never again would Israel be threatened, though the price was high: eight hundred Jews dead, twenty-five hundred wounded.

Tamara turned the radio off.

"Water," Arie muttered, running his tongue over his lips. Tamara filled the glass and held it to his mouth. "Drink," she said. "The more the better."

Carmel moved to his other foot. "You like?" He smiled weakly. "More oil?" He nodded, sighing. His daughter poured massage oil from a bottle, rubbed her hands, and began at the ankle, smiling dreamily.

"You're a lucky man," said the soldier in the next bed. Arie tried to move his head in acknowledgment, but he was too tired.

Tamara moved closer to him and whispered, "Do you want to move to Assuta? It's a private hospital, you can have your own room."

He shook his head weakly. His voice was thin, he had breath for only a few words. "I want to go home."

A nurse moved some chairs and curtained off his bed. "I'm going to remove the dressing so the doctor can take a look. Maybe you'd like to leave?"

"Carmi, go outside and get some air, all right?" Tamara said. Carmel made a face and left, rubbing excess oil into her arms.

There was a rustling, and Doctor Shimon pulled the curtain aside, reading Arie's file, while the nurse delicately unwound bandages that covered half of Arie's face and head. "It will look much worse than it is," the doctor warned Tamara, who shifted nervously. "All superficial, we took out seventeen small pieces of metal, from the face, head, and shoulder. They'll leave very small marks, nothing remarkable. Most didn't even need stitches. A very lucky man. Hair will grow back over the burn marks on the head."

He leaned into Arie's bruised face and half-shaved head, examined each puncture mark, and moved to the shoulder. "We had to stitch it up here, but it's doing just fine, excellently, in fact, just keep it immobile so the stitches don't come out."

"That's good," Tamara said, trying to control her shock. Arie's face was red and yellow and blue, and swollen with pockmarks all over the right side, like a side of pounded meat.

"We were very concerned at first about the infection and fever, but it is under control," the doctor said. "No need to worry."

"How long . . . till I go home?" Arie asked.

"Not long at all. In fact, I think the quicker we get you out of here, the better. The risk of another infection is higher than the value of keeping you here. And the wounds we can treat as an outpatient. You can go home tomorrow. Frankly, we need the bed."

Arie grimaced when he tried to smile and squeezed Tamara's hand.

"Just keep him rested, clean, away from germs, feed him light food, plenty of water, the swelling will go down quickly. I guarantee you no scars on the face, maybe this one above the eyebrow," he said, squinting into Arie's face. "It bled a lot, eyebrows always do."

"Knock, knock," a voice said from behind the curtain, "can I come in?"

"Peter," Tamara jumped up, pulling the curtain aside, "I haven't seen you, I haven't thanked you."

"I've been busy, and no need. How's the patient? A bit beat-up, I see."

"Going home tomorrow." Tamara said.

"Really, already?"

"That's all, then," the doctor said. "The nurse will take care of everything. We can have the dressing off in a few days. Let the wounds breathe. You've done very well, Arie. The fever is down, the infection's almost gone, just make sure you don't get another one. In a week, ten days, you'll be back on your feet, ready for the next war, God forbid. Good-bye."

"Thank you, Doctor," Tamara said. "Arie, I'll have your bed ready, flowers, fruit, chicken soup, whatever you want." She looked up at Peter with a sad smile. She wanted to take his hand, to fall into his arms. She had cried when Gingie told her what Peter had done. He had faced death alone to save his brother. That was the truth, Gingie told her, reading between the sparse lines Peter had written in his report to justify his sudden absence from the Office, just when he was needed to prepare Amit for his prime minister's briefing. She had also seen Colonel Uri's account, which, in terse military jargon, had filled in the details. The Mossad agent had acted with great

responsibility to prevent what could have been a firefight in a densely popu-
lated area with many civilian casualties. Who knows, Tamara thought,
how conflicted Peter had been, and what love he had shown, bringing back
his brother, her husband, his rival.

She couldn't help herself. She sprang up and embraced Peter, kissed him
on the cheek. "We owe you so much, thank you for bringing Arie home to
us." He tried not to respond, not to look at Arie, but he felt her lushness
through her flimsy summer dress, while she kissed him again.

He shook his head. "It wasn't like that, really. I promise you, Arie would
have done the same for me."

Arie, whose eyes had not left Peter since he'd entered the room, feebly
raised his hand for Peter to take. Peter sat on the bed, holding Arie's hand.
"You look great," Peter said with a smile. "Better than the last time I saw
you, anyway. Here, I brought you some flowers."

Arie nodded, he was breathing heavily, he tried to raise himself but
didn't have the energy. He pulled Peter closer by the hand, until his mouth
touched his brother's ear, but his whisper was so weak Peter couldn't hear.
"I'll put these in water," Tamara said, standing to fetch a vase.

Arie gripped Peter by the arm and whispered again, and this time Peter
heard him: "Stay away from my wife."

THE FAMILY

Ido and Alice, arms comfortably around each other, waved good-bye as the family drove off on their mystery tour. Arie had promised them a fun day out, resisting all the children's entreaties to divulge their destination. "Somewhere interesting" was all he would say. No need for bathing suits, just their ID cards.

"East Jerusalem, of course," Daniel guessed. "I'm the only one of my friends who hasn't been there yet."

"That's because Daddy needed to recover properly," Tamara said, looking back. "We'll arrive soon."

Ever since the conquered territories had been bared to the victors, Jews had swarmed across the erased borders, touring their holy places and cramming into the Arab bazaars of Jerusalem's Old City, hunting for exotic bargains: fabrics and rugs, wooden toys and carvings, spices and coffees sold by delighted merchants at double the prewar price. In his column, Moshe quoted Prime Minister Eshkol, who asked Defense Minister Moshe Dayan in exasperation, "Why are our people buying all this cheap rubbish?"

"Because they can," Dayan replied.

Ido and Alice closed the door behind them. "Great," Ido said. "We have the whole house to ourselves. Let's go into the garden, look at the waves." He took her hand, but halfway through the living room, felt resistance.

"Wrong way," Alice said, pulling him toward the staircase. "No garden?" Ido said with a smile. "Yes, garden," she said. "The Garden of Eden." Still holding hands they walked toward the guest bedroom where they had been staying for the past week, but again he felt a tug. "Now what?"

"Come." She took him through Arie and Tamara's immense bedroom, into their bathroom. It was all marble and mirrors, with steps to a raised bath and a shower large enough to host the family meal. "I've always wanted to do this," Alice said, with a shy smile. With her back to him, looking in the full-length mirror at Ido looking at her, she slipped out of her shorts and then out of her T-shirt. She contemplated her naked body, the orbs of her breasts and the sudden darkness between her legs. She leaned forward and ground gently against him, smiling at Ido's serious face in the mirror. Turning, she slowly pulled off his shorts and stood on tiptoes to kiss him. "Pick me up," she whispered. "Let's watch ourselves."

Just south of Tel Aviv, where the last houses gave way to fields and orange groves, Tamara saw the Road 1 sign to Jerusalem slip by. "You missed the turn," she called out. Arie, at the wheel, glanced at Peter by his side, and grinned. "You said Jerusalem," he said, "I didn't."

"Where are we going, then?"

Arie was enjoying himself. "Gaza."

"Gaza?" Carmel shrieked. "Why didn't you say so? I don't want to go to Gaza!"

"Nor do I!" Daniel shouted.

"That's why I didn't tell you."

"Is it open to civilians?" Tamara asked.

"Yes, it is. From today."

"That's interesting," Moshe said. "That's why you wanted me to come. I know where we're going. You want me to translate?"

Arie glanced at him with a half-smile and nodded.

"It's good that Rachel didn't come," Moshe said.

"Yes," Peter said. "It may be a bit much for her." It was almost too much for him too: he had unresolved business with Arie.

"Isn't it dangerous?" Tamara said. "And what will we do, you want to eat fish on the beach?"

"Maybe," Arie said. "But first, there's something I want to do. And I want you all to come with me. I want to thank the couple who saved my life."

"It's safe," Peter assured them. "We'll have an escort; I arranged it."

Carmel and Daniel exchanged glances. "I'd like that too," Carmel said. "To thank them." Tamara turned to the backseat and gripped her daughter's hand, making a kissing sound. "Me too," she said. "It will be extraordinary to meet the people who saved Daddy."

She could hardly breathe when he told her: how he and Peled were trapped in the alley, facing certain death. With Arabs inching toward them, bullets all around, he had shot off the metal bolt of a door, barged into someone's home, run right through and out the other side, run up another alley, and had kept on running, one twisting narrow lane leading to another, holding his head, stanching the blood, until he had no strength left. Along the way he lost contact with Peled.

He hid in a stinking empty chicken coop. His head hammered and wouldn't stop bleeding. At night he tried to walk east, toward Israel, but was dizzy from thirst and disoriented, and collapsed in an alley. He couldn't stay like that or he would be caught in the morning and killed, he had to act, trust in luck and God. He'd knocked softly on the nearest door, until it opened. He remembered an old man pulling him into a room. A woman feeding him olives and tomatoes, bread and hummus. He tried not to drink much water, it was too smelly. He woke up once to find the old man smothering his mouth. At first he fought, thinking he was being choked, until the man put his finger to his lips and he realized: he was just trying to stop him shouting in his sleep so nobody would know there was an Israeli soldier. And then he must have drifted in and out of consciousness; he was delirious. He remembered a child, the old woman, water, the muezzin's call to prayer. And then, somehow, Peter was saying something. Next he awoke in the hospital, with Tamara holding his hand.

What kind of people would shelter a helpless wounded enemy while they were fighting a war? they wondered together. If a wounded Arab soldier fell into the home of a Jewish family, would that family save the Arab from the Jews? They mulled it over and always reached the same conclusion: good, decent, brave people would, that's who. Like the Christians who hid Jews from the Nazis. Arie had said he wanted to repay them somehow, now Tamara understood why he had brought a backpack stuffed with cigarettes, whisky, medicines, and food, and probably, knowing Arie, a pocketful of money.

They made good time along mostly empty roads. Where the road curved east to the poor young Israeli towns of Sderot and Netivot, Arie continued south through farmland, skirting the Gaza Strip until its very southern tip on Egypt's border, which had now been erased. There he found the track that led into the now-occupied Arab town of Rafah. Israeli Jeeps and military convoys reassured them.

They drove in silence, each lost in thought. Arie looked for clumps of trees, inclines and ditches, rows of prickly pears, anything familiar to him from not one war but two. They passed a burned-out Jeep and in a plowed-up field, probably a former army staging post, a vast pile of Egyptian ammunition crates with two soldiers standing guard. "I wouldn't smoke if I were them," Moshe said.

Never again, Arie was thinking. Never again will I get into a tank. Two wars, two disasters. Three from this tank had died, two in '56. He was still in touch with Shelly, the wife of Itamar, who was burned alive in the *Queen of Sheba*. Poor old Itamar. Arie sent Shelly money and flowers for the high holidays.

Peter's mind was elsewhere, with Tamara. He had tried hard to control himself these past weeks, every day he had wanted to phone and invite her to his apartment, but the scale of the betrayal of his brother, recovering from near death, stopped him every time. He didn't know how to reconcile that truth with another, that there was always a reason to feel sorry for Arie, always an excuse not to follow through with his love for Tamara. Or was that in itself an excuse? Did she not really want to leave Arie? Did he not really want her to? And what about Arie, why doesn't he leave her, or let her go? Their marriage was a sham, and they all knew it. Yes, that was it, the essential truth.

Their marriage was a fiction, she wanted Peter, he wanted her, that was where things stood. Now they had to square the circle. But it was up to Tamara, she was in the middle, she was the one to decide. Suddenly he thought of his parents, what would they think of him, how he was letting them down. He shut them out. He looked over his shoulder and his eyes met with Tamara's, and held. Just long enough for Arie to note in the mirror.

Tamara glanced at the children in the back row of the van. They were staring at the scarred landscape of arid farms and burned-out Jeeps, smashed carts and cars. The dirt roads, piles of garbage, pools of still water in ditches, the stench of dead animals. This will be good for them, she thought, to see the real world, not just the privileged life they lead. How would Carmel and Daniel have coped with the freezing transit camp she had lived in for most of a year? The abuse and the humiliation of losing everything. Their father jailed and beaten. God forbid they should ever experience that. If we had lost the war, who knows what would have happened? Well, she knew, she was Egyptian after all. The Arabs would have slaughtered the Jews like dogs. They promised they would, and they meant it.

Arie looked into the mirror at Tamara, who was staring at the passing countryside. "What are you thinking, Tamara?" She shook her head. Nothing.

She gazed at the back of Arie's head, and Peter's, her two lovers, the only ones she had ever had. They were sitting silently next to each other, eyes fixed on the road. As she contemplated the banal: the shape of their ears, the shade and length of their hair, the curve of their necks, knowing the warmth of their bodies, she asked herself bitterly, what devilish design was this? King Solomon had it easy.

She hadn't slept with Peter since Arie had been called up for reserve duty. And after he had visited Arie in the hospital, Peter had, with great care, presented her with an ultimatum. She had to choose who she wanted, and if it was him, they would face the consequences together. But Peter could not continue cuckolding his brother.

She knew he was right.

And now finally, here, on the edge of the Gaza Strip, staring out at this poverty-stricken battleground, she allowed herself to admit the obvious, with all the clarity imposed by war and death. She didn't love Arie as she loved Peter, far from it, but he was her husband: troubled, difficult, selfish, nevertheless hers. The father of their dear children. Could she really leave him for his brother?

For she knew with certainty that right now, it was Peter's neck she wanted to stroke, Peter's hair she wanted to run her fingers through, Peter who made her heart beat faster.

If it was a choice between luxury, the house, the jewelry, the cars and Peter, she chose a loving, loyal, devoted man over a husband who didn't know what love was, whom she could never trust. She finally accepted what she had long known: if she didn't leave Arie and marry Peter she would regret it all her life.

So now she must act. She would tell them tonight, when they got home. Done.

She felt a lump rising in her chest, a sob almost escaped, a sob of relief and love. The agony was over. Whatever happened next, so be it. Another sob, barely contained. Her father shot a questioning look, laid his hand on hers. She turned to the window, the glint of a smile in her reddening eyes.

They found their way to Peter's rendezvous in a villa above the grand sweep of water and golden beach. Below them fully dressed Arab women splashed in the low waves, their children ran and yelled, while fishermen sat on colorful rowing boats fixing nets between catches.

"I've never seen so many Arabs," Daniel said.

"I don't think I've ever seen one," his sister said.

"Don't exaggerate, both of you," Tamara said. "Here's your father."

Arie and Peter returned with their escort for the refugee camp, four tough young men, each wearing khaki pants, a khaki shirt over a white T-shirt, sunglasses and caps, with backpacks.

"They'll blend in nicely with the Arabs," Moshe said.

"Should we be doing this?" Tamara asked Peter when he was alone. "Isn't it dangerous, especially for the children?"

"Arie needs to do this, he wants the children to be there. We'll be fine.

Nobody is expecting us, we'll just knock on the door and stay a few minutes. And anyway we have the area under complete control. Not a problem."

She nodded. "All right, I trust you. With Arie you never know, but if you say so."

They split up, Moshe and Tamara in the Jeep with two of the security guards, the rest in the van. She didn't want to leave the children but was persuaded that with Arie and Peter, who had pistols, and the two armed guards, the children were safer than she was. Nevertheless, she gripped Moshe's hand all the way and only noticed halfway that a second Jeep was following with soldiers. It was the only way the commander would permit Peter to enter the refugee camp with his family, and even then only because he was backed by the weight of Mossad.

The children took in the scenery with growing horror. They knew Herzliya, where they lived in one of the grandest homes in the country. They knew Tel Aviv, one of the most modern towns in the Middle East. A trip meant a hike in the desert with picnics and a bathe in a spring, or a trek along the coast to eat hummus and falafel in a café by the water.

But this? Barefoot infants in rags with runny noses and dirty faces? Four-year-olds scampering alongside the van, knocking on the window, begging for money? Old men in torn shirts and women in scarves with vacant eyes and rotting teeth? Donkeys urinating where children played, rows of shacks with cardboard windows and tin roofs?

The deeper they entered the camp, the more concerned Tamara became. Moshe tried to calm her. "You see how few young men there are? It's all old people, women, and children. Don't be frightened. How many people get to see this? Israel's celebrating, having fun in the Arab towns, shopping, eating, hunting for bargains, but this is the reality. This is our future, dealing with this. If we don't give up the Gaza Strip, and the West Bank, we'll have to find a solution for these people."

"They're refugees. Where from?"

"Israel of course. Ashkelon, all the towns in the south. When we won in '48 the Arabs ran away to Gaza, or we made them run. We proudly call it the War of Independence, they call it 'the Catastrophe.' Either way, here they are. If we occupy Gaza we're stuck with them. And it looks like we're staying."

"Will you write about this trip?"

"Of course. Business tycoon Arie Nesher thanking the Arabs who saved his life? You bet. Look."

He had brought a copy of the newspaper with a large portrait of Arie, one of very few that Arie had ever allowed to be published. For all his business success, wary of his past, he avoided personal publicity. However, reporters had gone to town with the story of the business tycoon MIA saved by Arabs, rescued by the army, and they needed a photo to go with the story. It was a two-page profile, tracing his comet-like career beginning before he changed his name from Aren Berg to Arie Nesher. There was no mention of Peter, the censor had banned any mention of the Mossad agent. It was as if he had never been there.

"I don't know if I'll show it to them though," Moshe said. "They may not like it. I'll play it by ear."

They parked the cars at the end of the alley, on the spot where the armored car had waited with Colonel Uri. "You remember this?" Peter asked Arie.

"Not a thing. It was dark, I could hardly walk, let alone see. Come on, I'm looking forward to this."

Surrounded by the bodyguards, Arie shouldered his backpack of gifts and holding a child by either hand, led the way along the silent dirt lane, stepping over pools of dirty water that had seeped over the shallow ditch. As soon as their cars had pulled up the alley had emptied of children. Women peered through windows, on a roof a young man followed their progress with a cold stare, and vanished.

Peter pointed out the door, planks of wood painted green and corrugated iron nailed together, and Arie knocked, with Moshe at his side to translate. A woman's voice called from inside, *"Meen bara?"* Who is it?

"Salamu alaykum," Moshe said, his mouth almost touching the wood. Peace upon you. "I have come with the man you saved a month ago, he wants to thank you, and he has brought some gifts. He is here with his family."

They heard murmuring from inside.

"*Salamu alaykum*," Moshe said again. The family stood in a tight group, shifting nervously by the guards, scanning the alley. Tamara glanced at Peter: maybe this was not such a good idea after all.

The door opened an inch, and then wider, enough to reveal half the lined face of the old woman. She looked frightened and shook her head ferociously.

"My friend just wants to thank you, he . . ."

She interrupted him with a flow of Arabic, speaking so fast Moshe had trouble following her. He answered her, she continued, fearfully looking up and down the alley.

"Arie," Moshe said, "I'll translate in a minute, do you want to give her some money?"

"Yes, I have an envelope with cash."

"Give it to me, don't let anyone see."

Arie looked around and Peter moved to him, shielding him, as Arie took the envelope from his trouser pocket and gave it to Moshe. He leaned against the door as close as he could and pressed the money into the lady's hand.

"What about all this," Arie said. "The backpack. Tell her I want to give . . ."

"She can't take it. I'll tell you why later. We have to go."

Another stream of Arabic followed from the woman, at the end of which she looked at the family, and said something else, more gently now. When her eyes met Carmel's, she smiled, and put her fingers to her mouth, as if blowing Carmel a kiss. Automatically Carmel made a kiss too, and the woman closed the door.

"What just happened?" Daniel said.

"Come on," Moshe said. "Quickly." He explained as they hurried back to the vehicles. "Her husband is in the hospital, he was badly beaten, she says they're lucky he wasn't killed. It was a warning from Fatah not to help the Israelis. No cooperation. She said if he wasn't old they would have killed him. She's terrified."

"Should we find him in the hospital?" Carmel said. "She seemed a nice old lady."

"That would make it worse for him," Moshe said. "Come on, let's go."

The hostility and the poverty of the life they had stumbled upon smothered them. They drove home in silence, but for Tamara trying to get Arie to slow down. It was as if he couldn't get away fast enough.

At last he spoke. "Did she ask for money or did you offer it?"

"I offered," Moshe said. "She didn't want anything."

"Did you ask her why she helped me?"

"I didn't have time."

"That's what I wanted to know, most of all," he sighed. "I'll find a way, one day, to repay them."

Next to him, Peter nodded. "You'll have plenty of time. We'll be stuck in Gaza for years."

"You think so?" Moshe said. "Why? The government is split."

"Because giving it back is the only card we have to make peace with the Arabs. And they don't want peace with us. So we'll hang on to the card in case that changes. Which it won't. So we'll have to swallow another million Arabs and, mark my words, we'll choke on their bones."

"For once we agree," Moshe said. "Can I quote a senior intelligence official?"

"No."

"When the Orthodox Jews get to pray in Rachel's Tomb in Bethlehem and Abraham's Tomb in Hebron, they'll never leave, even I know that," Daniel said. "And Joseph's Tomb in Shechem. Lots of tombs."

"At least we destroyed their armies, they can't fight us again," Carmel said.

"They'll rebuild," Moshe said. "Russia will help them. We'll never have peace. We won the battle, we'll never win the war."

"Nor will they," Peter said.

The road slipped by, from one world to another. At the line that marked the border with Israel, as if by a miracle fallow fields became green, trees blossomed, and in Carmel's mind, flies turned into butterflies. After a late lunch of grilled fish on the beach in Ashdod and dropping Moshe off, they arrived home, tired and not a little relieved.

"I bet they haven't even got a shower down there," Daniel said as the van pulled up in their tree-lined driveway. "We've got five. I can't wait to have one."

As the engine cut off, Ido appeared at the door. "There's a lady to see you, Arie. She telephoned twice and then she came here two hours ago. I said you'd be late but she wouldn't leave, she insists on seeing you."

"What? Who?" Arie said, taking his backpack from the trunk as everyone stretched and yawned.

"I don't know; she wouldn't say."

"She won't say who she is, but you let her stay two hours? What's she doing?"

"She's very nice, elegant, she's sitting at the bottom of the garden on the bench, waiting for the sunset. Her daughter is with her, they're English, they're talking with Alice. They had some tea."

"I'll make some more," Tamara said. "What a day. Peter, you'll stay? You said you had to go on to Haifa."

"Mint tea? A glass, thanks, and then I'll be on my way."

They delayed at the van until they were alone. Peter forced himself to ask the question that had tormented him all day. All month. "Tamara, did you decide? Enough of this, it isn't fair to anyone. I have to know. My life is on hold. I'll tell him if you like, but you have to say if you want me to." He hesitated. "If you want me." He breathed deeply, held Tamara's gaze. "Just tell me."

She swallowed, and with two words decided her life. "I do. I do, Peter, I want you. But I'll tell him. It's better that way."

He moved toward her but thought better of taking her hand. There were too many people around. He felt relief but no joy. The good news brought much bad. The path forward would be hard, more than hard, with Arie, with the children, but it was time. "I don't know. Maybe we should tell him together. I'm afraid for you, what he may do."

"No. The children are going out. I'll tell him tonight. Come on, darling, let's go inside." As they walked into the house she slipped her arm inside his.

While Peter went off to use one of the other five showers, Arie came out of his bathroom and stood behind Tamara, gazing at the lady and her daughter through the kitchen window. Beyond them, the cooling sun hung low over the horizon in a clear blue sky. "It's going to be a glorious sunset," Tamara said. They watched Alice talking with great animation. "But who is the woman? Look at Alice, she's probably telling them about her work in the hospital. What a brave girl. She grew up. She won't be the same girl when she goes home." ·

"If she goes home," Arie said. "Ido said she wants to stay, and he wants her to."

"She's only seventeen."

"Have you seen them together? Believe me. Either she stays or Ido goes with her to America."

Tamara filled the kettle and lit the gas. "You should go and see what that lady wants. She looks quite elegant. Beautiful wide hat. Straw?"

Her heart ached as she watched Arie walk to the end of the garden. What an image, she thought, Arie walking off into the sunset. She couldn't bear the thought of hurting him, but she would have to tell him tonight. Who knows, he may even be relieved. His anger was more about possession than love; he's afraid of being alone. And he knows that she loves Peter, it scares him. It scared her too, but she needed to think about herself at last, and Peter, and not always about Arie. With all her soul she prayed the brothers would stay close. Maybe with time.

She saw Arie approach the woman, who rose slowly, with her hand to her mouth. They exchanged words, then stood in silence. Tamara leaned on the sink, peering through the window, shielding her eyes from the setting sun. Suddenly she heard Arie shout and fall into the woman's arms. All the way from the kitchen she could see her husband's shoulders shaking. Now Alice and the daughter were embracing too.

She hurried out. Was Arie crying? She had never seen that. He was made of stone or, less charitably, didn't have a heart. What's going on? Had he lost the Peugeot contract?

She rushed to them, put her hand on Arie's shoulder. "Are you all right, Arie? What's going on?"

"Tamara," he said, between gasps. "Tamara, I can't believe this, oh my God, this is Renata. Renata, my sister."

Tamara's hand flew to her mouth. Renata? Dead Renata? Renata and Ruth, the little sisters? Who'd vanished in the concentration camps? Renata was still hugging Arie, tears streaming down her cheeks. She freed one arm and held it wide for Tamara to join their embrace.

Now Peter was walking toward them, looking puzzled. They were all crying, surely Tamara hadn't told Arie yet. And who was the lady and the girl?

"I can't believe it," Arie kept saying, "I can't believe it. And now I have a surprise for you." He turned his sister toward Peter. "Do you know who this is?"

The lady stood with her mouth open. Her chest was heaving, her eyes wet but unmoving, fixed on Peter's face.

"No, I don't believe we've met," Peter said, putting out his hand to shake hers.

She took his hand and held it. "We have. It's been a long time. Peter, I am your sister. Renata."

Peter went cold, the blood drained from his face, he felt his knees buckle. "Renata?" She threw her arms around him, kissing his cheeks, his neck, as the hands of time wound back, to two little girls crying on the step, and a boy in short trousers climbing into a big black car, waving through the window to his sobbing mother and his little sisters. Now Peter began to weep. When he could, he whispered, "Ruth?"

"Dead."

"Mama and Pappi?"

"All dead."

The sun sank quickly, the air chilled. Peter stared at his father's watch, as if it had stopped.

"I've got an ending for your story on me!" Arie shouted to Moshe on the phone. "Get over here right now."

"Now? I'm dead tired. Can't it wait till tomorrow?"

"Trust me, Moshe, it can't wait. You'll thank me. Get over here right now and bring Rachel. We're waiting. And on the way, go to Peter's place and pick up Noah and Ezra, I spoke to them already, they'll be waiting at the door."

"I can't believe I have a new niece," Ido was saying. "With an English name like Susie. And she's older than me."

"No I'm not, I'm thirteen," Susie said. "You're much older." They all roared with laughter. "And I have such lovely new cousins, twins even," Susie continued, smiling at Carmel and Alon. "And more twins, nobody will believe me. And so handsome." Noah and Ezra punched each other. What is it with girls, Peter thought, they make boys look like infants.

They drank orange juice and beer and ate sandwiches, wandering the garden, enjoying the orange-streaked sky, until Tamara asked everyone to gather together. They pulled all the chairs into a circle on the veranda. "This is the largest family gathering we have ever had, from Arie's side," she said.

"That's not hard," Peter put in.

Renata related how she had found Arie. "I looked for years, but I was looking for Peter, I thought you had died along with everyone else, Aren. I mean Arie. I knew Peter had gone to America, but that's all I knew. I was only seven when you left, and Ruth was nine. I didn't have any papers or information. Can you all follow my English?"

They nodded.

"Well, of course I had a bad war. And when I finally made it to London so many years had passed and I was struggling so much, I didn't know where to start. I asked a few organizations, but nobody had your name. I went through telephone directories at the American embassy but you weren't in any of them." She smiled sadly at Peter and took his hand. They waited while she had to collect herself.

"And then yesterday, I was in London, reading *The Jewish Chronicle*, and they had your story in it, Aren. Arie. The photo rang a bell, there was something familiar about the face, and then I read the story and there it was—Aren Berg." She burst into tears, she couldn't continue. Susie took over. "Mummy couldn't wait, we flew here this morning, found your new name, Nesher, in the phone book and telephoned from the hotel, but you weren't home. If you know my mother, you know she can't sit still, sometimes she's a nervous wreck . . ." Renata objected with an exaggerated shake of her head, and everybody chuckled. ". . . so we took a taxi here. Luckily Ido and Alice were home, because otherwise Mummy would have sat on the steps all night if necessary."

They ate, they drank, Susie spat out a green olive: "Ah, disgusting!" Renata told them about her early life alone in London, how she had studied and became a translator. She'd married a salesman in the fur trade and gave birth to Susie, but her husband, sadly, passed away four years earlier from pneumonia. "To be honest, our marriage was as good as over long before that, though." She sighed. "I may not be very easy to live with."

"Ha!" Susie said. "Let me tell you about when Mummy . . ."

"That won't be necessary, my dear," her mother said, restraining her with a hand on her arm. Everybody laughed.

In a lull, as the family savored a silent moment, content with the light sea breeze that cooled the muggy summer night, and Arie had stopped saying, "I can't believe it," Peter took his sister's hand.

"Renata, please, can you tell us what happened? How you survived? The war."

All eyes turned to Renata. She sighed, taking Susie's hand. "I'll try. It is so very hard."

Susie looked sharply at her mother. "Mummy never talks about it," she said. "Never. Not a word."

"Because I didn't want to hurt you, my dear. But it's time. This may be hard for you, darling. But you should know." Susie stared at her mother, her eyes tearing.

Alice trembled in Ido's lap. With her dread for him in the war, the distress of comforting the wounded, and now this, she felt untied, adrift. She could scarcely relate to who she had been only weeks earlier, to her life in Taos, New Mexico, where all she had truly cared about was Gadi Bronson, the boy opposite, and the ski conditions in the mountains. Her gaze wandered from face to anguished face and she saw her own bland, smug family back home:

We take everything for granted, she thought, while these Jews have to fight so hard just to survive. How easy it is for us. How hard it is for them.

Ido wiped a tear from her cheek and brought her hand to his lips.

"When you left, Peter," Renata began, fighting to compose herself, "the house became a silent place. It got worse and worse for the Jews. But I won't give you a history lesson, you know all that, and anyway, Aren, I mean Arie, must have told you." They both shrugged.

Renata and the rest of the family had continued living in their home for two years into the war, until finally the Nazis had come for them. "I was separated right away," Arie put in.

"Yes," Renata said. "We thought they killed you. All Mama and Pappi could think of was saving Ruth and me, that's all that kept them going, they kept saying, 'One day you'll go to America and live with Peter.' Anyway, so this is our story."

Renata's voice became slow and heavy, as if the words themselves hurt. "At the end of November 1941, they put us in transports to Riga, where we lived in the ghetto. There were twenty thousand Jews and the only food we had was what the Latvians didn't want. People starved to death in the streets. At one point they started rounding people up and caught Pappi. He was taken away, to the Rumbula forest, and was shot. Next there was a typhoid epidemic. The Nazis refused to give us medicine and Ruth died. There was nowhere to bury her, so they took her away in a cart piled with bodies. Then Mama and I were taken to a concentration camp nearby; Kaiserwald." She paused, swallowed hard. "I'm sorry, I can't talk about what happened there. You can guess." She glanced at her daughter. After a moment she was able to continue. "You know, you have read of these things. What those brown brutes did to us. To the women. I was thirteen, fourteen then, just a child. But that didn't stop them." She had to pause. The only sound was from a buzzing mosquito and the whirl of the fans, until Renata collected herself and continued in her flat voice.

"Then, after about a year, the Germans began to lose the war and they panicked, they wanted to hide the evidence, the horrors they had committed. They made us dig up the mass graves in the forest and burn the bodies. They were half-skeletons in rags. I was like a zombie, I worked with eyes closed in case I dug up Pappi. We worked for a week, and then they killed us with machine guns. But not me. I fell into the pit, and covered myself with bodies. During the night, when the Nazis were gone, and before they burned us too, I dug myself out. I couldn't see anything, there was no moon, and all I could hear was groaning, the earth shifting, there must have been more survivors. I ran into the forest until I collapsed. I fell asleep, I ran farther, slept again, and the partisans found me."

She looked at her family. Their mouths were open. Nobody said a word.

"We lived in the forest, collecting berries and hunting rabbits, and at last we heard that the war had ended two weeks earlier. Nobody celebrated, we just sank to the ground and gazed at the sky, the puffs of clouds, the green trees, the beautiful birds, we saw freedom and life, and we all had the same thought, in our stinking rags, skin and bones, sick: We made it. We survived.

"But I was too weak to go anywhere, and when I finally found work on a nearby farm, I just stayed there, I had no way to get back to Germany, and, anyway, the Russians wouldn't let anyone leave. I was stuck behind the Iron Curtain. Only in 1952 was I able to make it to freedom. That's another story. I had no desire to return to Germany, and I was able to go to London, where I got a visa to study."

She turned to Susie and took her hands. "Don't cry, my little darling. It's all over." She tried a smile. "But you'll forgive me if I'm a little nervous sometimes."

Susie nodded, speechless.

Arie clapped a mosquito. "Got it!"

The smack hung in the air like a gunshot, until Renata turned to Arie with a sigh. "And Aren. Arie. What about you. Tell me—how did you survive?"

"Oh no. Not me. Another time."

An owl hooted, birds rose from the cliff with fluttering wings.

Renata tried to fill the silence. "Every survivor has an unbelievable story. Otherwise they wouldn't have survived."

She took Arie's hand, and Peter's, and held them in her own, studying them, and looked up to contemplate their faces. She saw little Peter climbing into the car, heard Aren crying after him, felt herself clinging to Ruth.

"So Susie and I have a family at last," she said in a tone of wonder, smiling at the gathering of stunned faces. "And so beautiful and such a happy family. This has always been my dream."

They were struck mute. Ido and Alice gripped each other, Moshe and Rachel did the same, the two sets of twins were numbed. Arie, Peter, and Tamara exchanged glances and stared at the ground.

Each had their story, but what could they say?

Glossary

aize bardak (**Hebrew**)–what a mess

Ashkenazi–Jew from Central and Eastern Europe

bezrat Hashem (**Hebrew**)–with the help of God

Botz–Israeli thick black coffee

boychik (**Yiddish**)–little boy

budke (**Yiddish**)–kiosk

bupkes (**Yiddish**)–very little; not worth much

boureka–Middle Eastern fluffy pastry, often filled with cheese, potato, or spinach

causus belli (**Latin**)–justification for conflict

chutzpah (**Yiddish**)–cheek, audacity

dunam–measure of land equivalent to about 900 square meters. About four dunams to the acre

Fatah–Yasser Arafat's Palestinian nationalist political party, the largest faction of the Palestine Liberation Organization

fedayeen–Palestinian guerrilla fighters

Golani–Israeli infantry brigade

hanukiah–nine-candle candelabra used for Hanukah services

HaOlam HaZeh–Israeli irreverent weekly news magazine

imam–Mosque prayer leader

inshallah (Arabic)–God willing

kapo–Jewish concentration camp block commander, condemned as Nazi collaborator

Kirya–Israel's military headquarters in Tel Aviv

kushari–Egyptian dish of rice and lentils and more

kushi **(Hebrew)**–derogatory slang for black person; means "blackie"

linsen and spätzle–South German lentils and noodle dish

Makim course–squad leaders course in the army

ma'abara–Israeli refugee absorption camps in the 1950s; became synonym for slum or shantytown

meshugge **(Yiddish)**–crazy person

Mizrahi–Eastern Jews from mostly Arab lands

mulukhiya–Egyptian vegetable dish

Palmach–pre-state Jewish underground that fought British mandate soldiers as well as Arabs

proteksia **(Yiddish)**–favoritism, using connections to get a job or to achieve something

schmatte **trade (Yiddish)**–rag trade

Sephardim–Jew of Middle Eastern origin as well as from Spain and Portugal

shlemiel (Yiddish)–dope; clumsy person

Shin Bet–Israel's domestic secret service. Also known as Shabak and GSS, General Security Service

Ya Allah **(Arabic)**–exclamation, Oh my God, my dear God!

yekke **(Hebrew)**–Jew of German-speaking origin. Used semi-humorously for someone who wears a tie and jacket on a hot day, who is punctual and precise